Adrian Mole:
THE LOST YEARS

Adrian Mole: THE LOST YEARS

Sue Townsend

Portions of this text appeared in *The True Confessions of Adrian Albert Mole*, while "Adrian Mole and the Small Amphibians" appeared in *Adrian Mole, From Minor to Major. Adrian Mole, The Wilderness Years* appears in its entirety. All were first published in Great Britain by Methuen London, an imprint of Reed Consumer Books Ltd.

ADRIAN MOLE: THE LOST YEARS

Published by
Soho Press Inc.
853 Broadway
New York, NY 10003

Library of Congress Cataloging-in-Publication Data
Townsend, Sue
Adrian Mole, the lost years / Sue Townsend
p. cm.
ISBN 1-56947-055-3:
1. Mole, Adrian (Fictitious character)—Fiction. I. Title
PR607.0897A6 1944 94-11276
823'.914—DC20 CIP

10 9 8 7 6 5 4 3

Book I

True Confessions of Adrian Albert Mole

Adrian Mole's Christmas

DECEMBER 1984

Monday, December 24th
Christmas Eve

Something dead strange has happened to Christmas. It's just not the same as it used to be when I was a kid. In fact I've never really got over the trauma of finding out that my parents had been lying to me annually about the existence of Santa Claus.

To me then, at the age of eleven, Santa Claus was a bit like God, all-seeing, all-knowing, but without the lousy things that God allows to happen: earthquakes, famines, motorway crashes. I would lie in bed under the blankets (how crude the word blankets sounds today when we are all conversant with the Tog rating of continental quilts), my heart pounding and palms sweaty in anticipation of the virgin *Beano* album. I would imagine big jolly Santa looking from his celestial sledge over our cul-de-sac and saying to his elves: 'Give Adrian Mole something decent this year. He is a good lad. He never forgets to put the lavatory seat down.' Ah . . . the folly of the child!

Alas, now at the age of maturity, (sixteen years, eight months and twenty-two days, five hours and six minutes) . . . I know that my parents walk around the town centre wild-eyed with consumer panic chanting desperately, 'What shall we get for Adrian?' Is it any wonder that Christmas Eve has lost its awe?

2.15 am Just got back from the Midnight Service. As usual it dragged on far too long. My mother started getting fidgety after the first hour of the co-op young wives' carols. She kept whispering, 'I shall have to go home soon or that bloody turkey will never be thawed out for the morning.'

Once again the Nativity Playlet was ruined by having a live donkey in the church. It never behaves itself, and always causes a major disturbance, so why does the vicar inflict it on us? OK so his brother-in-law runs a donkey sanctuary, but so what?

To be fair, the effect of the Midnight Service was dead moving. Even to me who is a committed nihilistic existentialist.

Tuesday, December 25th
Christmas Day

Not a bad collection of presents considering my Dad's redundant. I got the grey zip-up cardigan I asked for. My mother said, 'If you want to look like a sixteen-year-old Frank Bough then go ahead and wear the thing!'

The Oxford Dictionary will come in useful for increasing my word power. But the best present of all was the electric shaver. I have already had three shaves. My chin is as smooth as a billiard ball. Somebody should get one for Leon Brittain. It is not good for Britain's image for a cabinet minister to go around looking like a gangster who has been in the cells of a New York Police Station all night.

The lousy Sugdens, my mother's inbred Norfolk relations, turned up at 11.30am. So I got my parents out of bed and then retired to my room to read my *Beano* annual. Perhaps I am too worldly and literate nowadays, but I was quite disappointed at its childish level of humour.

I emerged from my room in time for Christmas dinner and was forced to engage the Sugdens in conversation. They told me in minute, mind-boggling detail, about the life-cycle of King Edward potatoes, from tuber to chip pan. They were not a bit interested in my conversation about the Norwegian Leather Industry. In fact they looked bored. Just my luck to have philistines for relations. Dinner was late as usual. My mother has never learnt the secret of co-ordinating the ingredients of a meal. Her gravy is always made before the roast potatoes have turned brown. I went into the kitchen to give her some advice, but she shouted, 'Bugger off out' through the steam. When it came the meal was quite nice but there was no witty repartee over the table; not a single hilarious anecdote was told. In fact I wish I'd had my Xmas dinner with Ned Sherrin. His relations are dead lucky to have him. I bet their sides ache from laughing.

The Sugdens don't approve of drink, so every time my parents even *looked* at a bottle of spirits they tightened their lips and sipped their tea. (And yes it *is* possible to do both, I've seen it with my own eyes.) In the evening we all had a desultory game of cards. Grandad Sugden won four thousand pounds off my father. There was a lot of joking about my father giving Grandad Sugden an IOU but father said to me in the kitchen, 'No way am I putting my name to paper, that mean old git would have me in court as fast as you could say King Edward!'

The Sugdens went to bed early on our rusty camp beds. They are leaving for Norfolk at dawn because they are worried about potato poachers. I now know why my mother turned out to be wilful and prone to alcohol abuse. It is a reaction against her lousy moronic upbringing in the middle of the potato fields of Norfolk.

Wednesday, December 26th
Boxing Day

I was woken at dawn by the sound of Grandad Sugden's rusty Ford Escort refusing to start. I know I should have gone down into the street and helped to push it but Grandma Sugden seemed to be doing all right on her own. It must be all those years of flinging sacks of potatoes about. My parents were wisely pretending to be asleep, but I know they were awake because I could hear coarse laughter coming from their bedroom, and when the Sugden's engine came alive and the Escort finally turned the corner of our cul-de-sac I distinctly heard the sound of a champagne cork popping and the chink of glasses. Not to mention the loud 'Cheers'.

Went back to sleep but the dog licked me awake at 9.30, so I took it for a walk past Pandora's house. Her dad's Volvo wasn't in the drive so they must still be staying with their rich relations. On the way I passed Barry Kent, who was kicking a football up against the wall of the old people's home. He seemed full of seasonal good will for once and I stopped to talk with him. He asked what I'd had for Christmas; I told him and I asked him what he'd had. He looked embarrassed and said, 'I ain't 'ad much this year 'cos our dad's lost his job.' I asked him what happened, he said, 'I dunno. Our dad says Mrs Thatcher took it off him.' I said 'What, personally?' Barry shrugged and said, 'Well that's what our dad reckons.'

Barry asked me back to his house for a cup of tea so I went to show that I bore him no grudge from the days when he used to demand money with menaces from me. The outside of the Kents' council house looked very grim. (Barry told me that the council have been promising to mend the fences, doors and windows for years) but the inside looked magical. Paper chains were hung everywhere, almost completely hiding the cracks in the walls and ceilings. Mr Kent had been out in the community and found a large branch, painted it with white gloss paint and stuck it into the empty paint tin. This branch effectively took the place of a Christmas tree in my opinion, but Mrs Kent said, sadly, 'But it's not the same really, not if the only reason you've got it is because you can't afford to have a real, plastic one.' I was going to say that their improvised tree was modernistic and Hi Tech but I kept my mouth shut.

I asked the Kent children what they'd had for Christmas and they said, 'Shoes.' So I had to pretend to admire them. I had no choice because they kept sticking them under my nose. Mrs Kent laughed and said, 'And Mr Kent and me gave each other a packet of fags!' As you know, dear diary, I disapprove of smoking but I could understand their need to have a bit of pleasure at Christmas so I didn't give them my anti-smoking lecture.

I didn't like to ask any more questions and politely declined the mince pies they offered . . . from where I was sitting I could see into their empty pantry.

Walking back home I wondered how my parents were able to buy decent Christmas presents for me. After all my father and Mr Kent were both innocent victims of the robot culture where machines are preferred to people.

As I came through our back door I found out. My father was saying, 'But how the hell am I going to pay the next Access bill, Pauline?' My mother said, 'We'll have to sell something George, whatever happens we've got to hang on to at least one credit card because it's impossible to live on the dole and social security!'

So my family's Christmas prosperity is a thin veneer. We've had it on credit.

In the afternoon we went round to Grandma's for Boxing Day tea. As she slurped out the trifle she complained bitterly about her Christmas Day spent at the Evergreen Club. She said, 'I knew I shouldn't have gone; that filthy communist Bert Baxter got disgustingly drunk on a box of liqueur chocolates and sang crude words at the Carol Service!'

My father said, 'You should have come to us, mum, I did ask you!'

Grandma said, 'You only asked me *once* and anyway the Sugdens were there.' This last remark offended my mother, she is always criticising her family but she hates anybody else to do the same. The tea ended in disaster when I broke a willow pattern plate that Grandma has had for years. I know Grandma loves me but I have to record that on this occasion she looked at me with murder in her eyes. She said, 'Nobody will ever know what that plate meant to me!' I offered to pick the pieces up but she pushed me away with the end of the hand brush. I went into the bathroom to cool down. After twenty minutes my mother banged on the door and said, 'C'mon, Adrian, we're going home. Grandma's just told your dad that it's his own fault he's been made redundant.' As I passed through the living room the silence between my father and my Grandma was as solid as a double-glazed window.

As we passed Pandora's house in the car, I saw that the fairy lights on the fir tree in her garden were switched on, so I asked my parents to drop me off. Pandora was ecstatic to see me at first. She raved about the present I bought her (a solid gold bracelet from Tesco's, £2.49) but after a while she cooled a bit and started going on about the Christmas house-party she'd been to. She made a lot of references to a boy called Crispin Wartog-Lowndes. Apparently he is an expert rower and he rowed Pandora across a lake on Christmas Day. Whilst doing so he quoted from the works of Percy Bysshe Shelley. According to Pandora there was a mist on the lake. I got into a silent jealous rage and imagined pushing Crispin Wartog-Lowndes's aristocratic face under the lake until he'd forgotten Pandora, Christmas and Shelley. I got into bed at 1am, worn out with all the emotion. In fact, as I lay in the dark, tears came to my eyes; especially when I remembered the Kents' empty pantry.

The Mole/Mancini Letters

JANUARY 1ST 1985

From
Hamish Mancini
196 West Houston Street
New York, N.Y.

Hi there Aidy!

How are you kid? . . . How's the zits . . . your face still look like the surface of the moon? Hey don't worry, I gotta cure. You rub the corpse of a dead frog into your face at night. Do you have frogs in England? . . . Your mum gotta blender? . . . OK, here's what you do:

1. You find a dead frog.
2. You put it in the blender. (Gory, but you don't have to look.)
3. You depress the button for 30 seconds. (Neither do you have to listen.)
4. You pour the resulting gunk into a jar.
5. You wash the blender, huh?

6. Last thing at night (clean your teeth *first*) you apply the gunk to your face. It works! I now gotta complexion like a baby's ass. Hey! It was great reading your diary, even the odd unflattering remark about me. Still, old buddy, I forgive you on account of how you were of unsound mind at the time you wrote the stuff. An' I got questions . . .

1. What does RSPCA stand for?
2. Who's Malcolm Muggeridge?
3. For chrissake, what are PE shorts?
4. Is the *Morning Star* a commie newspaper?
5. Where's Skegness? . . . What's Skegness rock?
6. 'V' signs? . . . Like Churchill the war leader?
7. Toad in the Hole, is it food or what?
8. Woodbines? . . . Bert Baxter smokes flowers?
9. Family Allowance . . . is this a charity handout?
10. Kevin Keegan . . . who is he?
11. Barclaycard . . . what is it?
12. Yorkshire Puddings . . . what are they?
13. Broadcasting House?
14. How much in dollars is 25 pence?
15. Is a Mars Bar candy?
16. Is Sainsbury's a hypermarket?
17. What's the PDSA, some kinda animal hospital?
18. GCEs, what *are* they?
19. Think I can guess what *Big and Bouncy* magazine is like . . . but gimme some *details,* kid?
20. Bovril—sounds disgusting! . . . Is it?
21. Evergreens? . . . Explain please.
22. Social Services?
23. Spotted Dick . . . jeezus! . . . This some sexual disease?
24. Is a 'detention centre' jail?
25. You bought your mother 'Black Magic'—what is she, a witch or something?

26. Where's Sheffield?
27. What's Habitat?
28. Radio Four, is it some local station?
29. 'O' level what?
30. What is a copper's nark?
31. Noddy? That the goon in the little car?
32. Dole . . . 'Social Security' . . . is this like our Welfare?
33. Sir Edmund Hilary . . . he a relation of yours?
34. Alma Cogan . . . she a singer?
35. Lucozade . . . did you get drunk?
36. What's a conker?
37. The dog is AWOL . . . what is or was AWOL?
38. Who is or was Noel Coward?
39. What is BUPA?
40. What are 'wellingtons'?
41. Who is Tony Benn?
42. Petrol . . . you mean gas?
43. Is *The Archers* a radio serial about Robin Hood?
44. Is the Co-op a commie-run store?
45. Is VAT a kinda tax?
46. *Eating* a chapati? . . . Isn't chapati French for hat?
47. Rouge? . . . Don't you mean blusher?
48. Is an Alsatian a German Shepherd?
49. What's a Rasta?

Send info back soonest,
Yours eagerly, your old buddy
Hamish

PS. Mum's in the Betty Ford Clinic.
She's doin' OK, they've cured everything but the kleptomania.

Leicester
February 1st 1985

Dear Hamish,

Thanks for your long letter but please try to put postage stamps on the envelope next time you write. You are rich and I am poor, I cannot afford to subsidise your scribblings. You owe me twenty-six pence. Please send it immediately.

I am not *so* desperate about my complexion that I have to resort to covering my face with purée of frog. In fact, Hamish, I was repelled and disgusted by your advice, and anyway my mother *hasn't* got a blender. She has stopped cooking entirely. My father and I forage for ourselves as best we can. I'm pleased that you enjoyed reading my diary even though many of the references were unfamiliar to you. I am enclosing a glossary for your edification.

1. RSPCA stands for: the Royal Society for the Prevention of Cruelty to Animals.
2. Malcolm Muggeridge: is an old intellectual who is always on TV. A bit like Gore Vidal, only more wrinkles.
3. PE shorts: running shorts as worn in Physical Education.
4. Yes, the *Morning Star* is a communist newspaper.
5. Skegness is a proletarian sea-side resort. Skegness rock is tubular candy.
6. 'V' sign: it means . . . get stuffed!
7. Toad in the hole: a batter pudding containing sausages.
8. Woodbines: small, lethally strong cigarettes.
9. Family Allowance: a small government payment made to parents of all children.
10. Kevin Keegan: a genius footballer now retired.
11. Barclaycard: plastic credit card.
12. Yorkshire Puddings: batter puddings minus sausages.
13. Broadcasting House: headquarters of the BBC.
14. Work it out for yourself.

15. Mars Bars: yes, it's candy, and very satisfying it is too.
16. Sainsbury's: is where teachers, vicars and such-like do their food shopping.
17. PDSA: People's Dispensary for Sick Animals. A place where poor people take their ill animals.
18. GCEs are exams.
19. *Big and Bouncy*: a copy is on its way to you. Hide it from your mum.
20. Bovril: is a nourishing meat extract drink.
21. Evergreens: a club for wrinklies over 65 years.
22. Social Services: government agency to help the unfortunate, the unlucky, and the poor.
23. Spotted Dick: is a suet pudding containing sultanas. I find your sexual innuendos about my favourite pudding offensive in the extreme.
24. Detention Centre: jail for teenagers.
25. Black Magic: dark chocolates.
26. Sheffield: refer to map.
27. Habitat: store selling cheap, fashionable furniture.
28. Radio Four: BBC-run channel, bringing culture, news and art to Britain's listening masses.
29. 'O' level: see GCE's.
30. Copper's nark: rat fink who gives the police information about criminal activity.
31. Noddy: fictional figure from childhood. I hate his guts.
32. Dole: Social Security: yes, it's Welfare.
33. Sir Edmund Hilary: first bloke to climb Everest.
34. Alma Cogan: singer, now alas dead.
35. Lucozade: non-alcoholic drink. Invalids guzzle it.
36. Conker: round shiny brown nut. The fruit of the horse chestnut. British children thread string through them, and then engage in combat by smashing one conker against another. The kid whose conker gets smashed loses.
37. AWOL: British Army expression. It means absent without leave.

38. Noel Coward: wit, singer, playwright, actor, songwriter. Ask your mother, she probably *knew* him.
39. BUPA: private medicine, a bit like the Blue Cross.
40. Wellingtons: rubber boots. The queen wears them.
41. Tony Benn: an ex-aristocrat, now a fervent Socialist politician.
42. Petrol: OK . . . OK . . . gas.
43. The Archers: a radio serial about English countryfolk.
44. The Co-op: a grocery chain run on Socialist principles.
45. VAT: a tax. The scourge of small businesses.
46. Chapati: *not* a French hat. It's a flat Indian bread!
47. Rouge: *you* can call it blusher if you like. *I* call it *rouge.*
48. Alsatian: yes, also called German Shepherd, terrifying whatever they're called.
49. Rasta: a member of the Rastafarian religion. Members are usually black. Wear their hair in dreadlocks (plaits) and smoke illegal substances. They have complicated handshakes.

Look Hamish, I'm at the end of my patience now. If there is anything else you cannot understand please refer to the reference books. Ask your mother or any passing Anglophile. And please! . . . please! . . . send my diaries back. I would hate them to fall into unfriendly, possible commercial hands. I am afraid of blackmail; as you know my diaries are full of sex and scandal. Please for the sake of our continuing friendship . . . send my diaries back!

I remain, Hamish,
Your trusting, humble and obedient servant and friend.
A. Mole

A Letter to the BBC

Leicester
February 14th

Dear Mr Tydeman,

I am sending you, as requested, my latest poem. Please write back by return of post if you wish to broadcast the said poem. Our telephone has been disconnected (again).

I remain, Sir, your most humble and obedient servant,
A. Mole

THROBBING

Pandora,
I am but young
I am but small
(with cratered skin)
Yet! Hear my call.
Oh, rapturous girl

With skin sublime
Whose favourite programme's 'Question Time'
Look over here
To where I stand
A throbbing
Like a swollen gland.

A. Mole

Adrian Mole on 'Pirate Radio Four'

Art Culture and Politics

AUGUST 1985

I would like to thank the BBC for inviting me to talk to you on Radio 4. It's about time they had a bit of culture on in the morning. Before I begin properly I'd just like to take this opportunity to reassure my parents that I got here safely.

Hello, Mum. Hello, Dad. The train was OK. Second Class was full so I went into First Class and sat down and pretended to be a lunatic. Fortunately the ticket inspector has got a lunatic in his family so he was quite sympathetic and took me to sit on a stool in the guard's van. As you know I am normally an introvert, so pretending to be a lunatic extrovert for an hour and twenty minutes wore me out, and I was glad when the train steamed into the cavernous monolith that is St Pancras Station. Well to be quite honest the train didn't steam in because as you, Dad, will know, steam has been phased out and is now but an erotic memory in a train spotter's head.

Anyway I got a taxi like you told me, a black one with a high roof. I got in and said, 'Take me to the BBC'. The driver said, 'Which BBC?' in a surly sort of tone. I *nearly* said, 'I don't like your tone my man', but I bit my tongue back and explained: 'I'm speaking on

Radio Four this morning'. He said, 'Good job you ain't goin' on the telly wiv your face.' He must have been referring to the bits of green toilet paper sticking to my shaving cuts. I didn't know what to say to his cruel remark, so I kept quiet and watched the money clock like you told me to do. You won't believe it, Mum, but it cost me two pounds forty-five pence! . . . I know . . . incredible isn't it? Two pounds forty-five pence! I gave him two pound notes and a fifty pence piece and told him to keep the change. I can't repeat what *he* said because this is Radio Four and not Radio Three but he flung his five pence tip into the gutter and drove off shouting horrible things. I grovelled in the gutter for ages, but you'll be pleased to hear that I found the five pence.

A bloke in a general's uniform barred my way to the hallowed portals of Broadcasting House. He said, 'And whom might you be sunshine?' I said quite coldly (because once again I didn't care for his tone), 'I am Adrian Mole, the Diarist and Juvenile Philosopher'. He turned to another general . . . in fact, thinking about it, it could have been the *Director* General because this second general looked sort of noble yet careworn. Anyway, the first general shouted, 'Look on the list under Mole will you . . . ?' The second general replied (in cultivated tones, so it must have been the Director General) 'Yes I've got a Mole on the list . . . Studio B 198'. Before I knew it, a wizened-up old guide appeared at my elbow and showed me into a palatial lift. Then, once out of the lift—which was twice as big as my bedroom by the way—he took me down tortured, turning corridors. It was like George Orwell's Ministry of Truth in that book called 1984. No wonder DJs are always late turning up for work.

Eventually, exhausted and panting, we arrived outside the door of Studio B 198. I was a bit worried about the old guide. To tell you the truth I thought he'd force me to give him mouth to mouth, such was his feeble condition. I really think that the BBC ought to provide oxygen on each floor for their older employees; and a trained nurse wouldn't be a bad idea either. It would save them money in the long run; they wouldn't have to keep replacing staff all the time and collecting for wreaths and things. Anyway, just thought I'd tell you that I got here all right. Oh, you know the BBC bloke I've been writing to, that producer John Tydeman. Well he's dead scruffy. He looks like he *writes*. You know, with a beard and heavy horn-rimmed glasses. Need I say more? I'd better stop talking to you now Mum and Dad, because he's making crude signs at me through the glass—so much for the standard of education at the BBC!

Oh, before I forget, did you send that excuse to Pop-Eye Scruton telling him that I've gone down with an 'as yet unnamed' virus? If not, can you take one to school immediately after my broadcast? . . . Thanks, only, as you know, he refused me permission to come here today. How mean can you get? Fancy denying one of the foremost intellectuals in school the opportunity to talk about art and culture on the BBC. You'll be sure to mark the envelope 'for the attention of the Headmaster' won't you Dad? Don't forget and put 'Pop-Eye Scruton' on, like you did last time.

Well I'd better start properly now . . . I've got my notes somewhere . . . (*pause . . . rustling . . .*) Oh dear . . . I've left them in the taxi. Oh well, it's quite lucky that I'm good at doing 'ad hoc' spontaneous talking isn't it? . . . So, Art and Culture. Are they important?

Well, I think Art and Culture *are* important. *Dead* important. Without Art and Culture we would descend to the level of animals who aimlessly fill their time by hanging around dustbins and getting into fights. The people who don't allow Art and Culture into their lives can always be spotted. They are pale from watching too much television, and also their conversation lacks a certain *je ne sais quoi;* unless they are French of course. Cultureless people talk about the price of turnips and why bread always falls on the buttered side, and other such inane things. You never hear them mention Van Gogh or Rembrandt or Bacon (by Bacon, I'm talking about Francis Bacon the infamous artist, I don't mean streaky bacon or Danish bacon . . . the sort you eat). No, such names mean nothing to cultureless people, they will never pilgrimage to the Louvre Museum to see Michaelangelo's Mona Lisa. Nor will they thrill to a Brahms Opera. They will fill their empty days with frivolous frivolity, and eventually die never having tasted the sweet ambrosia of culture.

I therefore feel it incumbent upon me to promote artisticness wherever I tread. If I meet a low-browed person I force them into a philosophical conversation. I ask them, 'Why are we here?' Often their answers are facetious. For instance last week I asked a humble market trader that very question. He answered, 'I dunno why you're 'ere mate but I'm 'ere to flog carrots'.

Such people are to be pitied. We of superior intellect must not judge them too harshly, but gently nudge them into the direction of the theatre rather than the betting shop. The art gallery instead of the bingo hall. The local madrigal society as opposed to the discotheque. I know that there are cynics who say 'England is governed by philistines, so what do you expect?' but to those cynics I say yes, we may be governed by philistines at the moment but I'd like to take this opportunity to talk about a political party that I've started up. It is called the Mole Movement. As yet we are small, but one day our influence will be felt throughout our land. Who knows, one day our party could be the party of government. I could end up as Prime Minister. Is it so inconceivable? Not in my opinion. Mrs Thatcher was once a humble housewife and mother. So, if she can do it, why can't I?

The 'Mole Movement' was formed on Boxing Day, 1985. You know what it's like on Boxing Day. You've opened the presents, you've eaten all the white meat on the turkey, your half-witted relations are bickering about Aunt Ethel's will, and why Norman didn't deserve to get the scabby old clock: a general feeling of *ennui* (*ennui* is French for bored out of your skull by the way). Yes, *ennui* hangs around the house like stale fag smoke. Anyway it was Boxing Day and my girlfriend, Pandora Braithwaite, had come round so that we could exchange belated Christmas greetings. Her family took her to stay in a hotel for Christmas because Mrs Braithwaite said that if she had to stare up the rear of another turkey she would go berserk.

Anyway, we exchanged presents; I gave her a fish ash tray I made in pottery at school, and she gave me a Marks and Spencers voucher so that I could replace my old underpants. The elastic's gone . . . yes . . . so we thanked each other and kissed for about five minutes. I didn't want us to get carried away and end up as single parents . . . not in our 'A' level year. It wouldn't be fair to the kid with us both studying . . . er . . . what did I start to . . . ? Yes. Well, after the kissing stopped I started to talk about my aspirations, and Pandora smoked one of her stinking French fags and listened to me with grave attention. I spoke passionately about beauty and elegance, and bringing back the old branch lines on the railways. I thundered against tower blocks and leisure centres, and ended by saying 'Pandora, my love, will you join me in my Life's Work?' Pandora moved languidly on my bed and said, 'You haven't said what your life's work is yet, *chéri*'.

I stood over her and said, 'Pandora, my life's work is the pursuit of beauty over ugliness, of truth over deceit, and of justice over rich people hogging all the money'. Pandora ran to the bathroom and was violently sick, such was the dramatic effect my speech had on her. To tell the truth I was a bit misty-eyed myself, and while she was throwing up I studied my face in the wardrobe mirror and definitely saw a change for the better. For where once was adolescent uncertainty was now mature complacency.

Pandora emerged from the bathroom and said 'My God, darling, I don't know what's going to happen to you'. I pulled her into my arms and reassured her about my future. I said, 'The way ahead may be stony but I will walk it barefoot if necessary'. Our oblique conversation was interrupted by my mother making mundane enquiries about how many spoons of sugar Pandora took in her cocoa. After my mother had stamped off down the stairs I turned in despair and cried, 'Oh save me from the *petit bourgeoisie* with their inane enquiries about beverages'. We tried to continue the conversation but it was again interrupted when my father went into the bathroom and started making disgusting grunting noises. He is so uncouth! . . . He can't wash his face without sounding like two warthogs mating in a watering hole. How I managed to spring from his loins I'll never know. In fact sometimes I think that it wasn't *his* loins I sprang from; my mother was once very friendly with a poet. Not a full-time poet: he was a maggot farmer during the day, but at night, after the maggots had been shut up in their sheds, he would pull a pad of Basildon Bond towards him and write poems. Quite good poems as well; one of them got into the local paper. My mother cut it out and kept it . . . surely the action of a woman in love. When my mother came in with the cocoa I quizzed her about her relationship with the maggot poet. 'Oh Ernie Crabtree?' she said, pretending innocence. 'Yes', I said, then went on with heavy emphasis: 'I am like him in many ways aren't I . . . ? The poetry for instance'. My mother said, 'You're nothing like him. He was witty and clever and unconventional and he made me laugh. Also he was six foot tall and devastatingly handsome'.

'So why didn't you marry him?' I asked. My mother sighed and sat down on my bed next to Pandora. 'Well, I couldn't stand the maggots. In the end I gave him an ultimatum. "Ernie", I said, "It's me or the maggots. You must choose between us." And he chose the maggots.' Her lips started to tremble and so I left the room and bumped into my father on the landing. By now I was determined to sort out my paternity so I quizzed him about Ernie Crabtree. 'Yeah, Ernie's done well for himself', he said. 'They call him the Maggot King in fishing circles. He's got a chain of maggot farms now and a mansion with a pack of Dobermans running in the grounds . . . yeah, good old Ernie.' 'Does he still write poetry?' I enquired. 'Listen, son', said my father, and bent so close that I could see his thirty-year-old acne scars. 'Listen, Ernie's bank statements are pure poetry. He doesn't need to *write* the stuff.' My father got into bed, took his vest off and reached for the best-selling book he was reading. (Myself I never read best-sellers on principle. It's a good rule of thumb. If the masses like it then I'm sure that I won't.)

'Dad', I said, 'what did Ernie Crabtree look like?' My father cracked the spine of his book open, lit a disgusting fag and said 'Short fat bloke with a glass eye, wore a ginger wig . . . now clear off, I'm reading'. I went back to my room to find Pandora and my mother having one of those sickening talks that women have nowadays. It was full of words like 'unfulfilled', 'potential', and 'identity'. Pandora kept chipping in with 'environment' and 'socio-economic' and 'chauvinistic attitude'. I got my pyjamas out of my drawer, signalling that I wished their conversation to desist, but neither of them took the hint so I was forced to change in the bathroom. When I came back the air was full of French cigarette smoke, and they were gassing about the Common Market and the relevance of something called 'milk quotas'.

I hung about tidying my desk and folding my clothes, but eventually I was forced to climb into bed while the conversation continued on either side of me. When they got on to cruise missiles I was forced to intercept and plead for a bit of multilateral peace.

Fortunately the dog got into a fight with a gang of dogs outside in the street so my mother was forced to run outside and separate it from the other canines with a mop handle. I took this opportunity to speak to Pandora. I said, 'While you may have been idly chatting with my mother I have been formulating important ideas. I have decided that I am going to have a party.' Pandora said, 'A fancy dress party?' 'No', I shouted, 'I'm forming a *political* party, well more of a Movement, really. It will be called the Mole Movement and membership will be £2 a year.' Pandora asked what she would get for £2 a year. I replied, 'Arresting conversation and stimulation and stuff'. She opened her mouth to ask another question so I closed my eyes and feigned sleep. I heard the squelch of Pandora's moon boots as she tip-toed to the door, opened it and went off, squelching, down the stairs. Thus was the 'Mole Movement' born.

The next morning, I woke with an epic poem thundering inside my head. Even before I had cleaned my teeth I was at my desk scribbling feverishly. I was interrupted once when a visitor called from Matlock, but I declined the encyclopaedias he was selling, and returned to my desk. The poem was finished at 11.35am Greenwich Mean Time. And this is it.

THE HOI POLLOI RECEPTION
By A. Mole

The food stood on the table
The drink stood on the bar
The crisps lay in the glass dish
'Twixt the gherkins in the jar.
The poets were expected
The artists had sent word
The pianists and flautists
Were bringing lemon curd.

The novelists were travelling
From dim and distant lands
The journalists were trekking
O'er deep and shifting sands.
The *hoi polloi* stood standing
Outside the party room
Which glowed with invitation
Like a twenty-year-old womb.
Yet they dared not cross the portal
To taste the waiting feast
For fear of what would happen
If they dared to cross the beast.

The *hoi polloi* grew weary
And sat upon the floor
And told each other stories
Until the clock struck four.
They drew each other pictures

One person sang a song
But was careful at the end
To say, 'Of course *they* won't be long'.

The artists and the poets
And the people who write books
The musicians and the journalists
And the Nouvelle Cuisine cooks
Sent word they couldn't make it
They couldn't leave the town.
They were meeting VIP's for drinks
And couldn't make it down.

The gherkins went untasted
The crisps were never crunched
The Chablis kept its cork in
The Twiglets went unmunched
But still the people waited
For a hundred million days
And just to help to pass the time
They wrote and acted plays.

They carved a pretty pattern
On the panel of the door.
They painted lovely pictures on the
Coldly concrete floor
They sang in pretty harmony
About the epic wait.
Then hush! . . . Was that a car we heard
Was that a creaking gate?

It's the sculptors on the gravel
It's the poets wild-eyed
Quick open wide the door to
Let the journalists inside.
Oh welcome to our party!

We thought you'd never come
So sad we ate the food though
We haven't left a crumb!

For in the time of waiting
The *hoi polloi* grew brave
They went into the room
And took the things they craved.
And the poets and the sculptors
And the artists and the cooks
And the women good at music
And the men who wrote the books
And the journalists and actors
And the people trained to sing
Stood waiting ever after for the party to begin.

A Mole in Moscow

SEPTEMBER 1985

Woke up at 6am in the morning. Got out of bed carefully because the dog was spread-eagled across the bed, flat on its back, with its legs in the air. At first I thought it was dead, but I checked its pulse and found signs of life, so I just slid out from underneath its warm fur. The dog's dead old now and needs its sleep.

After measuring my chest and shoulders I had a thorough wash in cold water. I read somewhere (I think it was one of Mr Paul Johnson's articles) that 'cold water makes a man of you'. I've been a bit worried about my maleness lately, somewhere along the line I seem to have picked up too many female hormones.

I've been to see the doctor about it, but as usual he was most unsympathetic. I asked if I could have some of my female hormones taken out. Dr Grey laughed a horrible, bitter laugh and gave his usual advice, which was to go out and have my head kicked about in a rugby scrum. As I was leaving his surgery he said 'And I don't want to see you back here for at least two months'. I asked, 'Even if I'm taken seriously ill?' He muttered, '*Especially* if you're taken seriously ill'. I'm considering reporting him to his superiors; all this worry has affected my poetry output. I used to be able to turn out at least four poems an hour, but now I'm down to three a week. If I'm not careful I'll dry up altogether.

In my desperation I went to the Lake District on the train. I was struck down by the beauty of the place, although saddened to find that there were no daffodils flashing in my outer eye as in William Wordsworth the old Lake poet. I asked an ancient country yokel why there were no daffodils about. He said, 'It's July, lad'. I repeated loudly and clearly, (because he was obviously a halfwit) 'Yes I know that, but why are there no *daffodils* about?' 'It's July,' he roared. At that point I left the poor deranged soul. It's sad that nothing can be done for such pathetic geriatric cases. I blame the government. Since they put rat poison in the water supply most of the adult population have gone barmy.

I sat on a rock that Wordsworth once sat on and thrilled to think that where my denim was now was where his moleskin used to be. A yob had scrawled on the rock, 'What's wiv this Wordsworth?' Another, more cultivated hand, had written underneath: 'You mindless vandal, how dare you bespoil this precious rock which has been here for millions of years. If you were here I'd flog you to within an inch of your life. Signed, A. Geologist'. Somebody else had written underneath, 'Flog *me* instead. Signed, A. Masochist'. After eating my tuna-fish sandwiches and drinking my low calorie orange drink, I walked around the lake trying to feel inspired, but by tea-time nothing had happened so I put my pen and exercise book back into my carrier-bag and hurried back to the station to catch the train back to the Midlands.

It was just my luck to have to share a compartment with hyperactive two-year-old twins and their worn-out mother. When the twins weren't having spectacular tantrums on the floor they were both standing six inches away from me, *staring* at me with unblinking evil eyes. It used to be my ambition to have a farmhouse full of Hovis-like children. I would imagine looking out of my study window to see them all frolicking amongst the combine harvesters. With Pandora, their mother, saying; 'Shush! . . . Daddy is working', whereupon the children would blow me kisses with their podgy fingers and run into the stone-flagged kitchen to eat the cakes that Pandora had just taken from the oven. However since my experience with the mad twins I have decided *not* to spread my seed. Indeed I may ask my parents if I can have a vasectomy for my eighteenth birthday.

When I got home I hurried round to Pandora's house to tell her about this change in my future plans. Pandora said, '*Au contraire, chéri,* should we still be having a long term relationship. I should like to have one child when I am forty-six years of age. The child will be a girl. She will be beautiful and immensely gifted. Her name will be Liberty.' I said, 'But do women's reproductive organs still reproduce at the age of forty-six?' Pandora said, '*Mais naturellement, chéri,* and anyway there is always the test tube option'.

Mr Braithwaite came into the room and said, 'Pandora, make your mind up. Are you going to Russia or are you not?' Pandora said, 'Not. I can't leave the cat.' They then had a furious row. I could hardly believe my ears. Pandora was turning down a week in Russia with her father just because her stinking old moggy was about to give birth for the fourth time! During a pause in the argument I said, 'I would give my right leg to go to the country of Dostoyevsky's birth'.

However Mr Braithwaite didn't respond with an invitation for me to accompany him. How mean can you get? The Co-op Dairy had given him two tickets to go on a fact-finding tour of milk distribution in Moscow. (Mrs Braithwaite had refused to go because she'd recently joined the SDP.) So a ticket was going spare. Yet the tight git was denying me the glorious opportunity of studying revolution in the raw. When Mr Braithwaite had gone into the garden to savagely mow the lawn Pandora said, 'You *shall* go to Russia'. She worked on her father for a whole week. She refused to eat, she played her stereo at full decibels. She invited her 'Hell's Angels' friends for tea every day. Her punk friends came to supper and I had breakfast with the family most mornings. By the end of the week Mr Braithwaite was a broken man and Mrs Braithwaite was begging him to take me behind the Iron Curtain. Eventually, after Pandora held an open air reggae concert on the back lawn, Mr Braithwaite relented.

He came to our house at 11 o'clock one Sunday morning, so I got my parents out of bed and we had a meeting at our kitchen table. They enthusiastically agreed to me going to Russia for a week. My mother said, 'Great, George, we could have a second honeymoon while Adrian's away!' My father said, 'Yeah, mum'll look after the baby. We can rediscover ourselves, eh, Pauline?' They slopped over each other for a bit and then turned their attention back to the proceedings for, knowing that I was a virgin traveller, Mr Braithwaite had brought a passport form with him and I filled it in carefully under his supervision. I only made one mistake. Where it said 'sex' I put 'not yet', instead of putting 'male'.

We turned the house upside down looking for my birth certificate before my mother remembered that it was framed and hanging on Grandma's front room wall. My father was sent round to fetch it while Mr Braithwaite took me to have my passport photographs taken in a slot machine. On the way, in the car, I practised facial expressions. I wanted my photographs to show the *real* Adrian Mole. Warm and clever, yet enigmatic and with just a hint of sensuousness. In the event, the photographs were disappointing. I looked like a spotty youth with just a hint of derangement in my sticking-out eyes. After everyone, apart from me, had had a good laugh at the photographs my mother reluctantly wrote a cheque out for fifteen pounds and then the documents were checked and double-checked by Mr Braithwaite before being put into a large envelope. While he did this I examined him carefully, for he was to be my travelling companion and room mate for a week. Would I be able to stand the shame of being seen in the company of a man wearing flared trousers and a paisley patterned waistcoat? Too late! The die was cast! Fate had thrown us together!

As he left, clutching my documentation, he said: 'Adrian, during the week we are in Moscow do you promise, swear, give me your word, that you will not utter *one* word about the Norwegian leather industry?' Astonished I said, 'Of course. If, for some reason, you find my mini-lectures on the Norwegian leather industry *offensive,* then of course I won't mention it'. Mr Braithwaite said, 'Oh I don't find your constant monologues on the Norwegian leather industry *offensive,* just deeply, deeply boring'. Then he got into his car and went to put the documents through the door of the Passport Office.

If this was a film, then leaves would blow across the screen and pages of diaries would riffle, trains would roar and calendars would have months torn from them by unseen hands. But as this is just me speaking then all I need to tell you is that time went by, and I got my passport and my visa by second-class post. In the days before I left England for Russia I also got advice. My Grandma said, 'If the Russians offer to show you the salt mines refuse and ask to be shown a shoe factory instead'. My mother advised me *not* to mention that at the age of fourteen she had been thrown out of the Young Communist League (Norwich Branch) for fraternising with American soldiers. Pandora advised against buying her a light amber necklace saying she preferred the *dark* amber, and Mr O'Leary from over the road advised me not to go at all. He said. 'The Russians are godless heathens, Adrian'. Mrs O'Leary said, 'Yes, and so are you, Declan, you haven't been to Mass for over two years'.

The worst part of the journey to Russia was the M1 motorway. Mr Braithwaite's Volvo was almost sucked under the passing lorries several times. In fact at Watford Gap Mr Braithwaite lost his nerve and the capable hands of Mrs Braithwaite took the wheel. It was the first time I had flown in a plane so I was expecting sympathy and a bit of cherishing from the air-stewardesses who stood by the plane door. I said: 'This is the first time I've flown, I may need extra attention during the flight'. The woman said in broken English, 'Well you won't get it from me, Englishman, I will be too busy flying the plane'. Mr Braithwaite went pale when I told him that the pilot was a woman. Then he remembered that he was an avowed feminist and said, 'Jolly good'. Apart from my putting my seat belt around my neck, the flight was uneventful. The passengers concentrated on hiding or eating the garlic sausage and cream crackers they were served for lunch; but they warmed up a bit when the vodka came round, and by the time we landed at the airport just outside Moscow some of them were disgustingly drunk and were not good examples of Western Capitalist Society.

The airport was ill-lit and a bit chaotic, especially when it came to collecting luggage. Nearly everybody had brought Marks and Spencers luggage so quite a few arguments ensued and suitcases had to be opened on the floor, and underwear examined before the rightful owners managed to sort out the 'Y' fronts from the silk culottes.

A big blonde woman stood in a gloomy corner of the arrival lounge, holding a placard saying 'Intourist'. Five hundred people milled around her asking her questions.

Mr Braithwaite was bleating, 'I'm here to study milk distribution; my name is Ivan Braithwaite; am I in the right place?' The big blonde woman threw her placard down, clapped her hands and yelled 'All you foreigners are to be quiet. I am thinking I am in Moscow Zoo. Now you are to sit on your suitcases and wait.'

We waited and waited, more light bulbs went out and then in the gathering gloom four people arrived holding placards. One said, 'Siberia', one said 'Moscow'. Another one said 'Milk'. Mr Braithwaite and I stood by the 'Milk' placard and were eventually joined by two German dairy farmers, three retired English milkmen and a dyslexic American family who thought the sign said 'Minsk'. We were invited aboard a coach and our guide gave us a commentary on the Moscow suburbs we were passing through. The dyslexic American daughter peered out of the window and said, '*Gross* . . . where's the shops for chrissake?' Her mother said, 'Honey we're in the suburbs, the shops are downtown'. No shops could be seen, although one of the English ex-milkmen spotted a dairy and applauded, which made our guide smile for the first time.

The hotel we stopped in was monolithic and swarming with every nationality on earth. Our guide screamed above the babble of languages, 'Be patient please while I am wrestling with your room keys. If I am lost forever you must ask for Rosa. It is not my name but it will do. My name in Russian is too difficult for your clumsy tongues'. I fell asleep on the marble floor and woke hours later to the sound of a heavy metal key jangling in my ear.

Having checked the room for hidden microphones, I got into bed in my underwear because my grandma had warned me that secret television cameras were behind every mirror and I did not like the thought of my English genitals being mocked by unseen viewers. Mr Braithwaite fell instantly asleep in the bed next to me but I lay awake for hours listening to the trams outside the hotel and composing a poem in my head:

OH MOSCOW TRAMS

Are your wheels revolutionary?
Are your carriages forged from the steel
  of conflict?
Are there bloodstains on the uncut moquette
  of your seats?
Do your passengers keep to the tracks of
  sacrifice and denial?
I, Adrian Mole will soon know
For in the morning I will be a fellow traveller.

In the morning Mr Braithwaite was nowhere to be seen. My first thought was of abduction, but then I found a note on the toilet seat, it said 'Enjoy your day, see you late tonight'. So, I was alone in

Moscow. I put a towel over the bathroom mirror before attending to my toilette. Then, dressed in my best, I went down in the lift to breakfast. The dining room was like an aircraft hangar and was full of Communists eating black bread and drinking coffee. I sat next to a very dark man in robes who was in Moscow to buy gear-levers for his tractor factory in Africa. We chatted for a while but we had little in common, so I turned to my neighbour who turned out to be a Norwegian . . . what a stroke of luck! I spoke at great length about the Norwegian leather industry but instead of being interested he got up and left abruptly, leaving his breakfast half eaten. What a strange moody race are the Scandinavians!

Rosa stomped into the dining room and ordered her party to get on a coach. The American family, the three milkmen, the two German farmers and me were taken to see the sights. We had ten minutes at the Kremlin during which the American girl sold her camera, boots and umbrella to a disaffected whining youth who complained about his country, until Rosa hit him round the head and said, 'No other country would let you in anyway. You are a disgraceful *pretty crook*.' I think she must have meant *petty crook* because the youth was very unattractive. Then we got back into the coach and went to see the Bolshoi Theatre and the Olympic Stadium and the residence of the British Ambassador and museums gálore until it was time for lunch.

The milkmen, Arthur, Arnold and Harry reeled across the foyer and complained that they hadn't visited any dairies. They had been drinking and it wasn't milk. Vodka I suspect. Rosa was involved in a bitter argument with the American family who wanted to know when they would be leaving for Minsk, so she didn't listen to the milkmen's wild ramblings.

For lunch I joined a table of old aristocratic Englishwomen who were moaning that, for some inexplicable reason, they had spent the day touring Milk Distribution Centres. A deputation of them approached Rosa pleading to be taken to the Ballet.

The afternoon was free so I went for a walk in Gorky Park and looked for bodies. Loads of Russians were there walking about like English people do. Some were licking ice-creams, some were talking and laughing and some were sunbathing in their underwear with rouble notes on their noses to prevent sunburn. Indeed such was the heat that I was forced to go back to the hotel and take off my balaclava, mother's fur hat, mittens, big overcoat, four sweaters, shirt and two T-shirts.

In the evening we were coached off to the Opera where I and most of the Russians in the audience fell asleep, and the American girl sold her Sony headset. Mr Braithwaite came back very late and very drunk. Vodka doesn't smell but I *knew*. He got into bed without a word and snored very loudly. By now I was convinced he was a spy. The pattern continued throughout our three days in Moscow. I would wake up, find a note from Mr Braithwaite and so would be forced to throw myself on the mercy of 'Intourist'. By this time I was boggle-eyed with culture and longed for a bit of English apathy and gross materialism.

So, on my last afternoon in Moscow I did a brave thing. I went down into the bowels of the chandeliered metro in an attempt to find Moscow's shopping centre. I put a five kopek coin in a machine, got my ticket and descended into splendours of marble and gilt. Trains arrived every three minutes and took me and crowds of Russian people speeding along towards the shops. I attracted a few curious glances (spotty complexions are rare in Russia); but most people were reading heavy intellectual books with funny writing on them or learning piano concertos by Tchaikovsky.

I got out OK, found the shops and four hours later was returning to the hotel with a giant Russian doll which contained thirty other shrinking dolls inside it. Just like *Tinker, Tailor* on TV. Pandora will get the biggest doll, and my father will get the smallest. As I entered the hotel lobby I saw Mr Braithwaite sitting on a sofa with a voluptuous Russian woman wearing a lime-green trouser suit and platform shoes. She was toying erotically with the flares of Mr Braithwaite's trousers, and I saw him catch her hand and lick the palm. God! It was a revolting sight! I felt like shouting 'Mr Braithwaite, pull yourself together, you're an Englishman'. When they saw me coming they sprang apart. She was introduced as Lara, an expert on the diseases of cow's udders.

I smiled coldly, then left them together, unable to witness the naked lust in their middle-aged eyes. Three roubles were burning a hole in my sock, so I removed my shoe, took the money out and summoned a taxi. 'Take me to Dostoyevsky's grave,' I cried. The taxi driver said: 'How much money do you have?' 'Three roubles' I replied. 'It ain't enough, sunshine' he said, 'Dostoyevsky's grave is in Leningrad'. I complimented him on his English and slunk back into the hotel, did my packing and prepared to fly back.

Lara was at the airport. She gave Mr Braithwaite a single carnation. There was a lot of palm licking and sighing and talking about their 'souls'. Mr Braithwaite gave Lara a copy of *The Dairy Farmer's Weekly*, two pairs of Marks & Spencers socks, a toilet roll and a packet of Bic razors. She wept pitifully.

Mrs Braithwaite and Pandora were waiting beyond the barrier at Gatwick. As we walked towards them Mr Braithwaite sighed in a deep Russian Chekhovian way and said, 'Adrian, Mrs Braithwaite may not understand about Lara'. I said 'Mr Braithwaite, I do not understand about Lara myself. How *anyone* could have an affair with a woman wearing a lime-green trouser suit and platform shoes is beyond me'. This speech took me through the barrier and into the arms of Pandora and England. Oh, Leicester! Leicester! Leicester!

Mole on Lifestyle

OCTOBER 1985

I often look back on my callow youth, and when I do a smile flits across my now mature but pitted face. I hardly recognize the naïve boy I once was. To think that I once believed that Evelyn Waugh was a woman! Of course now, with a couple of 'O' levels under my belt, I am far more sophisticated and I know that Evelyn Waugh, should he be alive today, would be very, indeed, *dead* proud of his daughter, Auberon; because of course Evelyn is the *father* of Auberon and not as I once thought, the mother.

I occasionally glance through my early diaries and mourn for my lost innocence, for at the age of thirteen and three quarters, I thought it was sufficient to just have a *life*. I honestly didn't know then that you *can't* just have a life. You have to have a *lifestyle*. So my talk today is about 'Lifestyle', with particular reference to my own.

I will take you through a typical day. I will introduce you to my friends and family. I will refer fleetingly to my diet, toilet habits and my style of dress. My tastes in Art and Literature will be dwelt upon. At the end of my talk perhaps you will have an overview of my lifestyle. Incidentally, and by the way, 'overview' is just one of the thousands of words in my vocabulary, and with a bit of luck I will introduce other uncommon words to you, the listening masses. For I am solely aware of my duty via Radio Four to *educate* and entertain the great British public. For how else are they to rise up and take power if they don't understand the words of power? Or the power of words?

I have been told by my contemporaries that I am quite a trendsetter, although Pandora, the love of my life, maintains that *trendsetter* is a word only used by crumblies and people with one foot in the crematorium.

For instance my style of dress is idiosyncratic. Indeed it is personal to myself. Since radio is not television I will describe what I am wearing at the moment. I will start at the head and work down, to save any confusion. On my head I am wearing a balaclava helmet knitted by my ancient yet nimble-fingered Grandma. I am wearing the balaclava because my Father refuses to switch the central heating on until November 1st every year. He cares not that English summer does not exist anymore. As usual he is being selfish and thinking about paying the boring gas bill.

We move down. Around my neck is a silken cravat which was formerly owned by my dead Grandfather. It is a lucky cravat. My grandfather wore it at Epsom and won half-a-crown on a horse (whatever half-a-crown is). My shirt is proudly, indeed unashamedly, from a CND rummage sale. It once belonged to a Canadian lumberjack who had a sweat or, more politely, a perspiration problem, at least so my mother maintains. The smell doesn't bother me as I am used to it, although other people have complained. Under the shirt I wear an 'I love Cliff Richard' T-shirt. A reminder of when I was young and stupid. I *never* unbutton the Canadian shirt. My legs are clad in a pair of executive striped trousers bought at the closing down sale at Woolworths. On my feet are designer training shoes given to me by my best friend Nigel. Poor Nigel suffers from an obsession; he compulsively buys training shoes. The reasons are manifold:

a. He has to be the first in our small town to have the latest style.
b. Because of his inner rage Nigel is always yanking on laces too hard so that they break. He then passes the shoes on to me, claiming he can't be bothered to rethread the new laces.

My own improverished family benefit from Nigel's impetuousness. We are all walking around in Nigel's new old shoes. Even Grandma is wearing a pair. They are too big for her but, with the wisdom of the old, she found a way of making them fit by stuffing the toes with toilet paper.

Under my training shoes I am wearing a pair of odd socks. One sock is white, one sock is black. No, think not that I am an absent-minded genius who doesn't notice what he puts on his feet. Perhaps I am a genius, but not an absent-minded one. No, my choice of hosiery is completely calculated. Indeed it is symbolic. The white socks stands for my inner purity and morality: for I am against violence and Polaris missiles and cruelty to battery hens. The black sock stands for the evil in my soul, such as wanting to go the whole hog with Pandora and fantasising about blowing up tower blocks (minus suicidal tenants of course).

Thus I am a walking dichotomy. On my feet I carry the problems of the world. Naturally the *hoi-polloi* do not recognise this salient fact. They cry out 'Eh . . . yer wearin' odd socks!' To these crude rejoinders I simply reply, in my modulated tones, 'No, 'tis you who is wearing the odd socks, my friend.' Some of them walk away marvelling, although some of them, to be quite honest, don't.

As to personal adornments. I am wearing a gold-plated chain and locket. In the locket are the remains of a dried up autumn leaf. The leaf represents the frailty of the human condition. It was given to me by Pandora in a moment of autumnal ardour. Round my left wrist I wear a copper bangle which hopefully will guard against me contracting arthritis in old age. On my right wrist I wear a plastic waterproof watch which will allow me, should I feel the need, to dive to a depth of a hundred feet.

I have one other personal adornment that nobody knows about apart from me and one other person. It is a tiny tattoo secreted in a private part of my body. The tattoo says 'Mum and Dad' and dates from a time of their marital instability. I now regret my impetuosity because this tattoo will prevent me from partaking in nude sunbathing in the years to come. So, when I am a poet millionaire and I am lying on my personal Greek island I will be the only person amongst my guests to be wearing trunks.

However, the Greek Island home is for the future. My present domestic abode is a semi-detached house in a suburban cul-de-sac in the Midlands. Yes, like many of my fellow Britons, I live with a party wall between me and another family's intimate secrets. I will never understand why it is called a 'party' wall because *when* our next door neighbours throw a party every celebratory sound is heard. Tonic bottles unscrewed, cherries dropping into cocktails, women making brittle conversation, men being sick. So, if the purpose of a party wall is to prevent party noise from spilling into the house adjoining then I have this to say to the builders of Britain, 'You have failed, Sirs'. Now I will take you through one of my typical days.

The dog usually wakes me up at 7 o'clock or thereabouts. It is dead old now and has a weak bladder. I get out of bed, and in my underpants and vest I open the back door and let it out to cock its leg on our next door neighbour's lawn. I make myself a cup of coffee and take it back to bed with me while I read an edifying work of literature. At the moment I am reading *Wittgenstein Primer* written by T. Lowes MA. Trin. Dub. Sometimes for amusement I may turn to something less intellectually straining; *Wings On My Suitcase: personal adventures of an air hostess* introduced and edited by Gerald Tikell, is a good example. Then again, even reminiscences of air hostesses may prove to be too demanding at such an early hour. So for even lighter relief I will turn to my old *Beano* annuals.

I have a baby sister now and she usually climbs out of her cot at 7.30 dragging her wet nappy with her. She barges into my room and gabbles some childish gibberish to which I respond curtly, 'Go and wake Mummy and Daddy up, Rosemary'. I refuse to bastardise her name and call her 'Rosie'. She staggers out on her wobbly legs and beats her tiny fists on my parent's door. Muffled curses tell me that my parents are awake, so I quickly get out of bed and run into the bathroom before anyone else. I lie in my bath and ignore rattlings on the door and demands for entry. I insist on a period of quiet before I start my day. Anyway it's not my fault that the only lavatory is placed in the bathroom, is it? I've lost track of the times I've told my father to install a downstairs lavatory. After completing a meticulous toilette, topped off with liberal lashings of my father's after-shave mixed with my mother's Yardley water, I emerge from the bathroom, have a row with my parents, who are standing cross-legged outside the door, and go down to breakfast. I warm myself a frozen croissant and make a cup of Earl Grey Tea *sans* milk and sit down to study the world news. We take the

Guardian and the *Sun* so I am quite an expert on the latest developments concerning 'whale conservation' and also the mammary development of Miss Samantha Fox. My parents are victims of Thatcherism so neither of them is working, which means they are able to hang about and linger over their breakfasts. Rosemary is a disgusting eater. I always leave the table before she starts on her porridge.

I go to my room, collect my books and study aids and go to college. I ignore most of my fellow students, who are usually thronging the corridors laughing about the previous night's drunken debauch. Instead I make my way to a classroom and quietly study before the lessons begin. For, while I am an intellectual (indeed almost a genius), at the same time I am not very clever and so need to study harder than anyone else.

I spend each break with Pandora. We usually talk about world events. Pandora only wears black clothes as she is in mourning for the world. This has led to her being called 'Barmy Braithwaite' by unthinking morons amongst the student body and also, I regret to report, some of the academic staff. We usually walk home together and on the way call in to see Bert Baxter who is now the oldest man on the electoral roll. Pandora takes Sabre the Alsatian for an angry prowl around the recreation ground, while I clean Bert up and listen to his incoherent ramblings about Lenin and the 'needs of the Proletariat to rise up'. (Bert refuses to die until he sees the fall of Capitalism so it looks as though Bert will be with us for quite a while yet, unfortunately.) When Bert and Sabre have been pacified and fed and watered, Pandora and I walk home together. We part at the entrance to my cul-de-sac and she strolls off to her tree-lined avenue and her detached, book-lined house and I go to my previously described more horrible domestic living unit.

The warm scent of home baking does not greet me as I enter the kitchen. So I create my own smell by baking scones. Here is my recipe but remember before you rush for pencil and paper that the recipe is copyright and owned by me, Adrian Mole. So, should you wish to bake scones to this recipe then you will need to send money to me.

A. MOLE'S SCONES

Ingredients

4 oz flour or metric equivalent
2 oz butter or metric equivalent
2 oz sugar or metric equivalent
1 egg (eggs are still only eggs)

Method

Beat up all the ingredients. Make a tin greasy, throw it all in. Turn over to number 5. Wait until scones are higher than they were. Should be 12 minutes, but keep opening oven door every 30 seconds.

So, crunching, on my fresh-from-the-oven scones, I wind down from my day. At this time I may give Rosemary a few moments attention. Last night I built the GPO Tower from her lego bricks, but while my back was turned Rosemary smashed it to pieces, and then had the nerve to laugh amongst the rubble. This is typical of her behaviour. I am sure she is going to grow up to be psychotic. She is already quite unmanageable. She empties drawers, switches the television knobs on and off, throws her soft toys down the lavatory pan and flies into a rage if she is restrained in any way. I have urged my parents to take her to the Child Guidance Clinic before it is too late, but my mother defends her saying, 'Rosie is quite normal, Adrian, all toddlers behave like Attila the Hun. Why do you think so many mothers are on tranquillisers?' In the early evening I make a point of watching a soap opera or two. I think it is very important for us intellectuals to keep in touch with popular culture. We cannot live in ivory towers, unless of course the ivory towers have a television aerial on the roof.

My parents are trying to save their marriage by playing badminton together on alternative Wednesdays. Otherwise, apart from this fortnightly outing, they clutter the house up in the evenings so I am forced to keep in my room or take to the streets. I honestly can't understand how they can bear each other's company. Their conversation consists of moaning about money and whining about wages—the wages they haven't got.

I make a few demands on them. All I require is a jar of multivitamins once a week plus clean linen and courtesy. However I wouldn't like you to switch off thinking that I'm not fond of my parents. In my own way I'm very close to them. It's hard not to be. We live in a small house. They do have their good points. My father is quite a wit after a couple of glasses of vodka, and my mother is known for her compassion towards other married women. In fact she is in the middle of organising a local group of them. I read somewhere that it is important for families to have bodily contact, so I make a point of patting my parents' shoulders as I pass by. It costs nothing and seems to please them. However at 8 o'clock, when the lounge is full of cigarette smoke, I make my excuses and leave for the outside world.

I sometimes meet up with Barry Kent and we chat about which of his friends is in court, and who's in Borstal. Occasionally we discuss Barry's poetry; he was taught to read and write during his last period in a detention centre. It was a progressive place that had a poet in residence so instead of breaking rocks Barry was forced to split infinitives and then put them together again. Some of his stuff is quite good, primitive of course, but then Barry is practically a certified moron so it is only to be expected. Still, at least he's making a living out of his poetry. In the guise of 'Baz the Skinhead Poet' he tours pubs and rock venues, and shouts poetry at the audience. Sometimes they shout back and then there's a fight. Barry always wins.

On my way home I call in to see Pandora who is usually sitting under the anglepoise lamp bent over 'A' level homework. On the wall above her desk are two notices written in pink neon marker pen. One says, 'GET TO OXFORD OR DIE' the other says 'GO TO

CAMBRIDGE AND LIVE'. There are five exclamation marks after each of them. We share a cup of cocoa, or if her parents are out, gin and tonic. Then we kiss passionately for about five minutes, longer if it's a gin night, and I make my way home racked with latent sexuality. On such occasions I am pleased to find it's raining. There's nothing like a cold shower to ease sexual frustration.

By 11 o'clock I am in bed with the dog, reading, with a digestive biscuit and a cup of cocoa on my bedside table. It isn't the lifestyle I would choose for myself. Given the choice I would opt for a mixture of Prince Andrew and Prince Edward's social life, Ted Hughes's working life and the Wham or Mick Jagger's romantic life. But at least I've *got* a life. Some people haven't. And I'm on the verge, the very kerb of the dual carriageway of Fate. Will I go one way towards London, celebrity and media attention? . . . Or will I go the other way, towards the provinces, and be forced to write letters to the local paper in order to see my name in print? A third possibility occurs to me. I could break down at a roundabout and remain, unsung, in limbo.

But I mustn't burden you, kind listener, with my introspective musings. And anyway I shall have to finish now—it's started raining and my jeans are on the line.

Mole's Prizewinning Essay

JANUARY 1986

Monday

Oh joy! . . . Oh rapture! . . . At last I have made my mark on the world of literature. My essay entitled 'A Day in the Life of an Air Stewardess' has won second prize in the British Airways Creative Writing Competition.

My prizes are: A Concorde-shaped bookmark inscribed in gold leaf by Melvyn Bragg, a hostess apron which has been donated by 'The Society for Distressed Air Stewardesses', and £50.

Here, for posterity, is my prizewinning essay.

A DAY IN THE LIFE OF AN AIR STEWARDESS
By A. Mole

Jonquil Storme opened her languorous blue eyes and looked at the clock. 'Oh drat and bother', she expectorated. The clock said seven o'clock and Jonquil was due at Heathrow Airport at seven fifteen, where she was in charge of Concorde.

Jonquil stretched out her lissome white hand and picked up

the phone. Her other hand dialled the number: with her other hand she fondled an orchid that stood next to her bed in a jam jar.

'Hi Brett!' she said into the receiver . . . 'Jonquil here, darling. I'm late, our night of passion wore me out and caused me to oversleep.' Brett's manly chuckle reverberated down the phone.

'OK Jonquil', he guffawed, 'I'll tell the passengers that there is snow on the runway. Take your time my darling!'

Jonquil put the phone down and sank into the pillows that were still impregnated with Brett's hair oil. She wondered if she would ever get to marry Brett, the Captain of Concorde, and whether the excuse about snow on the runway would be believed. After all it was *July*. Thus ruminating, Jonquil showered in the shower and dressed in the dressing room. Soon she was soignée and was climbing into her Maserati open-topped sports car to the gapes of ordinary dingy passers by.

Soon she was wriggling up the steps of Concorde in her high heeled shoes. Brett met her at the door of the plane and gave her a French Kiss. The passengers didn't mind at all, in fact they applauded and cheered. A jolly American shouted 'God bless you, Captain!'

Brett flashed his manly teeth and went to the front of the plane and switched the engine on. Jonquil went round smiling at the passengers and opening jars of caviar. Soon the champagne corks were popping and the passengers were lying about in stupors. The flight was smooth and without hazards and when Concorde reached New York Brett asked Jonquil to be his bride. So, after having blood tests for diseases, Brett and Jonquil were married in the elevator of the Empire State Building. Soon it was time to turn Concorde round and go home to London. Jonquil was dead proud of her new gold ring and Brett flew the plane better than he ever had before.

As Jonquil got into bed that night she said to herself, 'What a lucky girl I am. To think I almost became a Domestic Science teacher'. She looked at Brett's matted black hair on the Laura Ashley pillow and smiled. It had been the most exciting day of her life.

THE END

(Copywright World Wide owned by A. Mole)

The Sarah Ferguson Affair

JULY 1986

Thursday, July 17th

I'm sick of reading about how handsome Prince Andrew is. To me he looks like the morons studying bricklaying and plastering at college, there is something about his neck that cries out for a hod of bricks. And those big white ruthless teeth! It makes me shudder to think of them nibbling at Fergie's defenceless neck. So some women like tall, well-built men who can fly helicopters and have gob-smacking bank accounts and Coutts gold cards. But personally I think Fergie is throwing herself away on him.

Miss Sarah Ferguson was born to be the wife of Adrian Mole. I have written to tell her so, and to implore her to change her mind before 23rd July. As yet I have received no reply. She must be agonising over her decision: 'Riches, glamour and publicity with Prince Andrew, or poverty, introspection and listening to poetry with Adrian Mole'—not an easy choice.

Sarah Ferguson, oh Sarah Ferguson,
Your name is on my lips constantly.
Don't marry Andy, his legs are bandy.
Come to Leicester, come to Leicester, marry me!
Leave the palace, grab a taxi,
I'll be waiting at the end of the M1.
We'll go to my house, meet my parents,
I know the dog and you will get along.

Friday, July 18th

No letter from Sarah Ferguson today.

I have rung Buckingham Palace but the (no doubt powdered and bewigged) flunkey refused to let me speak to her. He said, 'Miss Ferguson is taking no calls from strangers.' I said, 'Listen, my man, I am no *stranger* to Miss Ferguson, she is my soul mate.' I'm not sure but I could have sworn the flunkey muttered 'Arsehole mate,' before he slammed the phone done. There is nothing else to do but go to Buckingham Palace and tackle her face to face.

I have sent a Telemessage to my ginger-haired love:

Sarah, I am coming to you. Meet me at the Palace gate at high noon.

Yours with unvanquished love,
Adrian Mole (18 1/4).

P.S. I will be wearing sunglasses, and carrying a Marks and Spencer carrier-bag.

Saturday, July 19th
Buckingham Palace, 1.30 pm.

She did not come. I asked a mounted policeman if Sarah was at home. He said, 'Yes, she's inside having waving lessons from the Queen Mother.' I asked him if he would deliver a note to her from me, but he got distracted by a coach-load of excitable Japanese tourists who were measuring his horse and taking down its specifications. No doubt they are going to copy it and flood the world with cheap police horses. Will we English never learn?

I made my way home to the dreary provinces by train. An old fat woman kept up a non-stop monologue about her plans for the royal wedding day. I wanted to cry out, 'You old fat fool, you will be watching an empty screen on the 23rd because *there will be no royal wedding.* So cancel your order for two dozen crusty cobs and a crate of assorted bottles of pop.' I *wanted* to cry these words out but, of course, I didn't; people would have thought I was a teenage lunatic obsessed with Sarah Ferguson, whereas of course I am anything but.

Sunday, July 20th

Sarah has not replied to my letter yet.

Perhaps she has run out of stamps.

Monday, July 21st

I asked the postman if there was anything for me from Buckingham Palace. He replied, 'Ho, has Ted Hughes croaked it? H'are you the next Poet Laureate? H'if you hare, may I h'offer my h'utmost congratulations?'

No wonder England's going to the dogs with public servants of his calibre.

7pm. Pandora Braithwaite rang from Leningrad tonight.

I asked her how she was getting on with her Russian lessons. She said, 'Oh, amazingly well, I joined in a most stimulating debate in the turnip queue this morning. Workers and intellectuals discussed the underlying symbolism of *The Cherry Orchard.* I ventured the opinion, in Russian of course, that the cherries represented the patriarchal balls of Mother Russia, thus proving that Chekhov was AC/DC.'

I asked how the assembled geniuses in the turnip queue had reacted to her analysis. Pandora said, 'Oh, they failed to understand it, bloody peasants!' The line started to go faint, so Pandora shouted, 'Adrian, video-tape the royal wedding for me, darling.' Then the phone went dead and Pandora was lost to me.

Tuesday, July 22nd

My Sarah was on the front page of the paper this morning, wearing a most indecent low-cut dress. That oaf Andrew was quite openly leering at her cleavage. When Sarah is my wife I shall insist that she wears cardigans buttoned up to the neck.

I'm with the Moslems on this one.

No letter. No hope left, the wedding is tomorrow, I shall not watch it. I shall walk the streets clutching my despair. Oh God! Oh Sarah!

Wednesday, July 23rd
My Sarah's Wedding Day

Sarah! Sarah! Sarah!

I sobbed into my pillow for so long this morning that the feathers stuck together and formed lumps like bits of dead chickens. Eventually I rose, dressed in black, and made a simple yet nutritious breakfast. My mother came down and through cigarette smoke said, 'What's up with your face?'

I replied quietly, yet with immense dignity, 'I am in the deepest despair, Mother.'

'Why, are your piles playing you up again?' She coughed.

I left the kitchen, shaking my head from side to side in a pitying fashion, whilst at the same time saying, *sotto voce*, 'Lord, have mercy on the philistines I am forced to live with, for they know not what they say.'

My father overheard and said, 'Oh, got bleedin' religion now, has he?'

I passed Grandma on her way to our house. She was carrying a tea-tray piled high with little fancy cakes, iced with the entwined initials 'FA'. Grandma was in her best clothes; her hat swayed with exotic and long extinct birds' feathers, she was wearing net gloves and a fox's claw brooch. She was ecstatically happy. She cried out, 'Hello, Adrian, my little love, have you got a kiss for your Grandma?' I kissed her rouged cheek and walked on before she saw the tears in my eyes. She croaked, 'Happy royal wedding day, Adrian.'

I passed the Co-op where the Union Jack hung upside-down, and the Sikh temple where it was hung correctly. I bought a commemorative Andy and Fergie mug and blacked Prince Andrew's big-jawed face out with a black marker pen, then I sat on the side of the canal, put some flowers in the mug and wrote a last letter to Sarah:

Dear Princess Sarah,

You will soon tire of the loon you married (he looks like the sort to hog the bedclothes to me). As soon as you grow even a *little* weary of him, remember I am waiting for you here in Leicester. I cannot promise you riches (although I have £139.37 in the Market Harborough Building Society) but I can offer intellectual chit-chat and my body, which is almost unsullied and is *years* younger than your husband's.

Well, Sarah, I won't keep you as I expect your husband is shouting oafishly for your attention.

I remain, Madam,
Your most humble and obedient servant,
Adrian Mole.

The Mole/Kent Letters

Leicester

APRIL 2 1987

To:
Barry Kent
ITK SR
Unit 2
Ridley Young Offenders Centre
Ridley-Upon-The-Dour
LINCOLNSHIRE

Dear Baz,

It was good to see you on Tuesday. The prison uniform suits you. You should wear more blue when you get out. Also Baz, non-smoking seems to agree with you, your breath was not as repellent as usual, why not give up for good? I'm sorry I have to be the bearer of bad news but somebody has to tell you that your fiancée Cindy is living with Gary Fullbright, the body builder, remember him? He won the 'Mr Muscle' competition in 1985. Cindy is expecting his baby in four months time. I expect you have just reeled back with the shock, so I'll give you time in which to recover.

Baz, Cindy isn't worthy of your love, don't for God's sake grieve over her. Her fingernails were never clean, and she had no dress sense at all. I will never forget that black rubber outfit she wore (with scuffed stilletoes and laddered fishnet tights) to your father's funeral. Also, Baz, she had the intellectual capacity of a withered rubber band. I was chatting to her once about Middle Eastern politics and it became clear to me that she thought Mr Arafat was the Arab equivalent to Mr Kipling—a type of foreign biscuit.

Onto other subjects. Nigel sends his regards, he would like to come and see you but doesn't trust himself not to burst into tears at the prison gate. Also he thinks his appearance might startle your fellow prisoners and leave you open to a certain amount of bullying in the dormitory. He is now a bald-headed Buddhist and wears orange robes and orange flip-flops (in all weathers). But, apart from these superficial changes he is still the same old Nigel, although, sadly, he got the sack from the bank: religious persecution is still alive and well in this country, I fear.

Nothing much has happened here; provincial life drags its weary way through the hours and days and months and years. I think it's time I left the library, Baz. The attitude of the general public towards the books they borrow is contemptuous. Yesterday I found a rasher of bacon inside *A Dictionary of Philosophy*. It had obviously been used as a bookmark. Further on, in the same book, I found a note addressed to a milkman:

Dear Milkman

I'd be most terribly grateful if, from now on you would be as kind as to leave one further pint of skimmed milk. That is to say dating from today (Tuesday) I would like you to deliver two pints of skimmed milk per day. I hope you will join me in my happiness at the news that my wife has returned to me. I know how much you and she enjoyed your little early morning doorstep chats. Alas, I fear I do not have my wife's common touch. However, I am fully appreciative of your achievement in delivering our milk in all weather conditions, and if, in the past, I have given the impression of being surly and uncommunicative, I'm sorry. I'm not at my best in the early morning. I am plagued with a recurring nightmare: I am lecturing to a Hall full of students when half-way through I realise I am naked. Perhaps you have similar disturbed nights? From what I've seen of you from my bedroom window, you seem to be a sensitive person. You have an intelligent mien.

Don't be offended, milkman, but I would guess that you have had little education, so, why not let us help you to educate yourself by browsing along our well stocked bookshelves? You are welcome to borrow any book—apart from the first editions which need *very* careful handling—normally I would suggest that the ill-educated use the library but our local branch is staffed by cretins.

Do think about this proposition and communicate either 'yea' or 'nay' at the bottom of this page.

With warmest regards,
Richard Blythe-Samson (No. 19)

Nay. You owe me 6 weeks money. Milkman.

Well Baz, I'll sign off now. Hope you don't take it too hard about Cindy, but somebody had to tell you and who better than your old mate,

Adrian 'Brains' Mole

P.S. It's my birthday today. I am nineteen and God am I weary of this life.

UNIT 2
April 9th 1987

Dear 'Brains'

Cindy as wrote to me and said it is lies about her and Gary Fullbright and she said she is not in the club she as just put on some wait because of working in the hot spud shop she swears on her dogs head that she stills love me and she is weighting for me. The reeason she as not bin to see me is becars she has had migraine you have got a nerv to critisize her you should look in the mirrer sometime at yourself I av herd bad things about Pandorra that she is having it off with allsorts including china men and yugoslavians their is a screw in hear who as got a son at oxford university he nows pandorra an he says she is a *slagg* wye did you tell me that stuff about the milkman it was drivval I am goinng mad in hear I want to now what is goinng on with the lads outside did spig get sentensed yet as marvin got parrole things like that do not bothur writin if you write drivvel and if you come to see me argain dress up smart I was ashammd last time and I got greif from the lads after visitting. I told them you was not all their but I still got greif my cell mate is a fat slob is name is clifton there is not room to move when he is standing up I am asking for a transferr he is the fart champion of the prison gary fullbright is lookinggg for you

stay cool
Baz

April 18th 1987

Dear Baz

How dare you infer that Pandora is a slag? She mixes with Chinese, Russians and Yugoslavians because she is taking Russian, Serbo-Croatian and Chinese at Oxford. She no doubt entertains them in her rooms until quite late at night, but believe me Baz she is not engaging in sexual intercourse with them. I know for a *fact* that Pandora is a virgin. Unlike you and Cindy, Pandora and I have a completely honest relationship. If she were no longer a virgin I would be the first to know. I will make no further comment on the Cindy / Gary situation apart from saying that I saw them *together* in *Mothercare* buying a *baby's bath* and two maternity bras, but from now on my lips are sealed. I'm sorry you are of the opinion that parts of my last letter were drivel. I thought the note to the milkman would amuse you and take your mind off your present surroundings. I don't blame you for being bitter, though. Two years imprisonment for criminal damage to a privet hedge does seem harsh. I'm scared to *cough* in the street these days in case I get done under the new Public Order Act.

I haven't had a poem from you for ages Baz. I hope you haven't given up scribbling. You have a rare, muscular sort of talent which you mustn't waste. You once had a lucrative career as 'Baz, the Skinhead Poet' on the poetry club circuit. Why not take this opportunity to write a new collection?

Yours
Adrian 'Brains' Mole

May 12 1987

Dear Brains

BANGED UP

Ok. I done it
I damaged a hedge
I broke a few twigs
A few leaves fell off
Hedges grow again.
They said it was privet
in court, in evidence.
Me, I didn't know

I was falling, drunk.
I grabbed this green thing
I fell in, got scratched
couldn't get out again.
The hedges owner called 999.
An old bloke he was
If he'd pulled me out I
woulda gone.
Instead the filth come.
'Hello Baz, you've broken
an hedge.
That's criminal damage, vandalism, wanton,
mindless'
Honest, it was a few twigs, a few green
leaves.
It needed cutting,
'I shan't press charges' said the old man.
But it was too late,
the law had started its machinery up.
It couldn't stop.
Not until the prison gate
opened and took me in.
'Criminal damage to an hedge'
I'm a joke in here.
Psychopaths get more respect
the old man, he was in court.
He wasn't happy. He looked at me
in the dock. His face said,
'I'm not happy.'
I gave him a salute one man to
another.
Then I went down.

BAZ KENT
(The Skinhead Poet)

June 30th 1987

Dear Baz

Its some months since I wrote to you I know but I've been very busy with my opus, 'Tadpole', which I am hoping to get published either in *The Literary Review* or *The Leicester Mercury*, whichever pays the most. 'Tadpole' is the story-in-rhyme of a tadpole's difficult journey to froghood. It is 10,000 words in length so far and the tadpole in question is still in the canal squirming about. So, Baz, as a fellow poet, you can see my problem. All my waking hours—apart from those in the stinking library where I am forced to earn my living—are spent writing. I care nothing for food or rest or taking hot baths. I haven't changed my clothes in months (apart from socks and underpants); what care I for the outward trappings of *petit bourgeois* society?

There have been complaints at work about my appearance: Mr Nuggett, Deputy Librarian, said yesterday, 'Mole, I am giving you the afternoon off. Go home, bathe, wash your hair and change into clean clothes!'

I replied (with dignity), 'Mr Nuggett, would you have spoken to Byron, Ted Hughes, or Larkin as you've just spoken to me?' He was dumbfounded. All he could think to say eventually was 'You used the wrong tense as far as Ted Hughes is concerned, because, unless there has been a tragic accident or a sudden illness, I believe Mr Hughes to be most vigorously alive.'

What a pedant!

Your poem 'Banged Up' was quite nice. Must stop now, 'The Tadpole' calls.

Hey ho.
A. Mole

P.S. Cindy has called the baby Carlsburg.

Adrian Mole Leaves Home

JUNE 1988

Monday, June 13th

I had a good, proper look at myself in the mirror tonight. I've always wanted to look clever, but at the age of twenty years and three months I have to admit that I look like a person who has never even *heard* of Jung or Updike. I went to a party last week and a girl of sixteen felt obliged to tell me who Gertrude Stein was. I tried to cut her off—inform her that I was conversant with Ms Stein, but I started to choke on a cheese and tomato pizza so the opportunity was lost.

So, the mirror showed me myself, as I am. I'm dark but not dark enough to be interesting: no Celtic broodiness. My eyes are grey. My eyelashes are medium length, nothing exciting here. My nose is high-bridged, but it's a Roman centurion's nose, rather than a senator's. My mouth is thin. Not cruel and thin, and it gets a bit sloppy towards the edges. I *have* got a chin, though. No mean achievement considering my pure English genes.

Since I was a callow youth I've spent a fortune on my skin. I've rubbed and applied hundreds of chemicals and lotions onto and into the offending pustulated layer of epidermis, but alas! to no avail. Sharon Botts, my present girl friend, once described my complexion as being like 'one of them bubble sheets what incontinent people use to protect their mattress'.

As can be seen from the above reproduction of Sharon's speech her knowledge of correct English grammar is minimal, therefore I have taken it upon myself to educate her. I am Henry Higgins to her Eliza Dolittle.

She is worth it. Her measurements are 42-30-38. She's a big girl. Unfortunately she measures thirty inches round the tops of her thighs, and fifteen inches round her ankles. But isn't that just like life? The most beautiful and exotic places on earth also attract mosquitoes don't they? Nothing and nobody is perfect, are they? Apart from Madonna, of course.

Anyway, I suggested to Sharon that she would look wonderful in floor length skirts but she said 'Who the bleedin' hell d'you think I am, sodding Queen Victoria?'

Summer will soon be here and I have a recurring nightmare that Sharon decides to buy and *wear* a miniskirt. In my dream she takes my arm and we stroll down the crowded high street. The public stop and stare, guffawing breaks out. A three-year-old child points at Sharon and says, 'Look at the lady's fat legs.' At this point I wake up swearing and with a pounding heart.

You may be wondering why I, Adrian Mole, a provincial intellectual working in a library and Sharon Botts, a provincial dullard, working in a laundry are having a relationship. The answer is, sex. I have grown to be rather keen on it and find it difficult to stop doing it now I've started.

Sharon and I were both virgins when we met which is a piece of good fortune too rare to overlook. What with AIDS and herpes rampaging round the world. But sex is where our relationship begins and ends. Sharon is as bored by my conversation as I am by hers, so we go elsewhere for that. She goes to see her mother and five sisters, and I go to see Pandora Braithwaite, who is the true love of my life.

I've loved Pandora since 1980. Two years ago we went our separate ways, Pandora to Oxford to study Russian, Chinese and Serbo-Croat, and me to stamp books in the library in the town where I was born. I chose library work because I wanted to immerse myself in literature. Ha! The library I work in could easily double as the headquarters of the local Philistines Society. I have never had a literary conversation at work, never. Neither with the staff nor the borrowers of the books.

My days are spent taking books off shelves and putting books back on the shelves. Occasionally I am interrupted by members of the public asking mad questions: 'Is Jackie Collins here?' To this I reply, after first glancing round the library in an exaggerated fashion. 'Highly unlikely, madam. I believe she lives in Hollywood.'

Sometimes my mother visits me at work, although I have given her strict instructions not to do so. My mother cannot modulate her voice. Her laugh could pickle cabbage. Her appearance is striking and now, in her forty-third year, merging on the eccentric. She has no colour sense. She wears espadrilles. Summer and winter. She disobeys the No Smoking signs and enters doors labelled, Private Staff Only.

My father never visits the library. He claims that the sight of so many books makes him ill.

Unfortunately, I am still living at home with my parents (and my five-year-old sister Rosie). This *ménage à quatre* co-exists in a sullen atmosphere. Half the time I feel like somebody in a Chekhov play. We've even got a cherry tree in the front garden.

I've tramped the streets looking for my own cheap apartment. I put an advertisement in the local paper.

> Writer requires a room, preferably garret.
> Non-smoker, respectable.
> Clean habits. References supplied.
> Rent no more than £10 a week.

I received three replies: the first from an old lady who offered me rent free accommodation in return for helping her to feed her thirty-seven cats and nine dogs. The second from an anonymous person who wished to 'thoroughly irrigate my colon'. The third from a Mr QZ Diablo.

I went to inspect the room offered by Mr Diablo. As soon as he opened the front door I knew I would not enjoy living in close proximity to him. Beards irritate me at the best of times and Mr Diablo's cascaded down from his chin and came to a straggling end somewhere near to his navel. However I allowed him to lead the way up the swaying staircase. The room was at the top of the house. It was part-furnished, with a bed and a structure resembling an altar. Purple cloaks hung from hooks in the walls. Mr QZ Diablo said, 'Of course I shall need this room on Thursday evenings for our meetings. We finish just after midnight, would that be too inconvenient?'

'I'm afraid it would,' I said. 'I'd prefer to sort of have the place to myself.'

'You *could* join us,' he suggested, helpfully. 'We're a jolly crowd, though cursed with a diabolical public image.'

I stared down at a red stain. It was on a multi-coloured carpet that only a mad man or mad woman could have designed, possibly in a workshop within the high walls of an institution.

'Only animal blood,' said QZ, reassuringly poking the stain with his bare big toe. 'We don't go in for human sacrifice,' he said comfortingly.

I said the words of the timid and cowardly: 'I'll think about it.'

'Yes you must,' said my host. He then led me down the stairs and out to freedom. I didn't want to tramp the streets on Thursday evenings and neither did I want to wear a purple cloak and mutter incantations over an animal sacrifice with a jolly crowd once a week. So I didn't go and live under Mr QZ Diablo's roof. This was last week.

Tonight my mother said, 'Look, when are you leaving home? We want to let your room'.

My mother is not an advocate of the tactful approach. It transpired that she had answered an advertisement from the University and arranged to act as a landlady to two male students. This would give her an income of seventy pounds a week. Fifty pounds more than she receives from me. No contest. The two students (of engineering) are moving into my room on Friday afternoon. A new single bed has been purchased and is leaning accusingly against the wall of my bedroom.

Tuesday, June 14th

I found it hard to concentrate on my work today. The Head Librarian, Mrs Froggatt (fat, fifty and with the colouring and features of a jaundiced badger), said at lunchtime, 'Mole you've moved all our Jane Austens from the great English Classics section to the Light Romance Section, pray explain.' I snapped, 'In my opinion they have been given their proper classification. Jane Austen's novels are merely trashy romances read only by snobbish, brainless cretins.' How was I to know that 'Jane Austen, Her Genius, Her Relevance to England in the 1950's' was the subject of Mrs Froggatt's dissertation for her degree in English Literature many years before I was born? As I've said earlier in my diary, we didn't discuss books or writers in the library.

That afternoon I was called into Mrs Froggatt's room. She informed me that the library was cutting down on staff due to Government financial restraints. I asked how many staff would be asked to leave. 'Just the one,' said the Jane Austen admirer, 'and, since you were the last to come, Adrian, you must also be the first to go.' Homeless and jobless!

Wednesday, June 15th

When I got home from work, where I was shunned and vilified (it turned out that all the library staff like Jane Austen), I went to my room to find that my mother had cleared out my toy cupboard.

Pinky, my pink and grey rabbit, was nowhere to be seen! I burst into the kitchen, where my mother was entertaining her neighbours to tea. Through a thick smog of cigarette smoke I looked my mother in the eye and said, 'Where's Pinky?' 'He's outside in the dustbin,' she said. She had the grace to drop her eyes. She knew she'd done me and Pinky a terrible wrong. 'How could you?' I said coldly. I flung open the door that led to the yard. Pinky's threadbare ears were visible sticking out of a black plastic bag. I pulled him out of the bag and dusted him down, then I re-crossed the kitchen and slammed the door. Huge gusts of female laughter could be heard behind me as I ran up the stairs.

Pinky is exactly the same age as me. He was purchased by my drunken father on the day of my birth. Pinky only has, only ever had, two legs; but he is still a rabbit. It is beyond my comprehension how anyone could even *think* about disposing of him. I packed my suitcase there and then. I placed Pinky carefully in a carrier bag. I went into the kitchen. I addressed my mother. 'I'm going. I shall send for my books.' I went.

Thursday, June 16th

Living here with Sharon and eight other Botts is a nightmare. I am supposed to be sleeping on the living room couch but the Botts don't go to bed. They stop up, in the living room, talking and shouting and quarrelling and watching violent videos. A few Botts, Sharon was one, went to bed at 3am but the remaining Botts had noisy discussions about babies, contraception, menstruation, death, funerals, the price of ice-cream, Clement Freud, The Queen, the man in the moon, dogs, cats, gerbils, various aches and pains they had suffered from, clothes they had tired of. Then, after an hour of malicious gossip about a woman I'd never heard of called Cynthia Bell, I closed my eyes, feigning sleep. Would they take the hint and go to bed? No.

'Funny looking bugger isn't he?' said Mrs Bott. 'What does our Sharon see in him?'

Was she referring to me?

'He's supposed to be dead brainy,' said her eldest daughter Marjorie, 'though I ain't seen no evidence of brains. He just *sits* there looking like a wet weekend.'

'He's a randy little sod,' said Farah, the youngest Bott, 'our Sharon reckons 'e can do it four times a night.'

'Do what?' screeched Mrs Bott, 'thread a needle?'

The Botts screeched and cackled for quite some time then finally, after a lot of noisy stair climbing, went to bed. Dawn was breaking as I stretched out on the couch and went to sleep.

At 6am Mr Bott, a timid and, not surprisingly, quiet man, came into the living room, and switched on breakfast television.

''Ope I'm not disturbin' you,' he said politely.

'Not at all,' I said. I got up, retrieved my suitcase from the hall, and walked out into the cool morning air.

I was on the first stage of my journey to Oxford, where I intended to fall on Pandora's neck and plead sanctuary.

Friday, June 17th

It was lunchtime when I got to Pandora's flat. Pandora wasn't in. She was having a tutorial. However, a languorous youth called Julian Twyselton-Fife *was* in. We shook hands. I've grasped firmer rubber gloves.

To make conversation I asked him what he was doing at Oxford.

'Oh I'm just farting about,' he said airily. 'I shan't sit my finals, only people who intend to *work* do that.'

He offered me Turkish coffee. I accepted, not wanting to appear provincial. When it came I regretted my inferiority complex. I asked if he shared the flat with Pandora.

'I'm married to Pandora,' he said. 'She's Mrs Twyselton-Fife. I did it as a favour to her last week. Pandora has this dinky little theory that first marriages should be gotten over with quickly, so we intend to divorce quite soon. We don't *love* each other,' he added. Then, 'In fact, I prefer my own sex.' 'Good,' I said, 'because I intend to be Pandora's second husband.'

Pinky had slid out of his carrier bag. 'I say, who *is* that divine creature?' brayed Twyselton-Fife. He grasped Pinky to his tweedy bosom. I said, 'It's Pinky.'

He crooned, 'Oh, Pinky, you're a handsome one, aren't you? Now, don't deny it, sir, accept the compliment!'

Pandora came in. She looked clever and lovely.

'Hello Mrs Twyselton-Fife.' I said.

'Oh, you know then?' she said.

'Can I stay here?' I asked.

'Yes,' she said.

So that was that. I am now in a *ménage à trois*. With a bit of luck it will soon be a *ménage à deux*. For ever.

Saturday, June 18th

I phoned home this morning. One of the engineering lodgers answered. 'Hello, Martin Muffet speaking.'

'Martin *Muffet?*' I said.

'Yes,' he said, 'and spare the jokes about tuffetts and spiders will you?'

'I wish to speak to my mother, Mrs Mole', I said.

'Pauline,' he bellowed before banging the phone down on the hall table. I heard the click of my mother's lighter, then she spoke.

'Adrian, where are you?'

'I'm in Oxford.'

'At the University?'

'Not *studying* at the University, no, that honour was denied me. If I'd had a complete set of Children's Encyclopedias perhaps I'd . . .'

'Oh don't start on that again. It's not my fault you didn't get your 'A' levels . . .'

'I'm here with Pandora and her husband.'

'Husband?'

I could image the expression on my mother's face. She would be looking like a starving dog which was being offered a piece of sirloin steak.

'Who? When? Why?' asked my mother, who in the unlikely event of being asked for her recreation by the publishers of *Who's Who,* would be honour bound to reply: 'My main recreation is gossiping.'

'Do Pandora's parents know that she's married?' asked my mother, still agog.

'No,' I replied. Then I thought, 'But it won't be long before they do, will it, mother?'

In the afternoon, Pandora and I went shopping. Julian Twyselton-Fife was lying in bed reading a Rupert Bear Annual. As we were leaving, he shouted, 'Don't forget the honey, darlings.'

Once we were outside, on the street, I told Pandora that she must start divorce proceedings. 'Right now, this minute.' I offered to accompany her to a solicitor's office.

'They don't work on Saturday afternoons,' she said. 'They play golf.'

'Monday morning,' I said.

'I've got a tutorial,' she said feebly.

'Monday afternoon,' I pressed.

'I'm having tea with friends,' she said.

'Tuesday morning?' I suggested.

We went through the whole week and then the following week. Pandora's every waking moment seemed to be accounted for. Eventually I exploded, 'Look Pandora, you do *want* to marry me don't you?'

Pandora poked at a courgette (we were in a green-grocer's shop at the time), then she sighed and said, 'Well actually darling, no; I don't intend to remarry until I'm at *least* thirty-six.'

'*Thirty-six!*' I screeched. 'But, by then I could be fat or bald or toothless.'

Pandora looked at me and said, 'You're not exactly an Adonis *now,* are you?' In my hurry to leave the shop I knocked a pile of Outspan oranges onto the floor. In the resulting confusion (in which several old ladies reacted to the rolling oranges as though they were hand grenades, rather than mere fruit coming towards them), I failed to see Pandora leaving.

I ran after her. Then I felt a heavy hand on my shoulder, then a growling voice: the greengrocer's.

'Runnin' off without payin' eh? Well I'm sick of you students nickin' my stuff, this time I'm prosecutin'. You'll be in a police cell tonight, my lad.'

It was with horror that I realised I had an Outspan orange in each hand.

Sunday, June 19th

I have been charged with shoplifting. My life is ruined. I shall have a criminal record. Now I will never get a job in the Civil Service.

Pandora is standing by me. She is feeling dead guilty because when *she* ran out of the shop she forgot to pay for a pound of courgettes, a lettuce and a box of mustard and cress.

Nothing has changed. It's still the rich what gets the gravy and the poor what gets the blame.

Mole at the Department of the Environment

JULY 1989

Monday, July 10th

I was called into Mr Brown's office today, but first I was kept waiting in the small vestibule outside. I noticed that Brown had allowed his rubber plant to die. I was scandalised by the sight of the poor, dead thing. Taking my penknife out of my pocket, I removed the decayed leaves until a brown, shrivelled stump was left.

Brown bellowed, 'Come'. So I went, though I was annoyed at being summoned in like a dog.

Brown was looking out of the window and jiggling the change in his pocket. At least I *think* that was what he was doing, the only other possible alternative doesn't bear thinking about.

He turned and glowered at me. 'I have just heard a disquieting fact about you, Mole,' he said.

'Oh,' I said.

'Oh, indeed' repeated Brown. 'Is there something you should tell me about your lavatorial habits, Mole?'

After a period of thought I said. 'No sir, if it's about the puddle on the floor last Friday, that was when I . . .'

'No, no, not at work, at home,' he snapped. I thought about the lavatory at home. Surely I used it as other men did? Or did I? Was I doing something unspeakable without knowing it? And if I was how did Brown *know?*

'Think of your lavatory *seat* Mole. You have been heard bragging about it, in the canteen.' As I was bidden I thought about the newly installed lavatory seat at home.

'*Describe* the aforementioned lavatory seat, Mole.' I fingered my penknife nervously. Brown had obviously gone mad. It was common knowledge that he wandered around on motorway embankments at nights, muttering endearments to hedgehogs.

'Well sir,' I said, edging imperceptibly towards the door. 'It's sort of a reddish brown wood, and it has brass fittings . . .' Brown shouted, 'Ha, reddish brown wood! . . . Mahogany! You are a vandal, Mole, an enemy of the earth. Consider your job to be on the line! Mahogany is one of the earth's most precious and endangered woods and you have further endangered it by your vanity and lust.'

Tuesday, July 11th

Pandora and I had an in-depth discussion about the mahogany lavatory seat tonight. It ended when she slammed the lid down angrily, and said, 'Well, I like it; it's warm and comfortable, and it's staying!'

I have started scanning the job pages in *The Independent.*

Wednesday, July 12th

Brown has sent a memo round to all departments ordering the expulsion of all aerosols in the building. A spot check will be carried out tomorrow. The typing pool are in an ugly mood and are threatening mutiny.

Thursday, July 13th

There were pathetic scenes throughout the day as workers tried to hang on to their underarm deodorants and canisters of hairspray. But by four o'clock Brown announced a victory. It was a perspiring and limp-haired crowd of workers who left the building. Some shook their fists at the sky and swore at the ozone layer, or the lack of it. One or the other.

Friday, July 14th
Bastille Day

Now there is trouble with the cleaning ladies! Apparently Brown has left a note in each of their mop-buckets ordering them to rid themselves of their Mr Sheen and Pledge. Mrs Sprogett who cleans our office was very bitter about Brown. ''E's askin' us to go back to the dark days of lavender wax,' she said. I tried to explain to the poor woman, but she said 'What's a bleedin' ozone layer when it's at home?'

Saturday, July 15th

Made a shocking discovery this morning. Our so called mahogany seat is made entirely of chip-board! I rang the bathroom fitments showroom and informed them that they had contravened the Trade Descriptions Act. I demanded a full refund.

Monday, July 16th

Went to Brown's office to appraise him of the latest facts regarding the lavatory seat, but he wasn't there. He has been suspended on full pay pending an enquiry into his wilful neglect and cruelty to a rubber plant.

Book II

Adrian Mole and the Small Amphibians

Monday, July 17th 1989

My father has just telephoned the office to say that he thinks my mother is having an affair with the lodger, Martin Muffet. I asked him what evidence he has for his suspicions. 'I found your mother in Martin Muffet's bed this morning,' he said. Apparently my mother claimed she had been 'testing the tog rate' of Martin Muffet's duvet. Will I never escape from my parents' perpetual domestic dramas? I have written to my mother, reminding her of her parental responsibilities.

Oxford
Monday July 17th

Mother,

My father telephoned me at 11.00 am this morning in some distress. He had just witnessed the unsavoury sight of you and Martin Muffet side by side in the aforementioned's bed. Your explanation 'testing the tog rate' etc seems a little, on the face of it, unsatisfactory. (Especially since we are all suffering from the highest temperatures since 1976; it was 93°F or 34°C last night. I was forced to take my pyjamas off.)

When I lived at home I was constantly complaining about *my* thin duvet, yet *not once* did you crawl into *my* bed to investigate further. My father and I are now convinced that your relationship with Martin Muffet is of a sexual nature. Though how you could bring yourself to be intimate with a man who has the complete works of Wilbur Smith by his bed baffles me. (That reminds me, you never did acknowledge the volume of Kafka's *Letters* I sent to you for your birthday.) Do I have to remind you that you have a small child in the house, namely my innocent sister, Rosie? I am confined here in Oxford with matters domestic and intellectual but as soon as I have fulfilled my commitments I will hasten home and attempt to sort out the mess.

I urge you to restrain your unseemly middle-aged passion until then.

Your son,
Adrian

P.S. May I remind you that Muffet is a mere twenty-two years of age, whereas you are forty-five.

Friday, July 21st

A reply from my mother:

Dear Adrian,

Keep your nose out, you pompous git! Martin and I are in love. He doesn't give a toss that I am twenty-three years older than him. He adores me. He says that I am a 'free spirit' and that it has been a crime to shackle me to suburbia. When Martin qualifies as an engineer he is going to build bridges in the Amazon Basin, and I will be there at his side, holding his slide rule, or whatever it is that engineers use.

Rosie is also in love with Martin; she hardly sees her father and when she does he complains that her voice gets on his nerves.

I enclose a photocopy of something Rosie had to write at school, 'My family'. By the way, did you know that Sharon Bott is pregnant? I saw her in Tesco's and she told me she is 'three months gone'. She asked me where she could contact you. I said I'd forgotten the address, but she is bound to come back to me.

Yours,
Pauline

MY FAMILY
by Rosie Mole. 6 yrs. 8 months

My family is my dog my mummy my martin my daddy my adrain and my grarndma who is old. I love my dog and my mummy and martin best aftar them comes daddy.

mummy and martin play at cards at night they do laurghing a lot. daddy shout to be quite. adrain do not live in are house he lives in annother house. I am glad. he does moane and he has got spotts on his face.

Saturday, July 22nd

Sharon Bott *swore* to me that she was on the pill. I even saw her take one now and again. Oh God! Oh God! Oh God!

pm. At last! Ken Dodd's ordeal at the hands of the Inland Revenue is over. He was acquitted of the charge of keeping £336,000 in cash in his attic. Dodd cried in the witness box and said his mother had told him not to trust banks. £336,000! It would buy a hell of a lot of tickling sticks.

Sunday, July 23rd

I am a little calmer today. My pulse rate is almost normal. I feared for my sanity last night. How much worry can somebody of my sensitivity *take?* There must be a point at which my frail human body cries, 'No more!'

WORRIES

Sharon Bott (pregnant)
Pandora (finding out)
Mother's adultery
Grandma (finding out)
Overdraft £129.08
Skin
Middle East
Rosie's treachery
Dog will die soon
Knocking in pipes
Third world
Ozone layer
Hole in shoes
Fridge on the blink

Monday, July 24th

The worst has happened! The fridge has broken down and two litres of ice-cream melted overnight and dripped through the cardboard wrapper onto the food below. Pandora came down to find me on my knees weeping into the salad crisper. She said, 'For Christ's *sake,* Adrian, get things into perspective,' but as I later pointed out to her, I can ill afford to throw food away, especially when I am already facing financial ruin. 'We're talking about a ten-day-old lettuce and half-a-pound of soggy tomatoes,' she said. She added, 'I hope you realise, Adrian, that you're well on your way to having a nervous breakdown.' She should know—most of her friends are having them, recovering from them or writing books about them.

No word from Sharon Bott.

Tuesday, July 25th

I received the following letter from Martin Muffet this morning. I have corrected the many multifarious spelling mistakes.

Dear Adrian,

OK, so you and me don't exactly hit it off, right? I know you don't rate me because I'm an engineering student. Well I'll tell you something mate. *I* don't rate floppy-wristed so-called intellectuals who fart-arse about reading books all day, right?

What's happening with me and your mother has got nothing to do with you. She is a grown woman.

I have put new washers on all the taps and re-hung the doors on the kitchen cupboards. Also I have bled all the radiators and mended the lawnmower, and your mother can now use the gas oven without stooping.

Your father is a lazy sod, and so are you. Do you realise that there was not even a *screwdriver* in the place when I moved in? It's a good job I have my own well-equipped tool box.

One day I will be your stepfather so we will have to get on, I suppose. Your dad is looking for a flat. We all had a talk last night and thought it was for the best. We are hoping to get married next December (not me and your dad, of course, I mean me and your mother). So I hope you will by then have thrown down your gauntlet and swallowed the pill.

Best wishes,
Martin Muffet (Lodger)

P.S. Wilbur Smith may not be Kafka but tell me this, what did Kafka know about the Laws of the Jungle? Also, would Kafka know which rifle to use to knock out an elephant at 500 paces? Like hell he would.

I read this moronic scrawl aloud to Pandora through the bathroom door. To my amazement she took Muffet's side! She said, 'I'm with Muffet there. *I've* lost all patience with Kafka, he lacks muscularity.'

Julian Twyselton-Fife passed by and whispered, 'Our beloved Pandora's on the turn, Aidy. She's been keeping company with those thick-necks at Rocky's gym! I smell trouble ahead.'

'She's your wife,' I snapped. 'Forbid her to go to the gym.'

'My, my,' sighed Julian. 'We *are* living in post-feminist times, aren't we? You're getting quite Wilbur Smithish. You'll be marching about in a safari suit next.'

Friday, July 28th

It's ridiculous that three sets of sheets are used every week. If I shared Pandora's bed it would save on washing powder. I've pointed this out many times but the last time I did so she replied, 'You're obsessed with the bloody laundry. Look at the fuss you kicked up over losing one single handkerchief.'

Julian said, 'If you're going to go *on* about that missing blue handkerchief again I shall go simply *berserk*.'

I shut up, but quite honestly, dear diary, I am still extremely annoyed. That handkerchief was one of a set of seven: a different colour for every day of the week. Pandora says that it's time I joined the Kleenex Culture. She said nobody uses disgusting snot rags these days: she should try telling that to Mr Brown at the Department of the Environment. His wife *left him* because Brown wouldn't let her use disposable nappies.

Saturday, July 29th

Visited my father in his new flat today. It is very sparsely furnished. It has got a single bed, a stereo, a bamboo table, two plastic stacking chairs and one high armchair designed to be used by back sufferers. 'Might come in handy if I ever get a bad back,' he said.

I sat on one of the plastic chairs and tried to think of something to say to him, words of comfort, that sort of thing, but nothing came. He looked around and said, 'Not much to show for over twenty years of marriage, is it?' He offered me a can of Pils, but I declined. (After a few sips I can feel myself turning into a lager lout, no telephone box in my vicinity is safe.)

'Is there no white wine?' I asked.

'White wine?' he mocked. 'White wine? Of course there's white wine; I've got crates of the stuff; or perhaps you'd prefer champagne.' His tirade continued, 'And how about a bit of caviar to go with the champagne, and out-of-season strawberries and profiter-bloody-roles, and a good Stilton, and Carr's bleeding water biscuits?'

Later on we talked about last week's cabinet reshuffle. Mrs Thatcher has cast Sir Geoffrey Howe aside, as though he were a used tea-bag. Sir Geoff is no longer Foreign Secretary. A bloke called John Major is. Nobody in England has heard of John Major, let alone foreigners, so I predict that he won't last long. He looks like Mr. Pratt, deputy manager of my building society. The one who refused me a hundred per cent mortgage.

Yeah, just wait, Pratt. When I am living in a country mansion with flamingos on my own personal lake I will invite you to take cocktails on the terrace. It will amuse me to see your jaw drop in amazement. Also, Pratt, I will take you on a tour of the house pointing out the many en-suite bathrooms, the fully equipped gym and the whirlpool baths. You will be sorry, Pratt, that you had such little faith in my poetic talent. Your claim that you 'had never heard of a rich poet' just proves your monumental ignorance. What about the best-seller, *Taking Cocoa with Wendy Cope* by Sir Kingsley Amis?

One day I will be England's best known poet. The *Restless Tadpole* opus is nearly finished; and *Lo! the Flat Hills of My Homeland*, my experimental novel, is flowing nicely. My next step is to find a literary agent. I wonder who acts for Prince Charles?

Monday, July 31st

The Writer's and Artists' Yearbook tells me that a person called Sir Gordon Giles is our Heir's agent. I have written to him offering him my work.

Dear Sir Gordon Giles,

As you cannot fail to see, I have enclosed samples of two works in progress. *The Restless Tadpole*, an opus. And *Lo! the Flat Hills of My Homeland*, an experimental novel. I would like you to act on my behalf and sell the aforementioned work, I had in mind Faber and Faber for *Tadpole* and Weidenfeld for *Lo!*

About finance, I cannot afford to pay you the usual ten per cent. How about five per cent? My work will sell in great numbers so you won't be out of pocket. Please send the contracts to me at the following work address:

A.A. Mole
c/o Newt Dept
Sml Amphibians Section
D.O.E.
18–21 Lord David Cecil Street
OXFORD
OX1 7SD

P.S. Please do not telephone with your congratulations. My immediate supervisor Mr Brown does not allow us incoming private calls (unless it involves the death of a close relative). I do not have a telephone in my domicile at present, due to previous profligate abuse by my fellow tenants. Please excuse the purple ink that I have used to scribe this letter; I have run out of my usual green.

Thursday, August 3rd

I received the following letter this morning:

ADRIAN MOLE
NEWT DEPT
D.O.E.
OXFORD

Sir Gordon Giles Associates
372 Doughty Street
London

Dear Adrian Mole,

Thank you for sending me your two manuscripts, the *Restless Tadpole* opus and *Lo! the Flat Hills of My Homeland.* As you cannot fail to see, I have sent them back to you. Frankly, Mr Mole, I found it enormously difficult to read your manuscript. Your miniscule handwriting and your use of green ink does not make for trouble-free reading. Did you know you had failed to put enough stamps onto your somewhat bulky (certainly heavy) parcel?

Whether you did or not, you owe my office one pound seventy-five pence. I will skip over the unpleasant objects that appeared between the pages of your manuscript as I flicked through it. Bacon rind, bus tickets, a pristine packet of condoms, a pressed wild flower . . . I fear that your novel is *too* experimental to be of any interest to the general public and the fact that it lacks all vowels makes it incomprehensible at times.

I suggest you send *The Restless Tadpole* to the Natural History

Unit at the BBC, Whiteladies Rd, Bristol. They may know what to make of it. I don't.

I send you my good wishes,
Sir Gordon Giles, Literary Agent

So that's where those condoms went. I note he didn't send them back!

Friday, August 4th

The Queen Mother is eighty-nine years old today! God bless her! A certain Ms Alison Watt has unveiled her portrait of the Queen Mother. Words fail me. The Queen Mother's head looks like a turnip. Ms Watt is twenty-three years old. Enough said, perhaps. I too am an experimental artist but I draw the line at experimenting with our most revered royal.

Oh Queen Mother
There will never be another
It is really true that your eyes are blue
Your charm and grace
And your lin-ed face. . . .
(Unfinished, got bored.)

2.00 a.m. Pandora not yet back from the gym. If she is not careful she will have more muscles than Dublin Bay.

Saturday, August 5th

At last! The *Restless Tadpole* opus is finished! I was lying in bed thinking about sex when the ending came to me.

So! Squiggling Squirming Sensuous one
Dweller of pond and canal
Stretch, stretch, to daylight and t'ward air!

Oh Creature of Darwin, leap, leap, onto land!
Hop Hop Hop 'tis England you inhabit!
Arise! Frog. Arise! A tadpole no more!
Your journey's done, your form is changed
Oh that I could do your trick
Transmogrified
Go! Go! Go! Croak your message to the world!

The End

I don't believe in false modesty, so I will state quietly, dearest diary, that I am certain it is a work of genius. One day schoolchildren will study it for GCSE. Perhaps I should send it to Andrew Lloyd-Webber. It would make a brilliant musical. Yes! *Tadpole!* would set the West End on fire.

TADPOLE! CAST LIST

Tadpole's Mother .... Julia McKenzie
Tadpole's Father .... Stephen Fry
Baby Tadpole .... Madonna
Wise Frog .... Bernard Levin

Query: has Bernard Levin got an Equity card?

Sunday, August 6th

Visited my mother's house today. I can no longer call it home. Muffet has transformed the place. She has got more shelves than a reference library. Everything works. There is even a chain on the plug in the bathroom washbasin. Muffet has always got a tool in his hand, looking for things to shorten, lengthen, tighten or loosen. My mother follows him around like a poodle performing obedience trials at Crufts. It is sickening to watch. They are still going ahead with their ludicrous plans to get married. Muffet asked me to be the Best Man! I gave as my answer an ironical laugh. Rosie has designed her own bridesmaid's dress. It is vulgar beyond belief. A paederast's delight:

off-the-shoulder pink chiffon, held together with satin rosebuds. Nabokov, that you should be alive on this day!

I cannot bring myself to sleep under the same roof as my mother and Muffet, so I begged lodgings from my grandma. I hadn't been inside the door two minutes before I was dragged into the kitchen and forced to admire more of Muffet's handiwork, this time a set of fitted cupboards. Is there no end to the man's interference? I preferred Grandma's old, unfitted kitchen, and I told her so in no uncertain terms.

She opened Littlewoods' catalogue and showed me the outfit she has ordered for the wedding. She is paying for it over two years. I wonder if Littlewoods realise the risk they are taking? Grandma is not in the best of health, she could go at any moment.

Nipped in to see Bert Baxter before fleeing back to Oxford. Bert was having his toenails cut by a peripatetic chiropodist. When Bert saw me he said, 'Well bugger me, if it ain't Master Mole. When you gettin' rid of them bleedin' spots?'

The chiropodist—a furtive-looking dwarf with dirty fingernails—asked me if I would like a pedicure. I declined with a shudder. When the dwarf had departed I made Bert's tea; a beetroot sandwich and a can of brown ale. He ate and drank with his customary lack of manners. Then he began to reminisce about his ex-dead wife Queenie. We both got maudlin and Bert confessed that he 'couldn't wait to join his gel'. Sabre has lost his ferocity (along with his teeth). Even his bark is considerably reduced in volume. I've never seen a dog go so grey so quickly. And I was concerned to see how much weight he has lost. His collar hangs round his neck like the ring round Saturn.

Wednesday, August 9th

FAX MESSAGE FOR THE ATTENTION OF:
John Tydeman Esq, Head of Radio Drama
DATE: August 9th

NO. OF PAGES: 739
SUBJECT: *Lo! the Flat Hills of My Homeland*

Here is my novel, please read it immediately and then adapt it for radio. I will charge £1,000. Please broadcast it before 8.30 pm. My grandma removes her deaf aid at 8.35 pm on the dot.

A Mole

Friday, August 11th

BROADCASTING HOUSE

Dear Adrian Mole,

Have you gone off your head, boy? You clogged my fax machine up for eight solid hours. You do *not* fax 739 pages of manuscript. You parcel it up nicely and send it through the post.

Either you or my fax seems to have gobbled up the vowels of your novel, *Lo! the Flat Hills of My Homeland.* Your manuscript is awash with consonants, but vowels are very thin on the ground, thin to the point of non-existence. You expect a thousand pounds! This made me laugh quite a lot.

I do *not* adapt plays, my role at the BBC is Head of Drama. I dictate policy and encourage new writing etc. If you want your vowelless novel adapted, you must do it yourself.

Yours (but only just)
John Tydeman

PS I am going to Australia. I shall be gone for some time.

Thursday, August 17th

Tadpole has been rejected by the Bristol BBC. No reason was given. They will be sorry one day, the moronic philistines. I have sent it to Craig Raine, who is the poetry editor of Faber and Faber. He is a very hirsute man, and he is sure to understand that I am trying to move English Poetry into the twenty-second century single-handedly. I was lucky; there were only just enough stamps in Brown's drawer.

Harry Corbett, the father of Sooty the glove puppet, died today.

Friday, August 18th

I was working on a projection of newt births (1995) when Brown burst into my cubicle and started ranting on about postage stamps. He virtually accused me of theft! From now on everybody in the Newt Dept has to sign in a little book, and give the destination and reason before taking a stamp. The stamps are now kept in a locked box, and only Brown has a key. I'm surprised he doesn't hire Securicor to keep a twenty-four-hour watch over his stupid box. All this is most inconvenient; Brown has a weak bladder and visits the lavatory at least ten times a day. His visits usually coincide with the times I urgently require a stamp. I will have to start *buying* stamps from the post office now. It is essential that my manuscripts are perused. It can only be a matter of time before I am discovered.

Wednesday, August 23rd

The government is selling off our water, surely this is illegal? If a cloud bursts over my house and rains over my garden does the water belong to me, God or Mrs Thatcher? An interesting legal point. Perhaps I will write to John Mortimer of Rumpole fame. It is sure to interest his legalistic brain. He may use the argument in one of his amusing TV episodes. I will have to protect my copyright of course.

I really *must* get a literary agent.

Pandora was seen getting into Rocky Armstrong's Cadillac last night. My informant was Mr Brown. He disapproves of Cadillacs because of their high fuel consumption.

Monday, August 28th

I have sent *Lo!* to Ed Victor, who is Iris Murdoch's literary agent. He will appreciate it, I am sure. After all, me and Iris are both concerned with the metaphysical world.

Thursday, August 31st

Princess Anne's marriage is over! Captain Mark Phillips has moved out of the main part of Gatcombe House and into a sort of prefab in the grounds. I expect he has taken the stereo with him.

A point of interest: 'Captain' is the name of Jack Woolley's dog in 'The Archers'.

Wednesday, September 20th

When I got home from work today I was astonished to find Rocky, the monolithic body builder, sitting at the table holding a cucumber sandwich between his massive cruise-missile-like fingers. He rose to his feet as I entered the room, but I hastily urged him to sit down. I had no wish to be dwarfed by his six-foot-four frame. Pandora said, 'Rocky and I are in love.' Rocky dipped his head bashfully and then looked at Pandora, and I swear, dear diary, there truly *was* love-light in his eyes. I somehow managed to croak out, 'I'm very happy for you,' before stumbling from the room and throwing myself onto my bed. I fantasised about Rocky choking on a piece of cucumber rind (Pandora never cuts the skin off). Or of him being allergic to cucumber and dying hideously swollen, surrounded by baffled helpless doctors.

Saturday, September 30th

Three hundred thousand Scottish people have failed to pay their Poll Tax. Mrs Thatcher will never dare to introduce it to England. It would be political suicide. Pandora is in her bedroom. I can hear

Rocky pleading with her in his surprisingly high-pitched voice. 'But it's been ten days, I fort you loved me, Pan.'

I can hear her saying, 'I do, Rocky, but I prefer to keep my body to myself, now go to sleep.'

Ha Ha Ha Ha Ha!

Sunday, October 1st

Julian was furious this morning, he couldn't get into the bathroom where his creams and lotions were waiting for him. Rocky could be heard floundering in the bath like Moby Dick. Julian came into my room and sat on the end of my bed. He confessed that it was no longer amusing being married to Pandora. He said, 'I may divorce her.'

I urged him to do so.

Monday, October 2nd

A letter from Barry Kent:

> Yo!
>
> I get my parole next week so Ime coming too see you ok? Get some beer in. Have you heard of a bloke called Blake he has wrote some real hard poems. Tiger Tiger is one. Nigel come to see me last week. He is not a buddhist monk now, he is joined the Socialist Worker he made me buy a magazine. I am writin' a poem for it.
>
> Yo!
> Baz

Barry Kent may be well known on the poetry reading circuit (Baz, the Skinhead Poet) but he is still a moron. Anyone who is remotely educated knows that Rupert Blake's poem is entitled 'Tyger! Tyger!' A 'y' not an 'i'.

I have sent a Telemessage via the phone at work ordering Kent *not* to come here next week.

Yo! Baz.

Regret, have to go on newt ringing expedition next week. So won't be here. It is *Tyger* not Tiger.

Yo!
Aidy

Monday, October 9th

Our household now consists of Julian Twyselton-Fife, Pandora Braithwaite, Rocky (Big Boy) Livingstone, Barry Kent and me, Adrian Mole. It is prison regulations that prisoners cannot receive Telemessages or something; also I had forgotten to tell British Telecom to put Barry's prison registration number on the front of the envelope, so he turned up. We are all squeezed into one living room, a kitchenette, two bedrooms, a box room and a bathroom. I am a person who needs my personal space. Sharing a box room with Kent is abhorrent to me; he takes up all my remaining floor space. There is nowhere to put my slippers. Also he reads all night.

But, dear diary (I would got *mad* without you to confide in!), what is sending me *insane* is that he has been taken up by the Oxford literary crowd! Those weak-chinned knobheads have invited him to every function going. He *Barry Kent!!!* has dined *in hall* at Pandora's college! Pandora said the dons thought him an 'absolute darling'. Also he has been spouting his vile poetry to crowds of impressionable undergraduates at £75 a session. Thank God he goes back to prison tomorrow. This is what he ranted at the finest in the land last night to tumultuous applause and requests for his autograph:

EDUCATION

So what?
So you know things
So you're clever
So what?

Know how to put the boot in?
Steal a car?
Slop out?
Start a riot?

You know nothink!
Nothink!
Nothink!
You. No. Think. No. Know.
Think!

Friday, October 13th

My mother telephoned the office this morning, Brown came into my cubicle to tell me that he was allowing me to take the call because it was a 'matter of life and death' that my mother speak to me. Life or death? If *death,* who had died? If *life,* had Sharon Bott decided I was the father of her unborn child? The colour drained from my face, Brown had to help me to my feet and guide me towards the instrument of my fate, namely the telephone. As I picked it up I hesitated before speaking, savouring for a moment my innocence, my ignorance, my former carefree existence. Oh how sweet life was! Oh how I had wasted those so few precious moments! Brown barked, 'Well go on, Mole, speak!'

ME (*weakly*): Hello?
MOTHER: Who's that?
ME: It's your son. Who's dead? Is it Grandma?
MOTHER: Nobody's dead.
ME: So, it's *life.* She swore she was on the pill . . . I'll pay maintenance towards the child's upkeep, but I won't marry her . . .
MOTHER: For Christ's sake, what are you wittering on about? All I wanted you for was to ask if you want a carnation or a rose?

ME: A carnation or a rose?
MOTHER: Yes.

Brown jiggled the change in his pocket impatiently as I tried to understand the significance of my mother's horticultural ravings. Had she gone mad? Had I? A rose? A carnation? Was she speaking in code?

MOTHER: Hurry up, Adrian, Martin's under the sink shouting for the mole grips.
ME: Mole grips?
MOTHER (*screeching*): A carnation or a rose!
ME: How can I possibly decide? I don't know in what context . . .
MOTHER (*berserk*): Buttonholes! Buttonholes! What do you want in your sodding buttonhole?
ME: I haven't got a buttonhole?
MOTHER: Don't be ridiculous, of course you've . . .
ME: My duffle coat is fastened by *toggles.*
MOTHER: You are not wearing that vile duffle coat to my wedding!

Brown sat down behind his desk and pretended to read a report, *The Effects of the Destruction of the Ozone Layer on the Newt Population of England, Scotland and Wales.*

ME: I have to go now . . .
MOTHER (*going barmy*): A carnation or a rose?! . . . Answer me! One or the other?
ME: I can't possibly decide right now, aesthetics are involved . . .
MOTHER (*screaming*): Answer me!

Brown frowned and cleared his throat. He doodled on the cover of the report. The doodle looked like a cruise missile, it was aimed at a circle. Inside the circle Brown printed: 'AM'. Did this mean 'a.m.' as in morning, or 'A.M.' as in my initials? Was the significance of the doodle that Brown wished me dead?

ME: All right, a rose!
MOTHER: Thank you!

I put the phone down and Brown pounced on me (not literally pounced, not like a jaguar or a lion would pounce) and said, 'From now on you are forbidden to touch that phone, and should your whole family end up in intensive care you will enquire of their relative conditions via a public phone booth!'

Saturday, October 14th

I couldn't face staying in my flat tonight, so I went to the cinema and watched *Annie* (a sign of my desperation). I ate two giant tubs of popcorn, three Bounty bars, one drink on a stick, one choc-ice, two Jumbo hot dogs and a quarter pound of Devon toffees. My skin will react tomorrow but I don't care. Even when my skin is relatively unblemished it doesn't seem to make any difference to my life: women do not seem to be attracted to me, and men do not seem to notice my existence. What am I doing wrong? Have I got halitosis? Should I use an underarm deodorant? Am I without dress sense? Should I stop wearing plastic shoes? I walked past a public house which was full of uncouth men laughing and back-slapping, and talking in confident voices of masculine things. God, how I envied them. None of them gave a toss about the future of English poetry.

I have never been into a pub on my own. I feel that I am trespassing somehow. Am I a normal man? Perhaps I am a bisexual? Will I be buying my underwear from the Marks and Spencer's lingerie range in future?

Sunday, October 15th

How I laughed at last night's entry regarding my sexuality! I could never wear women's underwear. It takes forever to iron; all those frills and lace bits! Rocky doesn't wear underpants, 'Y' fronts or boxer shorts. He wears thongs; there were ten of them on the bathroom towel-rail the other day, and there was still room for Pandora's 'NO POLL TAX' XXL T-shirt.

Wednesday, October 18th

Julian's sister is a qualified solicitor, her name is Davina Belling. She has informed Julian that his marriage to Pandora can be annulled on grounds of non-consumption. Pandora will have to be medically examined to prove that she is still a virgin. Davina Belling is not giving her services free: she is giving her brother a ten per cent discount. According to Julian this is because he threw Davina's Tiny Tears doll over the cliffs at Beachy Head fifteen years ago. My God! Women certainly have long memories. Mr Honecker, the East German Communist Party leader, was thrown out of office today. The East Germans are sick of him. They want the Berlin Wall to come down. Poor idealistic fools! The Wall will never come down in their lifetime or mine.

Thursday, October 26th

Sabre is dead, knocked down by a milk float. Bert telephoned the office this morning. Luckily, Brown was in the toilet at the time and I knew he'd be at least five minutes because he'd taken the *Daily Telegraph* in there with him. So I was able to give Bert my sincere condolences. I promised to go and visit him at the weekend and I said I would personally bury Sabre in Bert's little garden. He will be kept in the vet's fridge until I arrive. Pandora was distraught when she heard the news. It brought us together, briefly.

Nigel Lawson, the Chancellor of the Exchequer, has resigned. He had a row with Mrs Thatcher at breakfast. He is jealous because a certain Professor Alan Waters has been hanging about. John Major has got Lawson's job. Apparently John Major's father was a knife-thrower in the circus. I wonder if John Major stabbed Lawson in the back? Ha! Ha! Ha!

Friday, October 27th

Rocky has broken Pandora's pine bed. She is extremely angry. He is already responsible for the springs on the sofa going, and all the cupboard doors have lost their knobs. The man just doesn't know his own strength. Teaspoons crumple in his hands. Curtains and curtain tracks fall to the carpet. Doors are wrenched from their hinges.

Saturday, October 28th

Pandora and I picked up the box containing Sabre's deep chilled body from the vet's. We then drove in a taxi to Bert's bungalow where my mother and Mrs Braithwaite were waiting for us. Bert was in his wedding suit, I could tell he'd been crying because his nose and eyes were the colour of cough linctus (Halls). While the others had a cup of tea I went out to the garden to dig a grave. There was no spade, *naturellement*, so I was forced to grovel in the dirt and hack at the earth with a garden trowel. It wasn't long before I was filthy, sweating and totally exhausted. A horny-handed man of the soil I am not. My skills are intellectual and artistic.

Bert came out to the back door in his wheelchair and shouted, 'Hurry up, yer lazy bleeder. Sabre's starting to go off.'

I cursed the day I ever set eyes on Bert. He has caused me nothing but grief. It's because of him I failed my 'A' Levels. When my fellow classmates were revising under their angelpoises, I was helping Bert by cutting his corns, or taking his bottles back to the off licence. Why, God, why? Why me?

Anyway, I eventually got the hole dug. It took all three of us to carry Bert out to the garden. 'Looks like a bleedin' artillery shell's exploded,' said Bert nastily when he saw the hole. 'I wanted a proper, oblong grave.'

I choked back comment, though my eyes filled with tears of self-pity. Luckily, Pandora took my glistening eyes to be a sign of grief for Sabre, and she took my hand and squeezed it and said, 'There, there, my pet, I think it's a splendid hole, I mean grave.'

I was almost glad that Sabre had died. I love Pandora. She released my hand and we put Sabre in the hole, then everyone took it in turns to throw earth onto the corpse and Mr Braithwaite emptied a bag of John Innes Compost on top. Then my mother pressed some daffodil bulbs into the mixture and that was that. We went inside and had a drink; vodka and Slimline tonic for the women, and a can of Newcastle Brown for the men. I *hated* leaving Bert but on the other hand I also *hate* Bert, so I did. Pandora promised that we would call round again tomorrow. Jesus! When is Bert going to die? He must surely be one of the oldest men in Great Britain by now. He was eighty-six when I first met him and that was *years* ago.

Sunday, October 29th

How could I have written the above? Bert was sad and pathetic today, I don't really hate him. It's just that he disgusts me. I have written a poem about Sabre, I hope Bert likes it.

SABRE

Fearless Sabre, vicious, faithful,
furry friend of man,
you really should have looked, and seen that
quiet Co-op van.

I know this is a terrible poem, but Bert won't know or care.

Monday, November 6th

A letter from Ed Victor, the literary agent:

> My dear Mr Mole,
>
> Are you *serious?* Is this some kind of *joke?* Your novel lacks vowels of any kind. Is this deliberate or do you have a rare form of dyslexia? You send me a handwritten manuscript in *green* ink, which is bristling with consonants, yet utterly devoid of vowels, and you expect me to *read* the goddamn thing?
>
> Listen, I'm a busy man. I have houses to furnish, planes to catch. Douglas Adams is one of my authors. My hands are full, OK? Buy yourself a typewriter, kid.
>
> All my good wishes,
> Ed

Wednesday, November 8th

I have seriously burned my hand on a rogue catherine wheel at tonight's belated Bonfire Party. It is all Rocky's fault, he is very religious and said, 'It wun't be right to have it on a Sunday.'

I said, 'I doubt if God gives a toss *when* we earthlings let off our fireworks!'

Rocky shouted, 'Hey, less of the *language,* man! I mean 'e can 'ear you, you know.' He looked up to the sky as if expecting to see God frowning down because an earthling had said 'toss'.

Friday, November 10th

As I have been predicting for some time, the Berlin Wall has come down! Both types of Germans, Communist and Non-Communist, danced in the streets. Sprayed champagne (a waste, in my opinion) and stayed up late. World leaders are ecstatic, except for Mr Kohl, the German Chancellor, who is worried that the East Germans will go mad in the shops. Talking about shops; there are Christmas trees in all the shop windows. This is a bad sign. By Christmas Day I will be Martin Muffet's stepson.

Saturday, November 11th

A report was released today that England's cattle feed has been contaminated by lead. I have emptied the fridge of all cow-related products. I poured the milk down the toilet. (The sink is blocked up again.) My fellow tenants went mad because there was no milk for their tea or cornflakes. I received no thanks whatsoever for my life-saving actions. I am looking forward to alternative accommodation. Rang Rosie to wish her a happy birthday, but she was out at the cinema with Muffet.

Sunday, November 12th

It is Remembrance Sunday today. I watched some old men march past in Oxford town centre. I removed my balaclava as a sign of respect.

Saturday, November 18th

Barry Kent is out of prison. He turned up here today, trying to sell pieces of the Berlin Wall. Rocky bought four pieces. When asked why he said, 'It's 'istory, man. I'm gonna give 'em to my kids.'

Pandora looked up from her Russian language edition of *Tales of the Underground* by Dostoyevsky and said, 'Kids?' It was only one word, but it was the way she said it. It chilled us three men to the bone.

Rocky was the first to recover, he said, 'Yeah, I sorta' want kids one day, Pan.'

'Not with me you won't, dearie,' she said. 'No sex, I'm British.'

Then she gave a wild laugh and went back to her book. I've got to get out of here.

Thursday, November 23rd

Barry Kent has appeared on television. The great big oaf was interviewed by a big-earringed woman about his cretinous poetry. It was only a pathetic regional arts programme but the woman carried on as though Barry was the new Messiah! Kent swore twice and the words had to be bleeped out. But we viewers could clearly see that Kent's lips had formed the letter 'F'. I have written to the TV company asking them to ban Kent from our screens.

Friday, November 24th

A picture postcard of Leningrad came back from Craig Raine. I quote the remarks on the back in full:

> Mr Mole,
> *The Restless Tadpole* is effete crap.

He did not send my manuscript back.

Saturday, November 25th

Woke up in a sweat. What if Craig Raine intends to keep *The Restless Tadpole* and *publish it as his own?*

Sunday, November 26th

Wyoming Homepride has flouted the Sunday Trading Laws. I am strictly against Sunday trading. However as I happened to be passing a branch of W.H., I nipped in and bought a sink plunger.

Monday, November 27th

I have been severely reprimanded by Brown. British Telecom have squealed on me regarding the Telemessage I sent to Kent ages ago. I took the reprimand like a man. But after he had dismissed me from his office I went into my cubicle and had a good cry. Janice Conlon (Ozone Dept) heard me and came in and patted my shoulder. This made me sob louder and she put her arms around me and squashed me to her (not inconsiderable) bosom. I felt my manhood stir and come up for air. About time! Who needs you, Pandora Braithwaite? Janice has asked me out for a Chinese meal. I've got one day to practice using chopsticks.

Tuesday, November 28th

Practised all morning, using two pencils and a piece of cheese covered in Branston pickle.

Wednesday, November 29th

I will never talk to Janice Conlon ever again. She has blabbed to the whole Ozone Dept that I drank the contents of the finger bowl and washed my fingers in the saki cup. I will never live this down.

Thursday, November 30th

The newt dept were in convulsions today as the news reached them about my gastronomic *faux pas.* Even Brown gave me one of his hideous half smiles when we met at the gents' urinals before lunch. He said, 'Don't forget to wash your hands after you've been to the toilet, Mole. I believe we have a cup of saki somewhere on the premises.' Ha! Ha! Ha! Brown. Ho! Ho! Ho! What a wit! Cor strike a light, guv! You ain't 'alf funny! Stand up, Brown, and accept your award for Funniest Quip of the Year! Move over, Les Dawson, your successor has arrived!

Friday, December 1st

Quite frankly, dear diary, I wouldn't give a toss if all of the newts in the world disappeared overnight. I am sick to death of them. I have asked Brown for a transfer. I have got myself in a rut lately.

work (boring)
sex (none)
home life (dull)
intellect (re-reading *Black Beauty*)

I have got nothing to look forward to in my life. Rocky suggested I become a member of his gym, but how can I possibly display my body in public? The suggestion is laughable. Would Kafka pump iron? Would A. N. Wilson jostle in a jacuzzi? Would Osbert Sitwell flick his towel in the shower? No, gyms are not for literary men like me. Sometimes I envy Rocky, he has only ever read two books in his life. (*Roar!* by Wilbur Smith, and *The Highway Code* by HMGP). He lives in a world of sights and sounds only. He does not lie awake at night worrying about the Palestinians.

Saturday, December 2nd

A letter from my mother:

> Dear Adrian,
>
> Have you decided what to wear to the wedding yet? I warn you, kid, if you turn up in that mangy duffle coat I will personally tear your head from your shoulders. Why don't you use that virgin Access card of yours and buy a new suit: navy-blue, three-button jacket, no vent, trousers with pleated front and turn-ups. A pale-blue suit with discreet stripe and a silk tie (red or pink). Black slip-on shoes, black socks?

Have you written your speech yet? You must remember to tell the Bridesmaid and Maid of Honour how pretty they look and thank the guests for coming and read out the telegrams. *Don't* ramble on about bloody Kafka or the Norwegian leather industry. *Do* welcome Martin to the family; a hearty masculine handshake would be certain to earn you a round of applause and help to convince his parents that he is doing the right thing. (He hasn't told them I am forty-five and got kids.) I meant to invite Pandora, Julian and Rocky. Will you do this for me? And if you run into Barry Kent, ask him. It will be exciting to have a celebrity at the wedding. Did you see him on television the other night talking to Melvyn Bragg? Wasn't he brilliant? (Kent not Bragg.) I was thrilled to see that his book, *So?*, is number five in the *Sunday Times* Best-Seller List. You must be so pleased. It was you who encouraged him, wasn't it?

Yours,
Pauline (Mum)

Sunday, December 3rd

Jason Donovan, Kylie Minogue, Bros, Bananarama and Wet Wet Wet have recorded a new version of 'Do They Know It's Christmas?' All the money from this record is going to the starving of Ethiopia. I would pay good money *not* to hear this record. I have sent £5 to Oxfam. I requested a receipt.

Monday, December 11th

I am in bed suffering from the flu that is sweeping Britain like a bush fire (Australian). Julian has been very kind. He went to Boots and bought me a bottle of Night Nurse and a packet of Tunes (blackcurrant). I have already used two Andrex toilet rolls in blowing my nose. Julian also rang the office to inform Brown of my incapacity. Brown was not sympathetic. He asked Julian to tell me that I may be 'prosecuted for stealing postage stamps belonging to Her Majesty's Government'. A new worry.

Tuesday, December 12th

9.00 a.m. Too ill to write. *Four* Andrex toilet rolls is the latest update. Query: I must have expelled at least two gallons of snot. Where does it all come from and where is it stored?

4.00 p.m. Managed a rich-tea biscuit.

5.00 p.m. Crumbs in bed but too weak to brush them out. I have been deserted. Pandora is at a tutorial, Rocky is at the gym, and Julian is doing his Christmas shopping.

A playwright is in charge in Czechoslovakia! A bloke called Vaclav Havel was sworn in. Let's hope he doesn't make a drama out of a crisis.

Friday, December 15th

Ate a little Readybrek for breakfast, and now feel that I will pull through. It has been touch and go. I have been near to death and yet have pulled back from the brink. I am a better person for the experience. A calmness has descended on me. I have put things into perspective. I am now above caring about the petty things of life.

3.45 p.m. Where is my brown comb? Who has had it? I have looked after that comb for six years, man and boy.

Saturday, December 16th

The Wedding is next week and I have got nothing to wear. Should I buy or should I hire? Pandora has bought a new Gothic outfit from

Miss Selfridge. Rocky has got nine suits already and Julian is going in his nineteen-twenties blazer, Oxford bags and cravat. I have asked him not to wear his monocle. If there is a fight at the wedding it could prove to be a hazard.

Monday, December 18th

Pandora has had her beautiful treacle-coloured hair shaved off. She hasn't got a hair on her head. She ran into the bathroom and slammed the door, but I clearly saw her bald bonce shining under the ceiling light as she passed by the kitchen door. She has been sobbing in a heartbroken manner all night, but she refused to unlock the door. I slipped a note under the door, 'Dinner is ready; do you want tinned pears after?' but I received no response. Why has she emasculated herself in such a manner? Julian, Rocky and I are baffled. Her ears will stick out more than ever now.

Went back to work today. Brown is away with the flu. I hope he is ill for a long time, develops complications etc. The police haven't been to the office to question me about the stamps so perhaps Brown has decided against prosecution. I have sent him a 'Get Well' card. The queue in the post office was snaking out of the door, so I went back to the office and took a stamp from his box, put it on his card and ran to the post box to catch the four o'clock post.

Tuesday, December 19th

Bought a suit with some difficulty. The salesman said I had 'unusually short legs'. I hadn't signed the back of my Access card, so there was a ridiculous fuss at the cash till. The manager was called. The shop was full of women buying boxer shorts, but they all stopped to watch my humiliation. After I had given my grandmother's date of birth and my mother's maiden name, the manager agreed with me that I was indeed Adrian Albert Mole, born in Leicester, and he deigned to allow me to purchase a navy-blue suit, blue shirt and red silk tie. He said, 'We have to be careful, sir.'

I said that *I* would be careful not to come into his shop again. But I said it quietly, to myself. He could easily have snatched my goods back. He looked the type.

Pandora is wearing a woolly hat with a bobble. Her ears, as I feared, look like halves of pancakes stuck to the side of her head. She refuses to give a reason for her mad action. Apart from saying, 'It's something I *had* to do.'

Wednesday, December 20th

My scalp is very itchy. Scratched all night.

Mr Patel our newsagent came round with his bill early this morning. He said he wouldn't leave until it was paid. To my horror I found it to be one hundred and forty-three pounds, nine pence! It is Julian's responsibility to pay the bill every week; he has obviously been derelict in his duty. I made Mr Patel a cup of tea and sat him in the kitchen, then I knocked on Julian's door, entered and asked him where the paper money had gone.

'Spent, dear boy, spent. On a pair of Gucci loafers. I couldn't resist them. Sorry.'

I asked Mr Patel if he would accept the Gucci loafers in lieu of payment, but he looked at me as though I was an idiot and said, 'I got enough shoes, it's money I need.'

Julian appeared in his Noël Coward dressing-gown and said, 'These are not *shoes*, Mr Patel, they are works of art. With these on your feet, you will be the king of Oxford's newsagents. You will probably end up as the Chairman of the Newsagents' Federation or something.'

Mr Patel said, 'One hundred and forty-three pounds, please. I will forget the nine pence.'

'No can do, old darling,' said Julian with a smile. 'All my spondulicks are gone, I haven't a bean, I'm flat broke. In Cary Street.'

The toilet flushed and Rocky appeared, his left trouser pocket was bulging. Was this evidence of early morning sexual excitement or did the bulge mean money? I explained the situation to Rocky in words of one syllable. Rocky said, 'So Julian's a fief, what's had our money and spent it on some Guccis? That ain't on, Jule,' chided the Neanderthal, 'I ought to give you some serious grief.'

Julian fled into the bathroom as Rocky approached him. Then Mr Patel cowered in the corner under the hanging spider plant as Rocky turned and approached *him*. 'Woss the damage, Mr Patel?' he asked; and took out a large roll of banknotes.

Mr Patel left, but not before I had cancelled the majority of our magazines and papers: the *Spectator*, the *Economist*, the *Listener*, *Body Builder*, *The Stage*, *Punch*, *Vogue*, *Elle*, *Fast Car*, the *Guardian*, the *Sun*, the *Daily Mail*, *Interiors*. They have all gone. We are left with the *Independent*, the *Mirror*, the *London Review of Books*, *Viz* and *Private Eye*. Pandora agreed to read *Marxism Today*, *Interiors* and *Vogue* in W. H. Smith. Julian had the nerve to loaf about in the Gucci loafers today. He is entirely without shame.

Saturday, December 24th
My Mother's Wedding Day

The first shock was that my *father* had been invited to the Registry Office and the reception. The second shock was coming eye to eye with the dead fox hanging round my grandma's neck. Rocky drove us over from Oxford in his flash car. It is so big that, had we so wished, we could have played a game of badminton in the back. We parked outside the office on double yellow lines and went inside to wait. Grandma produced a handkerchief, spat on it, and used a corner to wipe a smut off my face. She said, 'You look a proper bobby dazzler in your suit.'

Everyone took a step back as Rocky (Big Boy) Livingstone stepped into the wedding room, only to step back yet again when Julian appeared, wagging his cigarette holder about. Pandora's parents were there with Bert Baxter. Mr and Mrs Singh were talking to Mr and Mrs O'Leary about the dustbin men's latest outrage and Martin Muffet's parents stood at the back of the room looking sad. He is their only child. My mother's parents were invited but didn't turn up. They were busy slaughtering turkeys in Norfolk.

The Registrar came into the room, a nice-looking bouncy woman in a purple leaf-printed dress. She indicated towards the doorway and my mother and Muffet appeared with Rosie behind them (she looking like a petulant Lolita). I saw several faces crumple: my father's, Mr Muffet's and Mrs Muffet's.

Muffet was dressed in an appalling suit (salmon-pink), a white shirt and a red polka dot tie. Given his height (tall), and weight (thin), he looked like a stick of Skegness rock. My mother looked *old,* quite frankly, diary. She had done her best with make-up and clothes; cream suit, black accessories, floppy hat etc, but nothing could disguise the ravages of time. She looked like Martin Muffet's *mother.*

I stepped forward and joined the wedding party. I was conscious that all eyes were on my back, so I tried not to scratch the back of my scalp (which had been driving me mad with irritation for some days). The Registrar droned on and before I knew it, it was time to sign the register and give my mother and stepfather my hypocritical good wishes. Mrs Muffet wept quietly at the back of the room. Bert Baxter said loudly, 'If I don't have a pee soon, I'll wet myself.' And Rosie, whom I had picked up in order to show her the register, screamed and said, 'Look, Mummy, Adrian has got *insects* in his hair.'

People moved away from us, except for my mother, who started to examine my hair, tuft by tuft. She said quietly, but venomously, 'Your bloody head is infested with nits! And some of them have got *wings!* Keep away from Rosie.' So, while the rest of the wedding guests were roistering in the Function Room at the British Legion, I was sitting in my grandmother's house having a foul-smelling lotion—Prioderm—applied to my hair. Grandma was wearing rubber gloves and a nasty expression on her face.

I am not in any of the photographs. Julian read my speech out and was rewarded with loud laughter and applause. (He failed to give me a credit.) There was a small fight in the gents between my father and Mr Muffet senior, but it was not personal; they were fighting over the last piece of shiny toilet paper. Rocky, Julian and Pandora picked me up from Grandma's. We drove back to Oxford in silence. The car was full of foul fumes from the lotion which has to be kept on for twenty-four hours. I have decided not to carry on with my diary. Why catalogue such misery? What purpose does it serve?

2.00 a.m. Pandora has just confessed to me that the reason she shaved her hair off was because her scalp was infested with head lice. I will never, ever, forgive her for passing them on to me. Never, ever. My love for her has gone. Kaput.

Monday, January 1st 1990

These are my New Year's Resolutions:

1. Finish *War and Peace*
2. Go to the dentist with aching molar
3. Take driving lessons
4. Change job
5. Make a diary entry every day

Tuesday, January 9th

Brown ordered me to take down the Christmas decorations in my cubicle today. He said he was 'sick of living under the dreadful spectre of Christmas'. Brown doesn't believe in Christmas. He spent Christmas Day classifying seaweed in Dungeness.

Friday, February 16th

My first driving lesson today. My instructor is a woman called Vanessa Partridge. She is no relation to my former best friend, Nigel Partridge, who is now in the army. I was expecting to spend my first lesson driving around a deserted airfield or something, but instead Ms Partridge ordered me onto the *roads!* Busy roads. I felt like an Iranian on a suicide mission. At least Iranians have their religion to comfort them, but, being an atheist, I had nothing. As I came to my first roundabout I prayed to God to protect me from all the nasty cars and lorries.

Friday, April 6th

I am getting the hang of the gears now, but I have a horrible suspicion that I am probably one of life's pedestrians. Pandora passed her test first time last week. She drives Rocky's car as though she is taking part in a *Grand Prix* race.

The inmates are still on the roof of Strangeway prison. Mrs Thatcher is having to be restrained from climbing up there and beating their brains in.

Friday, April 13th

Vanessa has got absolutely gorgeous legs. When she operates the dual controls (which is quite often), I can't take my eyes off them. I asked her when I can put in for my test. She looked shifty and said, 'Not for a while yet.' Why not? I have had *seven* driving lessons at ten pounds a time. I have very limited financial resources. I am still paying for my suit. In fact Access are hounding me for this month's payment.

Friday, April 27th

Still can't manage the clutch, and I can't stop driving too near to the kerb. I nearly wiped out a pensioner's shopping trolley today.

Vanessa has had streaks put into her hair—either that or she has gone grey more or less overnight.

Friday, May 4th

Brown was waiting for me when I got back from my driving lesson today (gears better but still can't bring myself to overtake anything. I was quite happy to follow that silage spreader, but Vanessa was, I thought, rather impatient.) Anyway, Brown said that two reams of Conqueror A4 paper had gone missing from the stationery cupboard since the last audit in 1989 (March). Did I know its whereabouts? I quipped, 'Perhaps it's gone on holiday, perhaps it's sick of being stationary.' Brown was not amused.

Friday, May 11th

Received the manuscript of *The Restless Tadpole* back from Craig Raine; after many letters and telephone calls, I might add. The manuscript was in a dreadful condition and was littered with Raine's notes in the margin. 'Laughably pretentious' and 'numbingly philistine' being two of the less offensive and non-obscene terms.

My novel, *Lo! the Flat Hills of My Homeland,* is currently in the office of the chief bloke at the National Theatre, David Aukin. I have suggested to him that it could easily be adapted for the stage. The Olivier would be ideal. There would be 144 in the cast and I would need a full orchestra, a lake, and a deer park, plus half-a-dozen live deer. But I don't see why it shouldn't be done—English theatre needs spectacle. I photocopied the script using A4 Conqueror. I hope Mr Aukin is impressed.

Thank God for the warmer weather. Vanessa has discarded her black woolly tights and taken to wearing sheer stockings. I could hardly control *myself* today, let alone the lousy stinking pigging car. These driving lessons are doing my head in.

Saturday, June 2nd

Lo! came back today. Mr Aukin's note was kind.

Dear Mr Mole,

Thank you for sending me your manuscript, *Lo! the Flat Hills of My Homeland.* I read it with considerable interest. However, we are operating under difficult financial constrictions, and therefore it would be impossible for us to employ a cast of 144 actors, plus six live deer.

I do wish you good luck,
David Aukin

P.S. There seems to be something wrong with your word processor. Does it object to printing out vowels?

I am restless today. Yesterday's collision with the tar spreading lorry has upset me more than I realised. I am suffering from delayed reaction. Phoned Vanessa, she was at the chiropractor's trying to get her neck back to its original angle.

Sunday, June 3rd

Perhaps I should put the vowels back in. The world of literature is obviously not ready for another James Joyce. Barry Kent has been asked to do 'With Great Pleasure' on Radio Four. I wept when I heard this. He has asked me to join him for the evening—in the audience.

Friday, June 15th

I can now steer in a straight line. Vanessa is still wearing the surgical collar. She hates it but I quite like to see a woman with a bit of white next to her face.

Friday, June 29th

Pandora is now entitled to call herself Dr Pandora Braithwaite. And she will, dear diary, she will.

Did a three-point turn. It took fifteen goes. I asked Vanessa if she thought I was near to taking my test. She said, 'How near is Jupiter to Earth?' I had no idea she was interested in astronomy.

Sunday, July 1st

Dr Pandora Braithwaite and Rocky (Big Boy) Livingstone have gone to Barbados to meet Rocky's parents. Rocky's dad is a bank manager, and his mother is an expert on marine life. Rocky is the only one out of four children *not* to go to university. He is also the only millionaire. Rocky opened his fifth gym yesterday, in Grantham. Somebody from *Coronation Street* performed the opening ceremony. The one who serves in the shop. Not the grocery shop, the other one. I can't remember her name, anyway a thousand middle-aged women blocked Grantham's traffic trying to catch a glimpse of—Mavis? Doreen? Bet? It will come to me.

Friday, July 13th

Dual carriageway. Got up to forty-five mph!

Thursday, July 19th
Oxford Playhouse, 7.30 pm Tonight

Barry Kent rambled his way through the BBC recording of 'With Great Pleasure' tonight. He had a famous actor and actress to read his favourite works of prose and poems. The actor used to be the big one in that television series to do with a Dutch policeman. The actress was the one who was always crying in the one about Victorian servants. To finish, Kent bellowed his own poem, 'Earwig'.

EARWIG

How to measure earwig poo?
How to find how much they do?
Are there scales to measure it?
Those tiny piles of earwig shit?

The BBC have agreed to transmit the word 'shit' providing they can bleep out the more obscene words used throughout the programme. I fear this points to a lowering of standards. Kent will be on 'Desert Island Discs' next!

Friday, July 20th

Did a three-point turn in five goes. I am absolutely thrilled with myself. I have started looking at second-hand cars with a view to purchasing one. Got a postcard from my mother and Muffet today, they are in Spain.

Dear Adrian,
Sun, Sand, Sex and Sangria!

Salutations!
Mum and Martin

Saturday, July 21st

Went to visit my father today, he has received an identically worded postcard from his ex-wife and Muffet. He is furious because my mother has dumped Rosie on him. Rosie is even more furious because she was not invited to go to España. My father has made no attempt to amuse Rosie, apart from buying her a packet of felt-tip pens, and a dot-to-dot book. She was going 'stir crazy' so I took her to see *Bambi*. She broke down and wept in such a heartbreaking manner that an usherette shone her torch on her heaving shoulders and ordered her to be quiet. I snapped, 'My sister is a sensitive, sweet little girl, how dare you try to repress her emotions!'

I lectured the usherette on the dangers of internalising others' feelings, how it can lead to constipation, ulcers and mental illness. The usherette said, 'Yer a bleedin' loony yerself, if you ask me. An' if you don't shut yer big yap you'll find yerself in the manager's office.'

Sunday, July 22nd

Rosie clung onto my legs today and begged me to take her back to Oxford with me. My father made no attempt to restrain her outburst. He carried on watching *Songs of Praise* out of the corner of his eye. He enjoys mocking the congregation. From today onwards I am going to make a daily diary entry.

Drought conditions prevail. England looks like the parched part of Tunisia.

Thursday, August 2nd

Iraq has invaded Kuwait. I'm not sure why. Something to do with oil.

Friday, August 17th

Practised doing a hill start. Rolled down the hill as often as the Duke of York's men in the song. Vanessa has developed several nervous mannerisms, she is obviously a deeply neurotic woman. Why do *I* always get them?

Friday, August 31st

I am coming to the (reluctant) conclusion that Vanessa is an incompetent driving instructor. I am making very little progress. I may defect and go to the British School of Motoring. I will miss her, but the facts must be faced. She is no good at her job. I'm still nowhere near to taking my test.

Saturday, September 1st

Julian has got a job as a researcher at the BBC. He is working on documentary called 'Living with Failure'. He has asked me if the producer can have a quick chat with me. Don't ask me why.

Sunday, September 2nd

Wrote to Vanessa this morning, telling her that I have decided to be a pedestrian. This is a lie but I don't want to hurt her feelings. It must be terrible to be such a failure.

Friday, September 7th

First lesson with 'Quick Pass' Driving School. My instructor is called Dave Crooks. My God! Talk about impatient! Talk about irritable! Talk about lack of self-control! He shouted at me constantly, and never took his foot off the dual controls. When I kangaroo'd to a halt outside the D.O.E. he wiped his brow and said, 'Who taught you to drive like that?' I told him and he said, 'I don't understand it. Vanessa Partridge is a brilliant instructor. Her pupils have an incredible first-time pass rate.'

Friday, September 21st

Dave Crooks and I have parted company. He said, 'I'm sorry, Adrian, but I am leaving Quick Pass: it's too dangerous. I am going to teach free-fall parachuting instead.'

Why is it that nobody has got *backbone* in England any more?

Friday, September 28th

First lesson with 'Sure Pass' Driving School. Instructor an old git called Harold Wainwright. Lesson stopped half way through. Wainwright drove off, leaving me stranded in an outer suburb. What *is* it about driving instructors? Are mad people attracted to the profession or are they sent mad by incompetent pupils? I rang 'Sure Pass' to report their employee's unprofessional behaviour, but Harold Wainwright answered the phone. It is his firm.

Friday, October 5th

'Drivepass', first lesson. 12.00 am to 1.00. Instructor's name, Dave Singh.

Friday, October 12th

'Drivesure', instructor Mr Chan.

Friday, October 19th

'Upass', instructor Mr Abdul bin Salman.

Mr Salman has advised me against buying a second-hand car. He said, 'It would be somewhat premature, Mr Mole.'

Saturday, October 20th

Rocky has gone off with another woman! Pandora is devastated. I pointed out to her that Rocky is a red-blooded man who needs to feel that he is desirable and sexually lusted over. 'In short,' I said, 'Rocky wants sex, you won't give him any, so, not unnaturally, he has gone elsewhere; namely to Carly Pick, the receptionist at Rocky's new gym in Market Harborough.'

Pandora rang for a taxi; there was murder in her eyes. When asked for the destination she snarled, 'Market Harborough, and make it snappy, I am a doctor and this is an emergency.' She didn't tell the taxi firm she is only a doctor of philosophy.

Sunday, October 21st

My plans for a quiet time at home putting the vowels back into *Lo! the Flat Hills of My Homeland* were thrown into disarray when Carly Pick turned up at the flat with Rocky, who had come round to pick up his thongs. Pandora came out of her room looking like a harridan. She threw curses at everyone in the room (including me, unfairly I thought). Then she threw the thongs in Rocky's face and told Carly Pick that she had a face like a warthog's armpit. And that she was welcome to Rocky (Big Boy) Livingstone because he farted in bed.

Hey Ho, Hey Nonny No. Such is life. Or is it Heigh Ho? Hay Ho?

Monday, November 5th

Remembering last year's incident with the catherine wheel (I still have the scar), I decided to stay in and work on the last chapter of *Lo!* Pandora is out at a bonfire party given by Professor Cavendish, the notorious drunkard and womaniser. How he does it I don't know. (I saw him in the off-licence, he looked at least forty-five). He is scruffy and has got a battered-up face. His third wife has just left him. She has written a full account of her reasons for doing so. It appeared in the *News of the World* last Sunday under the headline CLEVER CLOGS PROF SEVEN TIMES A NIGHT 'TOO MUCH FOR ME'—WIFE.

Seven times a night! I've just reckoned it up. I've only done it five times in two years. From now on I am going to make a daily record of my doings in my diary.

Some people are predicting that Mrs Thatcher will resign. As if!

Monday, November 12th

A letter from my mother:

> Aidy,
>
> Saw Sharon Bott and son today. He, Glenn, looks exactly, but exactly like you: lips, nose, ears, mad hairline—everything.
>
> I know this is awkward but am I a grandmother or aren't I? I think I should be told. Are you keeping something from me? Martin sends his best and asks when you are coming to see us? Why aren't you on the phone like normal people?
>
> Grandma is using a walking frame to get to the shops now . . . Do you miss Mrs Thatcher? I wish John Major would do something about his hair. It would look lovely brushed back. Grandma has found three World War II gasmasks in the shed . . .

The rest was drivel apart from a bit at the end about the dog missing me. Which is a lie. On my past visits the dog has completely ignored me. Two can play at that game, dog!

From now on I will make a daily entry in my diary.

Monday, December 24th

I have just bumped into Sharon Bott in Woolworths in Leicester, where I was purchasing Christmas presents. She had a strange-looking moon-headed toddler with her. 'Say hello to Adrian, Glenn,' she said. I bent over the buggy and the kid gave me a slobbery smile. Is Glenn the fruit of *my* loins? Did *my* seed give him life? I must know. The kid was sucking the head of a Ninja Turtle. He looked fed up.

Monday, December 31st

The Prime Minister, Mr John Major, is trying to negotiate with the bloke in charge of Iraq. Some alarmists are predicting war. How absolutely ridiculous! We live in modern times. War belongs to the Middle Ages. There is no need to go to war. Not now we've got fax machines. Must go now, Professor Cavendish has just come out of Pandora's bedroom. He has promised to read *Lo!* and *Tadpole.*

Book III

Adrian Mole: The Wilderness Years

Tuesday, January 1st 1991

I start the year with a throbbing head and shaking limbs, owing to the excessive amounts of alcohol I was forced to drink at my mother's party last night.

I was quite happy sitting on a dining chair, watching the dancing and sipping on a low-calorie soft drink, but my mother kept shouting at me: 'Join in, fishface,' and wouldn't rest until I'd consumed a glass and a half of Lambrusco.

As she slopped the wine into a plastic glass for me, I had a close look at her. Her lips were surrounded by short lines, like numerous river beds running into a scarlet lake; her hair was red and glossy almost until it reached her scalp and then a grey layer revealed the truth: her neck was saggy, her cleavage wrinkled and her belly protruded from the little black dress (*very* little) she wore. The poor woman is forty-seven, twenty-three years older than her second husband. I know for a fact that he, Martin Muffet, has *never* seen her without make-up. Her pillow slips are a disgrace; they are covered in pan-stick and mascara.

It wasn't long before I found myself on the improvised dance floor in my mother's lounge, dancing to 'The Birdie Song', in a line with Pandora, the love of my life; Pandora's new lover, Professor Jack Cavendish; Martin Muffet, my boyish stepfather; Ivan and Tania, Pandora's bohemian parents; and other inebriated friends and relations of my mother's. As the song reared to its climax, I caught sight of myself in the mirror above the fireplace. I was flapping my arms and grinning like a lunatic. I stopped immediately and went back to the dining chair. Bert Baxter, who was a hundred last year, was doing some clumsy wheelchair dancing, which caused a few casualties; my left ankle is still bruised and swollen, thanks to his carelessness. Also I have a large beetroot stain on the front of my new white shirt, caused by him flinging one of his beetroot sandwiches across the room under the misapprehension that it was a party popper. But the poor old git is almost certain to die this year—he's had his telegram from the Queen—so I won't charge him for the specialist dry cleaning that my shirt is almost certain to require.

I have been looking after Bert Baxter for over ten years now, going back from Oxford to visit him, buying his vile cigarettes, cutting his horrible toenails, etc. When will it end?

My father gate-crashed the party at 11.30. His excuse was that he wanted to speak urgently to my grandma. She is very deaf now, so he was forced to shout above the music. 'Mum, I can't find the spirit level.'

What a pathetic excuse! Who would be using a spirit level on New Year's Eve, apart from an emergency plumber? It was a pitiful request from a lonely, forty-nine-year-old divorcee, whose navy blue mid-eighties suit needed cleaning and whose brown moccasins needed throwing away. He'd done the best he could with his remaining hair, but it wasn't enough.

'Any idea where the spirit level is?' insisted my father, looking towards the drinks table. Then he added, 'I'm laying some paving slabs.'

I laughed out loud at this obvious lie.

My grandma looked bewildered and went back into the kitchen to microwave the sausage rolls and my mother graciously invited her ex-husband to join the party. In no time at all, he had whipped his jacket off and was frugging on the dance floor with my eight-year-old sister Rosie. I found my father's style of dancing acutely embarrassing to watch (his role model is still Mick Jagger); so I went upstairs to change my shirt. On the way, I passed Pandora and Bluebeard Cavendish in a passionate embrace half inside the airing cupboard. He's old enough to be her father.

Pandora has been mine since I was thirteen years old and I fell in love with her treacle-coloured hair. She is simply playing hard to get. She only married Julian Twyselton-Fife to make me jealous. There can be no other possible reason. Julian is a bisexual semi-aristocrat who occasionally wears a monocle. He strains after eccentricity but it continues to elude him. He is a deeply ordinary man with an upper-class accent. He's not even good-looking. He looks like a horse on two legs. And as for her affair with Cavendish, a man who dresses like a tramp, the mind boggles.

Pandora was looking particularly beautiful in a red off-the-shoulder dress, from which her breasts kept threatening to escape. Nobody would have guessed from looking at her that she was now Dr Pandora Braithwaite, fluent in Russian, Serbo-Croat and various other little-used languages. She looked more like one of those supermodels that prowl the catwalks than a Doctor of Philosophy. She certainly added glamour to the party: unlike her parents, who were dressed as usual in their fifties beatnik style—polo necks and corduroy. No wonder they were both sweating heavily as they danced to Chuck Berry.

Pandora smiled at me as she tucked her left breast back inside her dress, and I was pierced to the heart. I truly love her I am prepared to wait until she comes to her senses and realises that there is only one man in the world for her, and that is *me*. That is the reason I followed her to Oxford and took up temporary residence in her box room. I have now been there for a year and a half. The more she is exposed to my presence, the sooner she will appreciate my qualities. I have suffered daily humiliations, watching her with her husband and her lovers, but I will reap the benefits later when she is the proud mother of our six children and I am a famous author.

As the clock struck twelve, everyone joined hands and sang 'Auld Lang Syne'. I looked around, at Pandora; at Cavendish; at my mother; at my father; at my stepfather; at my grandma; at Pandora's parents, Ivan and Tania Braithwaite; and at the dog. Tears filled my eyes. I am nearly twenty-four years of age, I thought, and what have I done with my life? And, as the singing died away, I answered myself—nothing, Mole, nothing.

Pandora wanted to spend the first night of the New Year in Leicester at her parents' house with Cavendish, but at 12.30 a.m. I reminded her that she and her aged lover had promised to give me a lift back to Oxford. I said, 'I am on duty in eight hours' time at the Department of the Environment. At 8.30 sharp.'

She said, 'For Christ's sake, can't you have one poxy day off without permission? Do you have to kow-tow to that little commissar Brown?'

I replied, with dignity, I hope, 'Pandora, some of us keep our word, unlike you, who on Thursday the second of June 1983 promised that you would marry me as soon as you had finished your "A" levels.'

Pandora laughed, spilling the neat whisky in her glass. 'I was sixteen years old,' she said. 'You're living in a bloody time warp.'

I ignored the insult. 'Will you drive me to Oxford as you promised?' I snapped, dabbing at the whisky droplets on her dress with a paper serviette covered in reindeer.

Pandora shouted across the room to Cavendish, who was engaged in conversation with Grandma about the dog's lack of appetite: 'Jack! Adrian's insisting on that lift back to Oxford!'

Bluebeard rolled his eyes and looked at his watch. 'Have I got time for one more drink, Adrian?' he asked.

'Yes, but only mineral water. You're driving, aren't you?' I said.

He rolled his eyes again and picked up a bottle of Perrier. My father came across and he and Cavendish reminisced about the Good Old Days, when they could drink ten pints in the pub and get in the car and drive off 'without having the law on your back'.

It was 2 a.m. when we finally left my mother's house. Then we had to call at the Braithwaites' house to collect Pandora's overnight bag. I sat in the back of Cavendish's Volvo and listened to their banal conversation. Pandora calls him 'Hunky' and Cavendish calls her 'Monkey'.

I woke up on the outskirts of Oxford to hear her whisper: 'So, what did you think of the festivities at Maison Mole, Hunky?'

And to hear him reply: 'As you promised, Monkey, delightfully vulgar. I enjoyed myself enormously.' They both turned to look at me, so I feigned sleep.

I began to think about my sister Rosie, who is, in my view, totally spoilt. The *Girls' World* model hairdressing head she had demanded for Christmas had stood neglected on the lounge window sill since Boxing Day, looking out onto the equally neglected garden. Its retractable blond hair was hopelessly tangled and its face was smeared with garish cosmetics. Rosie was dancing earlier with Ivan Braithwaite in a manner totally unsuited to an eight-year-old. They looked like Lolita and Humbert Humbert.

Nabokov, fellow author, you should have been alive on that day. It would have shocked even you to see Rosie Mole pouting in her black miniskirt, pink tights and purple cropped top!

I have decided to keep a full journal, in the hope that my life will perhaps seem more interesting when it is written down. It is certainly not interesting to actually live my life. It is tedious beyond belief.

Wednesday, January 2nd

I was ten minutes late for work this morning. The exhaust pipe fell off the bus. Mr Brown was entirely unsympathetic. He said, 'You should get yourself a bicycle, Mole.' I pointed out that I have had three bicycles stolen in eighteen months. I can no longer afford to supply the criminals of Oxford with ecologically sound transport.

Brown snapped, 'Then *walk*, Mole. Get up earlier and *walk*.'

I went into my cubicle and shut the door. There was a message on my desk informing me that a colony of newts had been discovered in Newport Pagnell. Their habitat is in the middle of the projected new ring road. I rang the Environmental Office at the Department of Transport and warned a certain Peter Peterson that work on the ring road could be subject to delay.

'But that's bloody ludicrous,' said Peterson. 'It would cost us hundreds of thousands of pounds to re-route that road, and all to save a few slimy reptiles.'

That is also my own private point of view of newts. I'm sick of them. But I am paid to champion their right to survive (in public at least), so I gave Peterson my standard newt conservation lecture (and pointed out that newts are amphibians, not reptiles). I spent the rest of the morning writing up the Newport Pagnell case.

At lunchtime I left the Department of the Environment and went to collect my blazer from the dry cleaners. I had forgotten to take my ticket. (It was at home, being used as a bookmark inside Colin Wilson's *The Outsider.* Mr Wilson is Leicester-born, like me.)

The woman at the cleaners refused to hand over my blazer, even though I pointed to it hanging on the rack! She said, 'That blazer has got a British Legion badge on it. You're too young to be in the British Legion.'

An undergraduate behind me sniggered.

Enraged, I said to the woman, 'You are obviously proud of your powers of detection. Perhaps you should write an *Inspector Morse* episode for the television.' But my wit was lost on the pedant.

The undergraduate pushed forward and handed her a stinking duvet, requesting the four-hour service.

I had no choice but to go home and collect the ticket, go back to the cleaners, and then run with the blazer, encased in plastic, slung over my shoulder, all the way back to the office. I have got a blind date tonight and the blazer is all I've got to wear.

My last blind date ended prematurely when Ms Sandra Snape (non-smoking, twenty-five-year-old, vegetarian: dark hair, brown eyes, five foot six, not unattractive) left Burger King in a hurry, claiming she'd left the kettle on the stove. I am now convinced, however, that the kettle was an excuse. When I returned home that night, I discovered that the hem was down at the back on my army greatcoat. Women don't like a scruff.

I was twenty-five minutes late getting back to work. Brown was waiting for me in my cubicle. He was brandishing my Newport Pagnell newt figures. Apparently I had made a mistake in my projection of live newt births for 1992. Instead of 1,200, I had put down 120,000. An easy mistake to make.

'A hundred and twenty thousand newts in 1992, eh, Mole?' sneered Brown. 'The good citizens of Newport Pagnell will be positively inundated with amphibia.'

He gave me an official warning about my time-keeping and ordered me to water my cactus. He then went to his own office, taking my paperwork with him. If I lose my job, I am done for.

11.30 p.m. My blind date did not turn up. I waited two hours, ten minutes in the Burger King in the town centre. Thank you, Ms Tracy Winkler (quiet blonde, twenty-seven, non-smoker, cats and country walks)! That is the last time I write to a box number in the *Oxford Mail*. From now on, I will only use the personal column of the *London Review of Books*.

Thursday, January 3rd

I have the most terrible problems with my sex life. It all boils down to the fact that I *have* no sex life. At least not with another person.

I lay awake last night, asking myself why? Why? Why? Am I grotesque, dirty, repellent? No, I am none of these things. Am I normal-looking, clean, pleasant? Yes, I am all of these things. So what am I doing wrong? Why can't I get an average-looking young woman into my bed?

Do I exude an obnoxious odour smelled by everyone else but me? If so, I hope to God somebody will tell me and I can seek medical help from a gland specialist.

At 3 a.m. this morning my sleep was disturbed by the sound of a violent altercation. This in itself is not unusual, because this house provides a home for many people, most of them noisy, drunken undergraduates, who sit up all night debating the qualities of various brands of beer. I went downstairs in my pyjamas and was just in time to see Tariq, the Iraqi student who lives in the basement, being led away by a gang of criminal-looking men.

Tariq shouted, 'Adrian, save me!' I said to one of the men, 'Let him go or I will call the police.'

A man with a broken nose said, 'We *are* the police, sir. Your friend is being expelled from the country, orders of the Home Office.'

Pandora came to the top of the basement stairs. She was wearing very little, having just left her bed. She said in her most imperious manner: 'Why is Mr Aziz being expelled?'

'Because,' said the thuggish one, 'Mr Aziz's presence is not conducive to the public good, for reasons of national security. Ain't you 'eard there's a war on?' he added, ogling Pandora's satin nightshirt, through which the outline of her nipples was clearly visible.

Tariq shouted, 'I am a student at Brasenose College and a member of the Young Conservatives: I am not interested in politics!'

There was nothing we could do to help him, so Pandora and I went back to bed. Not the same bed though, worse luck.

At nine o'clock the next morning, I rang the landlord, Eric Hardwell, on his car phone and asked if I could move into the now vacant basement flat. I am sick of living in Pandora's box room. Hardwell was in a bad mood because he was stuck in traffic, but he agreed, providing I can give him a £1000 deposit, three months' rent in advance (£1200), a banker's reference and a solicitor's letter stating that I will not burn candles, use a chip pan, or breed bull terrier dogs in the basement.

I shall have to stay here in the box room. I need to use my chip pan on a daily basis.

Lenin was right: all landlords *are* bastards.

Somebody who looked like Tariq was on *Newts At Ten;* he was waving from the steps of an aeroplane which was bound for the Gulf. I waved back in case it was him.

Correction: I meant, of course, to write *News At Ten.*

Friday, January 4th

Woke up at 5 a.m. and was unable to get back to sleep. My brain insisted on recalling all my past humiliations. One by one they passed in front of me: the bullying I endured from Barry Kent until my grandma put a stop to it; the day at Skegness when my father broke the news to me and my mother that his illegitimate son, Brett, had been born to his lover, Stick Insect; the black day when my mother ran away to Sheffield for a short-lived affair with Mr Lucas, our smarmy neighbour; the day I learned that I had failed 'A' level Biology for the third time; the day Pandora married a bisexual man.

Then, after the humiliations came the *faux pas,* a relentless march: the time I sniffed glue and got a model aeroplane stuck to my nose; the day my sister, Rosie, was born and I couldn't remove my hand from the spaghetti jar where the five pound note for the taxi fare to the maternity hospital was kept; the time I wrote to Mr John Tydeman at the BBC and addressed him as 'Johnny'.

The procession of *faux pas* was followed by a parade of bouts of moral cowardice: the time I crossed the road to avoid my father because he was wearing red pom-pom hat; my craven behaviour when my mother was stricken with a menopausal temper tantrum in the Leicester market place—I should not have walked away and hidden behind that flower stall; the day I had a jealous fit, destroyed the complimentary tickets for Barry Kent's first professional gig on the poetry circuit and blamed the dog; my desertion of Sharon Bott when she announced she was pregnant.

I despise myself. I deserve my unhappiness. I am truly a loathsome person.

I was relieved when my travelling alarm clock roused me from my gloomy reverie and told me that it was 6.30 a.m. and time to get up.

NIPPLES BY A. MOLE

Like raspberries
taken from the freezer
Inviting tongue and lips
but warning not to bite
Not yet
soon
But not yet

I am on flexitime and had agreed to start work at 7.30 a.m., but somehow, although I left my box room at 7 a.m., I didn't arrive at work until 8 a.m. A journey of half a mile took me an hour. Where did I go? What did I do? Did I have a blackout on the way? Was I mugged and left unconscious? Am I, even as I write, suffering from memory loss?

Pandora is constantly telling me that I am in urgent need of psychiatric help. Perhaps she is right. I feel as though I am going mad; that my life is a film and that I am a mere spectator.

Saturday, January 5th

Julian, Pandora's upper-crust husband, has returned from his Christmas sojourn in the country with his parents. He shuddered when he walked through the front door of the flat.

'God!' he said. 'The pantry of Twyselton Manor is bigger than this bloody hole.'

'Then why come back, sweetie?' said Pandora, his so-called wife.

'Because, *ma femme*, my parents, poor, deluded creatures, are paying mucho spondulicks to keep me here at Oxford, studying Chinese.' He laughed his neighing horse's laugh. (And he's certainly got the teeth for it.)

'But you haven't been to a lecture for over a year,' said Dr Braithwaite (12 'O's, 5 'A's, B.A. Hons. and D.Phil.).

'But my lecturers are all such boring little men.'

'It's such a waste, husband,' said Pandora. 'You're the cleverest man in Oxford *and* the laziest. If you're not careful, you'll end up in Parliament.'

After Julian had thrown his battered pigskin luggage into his room, he returned to the kitchen, where Pandora was chopping leeks and I was exercising my new sink plunger. 'So, darlings, what's new?' he said, lighting one of his vile Russian cigarettes.

Pandora said, 'I'm in love with Jack Cavendish, and he's in love with me. Isn't it absolutely marvellous?' She grinned ecstatically and chopped at the leeks with renewed fervour.

'Cavendish?' puzzled Julian. 'Isn't he that grey-haired old linguistics fart who can't keep his plonker in his pants?'

Pandora's eyes flashed dangerously. 'He's sworn to me that from now on his lifestyle will be strictly non-polygynous,' she said.

She stretched up to replace the knife on its magnetic rack and her cropped tee shirt rode up, revealing her delicate midriff. I thrust the plunger viciously into the greasy contents of the sink, imagining that Cavendish's head was on the end of the wooden stick, instead of the black rubber suction pad.

Julian neighed knowingly. 'Cavendish doesn't know the meaning of the word "non-polygynous". He's a notorious womaniser.'

'*Was,*' insisted Pandora, adding, 'and *of course* he knows the meaning of the word "non-polygynous": he is a professor of Linguistics.'

I left the plunger floating in the sink and went to my box room, took my *Condensed Oxford Dictionary* from its shelf and, with the aid of the magnifying glass, looked up the word 'non-polygynous'. I then uttered a loud, cynical laugh. Loud enough, I hoped, to be heard in the kitchen.

Sunday, January 6th

Woke at 3 a.m. and lay awake remembering the time when Pandora and I nearly went All the Way. I love her still. I intend to be her second husband. And what's more, she will take my name. She will be known as 'Mrs Adrian Albert Mole' in private.

ON SEEING PANDORA'S MIDRIFF

The glorious shoreline from ribcage
To pelvis
Like an inlet
A bay
A safe haven
I want to navigate
To explore
To take readings from the stars
To carefully trace my fingers
Along the shoreline
And eventually to guide my ship, my destroyer, my
  pleasure craft
Into and beyond your harbour

6.00 p.m. Sink still blocked. Worked for three hours in the kitchen, adding vowels to the first half of my experimental novel *Lo! The Flat*

Hills of My Homeland, which was originally written with consonants only. It is eighteen months since I sent it to Sir Gordon Giles, Prince Charles's agent, and he sent it back, suggesting I put in the vowels.

Lo! The Flat Hills of My Homeland explores late twentieth-century man and his dilemma, focusing on a 'New Man' living in a provincial city in England.

The treatment is broadly Lawrentian, with a touch of Dostoievskian darkness and a tinge of Hardyesque lyricism.

I predict that one day it will be a G.C.S.E. set book.

I was driven out of the kitchen by the arrival of that wrinkled-up ashtray on legs, Cavendish, who had been invited to Sunday lunch. He hadn't been in the flat two minutes before he was pulling a cork out of a bottle and helping himself to glasses out of the cupboard. He then sat on *my* recently vacated chair at the kitchen table and began to talk absolute gibberish about the Gulf War, predicting that it would be over within months. I predict that it will be America's second Vietnam.

Julian came into the kitchen, wearing his silk pyjamas and carrying a copy of *Hello!*

'Julian,' said Pandora, 'meet my lover, Jack Cavendish.' She turned to Cavendish and said, 'Jack, this is Julian Twyselton-Fife, my husband.' Pandora's husband and Pandora's lover shook hands.

I turned away in disgust. I'm as liberal and civilised as the next person. In fact, in some circles I'm regarded as quite an advanced thinker, but even I shuddered at the utter depravity that this introduction signified.

I left the flat to get some air. When I returned from my walk around the Outer Ring Road two hours later, Cavendish was still there, telling tedious anecdotes about his numerous children and his three ex-wives. I microwaved my Sunday lunch and took it into my box room. I spent the rest of the evening listening to laughter in the next room. Woke at 2 a.m. and was unable to get back to sleep. Filled two pages of A4 devising tortures for Cavendish. Not the actions of a rational man.

Tortures for Cavendish

1. Chain him to the wall with a glass of water *just* beyond his grasp.
2. Chain him naked to a wall while a bevy of beautiful girls walk by, cruelly mocking his flaccid *and* aroused penis.
3. Force him to sit in a room with Ivan Braithwaite, while Ivan talks about the finer details of the Labour Party's Constitution, with particular reference to Clause Four. (This is true torture, as I can bear witness.)
4. Show him a video of Pandora getting married to me. She radiant in white, me in top hat and tails, putting two gloved fingers up at Cavendish.

Let the punishment fit the crime.

Monday, January 7th

Started my beard today.

Some of the Newport Pagnell newts have crossed the road. I telephoned Peterson at the Department of Transport, to inform him. There has obviously been a split in the community. I expect a female newt is at the bottom of it: *cherchez la femme.*

Wednesday, January 9th

For the first time in my entire life I haven't got a single spot, pustule or pimple. I pointed out to Pandora over breakfast that my complexion was flawless, but she paused in applying her mascara, looked at me coldly, and said, 'You need a shave.'

Spent ten minutes at the sink with the plunger before going to work, but to no avail. Pandora said, 'We'll have to get a proper man in.'

Does Pandora realise the impact the above words, so apparently casually uttered, have had on me? She has disenfranchised me from my gender! She has cut my poor, useless balls off!

Thursday, January 10th

Brown has advised me to shave. I refused. I may have to seek the advice of the Civil and Public Service Union.

Friday, January 11th

Applied to join the C.P.S.U.

Pandora found Cavendish's A4 torture list. She has made an appointment for me to see her friend Leonora De Witt, who is a psychotherapist. I agreed reluctantly. On the one hand, I am terrified of my unconscious and what it will reveal about me. On the other, I am looking forward to talking about myself non-stop for an hour without interruption, hesitation or repetition.

Saturday, January 12th

Pandora's most recent ex-lover, Rocky (Big Boy) Livingstone, came round to the flat today, asking for the return of his mini sound-system. At six foot three and fifteen stone of finely-honed muscle, Rocky is a 'proper' man, if ever I saw one. Pandora was out, meeting some of Cavendish's children at the Randolph Hotel. So, in her absence, I gave the sound-system to him. Since he and Pandora split up, Rocky has opened new gyms in Kettering, Newmarket and Ashby-de-la-Zouch. He and his new girl friend, Carly Pick, are still happy.

Rocky said, 'Carly's a real star, Aidy. I respect the lady, y'know.' I told Rocky about Professor Cavendish. He was disgusted.

He said, 'That Pandora is a *user.* Just 'cos she's clever, she finks she's . . .' He flailed about for the right word and finished, 'clever'.

Before he went he unblocked the sink. I was very grateful. I was getting sick of washing the pots in the bathroom hand basin. None of the saucepans would fit under the taps.

I went to the window and watched him drive away. Carly Pick had both her arms around his neck.

Sunday, January 13th

The Gulf War deadline expires on the 15th, at midnight. What will I do if I am called up to fight for my country? Will I cover myself with honour, or will I wet myself with fear on hearing the sound of enemy gunfire?

Monday, January 14th

Went to Sainsbury's and stocked up with tins of beans, candles, Jaffa cakes, household matches, torch batteries, Paracetamol, multi-vitamins, Ry-King and tins of corned beef and put them in the cupboard in my box room. Should the war spread over here, I will be well prepared. The others in the flat will just have to take their chance. I predict panic buying on a scale never seen before in this country. There will be fighting in the aisles of the super-markets.

Appointment with Leonora De Witt on Friday 25th of this month at 6 p.m.

Tuesday, January 15th

Midnight. We are at war with Iraq. I phoned my mother in Leicester and told her to keep the dog in. It is twelve years old and reacts badly to unexpected noises. She laughed and said, 'Are you going mad?' I said, 'Probably,' and put the phone down.

Wednesday, January 16th

Bought sixteen bottles of Highland Spring water, in case water supply is cut off owing to bombardment by Iraqi airforce. It took me four trips from the Spar shop on the corner to the flat, but I feel more secure knowing I will not go thirsty during the coming *Blitzkrieg.*

Brown has not mentioned my beard for some days now. He is preoccupied with the effect that 'Operation Desert Storm' will have on the desert wildlife. I said, 'I'm afraid I regard Iraqi wildlife as being on the side of the enemy. I'm more worried about my dog, at home in Leicester.'

'Ever the parochial, Mole,' said Brown, in a lip-curling manner. I was quite insulted. Brown reads nothing, apart from journals on wildlife, whereas I have read most of the Russian Greats and am about to embark on *War and Peace.* Hardly parochial, Brown!

Thursday, January 17th

I have hired a portable colour television, so I can watch the Gulf War in bed.

Friday, January 18th

The spokesperson for the U.S.A. military is a man who calls himself 'Colon Powell'. Every time I see him, I think of intestines and the lower bowel. It detracts from the gravity of the War.

Saturday, January 19th

Bert Baxter rang me up at the office today. (I will kill whoever gave him the number.) He wanted to know 'when you and my favourite gal are comin' to see me?' His 'favourite gal' is Pandora. Why doesn't Bert just *die* like other pensioners? His quality of life can't be up to much. He is nothing but a burden to others (me).

He was entirely ungrateful when I dug a grave for his dog, Sabre, last year, though I challenge anyone to dig a neater hole in compacted soil with a rusty garden trowel. If I'd had a decent spade at my disposal, then, *naturellement,* the grave would have been neater.

The truth is that I hated and feared Sabre. The day the wretched Alsatian died was a day of rejoicing for me. No more smelling its noxious breath. No more forcing Bob Martin's conditioning tablets between its horrible vicious teeth.

Bert burbled on about the war for a while, and then asked me if I had heard my old enemy Barry Kent on *Stop the Week* this morning. Apparently, Kent was publicising his first novel, *Dork's Diary.* I am now utterly convinced there cannot be a God. It was me that encouraged Kent to write poetry, and now I find out that the ex-skinhead, frozen peabrain has written a novel, *and got it published!!!*

Pandora told me this evening that Kent made Ned Sherrin, A. S. Byatt, Jonathan Miller and Victoria Mather laugh almost continously. Apparently the phone lines at the BBC were jammed with listeners asking when *Dork's Diary* will be published (Monday). This is absolutely and totally the last straw. My sanity hangs by a fragile thread.

Sunday, January 20th

I was passing Waterstone's bookshop when I saw what appeared to be Barry Kent standing in the window. I lifted my hand in greeting and said, 'Hello, Baz,' then realised that the smirking skinhead was only a cardboard cut-out. Copies of *Dork's Diary* filled the window. I'm not ashamed to say that curses sprang from my lips.

As I flicked through the pages of the slim volume, my eye was caught not only by the many obscenities with which the book is littered, but by the name—'Aiden Vole'—given to one of the characters. This 'Aiden Vole' is obsessed with matters anal. He is jingoistic, deeply conservative and a failure with women. 'Aiden Vole' is an outrageous caricature of me, without a doubt. I have been slandered. I shall see my solicitor in the morning. I shall instruct him or her (I haven't actually got a solicitor yet) to demand hundreds of thousands of pounds in damages. I couldn't bring myself actually to buy a copy of the book. Why should I add to Kent's royalties? But I noticed as I left the shop that Kent is giving a reading from *Dork's Diary* on Tuesday evening at 7 p.m. I will be in the audience. Kent will leave Waterstone's a broken man when I have finished with him.

Monday, January 21st *The Cubicle, D.O.E.*

Just listened to Kent on *Start the Week* on my portable radio. He has certainly extended his vocabulary. Melvyn Bragg said that the Aiden Vole character was 'wonderfully funny' and asked if he was based on anybody real. Kent laughed and said, 'You're a writer, Melv; you know what it's like. Vole is an amalgam of fact and fantasy. Vole stands for everything I hate most in this country, after the new five-pence piece, that is.' The other guests—Ken Follett, Roy Hattersley, Brenda Maddox and Edward Pearce—laughed like drains.

Spent the rest of the morning looking through the Yellow Pages for a solicitor with a name I can trust. Chose and rang 'Churchman, Churchman, Churchman and Luther'. I am seeing a Mr Luther at 11.30 a.m. on Thursday. I am supposed to be visiting the Newport Pagnell newts on Thursday morning with Brown, but he will just have to face them alone. My reputation and my future as a serious novelist are at stake.

Alfred Wainwright, who wrote guides to the fells of the Lake District, died today. I once used Mr Wainwright's maps when I attempted to do the 'coast to coast' walk with the 'Off the Streets' Youth Club. Unfortunately, I developed hypothermia within half an hour of leaving the Youth Hostel at Grimsby and my record-breaking attempt had to be abandoned.

Tuesday, January 22nd

Review of *Dork's Diary* in *The Guardian:*

> 'A coruscating account of *fin de siècle* provincial life. Brilliant. Dark. Hilarious. Buy it!' Robert Elms

Box Room 10 p.m. Couldn't get in to see Kent; all the tickets were sold. Tried to speak to him as he entered the shop, but couldn't get near to him. He was surrounded by press and publicity people. He was wearing sunglasses. In January.

Wednesday, January 23rd

Beard coming along nicely. Two spots on left shoulder blade. A slight pain in anus, but otherwise I am in superb physical condition.

Read long interview in the *Independent* with Barry Kent. He told lies from start to finish. He even lied about the reason for his being sent to prison, claiming he was sentenced to eighteen months for various acts of violence, when I know very well that he got four months for criminal damage to a privet hedge. I have faxed the *Independent*, putting the record straight. It gave me no pleasure to do this, but without the Truth we are no better than dogs. Truth is the most important thing in my life. Without Truth we are lost.

Thursday, January 24th

Lied on the phone to Brown this morning and told him that I could not visit the Newport Pagnell newt habitat on account of a severe migraine. Brown ranted on about how he had 'never taken a day off work in twenty-two years'. He went on to brag that he had 'even passed several massive kidney stones into the lavatory at work'. Perhaps that explains why the lavatory basin is cracked.

I was late for my appointment with Mr Luther, the solicitor, though I left the flat in plenty of time—another time warp or memory-loss—a mystery, anyway. As I told Luther (in great detail) about Kent's slander of me, I noticed him yawning several times. I expect he was up late; he looks the dissolute type. He was wearing braces covered in pictures of Marilyn Monroe.

Eventually he raised his hand and said, 'Enough, I've heard enough,' in an irritable sort of way. Then he leaned across his desk and said, 'Are you vastly rich?'

'No,' I replied, 'not vastly.'

He then asked, 'Are you desperately poor?'

'Not desperately. That's why I . . .'

Luther interrupted before I could finish my sentence, 'Because unless you are vastly rich, or desperately poor, you can't possibly afford to go to court. You don't qualify for Legal Aid and you can't afford to pay a barrister a thousand pounds a day, can you?'

'A thousand pounds a day?' I said, absolutely aghast.

Luther smiled, revealing a gold back molar.

I remembered my grandma's advice, 'Never trust a man with a gold tooth.' I thanked Mr Luther politely but coldly and left his office. So much for English justice. It is the worst in the world. As I passed the waiting room, I noticed a copy of *Dork's Diary* on the coffee table, next to copies of *Amnesty* and *The Republican*.

Got home to find a note from Leonora De Witt informing me that she is unable to keep our appointment tomorrow. Why? Is she having her hair done? Is double-glazing being installed in her consulting room? Have her parents been found dead in bed? Am I so unimportant that my time is a mere plaything to Ms De Witt? She suggested a new appointment: Thursday 31st January at 5 p.m. I left a message on her Ansafone, agreeing to the new arrangement, but announcing my displeasure.

Saturday, January 26th

I was awake all last night, watching 'Operation Desert Storm'. I feel it's the least I can do—after all, it is costing H.M. Government thirty million pounds a day to keep Kuwait a democracy.

Sunday, January 27th

According to the *Observer* today, Kuwait is not and has never been a democracy. It is ruled by the Kuwaiti Royal Family.

Bluebeard laughed when I told him. 'It's all to do with *oil*, Adrian,' he said. 'Do you think the Yanks would be in there if Kuwait's main product was *turnips?*'

Pandora bent down and kissed the back of his withered neck. How she could allow her young, vibrant flesh to come into contact with his ancient, wrinkled skin, I'll never know. I had to go into the bathroom and take deep breaths and control the urge to vomit. Why slobber over *him* when she could have *me?*

My mother rang at 4 p.m. I could hear my young stepfather, Martin Muffet, hammering in the background. 'Martin's putting some shelves up for my knick-knacks,' she shouted over the row. Then she asked me if I had read the extracts from *Dork's Diary* in the *Observer.* I was able to answer truthfully. 'No,' I said. 'You should,' said my mother. 'It's totally brilliant. When you next see Baz, will you ask him for a free copy, signed to Pauline and Martin?'

I said, 'It is highly unlikely that I will see Kent. I do not move in the same illustrious circles as him.'

'Which illustrious circles *do* you move in, then?' asked my mother.

'None,' I answered truthfully. Then I put the phone down and went to bed and pulled the duvet over my head.

Monday, January 28th

Britain's Jo Durie and Jeremy Bates won the mixed doubles in Melbourne. This surely points to a renaissance in British tennis.

PANDORA'S LITTLE PUSSY

I love her little Pussy
Her coat is so warm
But if I should stroke her

She'll call the police and identify me in
A line-up
And do me some harm

Wednesday, January 30th

Shocked to hear on Radio Four that King Olav the Fifth of Norway was buried today. His contribution to the continuing success of the Norwegian leather industry is something that is little appreciated by the vast majority of the Great British Public. Prince Charles was England's graveside representative.

Borrowed *Scenes from Provincial Life* by William Cooper from the library. I only had time to choose one book, because a 'suspicious package' was found in the Romantic Fiction section and the library was evacuated.

Sink blocked again. Plunged for the duration of *The Archers,* but to no avail.

Thursday, January 31st

I didn't arrive at the consulting room on Thames Street until 5.15 p.m. Leonora De Witt was not pleased.

'I'll have to charge you for the full hour, Mr Mole,' she said, seating herself in an armchair which was covered in old bits of carpet. 'Where would you like to sit?' she asked. There were many chairs in the room. I chose a dining chair which was standing against a wall.

When I was seated, I said, 'I was under the impression that our sessions were to be under the auspices of the National Health Service.'

'Then you were gravely mistaken,' said Ms De Witt. 'I charge thirty pounds an hour—under the auspices of the private enterprise system.'

'*Thirty pounds an hour!* How many sessions will I need?' I asked.

She explained that she couldn't possibly predict, that she knew nothing about me. That it depended on the cause of my unhappiness.

'How do you feel at the moment?' she asked.

'Apart from a slight headache, I feel fine,' I replied.

'What are you doing with your hands?' she said quietly.

'Wringing them,' I replied.

'What is that on your brow?' she asked.

'Sweat,' I answered, taking out my handkerchief.

'Are your buttocks clenched, Mr Mole?' she pressed.

'I suppose they are,' I said.

'Now answer my first question again, please. How do you feel at this moment?'

Her large brown eyes locked into mine. I couldn't avert my gaze.

'I feel totally miserable,' I said. 'And I lied about the headache.'

She talked at length about the *Gestalt* technique. She explained that it was possible to teach me 'coping mechanisms'. Apart from Pandora, she is probably the loveliest woman I have ever spoken to. I found it hard to take my eyes off her black-stockinged feet, which were slipped into black suede shoes with high heels. Was she wearing tights or stockings?

'So, Mr Mole, do you think we can work together?' she said.

She looked at her watch and stood up. Her hair looked like a midnight river pouring down her back. I eagerly affirmed that I would like to see her once a week. Then I gave her thirty pounds and left.

Friday, February 1st

Just returned from Newport Pagnell. My nerves are shot to pieces. Brown drove like a man possessed. At no time did he exceed the speed limit, but he drove onto the kerb, scraped against hedgerows and on the motorway section of our journey he left only a six-inch gap between our fragile Ford Escort and the monolithic juggernaut in front of us.

'It saves precious fuel if you can stay in the lorry's slipstream,' he said by way of explanation. The man is an environmental fanatic. He spent last Christmas Day classifying seaweed at Dungeness. I rest my case. Thank God for the weekend. Or *le weekend,* as our fellow Europeans say.

Saturday, February 2nd

Viscount Althorp, Princess Diana's brother, has confessed to his thin wife and the rest of the world that he had an affair in Paris. Prince Charles and Princess Diana must have been horrified to find out that there was an adulterer in the family. He should be stripped of his title immediately. The Royal Family and their close connections should be above such brutish instincts. The country looks to them to set the moral standard.

Had bath, shampooed beard, cut fingernails and toenails. Put hot oil on hair to nourish it and give it shine and the outward illusion of health.

11.45 p.m. Bert Baxter has just telephoned. He sounded pathetic. Pandora was out and in a moment of weakness I agreed to go and visit him in Leicester tomorrow. Wrote a note to Pandora, left it on her pillow.

Pandora,

Baxter rang in considerable distress, something about killing himself—I intend to visit him tomorrow. He intimated to me that he wished to see you too. I plan to rise at 8.30 to catch the train, or, should you wish to accompany me, my alternative *modus operandi* will be to rise at nine and be driven by you in your motor car, thus arriving in Leicester at approximately 11 a.m. Would you please inform me of your decision by the method of slipping a note under my door? Please do not disturb me tonight with the sounds of your wild love-making. The walls of my box room are very thin and I am sick of sleeping with my Sony Walkman on.

Adrian

Sunday, February 3rd

At 2.10 a.m., Pandora burst into my box room and hurled abuse at me. She flung my note to her into my face and screamed, 'You pompous *nerd*, you pathetic *dork! "Modus operandi"!* "Be driven by you in your motor car"! I want you out of this box room and out of my life, *tomorrow!*'

Bluebeard came in and led her away and I lay in bed and listened to them murmuring together in the kitchen. What brought on such an unprovoked outburst?

At 3.30 a.m. they went into Pandora's bedroom. At 3.45 a.m. I put Dire Straits into my Sony and turned the volume up to full.

Didn't wake until midday. 'Phoned Bert and said I was unable to visit him owing to being awake all night with intestinal pains. I could tell Bert didn't believe me. He said, 'You're a bleedin' liar. I've just spoken to my gal Pandora. She rang me on her car phone. She looked in your room before she set out for Leicester and she said you were sleepin' like a newborn.'

'Why didn't she wake me then?' I asked.

''Cos she 'ates the bleedin' sight of you,' said the diplomatic one.

Monday, February 4th

Inexplicably late for work by twenty-three minutes. Brown was practically frothing at the mouth. Also accused me of stealing postage stamps. He said, 'Every penny is needed by the D.O.E. if our wildlife is to be preserved.' As if! Are the badgers and foxes and tadpoles and lousy, stinking newts going to pop their clogs because I, Adrian Mole, made use of two second-class postage stamps paid for out of my taxes in the first place? No, Brown. I don't think so.

Tuesday, February 5th

Pandora still in Leicester. Trimmed beard around mouth. Swallowed clippings. One lodged at back of throat; annoying.

Wednesday, February 6th

Brown came into my cubicle today and demanded to see my 'A' level certificates! He had heard on the office grapevine that I had failed 'A' level Biology three items. The only person in Oxford—apart from Pandora—who knows about my triple failure is Megan Harris, Brown's secretary. I confessed to her whilst in a drunken and emotional state at the D.O.E. Christmas party last year. She alone knows that my job as a Scientific Officer Grade One was granted to me under false pretences. Has Megan blabbed? I must know.

I told Leonora De Witt my family history tonight. It's a tragic story of rejection and alienation, but Leonora simply sat and picked balls of fluff from her sweater, which drew my attention to the shape of her comely breasts. It was obvious that she was not wearing a bra. I wanted to leave my chair and sink my head into her bosom. I went into some detail about my parents' deviant behaviour, but the only time she showed obvious interest was when I mentioned my dead grandfather, Albert Mole, whom I have to thank for my middle name.

'Did you see his dead body?' she asked.

'No,' I replied. 'The Co-op undertaker had screwed the coffin lid down and nobody could find the screwdriver at Grandma's house, so . . .'

'Continue,' ordered Leonora. So I did. Through fat, hot tears. I told about my feeling of exclusion from 'normal' life; of how I long to join my fellow human beings, to share their sorrows, their joys, their sing-songs in pubs.

Leonora said, 'People sing awful songs in pubs. Why do you feel a need to join in singing those mawkish lyrics and banal tunes?'

'I stood outside such pubs as a child,' I said. 'Everybody sounded so happy.'

Then the alarm went off on her watch and it was time to cough up thirty quid and leave.

On my way home I went into a pub and had a drink. I also initiated a conversation about the weather with an old man. There was no singing, so I went home.

Thursday, February 7th

I asked Megan outright this morning. I approached her in the corridor as she was being scalded by the Autovent tea/coffee/oxtail soup machine. She admitted that she had let it 'slip out' that I was totally unqualified for my position. Then she swore me to secrecy and informed me that she and Brown have been having an affair since 1977! Brown and the lovely Megan! Why do women throw themselves at worn—out old gits like Brown and Cavendish, and ignore young, virile, bearded men like me? It defies logic.

Megan was eager to talk about her affair with Brown. Apparently he had sworn to leave Mrs Brown in 1980, but has not yet done so. I feel sorry for Mrs Brown every time she comes into the office. It is not her fault that she looks like she does. Some women have got good dress sense and some women haven't. Mrs Brown obviously does not know that pop socks should only be worn under trousers or long skirts. Also, somebody should tell her that warts can be cured nowadays.

Friday, February 8th

Pandora is back in Oxford, but not speaking to me much, apart from the bare facts that Bert is no longer suicidal. She bought him a kitten and also installed a cat flap in his back door. Brown asked me again for my Biology 'A' level certificate. I looked at him enigmatically and said, 'I think you'll find that Megan has the information you require.' God, blackmail is an ugly word. I hope Brown doesn't force me to use it.

I have thrown my condom away. It had exceeded its 'best before' date.

Monday, February 11th

Megan came into my cubicle today, sobbing. Apparently Brown forgot her birthday, which was yesterday. Alack, alas! It looks as if I am cast into the role of Megan's only confidant. I put my arms around her and kissed her. She felt lovely and soft and squashy. She pulled away quite soon, however, and said 'Your beard is scratchy and horrible.'

But was my beard the *real* reason?

Does my breath stink? Does my body stink?

Who can I trust to tell me the truth?

I can certainly see what Brown sees in Megan, but I will never in a billion years see what she sees in him. He is forty-two, thin, and wears atrocious clothes from 'Man at C&A'. Megan says he is good in bed. Who is she trying to kid? Good at what in bed? Doing jigsaws? Sleeping? Perhaps she means that he is unselfish with the duvet? If Brown is good in bed, then I am a tractor wheel.

Tuesday, February 12th

Tried to visit newt habitat in Northamptonshire, but 'wrong kind of snow' caused Class 317 engine to fail. Was forced to sit in freezing carriage whilst buffet bar attendant gave out continuous announcements in annoying adenoidal voice. Was pleased when buffet car ran out of all supplies and closed. Got back to Oxford at 10.30 p.m., to find message from Megan. Rang her to find out that she and Brown had had a row; their affair is over. I was distraught. This means I no longer have a hold over Brown. It could signal the end of my career with the D.O.E.

Wednesday, February 13th

Brown/Megan affair is on again. Apparently Brown cycled round to Megan's flat in the early hours, after telling Mrs Brown he was going bat-watching. Their reconciliation was very passionate.

I cannot imagine anything in the world more distasteful than seeing Brown in a state of orgasmic pleasure. Apart from *being* with Brown in a state of orgasmic pleasure.

Bought new condom—spearmint flavoured.

Also bought bunch of bananas. Megan says they are very good for those, like me, who suffer from an irritable bowel.

Thursday, February 14th

Valentine's Day card from my mother as usual. Megan in tears again. Brown forgot. Bought economy box of tissues at lunchtime for Megan's sole use. I can't afford to keep wasting Kleenex on her. Bluebeard has sent Pandora a disgracefully extravagant bouquet (it is disgusting when people are starving), and at seven o'clock this evening he called with champagne, an Art Nouveau brooch and a pair of satin pyjamas. Then, as if that wasn't enough, he took her out for dinner in a hired car with uniformed driver! Most unacademic behaviour.

Cavendish behaves more like a pools winner than a professor of Linguistics at an ancient seat of learning.

Left to myself, I ate a simple meal of bread, tuna and cucumber and went to bed, early. I am reading *English Love Poems*, edited by John Betjeman. Valentine's Day is a ridiculous charade, the ignorant masses are manipulated by the greetings card companies into forking out millions—and for what? For the illusion of being loved.

Friday, February 15th

A Valentine's Day card! Signed 'A Secret Admirer'! I sang in my bath. I walked to work without touching the pavement! Who is she? The signature told me that she is educated and uses a felt-tip pen, like me.

Leonora had her hair pinned up today; she was wearing silver earrings so long that they brushed her slim shoulders. She was wearing a scooped-neck black top. A bra strap was visible. Black lace. She occasionally pushed it back inside her top. Every time she did so her sparkling bracelet fell down her arms towards her elbow. I am not in love with Leonora De Witt. But I am obsessed with her. She invades my dreams. She made me talk to an empty chair and pretend that it was my mother. I told the chair that it drank too much and wore its skirts too short.

Saturday, February 16th

I finally took my library books back today: *A Single Man* by Christopher Isherwood, *English Love Poems* by John Betjeman, *Scenes from Provincial Life* by William Cooper and *Notes from the Underground* by Dostoievsky. I owed seven pounds, eighty pence in fines. My least favourite librarian was on duty at the desk. I don't know her name, but she is the Welsh one with the extroverted spectacles.

After I'd written out my cheque and handed it to her, she said, 'Do you have a cheque card?'

'Yes,' I replied. 'But it's at home.'

'Then I'm afraid I cannot accept this cheque,' she said.

'But you know me,' I said. 'I've been coming here once a week for eighteen months.'

'I'm afraid that I don't recognise you at all,' she said and handed me my cheque back.

'This beard is quite recent,' I said coldly. 'Perhaps you could try to visualise my face without it.'

'I don't have time for visualisation,' she said. 'Not since the cuts.'

I showed her a small photograph of myself that I carry in my wallet. It was taken pre-beard.

'No,' she said, after giving it a cursory glance. 'I don't recognise that man.'

'But that man is *me!*' I shouted. A queue of people had built up behind me and they were listening avidly to the exchange. The librarian's spectacles flashed in anger.

'I have been doing the job of three people since the cuts began,' she said. 'And you are making my job even more difficult. Please go home and find your cheque card.'

'It is now 5.25 p.m. and the library closes in five minutes,' I said. 'Even Superman couldn't fly back in time to pay the fines, choose four books and leave before the doors close.'

Somebody behind me in the queue muttered, 'Get a bleedin' move on, Superman.'

So I said to the spectacled one, 'I'll be back tomorrow.'

'Oh no you won't,' she said, with a tiny smile. 'Due to the cuts this library doesn't open again until Wednesday.'

On my way home I railed internally against a government that is depriving me of new reading matter. Pandora has forbidden me to touch her books ever since I left a Jaffa cake inside her Folio Society edition of *Nicholas Nickleby*; Julian's books are in Chinese and I'm finding the last hundred pages of *War and Peace* heavy going. There is no way I can afford to buy a new book. Even a paperback costs at least a fiver.

I have to cough up thirty pounds a week for Leonora. I have even had to cut down on my consumption of bananas. I am down to one a day.

I have been forced to read my old diaries. Some of the entries are incredibly perceptive. And the poems have stood the test of time.

Sunday, February 17th

Pandora spoke to me today. She said, 'I want you to leave. You stultify me. We had a childhood romance, but we are both adults now: we have grown in different directions and the time has come to part.' Then she added, cruelly, I thought, 'And that bloody beard makes you look absolutely ridiculous. For God's sake, shave it off.' I went to bed shattered. Read page 977 of *War and Peace,* then lay awake staring into the darkness.

Monday, February 18th

I looked into the newsagent's on my way to work. I saw the following advertisement, written in a reasonably educated hand, on a Conqueror postcard:

> Large sunny room to let—in family house. Fire sign preferred. Use of W machine/dryer. £75pw inclusive to N/S male professional. Ring Mrs Hedge.

I rang Mrs Hedge as soon as I got to my cubicle. She asked for my date of birth. I told her it was April 2nd, which excited the response, 'Aries, good. I'm Sagittarius.'

I went to see her at 7 p.m. and inspected the room. 'It's not very sunny,' I said.

She said, 'No, but would you expect it to be on an evening in February?'

I like the cut of her jib. She is oldish (thirty-five to thirty-seven, i would guess), but has not got a bad figure, although it's hard to tell with the clothes women wear nowadays. Her hair is lovely; treacle-coloured, like Pandora's used to be before she started mucking about with Colour-Glo. She was wearing quite a bit of make-up and her mascara had smudged. I hope this is not a sign of sluttishness. She was recently divorced and needs to let the room in order to continue paying the mortgage. Apparently the Building Society (my own, coincidentally) has turned nasty.

She invited me to test the bed. I did so and had a sudden vision of myself and Mrs Hedge engaging in vigorous sexual intercourse. I said aloud, 'I'm sorry.'

Naturally Mrs Hedge was completely in the dark as to the reason for my apology and said, ' "Sorry"? Does that mean you don't like the bed?'

'No, no,' I gibbered. 'I love you; I mean, I love the bed.'

I was concerned that I hadn't made a good impression, so I rang Mrs Hedge when I got home (in an effort to impress her) and informed her that I was a writer; would the scratching of my pen in the small hours bother her?

'Not at all,' she replied. 'I am visited by the Muse myself in the night occasionally.'

You can't walk on the pavement in Oxford without bumping into a published or unpublished writer. It's no wonder that the owner of the stationery shop where I buy my supplies goes to the Canary Islands twice a year and drives a Mercedes. (He drives a Mercedes in *Oxford,* not the Canary islands, though of course it is perfectly feasible that he has the use of a Mercedes *in* the Canary Islands as well. But I doubt, given the comparative infrequency of his visits, if he actually *owns* a Mercedes in the Canary Islands though I suppose it could be leased.) I don't know why I felt the need to explain the Canary Islands/Mercedes confusion. I suppose it may be another example of what Leonora calls my 'childish pedantry'.

Tuesday, February 19th

My mother rang in a panic at 11.00 p.m., to ask if Martin Muffet, my young stepfather, had turned up at the flat. Quite frankly, I laughed out loud. Why would Muffet want to visit *me?* He knows I disapprove of my mother's foolhardy second marriage. Apart from the age difference (which is as wide as the mouth of the Amazon), they are physically and mentally incompatible.

Muffet is a six foot six bag of bones, who thinks the Queen works hard and that Paddy Ashdown is incapable of telling a lie. My mother is five foot five and squeezes herself into clothes two sizes too small for her and thinks that Britain should be a republic and that our first president should be Ken Livingstone, the well-known newt lover. On my last visit, I noticed that young Mr Muffet was far less attentive to my mother than of late. I expect he is regretting his mad rush into matrimony.

My mother said, 'He went to London this morning, to visit the Lloyd's building for his Engineering course.'

My mother's grasp of the geographical layout of the British Isles has always been minimal. I informed her of the distance from the Lloyd's building in the City of London to that of my box room in Oxford.

She said in a pathetic voice, 'I thought he might have popped in on his way back to Leicester.'

She phoned back at 2 a.m. Muffet was trapped in an underground train in a tunnel for six hours, or so he said.

Thursday, February 21st

This time Leonora invited me to imagine that the chair was my father. She gave me an African stick and I beat the chair until I lay limp and exhausted and physically unable to lift the stick again.

'He's not a bad bloke, my dad,' I said, 'I don't know why I went so berserk.'

Leonora said, 'Don't talk to me, talk to him. Talk to the chair. The chair is your father.'

I felt stupid addressing the empty chair again, but I wanted to please Leonora, so I forced myself to look the upholstery in the eye and said, 'Why didn't you buy me an anglepoise lamp when I was revising for my G.C.S.E.s?'

Leonora said, 'Good, good, take it further, Adrian.'

'I hate your Country and Western cassettes,' I said.

'No,' Leonora whispered. 'Deeper, darker, an earlier memory.'

'I remember when I was three,' I said. 'You came into the bedroom, yanked my dummy out of my mouth and said, "*Real* boys don't need a dummy." '

I then grabbed the stick from where it was lying on the floor and once again began to beat the chair. Dust flew.

Leonora said, 'Good, good. How do you *feel?*'

I said, 'I feel terrible. I've wrenched my shoulder beating that chair.'

'No, no,' she said, irritably. 'How do you feel *inside?*'

I cottoned on.

'Oh, at peace with myself,' I lied. I got up, gave my therapeutic dominatrix the thirty quid and left. I needed to buy some Nurofen before the late-night chemist closed. I was in agony with my shoulder.

Friday, February 22nd

Another split in the Newport Pagnell newts. There are now three separate habitats. Something fishy is happening in the newt world. Brown is phoning newt experts worldwide, droning on about this phenomenon.

Mrs Hedge has interviewed other potential tenants, but has chosen me! I was racked all night by erotic dreams, concerning me, Brown, Megan and Mrs Hedge. i am ashamed, but what can I do? I can't control my subconscious, can I? I was forced to go to the launderette, though it is not my usual day.

Saturday, February 23rd

Norman Schwarzkopf was on television tonight, pointing a stick at an incomprehensible map. Why he was dressed in army camouflage is a mystery to me:

a. there are no trees in the desert
b. there were no trees in the briefing room
c. he is obviously too important to go anywhere near the enemy; he could go around dressed like Coco the Clown and still not be shot at

Tuesday, February 26th

Visited Mrs Hedge today, to finalise arrangements for renting the room and to discuss our tenancy agreement. She had a picture of the charred head of an Iraqi soldier who was found dead in a vehicle held against her fridge by a Mickey Mouse magnet. I averted my eyes and asked her for a drink of water.

Wednesday, February 27th

Yesterday evening I informed Pandora that I am moving out of the flat at the weekend. I had hoped that she would fall on my neck and beg me to stay, but she didn't. At 1 a.m. I was woken by the sound of a champagne cork popping, glasses clinking and wild, unrestrained laughter from Pandora, Cavendish and Julian. The Infernal Triangle.

Thursday, February 28th

Leonora did most of the talking tonight. She told me that I expect too much of myself, that I have impossibly high standards. She told me to be kind to myself and made me draw up a list of ten things I enjoy doing. Every time I banish a negative thought about myself, I am allowed to treat myself.

She asked if I can afford the occasional self-indulgence. I confessed that I have savings in the Market Harborough Building Society. She gave me a piece of paper and a child's crayon and told me to write down ten treats.

TREATS

1. Reading novels
2. Writing novels
3. Sexual intercourse
4. Looking at women

5. Buying stationery
6. Eating bananas
7. Crab paste sandwiches
8. Watching boxing on television
9. Listening to Tchaikovsky
10. Walking in the countryside

I asked Leonora what her treats were.

She said in a husky low voice, 'We're not here to talk about me.' Then she smiled and showed her beautifully white teeth and said, 'We have a few things in common, Adrian.'

I felt a throb of sexual desire surge through me.

'I too like to watch the boxing on television,' she said. 'I'm a Bruno fan.'

Friday, March 1st

At breakfast this morning, I asked Cavendish if he would help me to move my things to Mrs Hedge's. He has got a big Volvo estate. He said, 'Can't think of anything I'd rather do, Aidy.' He offered to move me immediately, but I said, 'Tomorrow morning will do. Some of us have to *work*.'

He laughed and said, 'So you think teaching Linguistics is a soft option, do you, Aidy?'

I said, 'Yes, as a matter of fact, I do. I doubt if *work* is a four-letter word to you.'

'Speaking as a professor of Linguistics,' he snarled, 'I can assure you that work is indeed a four-letter word.' As he reached for the ashtray, his dressing gown fell open, revealing withered nipples and grey matted chest hair. I was almost physically sick. I could hardly swallow my Bran Flakes.

Took the portable TV back to the shop. On my return, I wrote a poem to Pandora and slipped it under her door. It was my last-ditch attempt to seduce her away from Cavendish.

PANDORA! LET ME! BY A. MOLE

Let me stroke your inner thighs
Let me hear your breathy sighs
Let me feel your silky skin
Let me make your senses spin
Let me touch your soft white breast
Let us stop and have a rest.
Let me join our beating hearts
Let me forge our private parts
Let me delve and make you mine
Let me give you food and wine
Let me lick you with my tongue
Let me do whatever's wrong
Let me watch you take your pleasure
Let me dress you in black leather
Let me fit you like a glove
Let me consummate our love.

At 1 a.m. Pandora pushed a note under my door.

Adrian,

If you continue to send such filth to me, I will, in future, pass it on to the police.

Pandora

Saturday, March 2nd

As I packed my belongings, I reflected that I have not acquired much in my life. A basic wardrobe of clothes. A few hundred books. A Sony Walkman. A dozen or so cassettes. My own mug, cup, bowl and plate. A poster by Munch, a cactus, a magnifying mirror on a stand, a bowl for bananas, and a lamp. It is not much to show for a year and a half of toil at the D.O.E. True, I have got £2,579 saved in the Market Harborough Building Society, and £197.39 in Nat West, but even so.

I found the blue plastic comb I have been searching for since last year. I was on top of the wardrobe. Why? How did it get there? I have never climbed on the wardrobe to comb my hair. I suspect Julian. He is a big fan of Jeremy Beadle's.

11 p.m. Too tired to write much, just to put it on the record that I am lying in Mrs Hedge's bed. It is very comfortable. My new address is now:

8 Sitwell Villas
Summertown
Oxford

Sunday, March 3rd

I didn't know where I was when I woke up, then I remembered. I smelt bacon cooking, but I didn't go downstairs. I felt like an intruder. I got up, tiptoed to the bathroom, got dressed, made my bed, then sat on the bed listening to sounds from below. Eventually, driven by hunger, I went downstairs. Mrs Hedge was not there. The breakfast plates were still on the kitchen table. The kitchen pedal bin was overflowing. There were eggshells on the floor. The cupboard under the sink was full of filthy yellow dusters. The fridge was full of little saucers containing mouldy leftovers. The grill pan was unwashed. The *Observer* was speckled with tinned tomato juice.

It is as I feared: Mrs Hedge is a slut. The phone rang non-stop. Took messages: 'Ted phoned.' 'Ian rang.' 'Martin called.' 'Call Kingsley back.' 'Julian rang: Are you going to the launch on Tuesday?'

I was mopping the kitchen floor when Mrs Hedge returned. She was carrying a large shrub and four tins of Carlsberg.

'Christ,' she said. 'It looks like I've struck lucky. Do you like housework, Mr Mole?'

'I find it difficult to tolerate disorder,' I said.

She went out into the garden to plant the shrub, then sat on the patio on an iron chair, swigging Carlsberg out of the tin. She didn't seem to notice the cold. When it started to rain, she came into the house, got a golfing umbrella from the jar in the hall, and went back out again. I went up to my room to work on my novel, *Lo! The Flat Hills of My Homeland.*

When I next went downstairs, there was no sign of Mrs Hedge. I was pleased to see three tins of Carlsberg still left in the fridge. She may be a slut and an eccentric, but, thank God, she is not yet an alcoholic.

Monday, March 4th

Mrs Hedge was still in bed when I got back from work. The kitchen was a disgrace. The Carlsberg was gone from the fridge. She must have drunk them in bed! It is the only conclusion.

Wednesday, March 6th

Went to Pandora's to pick up my post. Nothing exciting. Letters from the Market Harborough Building Society, *Reader's Digest* and Plumbs, a firm promoting stretch covers. How did Plumbs get hold of my name and address? I have never shown the slightest interest in soft furnishings. Pandora has turned my box room into a study. I opened a file on her desk marked, 'Lecture Notes'. Didn't understand a word. They were written in what was probably Serbo-Croat.

Thursday, March 7th

I walked into the bathroom tonight without knocking. Mrs Hedge was in the bath, shaving her legs. I will buy a bolt for the door tomorrow. I'd guess she is at least 38C.

Friday, March 8th

Mrs Hedge said, 'Feel free to invite your friends round, Mr Mole.' I told her that I hadn't got any friends. I walk alone.

When I told Leonora the same thing, she said, 'Before our next session, please try to speak to a stranger; smile and initiate a conversation; and make a new female friend.'

Saturday, March 9th

There was a stranger in the kitchen when I came down. He was eating Marmite on toast. He said, 'Hi. I'm Gerry.'

I smiled and said, 'Good morning. I'm Adrian Mole.'

That was the extent of our social intercourse. I found it difficult to initiate a conversation with a man wearing a woman's negligé and nothing else.

I made myself a cup of tea and left.

I wish I was back in my box room.

Monday, March 11th

Mr Major on the news. He said, 'I want us to be where we belong, at the very heart of Europe, working with our partners in building the future.'

A peculiar thing: Mr Major cannot say the word 'want' to rhyme with 'font', which is the correct English pronunciation. For some reason, he says *'went'*. I suspect that this disability stems from childhood. When little John lisped, 'I want some sweeties,' etc., etc. Did his father leap down from his trapeze and shout, 'I'll give you *want!*'? Or shout, 'Say *want* again and I'll beat you black and blue,' thus leaving little John sobbing into the sawdust of the Big Top and unable to pronounce that little English word?

My heart goes out to him. He is obviously in urgent need of therapy. It seems to me that we have both suffered for having embarrassing fathers. I will bring the subject up when I next see Leonora.

Tuesday, March 12th

Brown slipped down a grassy bank and bruised his coccyx at the weekend. He was collecting owl droppings. He has been incapacitated and is lying on a plank on his bedroom floor. Ha! Ha! Ha! Ho! Ho! Ho! Three cheers!

Wednesday, March 13th

Brown's deputy, Gordon Goffe, is throwing his weight (twenty stone) about. He is conducting an enquiry into 'postage stamp pilfering'. This is just my luck. I was about to send the opening chapters of my novel *Lo! The Flat Hills of My Homeland* off to Faber and Faber today. I shall have to fork out for the stamps myself. Once they have read these chapters, they will be panting for the rest.

Thursday, March 14th

The Birmingham Six have been released from prison.

Gordon Goffe is lumbering around the offices, carrying out spot checks on our drawers. Megan was found to have an illicit box of D.O.E. ballpoints. She has received an oral warning. No session with Leonora this week. She is attending a conference in Sacramento.

Friday, March 15th

Barry Kent was on *Kaleidoscope* reading from *Dork's Diary*. The little I heard was nihilistic rubbish. Goffe barged into my cubicle and said that I was not allowed to listen to Radio Four during office hours. I pointed out that Mr Brown had never objected.

Goffe said, 'I am not Mr Brown,' a statement so stupid that I was lost for an answer. I've got an answer now, at three minutes past midnight, but it is obviously too late.

Saturday, March 16th

Called round to Pandora's flat for my letters. Nothing of interest: circular for thermal underwear; *Reader's Digest* competition entry form—prize: a gold bar; Plumbs catalogue, offering discount on mock velvet curtains. I am twenty-four next month and I must confess, dear journal, that I had expected by now to be in correspondence with interesting and fascinating people. Instead, the world seems to think of me as a person who gets up in the morning, puts on his thermal underwear, draws his mock velvet curtains and settles down to read his new copy of *Reader's Digest.*

The cat looked thin, but was pleased to see me. I gave it a whole tin of cat food. Pandora was out, so I had a good look around the flat. Her underwear drawer is full of disgusting sex aids. Bluebeard is obviously not up to it.

Sunday, March 17th

Had an interesting talk about the Russian elections with the girl in the local newsagent's this morning. Then, as she handed me my *Sunday Times,* she remarked (joking, I presume), 'It's very heavy. Would you like me to help you carry it home?'

'No,' I jocularly replied. 'I think I can just about manage.' Though, as I took it, I pretended to buckle under its weight. How we laughed.

She is quite pleasant-looking in a sort of unassuming sort of way.

6.00 . . On rereading the above, I think I have been unfair to the girl in the newsagent's. A gingham nylon overall is not the most flattering of garments. And I didn't see her legs, as they were behind the counter at all times.

I have just read the *Sunday Times* Books section and was appalled, astonished and disgusted to see that *Dork's Diary* is at number ten in the hardback bestseller list today!

Monday, March 18th

Called in at the newsagent's for a packet of Polos on the way to work. The girl joked that I was paying for fresh air, i.e. the hole! This hadn't occurred to me before, so I handed the Polos back to her and said, 'Okay, I'll have Trebor Mints instead.' Again, we laughed uproariously. She has certainly got a good sense of humour. Legs still behind the counter. Brown still malingering at home. Goffe still rampaging in the office. Leonora will be pleased to hear about the girl in the newsagent's.

Tuesday, March 19th

A letter from Pandora, my first at Sitwell Villas:

> Sunday, March 17th
>
> Adrian,
>
> I have asked you many times to return the front door key to this flat. You have not yet done so. I'm afraid I must give you an ultimatum. Either the key is in my possession by 7 p.m. on Tuesday night, or I call out a locksmith, have the lock changed and send the bill to you. The choice is yours. I will no longer tolerate you:
>
> a. interfering in the cat's feeding pattern;
> b. snooping in my underwear drawer; or
> c. helping yourself to food from the refrigerator when I am not there.
>
> As I have said, I will continue to redirect your post (such as it is) and relay any messages that I consider to be urgent.

At 6.59 p.m., I pushed an envelope containing the key, a tenpence piece and a terse note under the door of Pandora's flat. The note said:

> Pandora,
>
> a. In my opinion, the cat is too thin and appears to be lacking in energy,

b. I vividly remember you saying that 'Suspenders, etc. are symbols of women's enslavement to men's lust.' Ditto vibrators;
c. The pot of crab paste in the refrigerator was *mine.* I purchased it on February 20th this year. I have the receipt to prove it. I admit that I did help myself to a slice of bread. I enclose, as you cannot fail to see, a tenpence coin, as remuneration for the slice of granary.

Wednesday, March 20th

How do I get the legs out from behind the counter?

Thursday, March 21st

Her name is Bianca. A strange name for somebody working in a newsagent's. They are usually called Joyce. I saw her carrying boxes of crisps from a delivery lorry into the shop. Legs okay, but ankles a bit bony, so, on a scale of one to ten, only five.

9.00 p.m. Leonora was in a strange mood tonight. She was annoyed because I was fifteen minutes late. I pointed out to her that she would be paid for the full hour.

She said, 'That's not the point, Adrian. Our sessions together are carefully structured. I insist that you are punctual in future.'

I replied, 'My chronic unpunctuality is one of my many problems. Shouldn't you be addressing it?'

She crossed her shapely legs under her black silk skirt and I saw a flash of white. From that point on I was helpless and could only nod or shake my head in answer to her questions. Speech was beyond me. I felt that if I opened my mouth I would utter crude inarticulate protestations of lust, which would frighten her and signal the end of our time together.

Ten minutes before the end of our session she said, 'You are displaying typically regressive behaviour at the moment, shall we take advantage of it?'

I nodded and she encouraged me to talk about my earliest memories. I remembered being bitten by a dog and my grandma applying iodine to the wound. I also remember my (now dead) grandad kicking the dog round the kitchen.

Then it was time to fork out £30 and leave.

Saturday, March 23rd

Mrs Hedge asked me if she should marry Gerry, sell up and move to Cardiff. I advised against it. I have only just settled in, found out how to work the grill pan, etc. I can't face looking for alternative accommodation. Anyway, why ask me? I've only spoken to the ugly brute a few times.

Sunday, March 24th

The lavatory seat was up, so I guessed that Gerry was *in situ*. I went to buy my newspaper from Bianca and, on my return, sure enough, Gerry and Mrs Hedge were in the kitchen eating eggs and bacon. Mrs Hedge didn't look pleased to see me. I threw a few Rice Krispies into a bowl and took them up to my room. But, by the time I'd got upstairs, they had stopped snapping and crackling and popping, which annoyed me considerably. I loathe soggy cereals.

Monday, March 25th

Gerry is now a fixture. I am like a cuckoo in the nest. A gooseberry in the strawberry patch. A piranha in the goldfish bowl. Conversation stops when I enter the kitchen or sitting room and they are there. I wanted to watch the Oscar ceremony on television tonight, but Gerry snatched the remote control and kept it on his lap, thus denying me the pleasure of *seeing* that gifted and modest actor Jeremy Irons win an

Oscar for Britain. I had to hear this wonderful news on Radio Four and visualise Mr Irons's delight myself. Whoever said that the 'pictures are better on the radio' was completely wrong.

Tuesday, March 26th

I have asked Bianca to give me prior warning, should a suitable-sounding postcard arrive at the shop offering accommodation. She agreed. I think she finds me personable. Haste has changed the meaning of the above sentence: postcards cannot walk into a newsagent's and talk suitably. Leonora cancelled tonight's appointment. 'An emergency,' she said.

Am I not an emergency? My sanity hangs by a gossamer thread. Leonora is the only barrier between me and the public ward in a lunatic asylum. How will she live with herself if I am admitted foaming at the mouth and struggling inside a strait-jacket?

Wednesday, March 27th

Mr David Icke, who is a famous Leicester person, has revealed that he is a 'channel for the Christ spirit'. He went on television and told the goggling press that his wife and daughter were 'incarnations of the archangel Michael'. He blamed the planet Sirus for bringing earthquakes and pestilence to the world. Gerry and Mrs Hedge mocked him and said he is barmy, but I'm not so sure. We Leicester people are known for our level heads. Perhaps Mr Icke knows something that we ordinary mortals cannot even guess at.

Thursday, March 28th

Bianca studied Astronomy in the sixth form. She said this morning, 'There is no such planet as Sirus.' But, as I pointed out to her, 'David Icke did say that Sirus was *undiscovered,* so naturally no reference *would* be found to it in the books, would it?'

A queue formed, so we were forced to break off our discussion. I called in on my way home from work, but Bianca was busy—some old git was complaining about his newspaper bill.

Friday, March 29th

The more I think about David Icke's predictions, i.e. that the world will end unless it 'purges itself of evil', the more it makes sense. He is a successful man, who was employed by the BBC, no less! He was also a professional goalkeeper for Hereford City. We should not be too quick to scoff. Columbus was once mocked for remarking that the world was round. Something that was verified by the first U.S. astronauts.

My mother rang tonight to ask me what I want for my birthday next week. I told her to get me the usual, a book token. She went on to say that Leicester was agog about David Icke, and that 'there has been a run on turquoise track suits' (worn by Mr Icke's followers). She said she felt sorry for his mother. Apparently, Mr Icke claimed he was born on the planet Sirus, whereas his mother said in the *Leicester Mercury* that she distinctly remembers giving birth to him in the Leicester General Maternity Hospital.

I ran out of bananas tonight. I had to walk to the outer suburbs before finding an off-licence that stocked them.

Saturday, March 30th

Posted two birthday cards to myself. I put second-class stamps on, so they should get here by Tuesday morning.

Monday, April 1st

A man with a Glaswegian accent rang me in my cubicle this morning and said, 'I have just finished reading the opening chapters of your novel *Lo! The Flat Hills of My Homeland* and I want to publish it next year. Would an advance of £50,000 be acceptable?'

I stammered out, 'Yes,' and asked to whom I was speaking.

'A. Fool!' laughed the imposter, and slammed the phone down.

How cruel can you get? For fifteen seconds, I had achieved my ambition. I was a professional writer living in my own house. I'd learned to drive. I had a car in the garage. I had a Rolex watch and a Mont Blanc pen. There was an air ticket to the U.S.A. in the pocket of my cashmere coat. Fan letters bristled inside my leather briefcase. Invitations to literary events were stacked on the mantelpiece. Then my dream was shattered by the hoaxer and I went back to being simple Adrian Mole, who was halfway through writing a report on newt movements, in a cubicle in a D.O.E. building in Oxford. I suspect Goffe.

Tuesday, April 2nd

Birthday cards from Mother, Rosie, Father, Grandma, Mrs Hedge and Megan. Six cards in all. Not bad. I needn't have posted two to myself.

PRESENTS

1. Ten pound book token from mother.
2. W. H. Smith voucher from father (fiver).
3. 2 pairs of socks from Mrs Hedge (white).
4. Cactus plant from Megan (obscene).

No surprise party. No candles to blow out. No singing. No Leonora until Thursday.

Wednesday, April 3rd

I am twenty-four and one day old. *Question:* What have I done with my life? *Answer:* Nothing.

Graham Greene died today. I wrote to him four years ago, pointing out a grammatical error in his book, *The Human Factor.* He didn't reply.

Thursday, April 4th

I trimmed my beard this morning. Mrs Hedge screamed when I came out of the bathroom. When she recovered, she said, 'Christ, you look like the Yorkshire Ripper.'

I had a terrible session with Leonora. I went into her room with the self-esteem of an anorexic aphid and came out feeling worse.

My low self-esteem on entering Leonora's room was due to an acrimonious phone conversation I'd had with my mother earlier. She had rung the office to ask me if I would like go to a party given by Barry Kent to celebrate the success of *Dork's Diary*. The venue is the North East Leicester Working Men's Club, and half of Leicester has been invited.

I said to my mother, 'I would sooner wash a corpse.'

My mother accused me of petty jealousy, and then had a tantrum and recited my faults: arrogance, overweening pride, snobbery, pretension, phoney intellectualism, wimpishness, etc., etc.

I recited this to Leonora who said, 'I suggest that you take on board what your mother is saying. I also suggest that you *go to the party.*' She said that she had bought five copies of *Dork's Diary:* for her husband, Fergus; for her best friend, Susan Strachan; for her therapist, Simon; for her supervisor, Alison; and for herself. I was totally gobsmacked. When Leonora said that it was time to go, I refused to leave my chair.

I said, 'I can't bear the thought of you enjoying Barry Kent's work.'

Leonora said, 'Tough, give me thirty pounds and leave.'

I said, 'No, I am totally sexually obsessed by you. I think about you constantly. I have revealed my innermost feelings to you.'

Leonora said, 'Yours is a standard reaction. You'll get over it.'

I said, 'Leonora, I feel betrayed. I refuse to be treated like an example from a text book.'

Leonora stood up and tossed her magnificent head and said, 'Ours is a professional relationship, Mr Mole. It could never be anything else. Come and see me next Thursday.'

'Okay,' I said. 'Take your thirty pieces of silver.'

I flung a Market Harborough Building Society cheque made out for thirty pounds onto the desk and left, slamming the door.

If my father had allowed me to abandon that dummy in my own time, I'm convinced I would now be enjoying perfect mental health.

Saturday, April 6th

Am I the only person in Britain who has an open mind re the David Icke sensation? Bianca described him as a 'barmpot' this morning—but as I pointed out to her, Jesus himself was reviled in his day. The press were against him and the money-lenders slagged him off to all and sundry. Also, Jesus was a bit of an eccentric as regards clothes. He would not have won a 'Best Dressed Palestinian of the Year Award'. But, had track suits been around in Christ's day, he would almost certainly have opted for the comfort and washability of such garments.

Sunday, April 7th

Dork's Diary is now at number eight. Glanced through my *Illustrated Bible Stories* tonight and was startled to find on page 33 (Raising Lazarus) that Jesus is wearing turquoise robes!!!

Monday, April 8th

Brown is back, but he is wearing a noisy surgical corset, which is quite useful (the noise, not the corset), because Megan is seeing Bill Blane (Badger Dept) on the side. I like Bill. He and I discussed David Icke at the Autovent today. Bill agrees with me that Sirus could have been overlooked by the astronomers. It could well have been hidden behind another, bigger planet.

The emir of Kuwait has promised to hold parliamentary elections next year. He has announced that women will be allowed to vote. Good for you, Sir!

Tuesday, April 9th

John Major has been cross-examined by the press about his 'O' levels. I hope this won't remind Brown about my own, nonexistent, Biology 'A' level. Why, oh why, couldn't I have been born an American? College students there are given multiple choice type exams. All the dumbos have to do is put a tick against what they think is the right answer.

Example: Question: Who discovered America?
Was it: a) Columbus?
b) Mickey Mouse?
c) Rambo?

Wednesday, April 10th

Bill Blane has asked me to go for a drink after work tomorrow. This could be the start of a new friendship.

Thursday, April 11th

Bill wanted to talk about Megan. In fact, he talked about her all night. I couldn't get a word in edgeways, apart from saying, 'Same again?' when it was my turn to buy a round. I drank far too much (three pints) and in my muddled state started walking back to Pandora's flat before realising my mistake and turning my steps towards the Hedge household.

Friday, April 12th

Worked on *Lo! The Flat Hills of My Homeland* tonight. Started Chapter Eleven:

As he skirted the top of the hill, he looked east and saw the city of Leicester glowing in the dying embers of the setting sun. The tower blocks reflected the scarlet rays and bounced them against the factory chimneys and the Royal Infirmary multi-storey car park. He sighed with the glorious anticipation of knowing that he would soon be tramping the reconstituted concrete streets of his home town. He could have entered the city by a more discreet route—turned off the motorway at Junction 23—but he preferred this, the route of the sheep drovers, and anyway, he hadn't got a car.

He had been away too long, he thought. He had grown tired of the world and its attractions. Leicester was where his heart was. He strode down the hill, his eyes were wet. The wind, perhaps? Or the pain of absence? He would never know. The sun slipped away behind the grand edifice of the Alliance and Leicester Building Society headquarters and he felt the stealthy black fingers of night collect around him. Soon it was dark. Still he descended. Down. Down.

Not many people know that Leicester lies in a basin, he ruminated. No wonder it is the bronchitis centre of the world, he thought. Before long, he had descended the hill and he was on flat ground.

I think this is probably the best writing I have ever done. It is magnificent. I hope I can maintain this standard throughout the novel.

Saturday, April 13th

Notes on *Lo!*:

a. Should I give my hero a name? Or should I continue to call him *'he'*, *'him'*, etc.?
b. Should the narrative be stronger? At the moment, not much

happens. *He* leaves Leicester, then comes back to Leicester. Should the reader know what *he* does in between?

c. Should *he* have sex, or go shopping? Most modern novels are full of references to one or the other—the reading public obviously relishes such activities.

Descriptions (to be slotted in somewhere):

The tree bent in the wind, like a pensioner at Land's End.

The fried egg spluttered in the frying pan like an old man having a tubercular coughing fit in a 1930s National Health Service hospital.

Her breasts were as full as hot air balloons.
Her face was infused with anger, her eyes flashed like a manic lighthouse whose wick needed cleaning.

The tea was welcome. *He* sipped it gratefully, like an African elephant which has previously found its waterhole to be dry, but then remembered, and walked to, another.

From now on, I shall write down these thoughts and ideas as they come to me. They are far too good to waste. Publication looks to be within my grasp.

Sunday, April 14th

Woke at 8.30, had breakfast: cornflakes, toast, brown sauce, two cups of tea. Collected *Sunday Times* and *Observer.* Bianca not there. *Dork's Diary* has gone to number seven. Changed into blazer. Walked round Outer Ring Road, came back. Brushed and hung up blazer. Lay on bed. Slept. Woke up, put on blazer, went out, had pizza in Pizza Hut. Came back, lay on bed, slept. Woke, had bath, changed into pyjamas and dressing gown. Cut toenails, trimmed beard, inspected skin. Tidied tapes into alphabetical order, Abba to Warsaw Concerto. Went downstairs. Mrs Hedge in kitchen, in tears at kitchen table. 'I've got nobody to confide in,' she cried. Made crab paste sandwiches. Went to bed. Wrote up journal.

I can't go on like this; I'd have more of a social life in prison.

Monday, April 15th

Went to see D.O.E. doctor, Dr Abrahams. I told him I was depressed. He told me he was depressed. I told him that my life was meaningless, that my ambitions remained unrealised. He told me that his dream was to become the Queen's gynaecologist by the age of 44. I asked him how old he was. He told me that he was 45. Poor old git. He gave me a prescription for my depression. I asked the chemist if there were any side effects.

She said, 'Well, there's lack of concentration. Your physical movement may be reduced. You'll notice an increase in heart rate. There'll possibly be sweating and tremors, constipation and perhaps difficulty in urinating. Bit depressing, really, isn't it?'

I agreed with her and tore the prescription into pieces.

Wednesday, April 17th

Rocky gave me a lift to work this morning in his limo. We discussed Pandora, how arrogant she is, etc. Rocky said, 'But, y'know, Aid, I'll always love the girl, she's, y'know, kinda like *unique.*'

I congratulated Rocky on his use of the word 'unique'.

Rocky told me that Carly Pick, his girl friend, is teaching him new words.

I said, 'So, she's extending your vocabulary, is she?' But he looked at me blankly, from which I inferred that she hadn't been at it for long.

When the car drew up outside the D.O.E., I was pleased to see that Brown was looking out of his office window. He ducked out of sight, but he couldn't have failed to see me exiting from the limousine. It won't hurt Brown to know that I mingle with the rich and powerful.

Robert Maxwell has saved the *Mirror.* He is a saint!

Thursday, April 18th

The Newport Pagnell newts seem to have settled down, thank God. The road plans are finalised and construction is due to start next month.

Mrs Brown came to the office today. She had lost her handbag in the Ashmolean Museum. Brown was entirely unsympathetic. Before he closed his office door, I heard him say, 'That's the second time this year, you stupid cow.' He would not have spoken to Megan like that. Mrs Brown is very pretty. It's just that her clothes are horrible. It's as though there is a lunatic living in her wardrobe who orders her what to wear every morning. She can get away with looking ridiculous in Oxford. People probably assume that she is just another barmy professor, but she would be a laughing stock in Leicester.

Saturday, April 20th

Mrs Hedge crying again this morning. I must away from this Vale of Tears. I need cheerful people around me.

Bianca handed me a card this morning. It said, in mad handwriting:

ROOM TO LET

> Academic household willing to let room free to tolerant person of either gender, in return for light household duties/babysitting/cat-sitting. Would suit working person with most evenings free. Please ring Dr Palmer.

I rang immediately from the phone box outside the newsagent's. A bloke answered.

DR PALMER Christian Palmer speaking.

ME Dr Palmer, my name is Adrian Mole. I've just seen your postcard in the newsagent's.

DR P When can you start?

ME Start what?

DR P Looking after the bloody kids.

ME But you don't know me.

DR P You sound okay and you've already proved you can use a telephone. So you can't be a total simpleton. Have you got all your faculties: four limbs, eyesight?

ME Yes.

DR P Ever been done for molesting kiddiewinkies?

ME No.

DR P Got any particularly nasty personal habits?

ME No.

DR P Good. So when can you start? I'm on my own here. My wife's in the States.

The telephone receiver was dropped. Suddenly I heard Palmer shout, 'Tamsin, put the top back on that bottle of bleach! Now!'

He came back on the phone and gave me his address in Banbury Road.

I went into the newsagent's and asked Bianca what newspapers and magazines Palmer read. This is a sure sign of character. It was a baffling list:

Newspapers: *The Observer, The Daily Telegraph, The Sun, The Washington Post, The Oxford Mail, The Independent, The Sunday Times, Today.*

Magazines: *Time Out, Private Eye, Just Seventeen, Vogue, Brides, Forum, Computer Weekly, Woman's Own, Paris Match, Gardening Today, Hello!, The Spectator, The Literary Review, Socialist Outpost, The Beano, Angler's Weekly, Canoeist, Viz, Interiors, Goal!*

I stopped her and said, 'Palmer's newspaper bill must be enormous. How does he pay it?'

'Infrequently,' she replied.

Sunday, April 21st

Dr Palmer is tall and thin and wears his hair like Elvis Presley did during his silver-cloaks-in-Los-Angeles phase. His first words to me were, 'On your way to a fancy dress party?' He laughed and fingered the lapels of my blazer.

I mumbled something neutral and he asked, 'Is that beard *real?*'

I assured him that I had grown it myself and he said, 'How old are you?'

I answered, 'Twenty-four,' and he laughed a strange laugh, like a dog's bark, and to said, '*Twenty-four:* so why the hell do you want to walk round looking like bloody Jack Hawkins?'

'Who's Jack Hawkins?' I asked.

'He's a film star,' he replied. 'Everybody's heard of Jack Hawkins.' He looked annoyed for some reason. Then he said, 'Well, unless you're twenty-four, that is.'

We were still standing on the doorstep of his decrepit house. A line of dirty, unrinsed milk bottles stood on the step. A little kid of unknown sex ran up the hall and tugged at Palmer's trousers. 'I've done a great big one! Come and look, Daddy!' it said.

We all three went into a gigantic room which seemed to be a kitchen, living-room and study combined. In the middle of the floor stood a potty in the shape of an elephant. Dr Palmer looked in the potty and exclaimed, 'Tamsin, that is a truly wonderful piece of shit.'

I averted my eyes as he carried the potty out of the room. Then I heard him shouting, 'Alpha! Griffith! Come and see what Tamsin's done!' There was a thundering on the stairs. I looked into the hall and saw two other androgynous children looking into the potty, saying, 'Wow!' and 'Mega shit!'

I adjusted my blazer in the mirror over the large fireplace and thought that the Dr Palmer household was unsuited to one of my temperament. I do not like to hear little children swear and I prefer them to be dressed in proper clothes and to have hairstyles which give a clue to their sexual orientation. However, when Dr Palmer came back from emptying the potty, I was pleased to see that he was drying his hands, which indicated to me that he knew the fundamentals of hygiene. I agreed to inspect the free room. We climbed the stairs, followed by Tamsin, Griffith and Alpha, who spoke to each other in a language I was not familiar with.

'Is it Welsh they're speaking?' I asked.

'No,' Palmer laughed. 'It's Oombagoomba. It's their own language. They're wearing their Oombagoomba clothes.'

I looked at the rags and bits f cloth and shawls, etc. with which the kids were festooned and was relieved to find out that it was not their usual mode of dress. I too used to have my own made-up language (Ikbak), until my father beat it out of me during a long car journey to Skegness.

The 'free room' turned out to be the whole of the attic floor. It had a kitchen at one end, and a private bathroom at the other. There was a proper desk. I could imagine reading the proofs of *Lo!* at that desk.

'You can do what you like up here,' said Palmer, 'apart from serial killing.'

'Are you a teacher?' I ventured.

'No,' he said. 'I'm leading a research project on popular culture. We are trying to establish why people go out to pubs, discos, bingo sessions, to the cinema, that sort of thing.'

'It's to enjoy themselves, isn't it?' I said.

Palmer laughed again. 'Yeah, but I've got to stretch that very simplistic answer into a three-year study and a seven-hundred page book.'

As we went down the stairs, I mentioned to Dr Palmer that as well as being an excellent tenant, I am also a novelist and a poet.

He groaned and said, 'So long as you *never* ask me to look at your manuscripts, we'll stay the best of friends.'

He made me a cup of coffee after grinding up some beans and he told me a bit about his wife, Cassandra, who is in Los Angeles directing a film about mutilation. She sounds horrific, although he claims to miss her. I am too tired and confused to write more. Dr Palmer has told me he must know by Wednesday if I want the room. He's got to go out on Friday to a darts competition.

Monday, April 22nd

Should I go, or should I stay?

Can I stand babysitting for three children, four nights a week?

I could save £75 a week. In a year, that is . . . ? As usual, when faced with mental, or even physical, arithmetic, my brain has just left my body and walked out of the room.

Thank God for calculators. Nine hundred pounds! It's not as if I would be sacrificing my social life. I haven't got one and, with a bit of luck, Mrs Palmer will stay in America, or fall over Niagara Falls, or something.

Thursday, April 25th

Rang Palmer from the office and told him that I would be moving in tonight. Rang Pandora; asked if Cavendish would help me to move.

'Moving?' she said. 'Again?' Then, 'You make more moves than a tiddlywink.'

Rang Mrs Hedge, asked her to take my Y-fronts out of the washer and hang them on my bedroom radiator to dry. Mentioned that I would be moving on.

She said, 'Everybody does, eventually.'

Rang my mother and gave her my new address in case of a family tragedy. She yakked on for half an hour about President Gorbachev's threat to resign and predicted that the U.S.S.R. was in danger of collapse. I cut in eventually and said, 'I no longer take an interest in world events. There is nothing I can do to influence them, so why bother?'

Rang Grandma, in Leicester. Had a long chat about Princess

Diana. Grandma doesn't think she's been looking happy lately. I voiced my own concern. Diana is too thin.

Rang Market Harborough Building Society to notify change of address.

Rang Waterstone's. Pretended to be irate reader; threatened to sue them for selling pornography, i.e. *Dork's Diary*.

Rang Megan. Pretended to be Brown. Said, 'God, I love you, Megan,' in his horrible squeaky voice.

Eventually, Brown burst in and demanded that I get off the phone. I sincerely hope he hasn't been listening outside the door.

I had a compulsion to visit Leonora again. She agreed to see me immediately. She was wearing a white dress. She looked like a sacrificial virgin. I wanted to deflower her, but I found myself talking about Bianca. Leonora leant forward in her chair, displaying her dark cleavage. I found myself saying that I was quite interested in Bianca, although I found her lack of cleavage disappointing.

Leonora said, 'But could you love Bianca?'

I said, 'The idea is ridiculous. The thought of *her* doesn't keep me awake at night, but the thought of *you* does.'

Leonora sighed and said, 'I suggest you cultivate this friendship with Bianca. I am a married woman, Adrian. Your obsession with me is typical of a therapist/client relationship. It is called transference. You must face the truth about your feelings.'

I said, 'The truth about my feelings is that I don't love you. I just want to go to bed with you.'

Leonora said, 'Thirty pounds please.'

I felt like a client paying a whore.

Friday, April 26th
Moving Day

Cavendish and Palmer are old friends. When they saw each other, they did that arms-clasped-on-each-other's-shoulders, then grin-and-shake, which so many men in Oxford seem to go in for these days. As I removed my possessions from the back of the Volvo and tried to stop Tamsin, Griffith and Alpha from interfering, I heard Cavendish and Palmer laughing like madmen in the living-room. I'm not sure, but I think I heard the word 'blazer' mentioned. The children spoke Oombagoomba all night until their father returned at 11.30 p.m. They flatly refused to go to bed, or to converse with me in English. Instead, they lay under the massive pine table on a pile of cushions and jabbered away in that made-up lingo. It was like being abroad; if you closed your eyes.

Saturday, April 27th

Bought *The White Hotel* by D. M. Thomas this morning. If it is even half as good as *The Great Babylon Hotel* by Arnold Bennett I will be more than satisfied. When Christian saw me take it out of the carrier bag, he raised his eyebrows and said, 'Don't leave it lying around. Alpha's got a reading age of thirteen.'

I said, 'You should encourage your child to read.'

Christian snapped, '*The White Hotel* is a bit heavy for a kid who still believes that fairies live at the bottom of the garden.'

I must say this surprised me. I went down to the bottom of the garden yesterday. It is covered in rusting toys and stinking garden rubbish. It is hardly Fairyland.

At 11.30 p.m., I opened *The White Hotel*, read for ten minutes, then got out of bed and bolted the door. It must never fall into Alpha's hands.

Monday, April 29th

Babysat. Christian is at the semi-final of a darts competition with his dictaphone and clipboard. Do the big-bellied darts players realise that they are taking part in a research project? I doubt it. They all seem to have tunnel vision, which I suppose is an advantage if you play darts for a living.

Christian told me today that Bianca was enquiring about me, asking if I'd settled in. He told her that the kids like me. I wish he'd told me. Christian asked me why I don't ask Bianca for a date. I answered nonchalantly that I was too busy. But, dear journal, the truth is that I'm afraid *she might refuse.* My ego is but a frail and fragile thing and furthermore am I sure I want to commit myself to a person who works in a newsagent's shop?

NOTES ON BIANCA:

Negative

1. She is pleasant-looking but certainly not a head-turner, unlike Leonora, who is capable of stopping the traffic.
2. When I mentioned that my walk to work was 'pleasantly Chekhovian', largely due to the blossoming cherry trees, she looked at me blankly and asked me what 'Chekhovian' meant.
3. Her hips do not look capable of bearing a child.
4. She wears Doc Marten boots.
5. She is a Guns 'n' Roses fan.

Positive

1. She is kind, especially to the children who linger over the sweets section in the newsagent's.
2. I seem to be able to make her laugh.
3. Her skin looks like white silk. I have a strange desire to stroke her face whenever I am close to her.

Tuesday, April 30th

I'm glad April is over. It is a bitter-sweet month. The blossom is out, but the wind still swells around and flaps the bottoms of your trousers unless you tuck them into your socks.

Beard bushy now. Food gets caught in it. Brown pointed out a piece of egg white at 9.30 a.m. I ate my boiled egg at 7.39 this morning. Since that time, I have spoken to, or been seen by, at least thirty people. Why did no one else point out that I had egg white in my beard? It is not as if it was a *small* piece. As egg white goes, it was quite a large piece, and as such, impossible to overlook. I will have to buy a small hand mirror and check my beard regularly after meals. I cannot risk such social embarrassment happening again.

Wednesday, May 1st

Babysat. Griffith asked me to help him with his model of a Scud missile, which he is making out of a toilet roll tube and cut-up bits of washing-up liquid bottle. I pointed out to him that I am a pacifist.

Griffith (six) said, 'If your sister was being threatened by a gang of vicious thugs, would you stand by and do nothing?'

I said, 'Yes.' Griffith doesn't know my sister Rosie. She is quite capable of seeing off a gang of vicious thugs.

Christian was back from his karaoke evening by 11 p.m. Apparently, he'd been forced to sing 'Love is a Many Splendoured Thing' in order to keep his cover. So his research project *is* an undercover operation. That explains why Christian changes out of his ragged denims and into his Sta-Pressed polyesters before joining his unsuspecting fellow low-culture vultures.

Thursday, May 2nd

Read through the whole of *Lo! The Flat Hills of My Homeland* manuscript so far. It is crap from start to finish.

Friday, May 3rd

Perhaps I was too harsh last night. *Lo!* has passages of sheer brilliance. About five.

Saturday, May 4th

Left *Lo!* on kitchen table overnight. No comment from Christian this morning, though Alpha said, 'You've spelt "success" wrong on page four. It's got two c's and two s's.' Christian didn't even look up from his *Sun*.

If there's one thing I can't bear, it's a precocious child. It's completely unnatural. I was tempted to tell Alpha that any fairy living in the Hell Hole at the bottom of her garden should have a tetanus jab, but I didn't.

I received the new Plumbs catalogue this morning, offering me four tapestry-look cushions with frilled edges at the bargain price of £27.99. How did they track me down? The envelope came direct from Plumbs to the Banbury Road. Are they watching me?

Sunday, May 5th

Put blazer on and went for my customary Sunday walk around the Outer Ring Road at 2 p.m. Some old git in a Morris Minor stopped and asked me for directions to the Oxford Bowling Club. As if *I*'d know! Returned to find house full of Christian's friends having what he described as a 'fondue party'. They were dipping raw vegetables into a stinking pot of what looked like yellow emulsion paint. I declined to join them.

Monday, May 6th

Bianca was passing as I left for work this morning, so we walked part of the way together. As we crossed at the lights, her hand brushed mine. An electric shock passed through me. I apologised and put my hand in my raincoat pocket to prevent another such occurrence. She took off her Sony headset and invited me to listen to her Guns 'n' Roses tape. After five minutes I handed it back to her. I couldn't stand the din.

Tuesday, May 7th

Bianca was there again outside the house this morning. I don't know why she keeps coming down this road. It's not on her route to work.

Babysat. The kids went to bed at 9.30 p.m., after I'd read them the first three chapters of *Lo!* For once, they seemed quite tired, yawning, etc.

Wednesday, May 8th

Bianca there yet again, tying the laces on her Docs. She told me that she gets bored in the evenings—she hasn't got that many friends in Oxford. She misses the cinema especially, but she is fed up with going on her own. She went on and on about Al Pacino. She has seen *Sea of Love* eleven times. I haven't seen it once. Personally, I can't stand the man. I told her that I too haven't seen a film in ages. When she left me and went into the newsagent's, she looked irritable. Premenstrual, probably.

Thursday, May 9th

Babysat. At 7.30 p.m. I offered to read more of *Lo!* to the kids, but they said, as one, that they were very tired and wanted to go to bed! I had a peaceful night washing my working wardrobe and shampooing my beard. Christian got back at 1 a.m. after observing a fight in an Indian restaurant. I advised him to put his trousers in cold water to soak overnight. Turmeric is one of the most stubborn stains known to man. It is a pig to shift once it has gained a hold.

Monday, May 13th

A terrible scandal at lunchtime today! Megan Harris and Bill Blane were caught in the act of photocopying their private parts! They would have got away with it, had the machine not jammed. They have both been suspended on full pay, pending an internal enquiry. I am quite pleased. It has saved me from having to photocopy two hundred pages of Newport Pagnell newt drivel.

Tuesday, May 14th

It is totally unfair. Because of Bill's suspension, I have been given responsibility for the entire Badger Department. Brown threw the badger case histories on my desk and said, 'You're a friend of Bill's. Sort this out.'

Just because Brown was the one to force the photocopy room door open yesterday, there's no need to take it out on me. He may have lost a mistress and a secretary, but he must remember what he learned on his managerial training course and keep his head.

Wednesday, May 15th

Up at dawn to catch taxi to badger set. I must learn to drive. On the return journey, the taxi driver kept complaining about the smell. I had the fresh badger droppings in a sealed D.O.E. jar, so how the aroma came in contact with the taxi driver's nose is a mystery to me. Personally, I found the fresh air 'pine tree' hanging from the roof of his taxi to be much more olfactorily offensive.

Friday, May 17th

I am already up to my ears in newts and badgers, and now Brown is hinting that I may also be given responsibility for *natterjack toads!* He is obviously trying to force me into resigning or having a nervous breakdown due to overwork.

Photocopies of Megan's and Bill's private parts are being passed around the office. I think this is absolutely disgusting—a total invasion of their private lives, not to mention their private parts.

Anyway the copies are so blurred that it is impossible to tell which is Bill's and which is Megan's. That photocopier never did work properly.

Bianca came round with Palmer's newspaper bill tonight. I answered the door and would have invited her in, but I didn't want her to think that sexual intercourse was on my mind—though, of course, it was. It's never off my mind. She had obviously gone to some trouble with her clothes, for a change. She was wearing tight denim jeans, high-heeled ankle boots and a white shirt which was tucked into a brown leather belt. She had recently washed her hair. I could smell Wash 'n' Go—the shampoos I use myself. It was on the tip of my tongue to ask her if she would come in for coffee, but something held me back.

She didn't seem to want to move off the doorstep—she kept talking about how fed up she was with having nothing to do in the evening. I was forced to stand in a cold wind, wearing only a shirt and trousers. This could result in a severe chill. I must check my temperature over the next few days.

Sunday, May 19th

As predicted, I woke up on Saturday feeling feverish, so I had three tablespoons of Night Nurse (thought it was only 8.30 in the morning) and went back to sleep. On Sunday, Christian knocked on my door at 12.30 a.m. and asked if I could watch the kids for three hours while he attended a 'Stag Strip' at a Working Men's Club. I reluctantly agreed and dragged myself out of bed.

I myself, personally, have never watched a strip show. I wouldn't know how to arrange my facial features. Would I watch with studied indifference like TV detectices when they are forced to interview scumbag low-life in strip joints? Would I smile and laugh as though *amused* by the sight of a young woman taking her clothes off? Or would I swallow frequently, pant and goggle my eyes and reveal to onlookers that I am sexually excited? I fear the latter.

When Christian returned, he went upstairs. The shower was running for at least three quarters of an hour. I suspect he was symbolically cleansing himself.

Today was an Oombagoomba day, so I didn't—indeed, *couldn't*—talk to the kids.

The Chancellor, Norman Lamont, is going to sue a sex therapist for damages. But *how* did she damage you, Lamont? The British people should be told.

A letter from *Reader's Digest* arrived on Saturday, informing me that my name has been shortlistd out of many hundreds of thousands to receive a huge cash prize! All I have to do is agree to subscribe to the *Reader's Digest* magazine! It is easy to sneer at *Reader's Digest,* but it has to be said that they are an extremely handy way for busy bibliophiles to keep abreast of matters literary.

Plumbs have also written to me, offering to supply a lace circular tablecloth, plus a plywood circular table, should I not already have one. I must say I was quite tempted by both.

Thursday, May 23rd

Christian held a drinks party last night and Cavendish and Pandora came round. I tried to engage Pan in conversation, but every time I did, I could see her eyes looking past me over my shoulder. Am I such boring company?

At 8 o'clock, Bianca turned up in a shiny, tight black dress. I introduced her to Pandora. Pandora said to her, 'That's a great dress, Bianca. God, don't you love lycra? What did we do without it?' They then yakked on about lycra for half an hour. In my opinion, Pandora's expensive education has been entirely wasted.

There must have been at least fifty people in the living-room/kitchen/study at one point. The majority of them were graduates, but you would never have known it from their conversation. The main topics were, in order:

1. *The Archers*
2. Football (Gazza)
3. Lycra
4. University cuts
5. Princess Diana
6. Alcoholism
7. The Oxford murder
8. Oats
9. Rajiv Gandhi being burnt
10. The Gossard Wonderbra

Call themselves intellectuals! My efforts to talk about my book, *Lo! The Flat Hills of My Homeland,* were met with cool indifference. Yes! The so-called 'best brains' in the land listened to me for a few minutes, then made feeble excuses to leave my company. At one point, just as I was telling him about my hero's apprenticeship to a cobbler in Chapter Eleven, a man called Professor Goodchild moved away, saying: 'Please spare me the sodding details.'

Yet only minutes later, I overheard him talking about his fish tank and how best to clean it.

Bianca left at 11.30 in the company of a dubious-looking type in a black leather jacket. He is something big in astrophysics, apparently, though in my opinion he looked like the type of moron who wouldn't know which end of a telescope to put his eye to.

As we were cleaning up after the party, Christian said, 'Adrian, take a tip from me, throw that bloody blazer away. Buy yourself some fashionable, young man's clothes!'

I replied (quite wittily, I thought), 'Lycra doesn't suit me.' He looked puzzled for a moment, then continued to wash the glasses.

Pandora also commented unfavourably, saying, 'That fucking awful blazer: give it to Oxfam, for Christ's sake.'

Perhaps I will.

I lay awake for hours imagining Bianca and the astrophysicist gazing at the stars together. Would he trust her with his telescope?

Friday, May 24th

A household on my route to work has acquired an American pit bull terrier. On the surface, it seems to be a friendly beast. All it does is stand and grin through the fence. But in future I will take a different route to work. This is a considerable inconvenience to me, but I cannot risk facial disfigurement. I would like the photograph on the back of the jacket of my book to show my face as it is today, not hideously scarred. I know that plastic surgeons can work miracles, but from now on I am taking no chances.

Brown was in a foul mood today. He has had a letter from Megan's solicitor. She is threatening to sue him for defamation of character, unless she is reinstated immediately. I hope Brown caves in. Megan's replacement, Ms Julia Stone, is one of those superior types who never lose their money in chocolate machines in railway stations.

Saturday, May 25th

Oxford is full of sightseers riding on the top deck of the tourist buses and walking along the streets gazing upwards. It is extremely annoying to us residents to be asked the way by foreigners every five minutes. Perhaps it is petty of me, but I quite enjoy sending them in the wrong direction.

I have just remembered! When I gave my blazer to the Oxfam shop yesterday, my condom was in the top pocket. This means that, should a sexual opportunity arise today, I will be unprepared. It also means that I can no longer go into the Oxfam shop—at least, not until Mrs Whitlow, the volunteer helper I gave it to, dies or retires. Mrs Whitlow has often congratulated me on being a 'decent, clean-living young man', though I have given her absolutely no grounds for thinking so.

Monday, May 27th

Why do the banks have to close just because it is a Bank Holiday? It is a day when people want to *spend* money, isn't it? Borrowed £5 from Christian for Durex and bananas.

Tuesday, May 28th

I have just finished Chapter Twelve of *Lo! The Flat Hills of My Homeland*, 'The Dog It Had To Die':

> He closed the front door of his mother's house with a sigh. He had left her slumped on the kitchen table surrounded by brimming ashtrays and empty Pilsner cans. Upstairs, his father was injecting heroin into his collapsed veins. The family pet, an American pit bull terrier, looked out from the front window of the squalid terraced house and growled, showing its fearsome jaws. He walked down the street and tossed off greetings to the stunted neighbours. A couple fornicated in an alley, their eyes dead, their motions automatic. He wept internally. Anguish gripped his soul. He rued the day he had been born. Then, suddenly, a shaft of sunlight fell across his path. He stood, mesmerised. Was it a sign, a portent, that his life would improve from now?
>
> He turned and went back to the house. He opened the front door. The dog, Butcher, growled at him, so he strangled it until the dog lay dead at his feet. He felt Evil, but at the same time strangely Good. The dog had been nothing but a nuisance and nobody ever took it for a walk. His conscience was clear.

Wow! Powerful writing, or what? I believe Dostoievsky would be proud of me. Canine murder is surely a first in English fiction. I expect I'll get a few letters from English dog lovers when *Lo! The Flat Hills of My Homeland* is published, but I shall write back and point out that I am an artist and must go where my pen takes me.

Wednesday, May 29th

Julia Stone and I had a brief conversation at the Autovent machine today, while my oxtail soup was pouring into my plastic cup. She asked me not to use the ladies' lavatory again. I pointed out to her that the men's lavatory had run out of toilet paper, but she said if I continued to 'invade female space', she would report me for sexual harassment. She also said that she had checked the post book and that I used more postage stamps than any other member of staff.

I told her in cold tones—though not as cold as my oxtail soup—that I wrote more letters, therefore I needed more stamps. But I fear I have made an enemy.

Ms Julia Stone is a daunting woman. My throat constricts whenever I have to talk to her. Lipstick might help. Her, not me.

Christian returned from the Golden Gate nightclub with a black eye. His crime was to look at a yob. Yes, the yob accused Christian of 'looking' at him. This is a frightening example of the disintegration of British society. Yobs used to *enjoy* people looking at them. From now on, I shall avert my eyes whenever I see a yobbish person approaching me.

After Christian had stopped fussing with his eye and gone to bed, I sat at the kitchen table and tried to get some sex into *Lo! The Flat Hills of My Homeland.*

Chapter Thirteen: Deflowering

He lay in bed in his Parisian bedroom. Fifi began to remove her lycra dress. His breathing rate increased. She stood revealed before him, her chest strained beneath her Gossard Wonderbra, her knickers were clean and nicely ironed. He reached out for her, but she said to him in her French accent, 'No, no, *mon amour,* I am thinking you must wait.' His ardour increased as he noticed that her bottom was smooth and had no pimples. He groaned and . . .

It's no good. I can't write about sex. Not even French sex in Paris.

Saturday, June 1st

Two letters, one from Plumbs, offering me a set of matching towels with my personal monogram embroidered on the hems; the other from Sharon Bott.

Dear Adrian,

I hope you are welllong time no seeI saw your mum in town and we had a talkshe said how much Glenn looked like you I said yes and she said is he our Adrians Sharon I must knowshe just came out with it like thatIdidn't know what to sayI have got to confess I was seeing someone else at the time as I was seeing you I didn't want to double time you Adrian but you was sometimes moody and I wanted some laffs I was only young. Glenn is going to school now and is a big boy. My mum says you should pay some money but I said no mum it would not be fair cause I dont no if Glenn is Adrians or notYour mum gave me this address to write to youI hope they're is not to many spelling mistakes and that but I never write anything now since I left school their is no need I saw Baz on the telly did youHe has done alright for himself I have not got a bloke now sinse Daryl run off with the video and £35 I had saved for the gasI have put a bit of wait on but I am going to go to Waitwatchers and get it offYou mum said she would babysitshe is so good to me.

Cheers,
Sharon

Sunday, June 2nd

I spoke to my mother this morning and ordered her to keep her nose out of my affairs. She said, 'Glenn is the *result* of one of your affairs,' and put the phone down. From then on, I got the engaged signal.

I was enraged by my mother's interference. How dare *she* pontificate about *anybody's* morals? I know for a fact that she was not a virgin on her wedding night. Grandma told me.

And anyway, my mother should not have spoken in the plural. I have not had *affairs*. I have had *an* affair. In the singular. With Sharon Bott, a simpleton who cannot differentiate between 'they're', 'there' and 'their' and is a virtual stranger to the comma and full stop. She probably thinks that a semi-colon is a partial removal of the intestines.

Memo to self: Is the kid mine? Blood test? Letter of denial?

2 a.m. Wrote to Sharon.

3 a.m. Destroyed the letter. (My reply to her must be carefully crafted. I need time to read up on the law relating to paternity.)

Tuesday, June 4th

Thank God, Prince William has made a full recovery after being bashed on the head by a golf club. When I think how close we came to losing our future King, my heart stands still. Well, not literally *still*, it doesn't *stop*, but I'm glad the kid is better. I phoned Grandma in Leicester. She wanted to know why Prince Charles didn't pick his son up from the hospital. She said, 'Doesn't he know that it is traditional in our English culture?' She thinks that the monarchy is losing touch with the common herd and she complained bitterly that the Royal Yacht *Britannia* costs thirty-five thousand pounds a week to run.

5.00 p.m. The *Oxford Mail* has just informed me that the emir of Kuwait has yet to announce the date for democratic elections to be held in his country. Puzzling, considering all the trouble and expense the allies went to only recently. Get a move on, emir! I'm also informed by the *Oxford Mail* that the Royal Yacht *Britannia* costs thirty-five thousand pounds *a day! A day!* I phoned Grandma immediately and put her right. She was disgusted.

Query: Why does the emir of Kuwait spell his name with a small 'e'?

Friday, June 7th

I spent the morning writing a report on a projection of newt births and the early afternoon on a report on the distribution of badgers. But I fear some of the paperwork has got mixed up. As I was photocopying the reports, I noticed that I had muddled a few facts. However, Brown was shouting down the corridor for the reports, so what could I do? His management meeting was due to start at 4 p.m., so I had no choice but to hand him the papers.

Saturday, June 8th

Wrote to Sharon:

> Dear Sharon,
>
> How very nice to hear from you after all this time.
>
> I'm afraid that there is no chance at all that I can be the father of your child, Glenn.
>
> I have recently had my sperm counted and I was informed by the Consultant Spermatologist that my sperms are too weak to transform themselves into a child. This is a personal tragedy to me, as I had planned on having at least six children.
>
> You mention in your letter that you were double-timing me. I was most upset to read this—our relationship was not ideal, I know; we came from different backgrounds: me: upper working/lower middle; you: lower working/underclass. And, of course, our educational attainments are worlds apart, not to mention our cultural interests. But despite these differences, I had thought that we rubbed along quite well sexually. I see absolutely no reason why you should have betrayed me and

sought out another sexual partner. I confess that I am devastated by your revelation. I feel cheap and used. I would be most obliged to you if you would stop seeing my mother. She is addicted to human dramas of any kind. She thinks of herself as a character in a soap opera. I suggest that you should go to Weight-watchers (not *Wait*watchers, by the way), and hire yourself a competent child-minder. My mother is not to be trusted with young children: she dropped me on my head at the age of six months, whilst taking a boiled egg out of a saucepan.

Anyway, Sharon, it was very nice to hear from you.

Regards,
Adrian

P.S. Who were you double-timing me with? Not that it matters, of course. I have had a constant stream of lovers since our relationship ended. It is simple curiosity on my part. But I would like to know the youth's name, though it is not in the least important. Don't feel obliged to let me know. I just think it may help you to get it off your chest. Guilt can eat away at you, can't it? So would you please write to me and let me know the youth's name? I think you would feel better about yourself.

Sunday, June 9th

I spent the day quietly, working on Chapter Fourteen of my novel.

He looked at the young boy, who was poking a stick at a natterjack toad. 'Stop!' he cried. 'It is one of an endangered species. You must be kind to it.' The young child stopped poking at the toad and came to hold his hand.

'Who are you?' lisped the child. He longed to shout, 'I am your *father*, boy!' but it was impossible. He looked at Sharon Slagg, the boy's mother, who weighed twenty-one stone and had numerous split ends. How could he have once enjoyed sexual congress with her?

He let go of the boy's hand and said, 'I am nobody, boy. I am a stranger to you. I am simply a person who loves the planet we live on—including the dumb creatures that we share our planet with.'

With that, he walked away from his son. The boy exclaimed, 'Please, stranger, don't go.' But he knew he must, before Sharon Slagg looked up from *Damage*, the book she was reading on the park bench. The boy said, 'I wish you were my father, stranger, then I too would have a daddy to come to parents' evenings.'

He thought his heart would break. Sobbingly, he walked away across the grass until the boy was the size of an ant in the distance.

I don't mind admitting that this piece of writing had me wiping my eyes. God, I'm clever. I can tug at the heart strings like no other writer I know. I do feel that my book is now vastly improved by these additions. It still lacks narrative thrust (or does it?), but nobody can say that it doesn't engage the reader's emotions.

Thursday, June 20th

Bianca came round tonight to borrow a cup of Basmati rice. She has stopped going out with the Stargazer: she said his breath smelled constantly of kiwi fruit.

She is a nicely spoken girl, with quite an extensive vocabulary. I asked her why she was serving in a newsagent's. She said, 'There are no jobs for qualified engineers.'

I was totally gobsmacked to learn that Bianca has an upper second degree in Hydraulic Engineering—from Edinburgh University. Before she left with the rice, I asked her to mend the leaking shower in my room. She said she would be pleased to come round tomorrow night and see to it for me. She asked if she should bring a bottle of wine with her. I said there was no need. She looked disappointed. I sincerely hope she is not an alcoholic or a heavy drinker who needs a 'nip' before she can do a job of work.

I am making good progress on the novel. I took out my epic poem *The Restless Tadpole* tonight. It is amazingly good, but I can't spare the time to finish it. The novel has to come first. There is no money in poetry. Our Poet Laureate, Ted Hughes, has been wearing the same jacket in his photograph for the past twenty years.

Friday, June 21st

Bianca came round *avec* tool box, but *sans* wine. She hung about after she'd fixed the shower and talked about how lonely she is and how she longs to have a regular boy friend. She asked me if I have a regular girl friend. I replied in the negative. I sat in the armchair under the window and she lay on my bed in what an old-fashioned kind of man could have interpreted as a provocative pose.

I wanted to join her on the bed, but I wasn't sure how she would react. Would she welcome me with open arms and legs? Or would she run downstairs screaming and ask Christian to call the police? Women are a complete mystery to me. One minute they are flapping their eyelashes, the next they are calling you a sexist pig.

While I tried to work it out, a silence fell between us, so I started to talk about the revisions I am making to my book. After about twenty minutes, she fell into a deep sleep. It was a most awkward situation to be in.

Eventually, I went downstairs and asked Christian to come and wake her up. He sneered and said, 'You're unbelievably stupid at times.' What did he mean? Was he referring to my inability to fix my own shower head, or to my timidity regarding sex?

When Bianca woke up she looked like a sad child. I wanted to put my arms round her but before I could she had grabbed her tool box and run down the stairs without saying goodnight.

Saturday, June 22nd

Had a most satisfactory shower this morning. The force of the water has improved considerably.

2.00 p.m. Worked on Chapter Fifteen. I have sent *him* to China.

11.30 p.m. I have brought *him* back from China. Can't be bothered to do all that tedious research. I just got him walking along the Great Wall, then flying back to East Midlands Airport. I went down to the kitchen to make myself a cup of hot chocolate and told Christian about my hero's trip to China. Christian said, 'But you told me that he is a pauper. Where would he get the money for his air ticket?' God, how I hate pedants!

1.00 a.m. Insert for Chapter Fifteen:

> What was this on the mat? He bent down and picked up a letter from the *Reader's Digest.* On the front of the expensively papered envelope was written 'OPEN AT ONCE'. He obeyed. Inside was a letter and a cheque for one million pounds! He was fabulously rich! 'How shall I spend it all?' he asked the cat. The female cat looked back at him inscrutably. 'China?' he said. 'I'll have a day trip to China!'

I hope this satisfies my pedantic landlord and my most critical of readers.

Sunday, June 23rd

At breakfast, I told Christian how my hero got the money to go to China. He now wants to know what my hero does with the *remaining* money. There is no pleasing him.

12 noon

> *Chapter Sixteen: A Gratuitous Act*
>
> The beggar outside Leicester bus station stared in disbelief as £999,000 showered down onto his head. *He* walked away, a pauper once again.

5.00 p.m. Saw Bianca walking towards me as I was returning from my perambulations around the Outer Ring Road this afternoon. She was wearing shorts and a tee shirt: her legs, apart from the ankles, looked superb, long and slim. I hurried towards her. To my astonishment, she crossed over the road and ignored me. So much for Christian telling me that she fancies me! It's certainly a good job I didn't join her on the bed the other night. I could be in prison now, on a sexual assault charge.

The next time I go to the library I will try to find a book that explains to the intelligent layman how women's brains work.

Wednesday, July 3rd

Brown reminded me today that I have two weeks' holiday entitlement which I will lose unless I take it within the next two months.

Rang my travel agent. Told her I want two weeks in Europe in a four star hotel with half board, but for no more than £300. She promised to ring back if anything turned up in Albania. I said, 'Not Albania, I hear the food is inaudible.' After I'd put the phone down, I remembered that the word for bad food is, of course, 'inedible'. I hope I'm not suffering from an early onset of senile dementia. Word-loss is an early signal.

Friday, July 5th

The travel agent rang today. Unfortunately, the call was put through to Brown's office, where I was being reprimanded because of a mix-up over the newt and badger reports. The Department of Transport had received the erroneous intelligence that a family of badgers had appeared on the route of the projected Newport Pagnell bypass. Naturally, I was constrained by Brown's presence, so I was unable to concentrate on what the travel agent was saying.

I said that I would ring her back, but she said, 'You must book it *now* if you want it.'

I said, 'Book what?'

She said, 'Your holiday. A week on the Russian lakes and rivers, and a week in Moscow. A fortnight for £299.99, full board.'

'Go ahead,' I said.

Saturday, July 6th

Rang 'Easy-pass' Driving School and booked a free lesson as advertised in the *Oxford Mail.* I take to the road on Thursday, July 18th.

I have taken driving lessons before, but have been badly let down by my previous instructors. They were all incompetent.

Sunday, July 7th

Babysat while Christian went to bingo. He won £7.50 and was near to winning the area prize of £14,000. He only needed two fat ladies.

Monday, July 8th

Worked on *Lo!* Shall I give *him* a name? If so, what shall it be? It needs to express his sensitivity, his courage, his individualism, his intellectual vigour, his success with women, his affinity with nature, his proletarian roots.

Tuesday, July 9th

How about Jake Westmorland?

Wednesday, July 10th

Maurice Pritchard?

Thursday, July 11th

Oscar Brimmington?

Friday, July 12th

Jake Pritchard?

Saturday, July 13th

Maurice Brimmington?

Sunday, July 14th

A decision will have to be made soon. I can't move on with my book until it has. Christian prefers 'Jake Westmorland'. However, the man in the greengrocer's likes the sound of 'Oscar Brimmington'. Whereas a bus conductor, whose opinion I sought, was very keen on 'Maurice Westmorland'.

Monday, July 15th

Spent the day babysitting. I got the kids to test me on the Highway Code. Somebody kept ringing the house tonight. A woman. All she said was, 'Hello.' But when I asked who was calling she put the phone down. It sounded like Bianca, but why should she behave in such a childish manner?

Tuesday, July 16th

Brown had to have his surgical corset adjusted at the Radcliffe Hospital this morning, so I took the opportunity to go into his office and look at my file: 'MOLE—ADRIAN.'

FORESIGHT—NONE
PUNCTUALITY—POOR
INITIATIVE—NONE
RELIABILITY—QUITE GOOD

HONESTY—SUSPECTED OF PILFERING POSTAGE STAMPS
ACCEPTANCE OF RESPONSIBILITY—POOR
RELATIONS WITH OTHERS—QUITE GOOD

I believe his 'A' level Biology qualification to be bogus.

Wednesday, July 17th

Dear Mr Brown,

It is with great regret that I write to inform you of my intention to resign from the Department of the Environment. I will of course serve out my statutory two months' notice. I have been unhappy for some time now with how the department is run. I feel that my talents have been wasted. Collecting badger faeces was not in my original job description.

Also, in my opinion, the protection of animals has reached ludicrous levels. The beasts have more rights than I do. Take bats. If I were to hang upside down and defecate in a church, I would be taken away to an institution. Yet bats are *encouraged* by conservationists such as yourself, Mr Brown. It's no wonder that our churches are empty of parishioners.

I remain, sir,
Adrian Mole

At 10.00 a.m. I wrote the above letter, put it into an envelope and wrote 'FOR THE ATTENTION OF MR BROWN'.

At 11.00 a.m., after staring down at the envelope for a full hour, I put it under my blotting pad. Thinking perhaps that I could brazen it out regarding the bogus 'A' level.

At midday, while I was at the Autovent, the envelope disappeared. I searched my cubicle but found nothing, apart from my little blue comb.

At 1.00 p.m., I was summoned to Brown's office and told to clear my desk and leave the premises immediately. He gave me an envelope which contained a cheque for £676.31 = two months' pay plus holiday money less tax and National Insurance.

Who delivered my resignation letter? I suspect the Sexually Harassed One.

So, like three and a half million of my fellow citizens, I am without work.

1 a.m. Christian got me drunk tonight. I had two and a half glasses of Vouvray and a pint of draught Guinness in a can.

Thursday, July 18th
Driving Lesson

Stayed in bed until 2 p.m. My driving instructor is a woman called Fiona. She is old (47) and has got lots of loose skin around her neck, which she pulls at in times of crisis. I did *tell* her that it is over a year since I was behind the wheel. I did *ask* if I could practise first on Tesco's Megastore out-of-town car park, but Fiona refused and forced me to drive on real roads with real traffic. So what happened at the roundabout was not my fault. Fiona should have been quicker with the dual controls.

Friday, July 19th

A letter from Faber and Faber:

> Dear Mr Mole,
>
> I am afraid that I am returning your manuscript, *Lo! The Flat Hills of My Homeland.*
>
> It is a most amusing parody of the English *naïf* school of fiction.

However, we do not have a place for such a book on our list at the moment.

Yours sincerely,
Matthew Evans

After reading the letter six times, I tore it in pieces. Mr Evans will be sorry one day. When my work is being auctioned in hotel rooms, I will instruct my agent to disqualify Mr Evans from the bidding.

There was no reason to get up, so I stayed in bed all day, wondering if there was any point in going on. Pandora despises me, I am out of work and I am incapable of driving a car in a straight line. At 7 p.m. I got out of my bed and rang Leonora. A man answered the phone: 'De Witt.'

'It's Adrian Mole,' I said. 'Could I speak to Leonora?'

'My wife's dressing,' he said; which threw me for a while. Images of Leonora in various lingerie outfits flashed into my mind.

'It's an emergency,' I managed to croak out. I heard him put the receiver down with a crack and shout, 'Darling, it's for you. Something about moles.'

There was a muttered oath, and then Leonora came on the phone.

'Yes?'

'Leonora, I'm in despair. Can I come round and see you?'

'When?'

'Now.'

'No, I'm giving a dinner party at eight and the first course is an asparagus soufflé.'

I wondered why she would think I was remotely interested in her menu.

'I need to talk to you,' I said. 'I've lost my job, my novel's been rejected and I crashed the driving school car yesterday.'

'They are all life experiences,' she said. 'You will come out of this a stronger man.'

I heard her husband shouting something in the background. Then she said, 'I have to go. Why don't you talk to that girl, Bianca? Goodbye.'

I did as I was told. I went and stood outside Bianca's house and looked up at her flat. Nobody went in or came out.

After watching for an hour I went home and got back into bed. I hope the De Witts and their guests all choked on their asparagus soufflé.

Saturday, July 20th

Cassandra Palmer turned up on the doorstep this afternoon. Christian's face turned white when he saw his wife. The children greeted her politely, but without much enthusiasm, I noticed. She looks as though she wrestles in mud for a living. I loathed her on sight. I cannot stand big women who shave their heads. I prefer them with hair.

Her first words to me were, 'Oh, so *you*'re the cuckoo in the nest.'

Sunday, July 21st

The dictatorship of Cassandra started this morning. Our household is not allowed to drink tap water, coffee, tea or alcohol, nor to eat eggs, cheese, chocolate, fruit yoghurt, Marks and Spencer's lemon slices . . . etc., etc. The list goes on forever. There are also things we mustn't say. I happened to mention that Bianca's boss, the newsagent, is a fat man. Cassandra snapped, 'He's not fat, he's dimensionally challenged.'

I laughed, thinking this was a good joke, but Cassandra's mouth turned into a grim slit and with horror I realised she was serious.

Christian remarked to his wife over lunch that he was losing his hair, 'going bald' were his words. Once again, Cassandra snapped into action.

'You're a little follicularly disadvantaged, that's all,' she said, as she inspected the top of her husband's head.

I cannot share this house with that woman, or *her* language. It is not as though she is pleasant to look at. She is as ugly as sin, or, as she might put it, she is facially impaired.

Monday, July 22nd

I asked Bianca if she would keep a lookout for suitable accommodation. She agreed, though there is nothing to keep me here in Oxford any more, apart from my unrequited love for Dr Pandora Braithwaite.

Tuesday, July 23rd

DR BRAITHWAITE

Since you gained your Ph.D.
You have had no time for me.
You loved me once, you could again.
Pandora, give up other men!
You swore to love me for all time.
As long as Moon and June would rhyme.
Please marry me and be my wife.
For you I'll sacrifice my life.
I'll stay at home, I'll cook and clean
In the background, never seen.
When you return from brainy toil,
I'll have the kettle on the boil.
While you translate from Serbo-Croat,
I will shake our coco doormat.
I'll gladly wash your duvet cover,
If only I can be your lover.

I put the poem through Pandora's door at 4 a.m. This is my last-ditch attempt to sound out Pandora's true feelings for me. Leonora has said that I must move on emotionally. What will Pandora's reaction be?

Wednesday, July 24th

I found this letter on the doormat.

> Dear Adrian,
>
> You woke me at 4 a.m. with your clumsy manipulation of my letter box. Your poem caused my lover and me much merriment. I hope, for your sake, that it was *meant* to be funny. If it was *not*, then I urge you to seek further psychiatric advice from Leonora. She told me that you have stopped seeing her regularly. Is it the cost?
>
> I *know* you can afford £30 a week. You don't drink, or smoke, or wear decent clothes. You cut your own hair, you don't run a car. You don't gamble or take drugs. You live rent-free. Withdraw some money from your precious Building Society and *get help*.
>
> Regards,
> Pandora
>
> P.S. Incidentally, I am *not* a Ph.D., as you state in your poem. I am a D.Phil. A subtle but important difference here in Oxford.

So that's it. If Pandora came to me tomorrow, begging to be Mrs A. A. Mole, I would have to turn her down. I have moved on. It's Leonora I must see. Must.

Thursday, July 25th

5.15 p.m. I have just phoned Leonora and insisted that she gives me an emergency appointment. I said I had something momentous to tell her. She agreed reluctantly.

9.30 p.m. I burst into Leonora's room this evening and found her with another client, a middle-aged man who was sobbing into a Kleenex (woman trouble, I suppose). I was ten minutes early and Leonora was furious and ordered me to wait outside. At 6.30 p.m. precisely, I knocked on her door and she shouted, 'Come.' She was still in a bad mood and so I tried to make conversation and asked her what had upset the sobbing middle-aged man. This angered her even more. 'What is said to me in this room remains confidential,' she said. 'How would *you* feel if I talked about *your* problems to my other clients?'

'I don't like to think about you having other clients,' I confessed.

She sighed deeply and curled a hank of black hair around her finger. 'So what's the momentous happening?' she said eventually.

'I've moved on from Pandora Braithwaite,' I said, and I told her about the poem and Pandora's reaction to it and my reaction to Pandora's reaction. At that moment, a tall, dark man wearing a suede shirt came in. He looked surprised to see me.

'Sorry, darling. I can't find the small grater, for the parmesan.'

'Second drawer down, darling, next to the Aga,' she said, looking up at him in rapt adoration.

'Terribly sorry,' he said.

When he'd gone out, I stood up and said, 'How dare your husband interrupt my consultation with his petty domestic enquiries?'

Leonora said, 'My husband didn't know you were here. I squeezed you in, if you remember.' Her tone was carefully measured, but I noticed that a vein was pulsating on the side of her temple and that she was wringing her hands.

'You should learn to express your anger, Leonora. It's no good for you to bottle it up,' I said.

She then said, 'Mr Mole, you are not making progress with me. I suggest you try another analyst.'

'No,' I said. 'It's you I want to see. You're my reason for living.'

'So,' she said. 'Think what you're saying. Are you saying that without me you would commit suicide?'

I hesitated. Noises of pans banging and glasses tinkling came up from the basement, as did a delicious smell that made my mouth water. For some reason I blurted out, 'Could I stay to dinner?'

'No. I never socialise with my clients,' she said, looking at her slim, gold watch.

I sat down and asked, 'How mad am I, on a scale of one to ten?'

'You're not madat all,' she said. 'As Freud said, "It is impossible for a therapist to treat either the mad or those in love." '

'But I *am* in love. With you,' I added.

Leonora sighed very deeply. Her breasts rose and fell under her embroidered sweater.

'That is why I think that seeing another therapist would be a good idea. I have a friend, Reinhard Kowolski, who has a superb reputation . . .'

I didn't wait to hear any more about Herr Kowolski. I left her room and put three ten pound notes on the hall table, next to the laughing Buddha and walked out into the street.

I felt angry, so I decided to express my anger and I kicked an empty Diet Coke can all the way home.

When I got to the attic, I laid out all my job-searching clothes ready for the morning. Then I lay on my bed with the *Oxford Mail* and ringed all the likely looking jobs in the situations vacant columns.

There was nothing that required one 'A' level in English.

Friday, July 26th

Went to the Job Centre, but the queue was too long, so returned to find Cassandra in the kitchen, examining the children's books, pen in hand. She picked one up and changed *Winnie the Pooh* to *Winnie the*

Shit. 'I hate ambiguity,' she explained, as she snapped the cap back on her Magic Marker.

Saturday, July 27th

Saw Brown in W. H. Smith's, buying the current wildlife magazines. He smiled and said, 'Enjoying your life of leisure, Mole?'

I forced a smile to my lips and said, 'On the contrary, Brown, I am working as hard as ever. I am a middle manager at the Book Trust in Cambridge, at £25,000 a year, plus car. I got the position thanks to my having English Literature at 'A' level.' Brown stormed off, forgetting to pay for his magazines. He was stopped on the pavement by a security guard. I didn't hang around to watch Brown's humiliation.

Sunday, July 28th

Stayed in room all day, out of Cassandra's way. She is insisting that everyone in the house meditates for half an hour each morning. Christian has stopped doing his research into popular culture. Cassandra objected to the smell of cigarette smoke on his clothes when he returned from his low-class haunts. If she is not careful, she will wreck his academic career.

I am living on my savings, but I cannot continue to do so. The State will have to keep me—after all, I didn't ask to be born, did I? And one day the State will be glad it supported me. When I am a high-rate taxpayer.

However, before I throw myself on its mercy, I am going to tramp the streets of Oxford tomorrow and look for a job, any job that doesn't involve driving or working with animals.

Next year, I will have lived for a quarter of a century and as yet I have made no mark on the world—apart from winning a *Leicester Mercury* literary prize when I was seventeen.

If I died tomorrow, what would be written on my tombstone?

Adrian Albert Mole
Unpublished novelist
and pedestrian

Mourned by few
Scorned by many
Winner of the *Leicester Mercury*
'Clean Up Leicester' Essay Prize

Tuesday, July 30th

Why do beggars *always* want money for a cup of tea? Don't any of them drink coffee?

Wednesday, July 31st

Why didn't palace flunkies arrange for Princess Diana to be kept dry at the open-air Pavarotti concert last night? If she develops pneumonia and dies, the country will be plunged into crisis and Charles will be devastated with grief. He obviously adores her. Somebody's head should roll.

Thursday, August 1st

Dear Adrian,
I was sorry to read about your poor cwallity seedthe person I was seeing on the side was barry kentI feel better now it is off my chest.

Yours sinserely,
Sharon

Barry Kent! I should have known! He is an amoral, talentless turd! He is lower than a cesspit. He has the prose style of a *Daily Sport* leader writer. He wouldn't know what a semi-colon was if it fell into his beer. The little I have read of *Dork's Diary* forced me to the conclusion that Kent should be arrested and charged with criminal assault on the English language. He deserves to burn in everlasting hell with a catherine wheel tied to his cheating penis.

Friday, August 2nd

Dear Sharon,

Many thanks for your commiserations regarding my 'seed', as you put it. May I suggest that you get in touch with Barry Kent (who, as you know, is now both *rich* and famous) and ask him to contribute to Glenn's upbringing? The least Kent can do is to send Glenn to a private school, thus giving his child an excellent start in life.

I remain,
Yours,
Adrian

P.S. I am absolutely sure that Barry will be thrilled to hear that he has a child.

P.P.S. Eton is quite a good private public school.

Sunday, August 4th

Cassandra announced at breakfast that she has taken the locks off the bathroom and lavatory doors. 'Inhibitions about nakedness and bodily functions are the reason why the English are no good at sex,' she said. She looked pointedly at her husband, who blushed and rubbed the side of his nose.

The Queen Mother is 91 today. I suppose she doesn't think it is worth getting her teeth seen to now. I can see her point.

Monday, August 5th

Contacted Foreign Parts, the travel agents, about my Russian cruise and explained that I have been made redundant and would like to cancel and have my money back. The travel agent told me that it was impossible and told me to refer to the small print on my documents. I peered in vain and eventually went to Boots and bought a pair of 'off the peg' reading spectacles for £7.99. The travel agent was right; I will have to go.

Tuesday, August 6th

Christian told me (shamefaced) that Cassandra requires my attic room. She is opening a reincarnation centre where people can get in touch with their former selves. She wants me out of the attic by mid-September. I couldn't help myself. I burst out, 'Your wife is a cow!' Christian said, 'I know, but she used to be a kitten.'

So, no job and, when I get back from the Russian cruise, nowhere to live.

Thursday, August 8th

Dear John Tydeman,

The last time I wrote to you, it was to apologise for clogging up the BBC's fax machines with my 700-page novel, *Lo! The Flat Hills of My Homeland*. You sent it back to me (eventually) and said, and I quote: 'Your manuscript is awash with consonants, but vowels are very thin on the ground, thin to the point of non-existence.'

You will, I am sure, be delighted to hear that I have now reinstated the vowels and have spent this year rewriting the first sixteen chapters, and I would value your comments on them. They are enclosed with this letter. I know you are busy, but it wouldn't take you long. You can read them in the BBC's coffee lounge during your coffee breaks, etc.

I remain, Sir,
Yours,
Adrian Mole

10.30 p.m. I have seen Leonora for the last time. She has dismissed me from my post as her client. I overplayed my hand and declared my love for her. In fact, it wasn't so much a declaration, it was more of a proclamation. It was probably heard all over Oxford. Her husband heard it because he came into the room with a tea towel and a little blue jug in his hand and asked Leonora if she was all right.

'Thank you, Fergus, darling,' she said. 'Mr Mole will be leaving soon.'

'I'll be outside if you need me,' he said, and left, leaving the door slightly open.

Leonora said, 'Mr Mole, I am calling a halt to our professional relationship, but before you leave I would like to reassure you that your problems are capable of being solved.

'You expect too much of yourself,' she said, leaning forward sympathetically. 'Let yourself off the hook. Be *kind* to yourself. You've expressed your worries about world famine, the ozone layer, homelessness, the Aids epidemic, many times. These are not only your problems. They are shared by sensitive people all over the world. You can have no control over these sad situations—apart from donating money. However, over your personal worries, lack of success with your novel, problems with women, you do have a certain amount of control.' Here she stopped and she looked as though she wanted to take my hand, but she didn't.

'You are an attractive, healthy young man,' she said. 'I have not read your manuscript, so I can't comment on your literary talent or otherwise, but what I do know is that there is somebody out there who is going to make you happy.'

I turned on my dining chair and looked out of the window. 'Not literally out there, of course,' she snapped, following my glance. She stood up, shook my hand and said, 'There will be no charge for this session.'

I said, 'It isn't transference: it's true love.'

'I've heard that at least twenty times,' she said, softly. She rose to her feet. Her rings sparkled under the light and she shook my hand. As I left, I passed her husband, who was still drying the little blue jug twenty minutes later. A suitable case for treatment if ever I saw one.

'I intend to marry your wife one day,' I said, before closing the front door.

'Yes, that's what they all say. Cheerio.' He smiled and went towards Leonora and I closed the door on a painful—and expensive—period of my life.

Friday, August 9th

Adrian,

What the fuck are you playing at, getting Sharon Bott to write to me and ask for money to send her sprog to fucking Eton? I'm down here at Jeanette Winterson's place, trying to finish my second novel and I can do without all this fucking rubbish.

Baz

Saturday, August 10th

I looked in the Job Centre window today. There were three vacancies in the window. One for a 'mobile cleansing operative' (road sweeper?), one for a 'peripatetic catering assistant' (pizza delivery?) and one for a 'part-time clowns enabler' (!). I didn't exactly reach excitedly for the Basildon Bond on my return to Stalag Cassandra.

Sunday, August 11th

Went to the newsagent's. Bianca is back from Greece. She has got a fantastic tan. She was wearing a low-cut white tee shirt, which displayed her breasts. They looked like small, ripe, russet apples. I asked her facetiously if she had had a holiday romance. She laughed and admitted that she had—with a fisherman who had never heard of Chekhov. I asked if she was going to continue the romance. She gave me a strange look and said: 'How would you *feel* about it if I did, Adrian?'

I was about to reply when a member of the underclass thrust a *Sunday Sport* into her hands, so the moment was lost.

10.00 p.m. How do I feel about Bianca's holiday romance? I'm always pleased to see her, but I can't stop comparing her to the lovely Leonora: Bianca is a Malteser: Leonora is an Elizabeth Shaw gold-wrapped after dinner mint.

Tuesday, August 13th

I leave for Russia on Thursday. I bought myself a new toiletry bag—it's time I treated myself. I hope there are some decent women of childbearing age aboard.

I spent the evening packing. I decided not to take any books. I expect there will be a library on the ship, well stocked with the classics of Russian literature in good translations. I hope my fellow passengers are cultured people. It would be intolerable to have to share the dining room and decks with English lager louts. I decided to include a huge bunch of semi-ripe bananas amongst my luggage. I am used to eating a banana a day and I have heard they are in short supply in Russia.

Saturday, August 17th
River camp—Russia

It is 7.30 p.m. There is no cruise ship. There are no passengers. Each member of our party is paddling their own canoe. I am crouched inside a two-man tent. Outside are swarms of huge, black mosquitoes. They are waiting for me to emerge. I can hear the river throwing itself over the rapids. With a bit of luck, I will die in my sleep.

The man I have been sharing my tent with, Leonard Clifton, is out chopping trees down with a machete, borrowed from Boris, one of our river guides. I sincerely hope that one of Clifton's trees falls on his horrible bald head. I cannot stand another night listening to his interminable anecdotes about the Church Army.

I told Boris earlier today that I would give him all my roubles if he would arrange for me to be airlifted to Moscow. He paused from repairing the hole in my canoe and said, 'But you must paddle now to the river's end, Mister Mole; there is no inhabitations, peoples or telephonings here.'

On my return to civilisation, I will sue Foreign Parts for every penny they've got. At no time did they mention that I would be paddling a canoe, sleeping in a tent, or drinking water from the river. The worst privation of all is that *I have got nothing to read*. Clifton lent me his Bible, but it fell overboard at the last rapids. As I watched it sink, I shouted 'My God, my God, why hast thou forsaken me?' To the bewilderment of the rest of the group and of myself, I must admit.

Monica and Stella Brightways, the twins from Barnstaple, are outside leading the singing of 'Ten Green Bottles'. Leonard and the rest of the gang are joining in lustily.

10.00 p.m. Tent. I have just returned from the forest, where I was forced to urinate into the darkness. I stood with the others round the fire for a moment, drinking black tea.

Monica Brightways had a serious argument with the scoutmaster from Hull. She claimed she saw him take two slices of black bread from the sack at lunchtime. He denied it vehemently and accused her of hogging the camp fire. Everyone took sides, apart from me, who loathes them both equally.

Capsized eleven times earlier today. The rest of the hearties were furious with me for holding them up. It is all right for them. They are all members of the British Canoe Union. I am a complete novice and crossing a lake in a force-nine gale is something out of my worst nightmare. The Waves! The Wind! The Water! The lowering black Russian sky! The Danger! The Fear!

I pray to God we may soon come to our journey's end. I long for Moscow. Though I will have to stay in my hotel room; the mosquitoes have attacked my face unmercifully. I look like the Elephant Man on acid.

Midnight The drinking of vodka is now taking place. From my tent I can hear every word. The Russians are maudlin. Every time they talk about 'our souls', the English snigger. I crave sleep. I also crave hot water and a flushing lavatory.

Moscow! Moscow! Moscow!

Wednesday, August 21st
Moscow train

The lavatory on the train defies description. However, I'll try. After all, I am a novelist.

Imagine that twenty buffalo with loose bowels have been trapped inside the lavatory for two weeks. Then try to imagine that an open sewer runs across the floor. Add an I.R.A. prisoner on dirty protest. Then concoct a smell by digging up a few decomposed corpses, add a couple of healthy young skunks and you come quite near to what the lavatory looks and smells like.

Leonard Clifton is writing to President Gorbachev to complain.

I said, 'I think Gorbachev has other things on his mind at the moment, such as preventing civil war and feeding his fellow citizens.'

A harmless remark, you might think, but Clifton went mad. He screamed, 'You have ruined my holiday, Mole, with your pathetic whingeing and nasty, cynical comments.'

I was totally gobsmacked. Nobody in the group came to my defence—apart from the Brightways twins, who had already informed the group at frequent intervals that they 'loved all living things'. So anything they had to say was irrelevant. They no doubt equate my life with that of a lugworm.

Thursday, August 22nd
Hotel room—Moscow

I am staying in the 'Ukraina', near the Moskva River. It looks like a hypodermic syringe from outside. Inside, it is full of bewildered guests of all nationalities. Their bewilderment stems from the hotel staff's reluctance to pass on any information.

For instance, hardly anybody knows *where* meals are being served, or even *if* meals are being served.

For breakfast this morning I had a piece of black bread, four slices of beetroot, a sprig of fresh coriander and a cup of cold, black tea.

An American woman in the queue behind me wailed to her husband, 'Norm, I gotta have juice.'

Norm left the queue and went up to a group of loitering waiters.

I watched him mime an orange, first on the tree and then off the tree. The waiters watched him impassively, then turned their backs on him and huddled around a portable radio. Norm returned to the queue. His wife shot him a contemptuous look.

She said, 'I just gotta have some fruit in the morning. You *know* that, Norm. You know how my system seizes up.'

Norm pulled a face indicating that he remembered *exactly* what happened to his wife's system when it seized up. I thought fondly about the bunch of bananas upstairs in my room.

They were worth their weight in gold.

At nine-thirty, most of our group gathered in the foyer of the hotel ready to start our visit to Red Square. I lurked behind a pillar, dabbing T.C.P. onto the fourteen mosquito bites which disfigured my face.

The Barnstaple twins, Monica and Stella Brightways, kept us waiting for ten minutes, claiming that they had to wait for the lift to ascend to where their room was on the nineteenth floor. Eventually we set off in a bus which seemed to have an interior exhaust pipe next to my seat at the back. I coughed and choked on the diesel fumes and made a futile attempt to open the window. The coach driver was wearing a Gorbachev badge and seemed to be in a bad mood. Our coach parked on the edge of Red Square and we got out and gathered around our Intourist guide, Natasha. She held up a red and white umbrella, and we followed behind like moronic sheep. When we got to the Square, it became obvious that something was happening, a protest march or a demonstration of some kind was taking place. I lost sight of the red and white umbrella and became lost in the crowd. I heard an ominous rumbling behind me, but was unable to move.

An old lady in a headscarf shook her fist towards the noise. She screamed something in Russian. Spittle flew out of her mouth and landed on my clean sweater. Then the crowd parted and the rumbling grew nearer and the tracks of a Russian army tank clanked past an inch away from my right shoe. The tank stopped and a young man clambered aboard and began to wave a flag. It was the hammer and sickle flag I'd been used to seeing everywhere. The crowd roared its approval. What was happening? Had Moscow Dynamo won at football? No, something more important was taking place.

A young woman who wore too much blue eyeshadow said to me, 'Englishman, today you have witnessed the end of Communism.'

'I nearly got run over by a tank,' I said.

'A proud death,' she said. I reached into my pocket for a banana to boost my blood-sugar level. I started to peel it. The young woman's eyes filled with tears. I offered her a bite, but she misinterpreted my gesture and shouted something in Russian. The crowd roared and cheered. She then turned and told me she was shouting 'Bananas for all under Yeltsin!' The crowd began to chant. Then the young woman ate my banana.

'A symbolic gesture, of course,' she said.

When I returned to my room, I found a hefty young Russian woman sitting on a chair outside the door. She was wearing a low-cut brown lamé minidress.

She said, 'Ah, Mr Mole, I am Lara. I come to your room, to sleep, of course.'

I said, 'Is this part of the Intourist programme?'

Lara said, 'No. I am, of course, in love with you.'

She followed me into my room and went to the bunch of bananas on the bedside table. She looked down at them with lust in her eyes and I understood. It wasn't me she wanted: it was the bananas. I gave her two. She went away. Intercourse with her might have done me some harm. She had thighs like Californian redwoods.

Friday, August 23rd

I lay awake most of the night, scratching at my mosquito bites and regretting my hasty decision and wondering how news about my bananas had spread. The next day the streets were full of rioting Muscovites and we were confined to the hotel.

After lunch (black bread, beetroot soup, a wizened piece of meat, one cold potato), I returned to my room to find that my bananas had gone. I was outraged.

I complained to Natasha, but she only said, 'You had *ten* bananas?' She looked misty-eyed and then snapped, 'You should, of course, have put them in the hotel safe. They will be changing hands on the black market by now.'

I found Leonard Clifton in the gloomy basement bar. There had been a coup against Gorbachev and then a counter-coup by Boris Yeltsin.

'This is bad news for Soviet Communism,' he said, 'but good news for Jesus.'

England! England! England!

I long for my attic room.

Monday, September 2nd
Oxford

I am in bed, exhausted and hideously deformed. Why do mosquitoes exist? Why? Cassandra said they are 'a vital component of the food chain'. Well, I Adrian Mole, would gladly *pull* the chain on them. And, if the food chain collapses and the world starves, so be it.

I have written to Foreign Parts, threatening to report them to A.B.T.A. unless I receive *all* my money back, plus compensation for the double trauma suffered from the mosquitoes and the revolution.

Tuesday, September 3rd

Christian passed by Foreign Parts today. He said it looked deserted. There was a pile of unopened letters on the doormat inside the shop.

Thursday, September 5th

A reply from John Tydeman, Head of Drama, BBC Radio.

Dear Adrian,

To be perfectly honest, Adrian, my heart sank when I returned from holiday and saw that your manuscript, *Lo! The*

Flat Hills of My Homeland had landed on my desk yet again. You say in your letter, 'I expect you are busy'. Yes, I damned well *am* busy, incredibly so.

What exactly is a 'coffee break'? I've never had a 'coffee break' during the whole of my long career with the BBC. I drink coffee at my desk. I do not go to a 'coffee break' lounge where I loll about on a sofa and read handwritten manuscripts, 473 pages long. My advice to you (without reading your wretched MS) is to:

1. Learn to type
2. Cut it by at least half
3. Supply a S.A.E. and postage. The BBC is suffering from a cash crisis. It certainly cannot afford to subsidise your literary outpourings.
4. Find yourself a *publisher.* I am *not* a publisher. I am the Head of Radio Drama. Though sometimes I wonder if I am Marjorie Proops.

I am sorry to have to write to you in such terms, but in my experience it is best to be frank with young writers.

Yours, with best wishes,
John Tydeman

Poor old Tydeman! He has obviously gone mad. 'Sometimes I wonder if I am Marjorie Proops' (!)—perhaps the Director General should be told that his Head of Radio Drama is suffering from the delusion that he is an agony aunt.

And he admitted that he hadn't even read the re-edited *Lo! What do we licence-payers pay for?*

Dear Mr Tydeman,

I would appreciate it if you could send my MS back, A.S.A.P. I do not want it circulating around the corridors of the BBC and being purloined by a disaffected freelance producer, anxious to make his or her mark on the world of broadcasting.

Adrian Mole

P.S. Allow me to inform you, sir, that you are *not* Marjorie Proops.

Saturday, September 7th

Spent most of the day in a futile search for a reasonably priced room. As I made my weary way back home, I passed Foreign Parts. There was a note on the door:

This business is closed. All enquiries to Churchman, Churchman, Churchman and Luther, Solicitors.

I didn't take down the telephone number. It was already in my filofax, under 'S'. A middle-aged couple *were* taking the number down, though. They were due to depart tomorrow on a cycling holiday in 'Peter Mayle Country', Provence. They were facing the awful realisation that they were not going to see the famous table on the infamous terrace, and possibly take tea with Pierre Mayle plus *femme*.

As the couple walked away, I heard her say to him: 'Cheer up, Derek, there's always the caravan at Ingoldmells.' A fine woman, indomitable in the face of disaster. Mr Mayle has been cheated of meeting a true Brit.

Sunday, September 8th

I have decided to go with Jake Westmorland.

Chapter Seventeen: Jake—A Hero of Our Time

Jake stood on top of the tank in Red Square. What a good job I took Russian at school, instead of French, he thought. Then, quieting the multitudes by a small gesture of his hand, he spoke.

'I am Jake Westmorland,' he shouted. The revolutionary hordes bellowed their grateful recognition. A sea of banners waved joyously. The sultry Russian sunlight glinted on the dome of St Basil's Cathedral as Jake tried to quieten the crowds and begin his speech. The speech that he hoped would prevent the disintegration of the Soviet Union. . . .

Monday, September 9th

I have written eleven speeches for Jake and thrown them all in the bin. None of them was capable of changing the course of world history.

. . . But before Jake could make the speech that would almost certainly have saved the Soviet Union, a shot rang out and Jake fell off the tank and into the arms of Natasha, his Russian mistress. She threw Jake over her shoulder and the silent crowd parted to let them through.

Thursday, September 12th

Cassandra has ordered me to be out of the house by noon on Saturday! The lousy, stinking undergraduates have hogged all the private rented accommodation. I had no choice but to throw myself on the mercy of Oxford Council. But the Council official I spoke to today maintained that I am 'intentionally homeless' and refused to help me. I have started collecting cardboard boxes. Either to pack my belongings in, or to sleep in—who knows?

Friday, September 13th

Christian has taken the children to see his mother in Wigan. He is a spineless coward. The hideous Cassandra is walking around the house in her absurd clothes, singing her ludicrous rapping songs. I asked her tonight if I could store my books in the attic until I've found a place of my own. She replied, 'Books?' as though she'd never heard the word before.

I said, 'Yes, *books*. You know, those things with cardboard covers stuffed with paper. People read them, for pleasure.'

Cassandra snorted contemptuously. 'Books belong in the past, together with stiletto heels and Gerry and the Pacemakers. This is the nineties, Adrian. It's the age of technology.'

She went to her word processor and pressed a button. A series of little green men wearing Viking helmets filled the screen and began to fight with little red men wearing baseball caps, who came out of a cave. Cassandra leaned eagerly towards the screen. I sensed that our conversation was over and left the room.

Query: Is the world going mad, or is it me?

Saturday, September 14th

8.30 a.m.

OPTIONS

1. Pandora (no chance)
2. Bianca (possible)
3. Mother (last resort)
4. Bed and breakfast (expensive)
5. Hostel (fleas, violence)
6. Streets

11.30 a.m.

1. Pandora turned me down flat. She is a true *Belle Dame sans Merci*.
2. Bianca is away attending a Guns 'n' Roses convention in Wolverhampton. Left note at newsagent's.

3. My mother is out gawping at a new crop circle just outside Kettering.
4. The cheapest B&B is £15.99 a *night!*
5. There is nothing under 'Hostel' in the phone book.
6. I hit the road at high noon.

11.35 p.m. Leicester. Bert Baxter's house So, it has come to this. I am reduced to sleeping on a Put-U-Up in a pensioner's living-room, which stinks of cats. Baxter is charging me £5 for tonight, plus £2.50 for bacon and eggs. My mother's house is locked and dark, and the key is not in its usual place under the drain cover. In normal circumstances I would have broken the small pantry window and climbed in, but my mother has had a security system installed. Delusions of grandeur, or what?

My father, supposedly penniless, is on holiday in Florida with a rich divorcee called Belinda Bellingham. I know I could go to my grandma's but I can't bear her to find out that I am unemployed and homeless. The shock could kill her. She has my G.C.S.E. certificates framed on the hall wall. My 'A' level English certificate is in a silver frame on the mantelpiece in her front room. Why give such anguish to an elderly diabetic?

Monday, September 16th

1.35 a.m. I am now trying to sleep on the sofa-bed in my mother's living room. As I write, the television in my mother's bedroom is blaring. The washing machine is on its spin cycle. The dishwasher is shrieking and somebody is taking a shower. Subsequently, the water pipes are banging all over the house. My stepfather, Martin Muffet, has just gone upstairs with his D.I.Y. toolbox. Does nobody sleep in this house?

Tuesday, September 17th

My grandma knows all. My mother has told her everything. She is disgusted. I hope she never finds out that Bert Baxter gave me a bed for the night.

Wednesday, September 18th

G. knows about B&B at B.B.'s. She saw B.B. in C&A.

Friday, September 20th

A postcard of Clifton Suspension Bridge came this morning.

> Dear Adrian,
>
> I've only just got your message! Sorry I didn't see you before you left. That Cassandra is a sad woman all right!
>
> I've never been to Leicester. Is it nice? Hope so for your sake!
>
> There's a floor here for you if you fancy coming back to Oxford! I know where I can borrow a double mattress.
>
> Let me know soon, please!
>
> Love,
> B.

The exclamation marks gave me some pain. Could I share a floor with a woman who was so profligate with them? And what would the sleeping arrangements be? This 'double mattress' she mentioned. Was it for me only? If so, why a double? I presume she has an adequate bed of her own. I decided to write an ambiguous reply, keeping my options open, but committing myself to nothing. My mother, who had brought the postcard to me in bed, wanted to know *everything* about 'B'. Height, weight, build, colouring, education, class, accent, clothes, shoes. 'Is she nice?' Have I 'slept with her'? 'Why not?' The Spanish Inquisition would be nothing compared to my mother. Nothing.

Dear Bianca,

It was most kind of you to write to me and offer the use of a double mattress and your floor.

I confess to you that when I asked you for your help in solving my temporary difficulty regarding my lack of accommodation, I was in somewhat of a panic.

I am surprised that you responded as you did. Ours has not been a long acquaintanceship. For all you know, I could have severe character faults or a psychotic personality.

I would urge caution in the future. I would not like to see you taken advantage of. I am not sure about my future plans. Leicester has a certain *je ne sais quoi:* it is quite pleasant in the autumn, when the fallen leaves give the pavements a little colour.

Yours,
Best wishes,
Adrian

Sunday, September 22nd

I was looking forward to a traditional Sunday dinner with Yorkshire pudding and gravy, etc. But my mother informed me at 1.00 p.m. that she doesn't *do* Sunday dinner any more. Instead, we were driven four miles in Muffet's car to a 'Carvery' where we paid £4.99 a head to be served with slices of cardboard and dried up vegetables by a moronic youth in a chef's hat. My sister Rosie spilt Muffet's half pint of Ruddles all over our table. I tried to come to the rescue with half a dozen beer mats—but the beer mats refused to soak up any beer. They repelled all liquid. In the end, the moronic one threw us a stinking dishcloth.

Query: What is the purpose of modern beer mats? Are they now merely symbolic, like the crucifix?

6.00 p.m. My mother has informed me that I have got to pay her board of 'a minimum of thirty-five pounds a week, or you're out on your ear'. Does blood count for nothing in 1991?

Tuesday, September 24th

My grandma has said I can move in with her, rent free, providing I cut the grass, wind the clocks and fetch the shopping. I agreed immediately.

Wednesday, September 25th

I read the first three chapters of *Lo!* aloud to Grandma tonight. She thinks it is the best thing she has ever heard. She thinks that the publishers who rejected it are barmy. And she has got nothing but contempt for Mr John Tydeman. She recently wrote to him to complain about the sex in *The Archers.* She claims that he didn't reply personally. Apparently he got a machine to do it for him.

Sunday, September 29th

Archers omnibus. Egg, bacon, fried bread, *The People.* Roast beef, roast potatoes, mashed potatoes, cabbage, carrots, peas, Yorkshire pudding, gravy. Apple crumble, custard, cup of tea, extra strong mints, *News of the World.* Tinned salmon sandwiches, mandarin oranges and jelly, sultana cake, cup of tea.

Monday, September 30th

Chapter Eighteen: Back to the Wolds

Jake settled back in the rocking chair and watched his grandmother making the corn dolly. Her apple cheeks glowed in the flames from the black leaded range. The copper kettle sang. The canary in the cage by the window trilled along with it. Jake sighed a deep, contented sigh. It was good to be back from Russia and all that unpleasantness with Natasha. Here, he could truly relax, in his grandma's cottage on the Wolds.

Tuesday, October 1st

My father brought Mrs Belinda Bellingham round to meet me at Grandma's house tonight. I was totally gobsmacked; she is a posh person! My father has started to pronounce his aitches religiously and to say 'barth' instead of 'bath'. And he has also discovered manners: every time my grandma came into the room, he leapt out of his chair.

Eventually she snapped, 'Sit *down*, George. You're up and down like a window cleaner's ladder.'

Mrs Bellingham is blonde and pretty, with those cheekbones that denote centuries of wise breeding. I thought she was very pale, considering she had just spent two weeks in the sun. Later in the evening, I found out that she lives in fear of skin cancer. Apparently she spent her holiday running from one patch of shade to another. Mrs Bellingham is the managing director of 'Bell Safe'—a burglar alarm company. My father starts work next Monday as Mrs Bellingham's sales director. They tried to persuade my grandma to allow them to install a burglar alarm at cost price, but she refused, saying, 'No, thank you. If I have to go out, I turn the volume up on Radio Four and leave my front door open.'

Mrs Bellingham and my father exchanged scandalised glances. Grandma continued, 'And I've never been burgled in sixty years, and anyroad up, if I had an alarm on the front of the house, folks'd know I've got something valuable, wouldn't they?'

There was an awkward pause, then my father said, 'Well, Belinda, I'll see you home, shall I?'

He fetched her coat and held it out while she put it on. He has obviously been having lessons in social etiquette. When they'd gone, my grandma shocked me by saying, 'Your dad's turned into a right brown-nosing bugger, hasn't he?'

Perhaps she is suffering from the early symptoms of senile dementia. I have never heard her swear before.

Sir Alan Green, the Director of Public Prosecutions, has been caught talking to a prostitute and has resigned. Under the 1985 Sexual Offences Act, a man seen approaching a woman more than once can be stopped by the police. This is news to me. I shall certainly be more careful whom I approach in the street from now on.

Friday, October 4th

Grandma and I have scoured the house from top to bottom today. Grandma has a fixation about germs. She is convinced that they are lying in wait for her, ready to pounce and bring her down. I blame the television advertisement for a lavatory cleaner which depicts 'germs' the size of gremlins, who lurk about in the 'S' bend, chuckling malevolently. Although I've seen this advertisement hundreds of times, I simply can't remember what the product is called.

Query: Is television advertising effective?

Later, Grandma sat down and watched the Labour Party singing 'We Are the Champions' as the finale to their conference in Brighton. Not many of the shadow cabinet knew the words. I hope Freddie Mercury wasn't watching—it would have stuck in his teeth, not to mention his craw.

Sunday, October 6th

Turning the pages of my *Observer* today, I saw Barry Kent's ugly face staring out at me. Apparently he is a new member of a place called the Groucho Club. I read the accompanying article avidly. It is exactly the sort of place I would like to be a member of. Should I ever reach that goal, I shall tell the manager (Liam) the truth about Kent's past and have him blackballed.

Elizabeth Taylor has married a bricklayer with a bad perm. He is called Larry Fortensky. Michael Jackson's ape, Bubbles, was the best man.

Chapter Nineteen: Time to Move On

Jake slipped out of the cottage as the village church struck midnight. He ran stealthily down the lane and towards the minicab which was waiting, as instructed, by the post office. As he threw his rucksack into the back of the car and climbed in after it, he sighed with relief. He never again wanted to see the apple cheeks of his grandmother and he vowed to burn the next corn dolly he came across.

'Put your foot down!' Jake barked to the minicab driver. 'Take me to the nearest urban conurbation.'

The minicab driver's brow was furrowed. 'What's an urban conurbation when it's at 'ome?' he said.

Jake snapped, 'Okay, dolt! You want specifics, take me to the Groucho Club.'

At the mention of the magic words, the cab driver's shoulders straightened. The dandruff stayed on his scalp. He had waited years to hear the words, 'Take me to the Groucho Club'. He looked at Jake with a new respect and he did as he was told. He put his foot down on the clutch and the minicab sped away from the Wolds and towards the great metropolis where, in the Groucho, the Great were no doubt quaffing the house wine and exchanging witticisms. Jake hoped Belinda would be there, at the bar, showing her legs and laughing hysterically at one of Jeffrey Bernard's jokes.

Monday, October 7th

Barry Kent is making a film for BBC2 about his 'roots'. The television cameras were in the Co-op, blocking the aisles. I couldn't get to the cat food, so I complained to the manager (who, incidentally, didn't look a day older than seventeen). He replied, 'Barry Kent's comin' here in person this afternoon.' It was as though he were talking about royalty.

I said, 'I don't give a toss. I want three tins of Whiskas, *now!*' The boy manager went off and, in crawling tones, asked the cameraman to pass him three tins of cat food. With what I thought was ill grace, the cameraman obliged and, after paying the starstruck child, I left the shop.

Tuesday, October 8th

My mother has been persuaded to give a talk to camera about 'the Barry Kent she once knew'. I urged her to tell the truth, about the bullying, lying, scruffy, thick youth we knew and despised.

But my mother said, 'I always found Barry to be a sensitive child.' The director made her stand by her overflowing wheelie bin in the side yard.

My mother said, 'Shouldn't I be made-up, by a proper make-up artist?' Nick, the director, said, 'No, Mrs Mole, we're going for actuality.' My mother touched the cold sore on her lip and said, 'I'd counted on a bit of camouflage to hide this.' A strong light was turned on her, which showed every line, wrinkle and bag on my mother's face.

Then the director shouted, 'Go!' and my mother went. To pieces. After seventeen attempts, BBC2 gave up, packed their gear and went off. My mother ran upstairs and threw herself on the bed. There is nothing so pitiful as a failed interviewee.

Saturday, October 12th

Kent is still poncing around the neighbourhood. I saw him being filmed walking up our street. He was wearing a floor-length overcoat, cowboy boots and dark glasses. I ducked out of sight. I have no wish to be publicly identified as the dork in *Dork's Diary.*

I took the dog for a walk to the field where Pandora used to ride Blossom, her pony. It tired very quickly. I had to carry it back.

I saw Mrs Kent, Barry's mother, on the way home. She was walking her pit bull terrier. I asked her if she had registered the beast yet (as required by law).

She said, 'Butcher wouldn't hurt a fly.'

I said, 'It's not flies I'm worried about. It's the tender flesh of small children.'

She changed the subject and told me that Barry had bought her the council house she now lives in. This made me laugh quite a lot. The Kents' house is a byword for squalor in our neighbourhood. They chop the internal doors up for firewood every winter.

Sunday, October 13th

Finished Chapter Nineteen tonight.

> Jake was sick of being interviewed. He ordered the journalists to leave the Groucho Club and leave him alone. He turned to Lenny Henry and said, 'Let's have a drink, Len.' Lenny smiled his thanks and Jake snapped his fingers. A waiter came running immediately and bent deferentially towards Jake. 'A bottle of champagne—a big one—and make that three glasses,' for Jake had just seen one of his best friends, Richard Ingrams, of *News Quiz* fame, come through the hallowed swing doors. 'Hey, Rich, over here!' shouted Jake. There was a sound of scuffling coming from the reception area. Jake turned his head round to see Liam, the manager, throwing Kent Barry, the failed writer, out of the club and into the gutter.

Monday, October 14th

> Dear Bianca,
>
> After further reflection, can I take you up on your offer? It would be most convenient for me to spend a few days sleeping

on your floor in Oxford. Quite honestly, I cannot tolerate another moment living with my family. It isn't just the noise level and the constant bickering; it's the small things—the encrusted neck of the H.P. Sauce bottle; the slimy soap dish; the dog hairs in the butter. You can telephone me on the above number, any time, night or day. Nobody sleeps in this house.

All my very best wishes,
Adrian Mole

Tuesday, October 15th

My sister Rosie told me that she hated me this morning. Her outburst came after I suggested that she comb her hair before going to school. My mother got out of bed and came downstairs. She lit her second cigarette of the day (she smokes the first in bed) and immediately took Rosie's side. She said, 'Leave the kid alone.'

I said, 'Somebody has to maintain standards in this house.'

My mother said, 'You can talk. That beard looks like a ferret's nest. I don't know how you can bear to have it so near to your mouth. A public health inspector would close it down.'

During the ensuing row, nasty things were said on both sides, which I now regret. I accused her of being a neglectful mother, with loose morals. She counter-attacked by describing me as 'a fungus-faced dork'. She said she had secretly read my *Lo!* manuscript and thought it was 'crap from start to finish'. She said 'in the unlikely event of it being published, I hope you will use a pseudonym, because, to be honest, Adrian, I couldn't stand the public shame.'

I put my head on the kitchen table and wept.

My mother then put her arm around me and said, 'There, there, Adrian. Don't cry. I didn't mean it, I think *Lo! The Flat Hills of My Homeland* is a very interesting first attempt.'

But it was no good. I wept until dehydration set in.

10.00 p.m. Why hasn't Bianca phoned? I used a first class stamp.

Thursday, October 17th

Drew more money out of the Market Harborough Building Society. My dream of being an owner-occupier has receded even further into the realms of fantasy.

I have received a postcard of the Forth Bridge, with no address but posted in London.

Dear Adrian,

I'm going to London to try for a proper job. I've got an interview with British Rail. In a rush. Please reply c/o my friend Lucy:

Lucy Clay
Flat 10
Dexter House
Coghill Street
Oxford

She has promised to pass on any messages. I hope you are well and happy. I miss you!

Love,
B.

P.S. How about a London floor when I find one?

Friday, October 18th

Chapter Twenty: The Reckoning

Jake pushed the earth wire out of the lawnmower plug, then screwed the plug together again. He could hear his mother on the telephone to her new lover (a schoolboy called Craig).

He waited for her to finish cooing her endearments down the phone and re-emerge on the terrace. 'I've cut half the lawn, mother,' he shouted, 'but I've got to go to the barber's now.'

His mother frowned and dropped ash all down her cashmere dress. 'But Jake, darling,' she remonstrated. 'You know I hate to see a job half done.' She went towards the lawnmower.

Jake chuckled inwardly. He had banked on this trait of his mother's. As he passed through the french windows, he heard the hover-mower whir into life, to be followed immediately by the high-pitched scream.

Jake immediately felt guilty, then comforted himself by thinking that he had advised his mother time after time to install a circuit breaker; advice she had foolishly chosen to ignore.

Sunday, October 20th

It was my father's access day today. He came to take Rosie out to McDonald's as usual. While she looked for her shoes, my father and I talked man to man about my mother. We agreed that she was an impossible person to live with. We had a good laugh about Martin Muffet, who was in the back garden building a lean-to conservatory with the assistance of his Black and Decker work bench. We agreed that, since marrying my mother, Muffet has aged ten years.

I congratulated my father on capturing Mrs Belinda Bellingham, and confessed that I didn't have much luck with women. My father said, 'Tell them what they want to hear, son, and buy them a bunch of flowers once a fortnight. That's all there is to it.'

I asked him if he intended to marry Mrs Bellingham, but before he could answer, my mother staggered into the room carrying a large cardboard box which contained the swag she'd bought from a car boot sale. She'd bought a painting of Christ on the cross; an ashtray with two scottie dogs painted on it; an aluminium toast rack;

twenty-seven bent candles; a chenille tablecloth; a Tom Jones LP; six cooking apples; and a steering wheel. As she excitedly unpacked the junk onto the kitchen table, I saw my father looking at her with what I can only describe as lovelight in his eyes.

Monday, October 21st

Bianca rang, but I was out cutting Bert Baxter's disgusting toe-nails. My mother wrote down a telephone number where I could contact Bianca, but then lost it almost immediately. We searched the house, but failed to find the scrap of paper. I expect the dog ate it. It has recently taken to scoffing whole pages of the *Leicester Mercury*, a sign of its increasing neurosis or a vitamin deficiency—who knows? Nobody can afford to take it to the vet to find out.

Tuesday, October 22nd

I sent a postcard of Leicester Bus Station to Bianca c/o Lucy Clay:

> Dear Bianca,
>
> Thank you for your postcard of the Forth Bridge.
>
> I was most surprised to hear that you were leaving Oxford and going to the 'Smoke', as the cockneys say.
>
> I wish you luck in your search for a 'proper' job. Keep me posted. I have had no luck yet, but I keep trying.
>
> It is very difficult living here with my family. There is a total clash of lifestyles. I strive to be tolerant of the noise and disorder, but it is hard, very hard.
>
> Yours,
> With very best wishes,
> Adrian

Mrs Bellingham has offered me a job selling security devices. It is evening work. I have to call on nervous householders after dark and put the fear of God into them until they sign up for a burglar alarm or security lights. I said I would think about it.

Mrs Bellingham said in her careful voice, 'There are three million unemployed. Why do you need to think about it?'

I said I hoped that beggars could still be choosers.

She is offering me £3.14 an hour. No commission, no insurance stamp, no contract of employment—cash in hand. I asked her if she objected to my belonging to a union. Her face went whiter than ever and she said, 'Yes, I'm afraid I do. Mrs Thatcher's greatest achievement was to tame the unions.' My father is a Thatcherite's lackey!

Thursday, October 24th

I despise myself. I have only been working for two nights, but I have already sold a whole house security system, six car alarms, four peepholes and half a dozen bike locks. My method is simple. I get into the house and show the householders the portfolio that Mrs Bellingham has assembled. It consists of lurid stories cut out of the tabloid newspapers and police press releases. After leafing through this alarming document, it would take great insouciance for the householder to deny that more security in the home is a desirable thing.

Mrs Bellingham has instructed me to ask the question, 'Don't you think your family deserves more protection from the dark forces of evil that are at large in our community?'

So far only one person has said, 'No,' and he was the defeated-looking father of six teenage boys.

Monday, October 28th

Shaved beard off. Mrs Bellingham said it made me look untrustworthy. I am completely in her power. If she ordered me to go to work wearing a Batman outfit, I would have to obey her. I have no legal rights of employment.

Thursday, October 31st

At last! The economic recovery is on its way! The Confederation of British Industry has reported that they expect outputs and exports to increase in the years ahead. According to the C.B.I., manufacturers are expecting huge new orders. I broke this good news to my mother. She said, 'Yes, and the dog is getting married on Saturday and I'm its Matron of Honour.' Then she and Martin Muffet went off into one of their mad laughing fits.

Ken Barlow of *Coronation Street* fame has been on trial for being boring. He was found 'Not Guilty' and awarded £50,000.

My mother has got a job as a security guard in the new shopping centre that has just opened in Leicester city centre. She looks like a New York City policewoman in her uniform. She told the security firm, 'Group Five', that she was *thirty-five years old!* She is now living in fear that her true age, forty-seven, will be revealed. Is everybody partially sighted at Group Five? Did her interview take place in a candlelit office? I asked her these questions.

She said, 'I bunged on rather a lot of Max Factor's pan-stick and sat with my back to the window.'

Friday, November 1st

In view of my continuing success in flogging her security paraphernalia, Mrs Bellingham has raised my hourly rate from £3.14 to the heady sum of £3.25! Gee whiz! Fire a cannon! Release the balloons! Open the Bollinger! Issue a press release! Inform the Red Arrows!

Saturday, November 2nd

> Jake used his Swiss Army knife to dismantle the burglar alarm and in a matter of moments he had circumnavigated the padlocks, bolts and chains on the front door and was standing in the front hall of Bellingham Towers.

Upstairs, sleeping after an hour of arduous lovemaking, were the owners of the historic country house, Sir George and Lady Belinda, and their daughter, the Honourable Rosemary. Jake chuckled as he stuffed silver and *objets d'art* into a black plastic bag. He felt no guilt. He was robbing the filthy rich to feed the filthy poor. He was the Robin Hood of Leicestershire.

My mother claims that I look exactly like John Major, especially when I am wearing my reading glasses. This is total rubbish: unlike Mr Major, I have got lips. They may be on the thin side, but they are distinctly there. If I were Major, I'd have a lip transplant. Mick Jagger could be the donor.

Tuesday, November 5th

Robert Maxwell, the mogul, has fallen overboard from his yacht, the *Lady Ghislaine*.

Went to Age Concern Community Bonfire Party. Pushed Bert Baxter there in his wheelchair. Baxter was asked to leave after half an hour because he was seen (and certainly heard) to throw an Indian firecracker into the bonfire. The organiser, Mrs Plumbstead, said apologetically, 'Safety has to be paramount.'

Baxter said scornfully, 'There were no such thing as *safety* when I were a lad.'

I pushed him home in silence. I was furious. Because of him, I missed the baked potatoes, sausages and soup. I had to wait for an hour for the district nurse to come and put him to bed.

Thursday, November 7th

Kevin Maxwell has denied that his deceased father's businesses have financial problems.

Query: Would our banks lend £2.5 billion to a man with money problems?

Answer: Of course not! Our banks are respected financial institutions.

Sunday, November 10th

To Grandma's for the Remembrance Day poppy-laying ceremony. I am proud of my dead grandfather, Albert Mole. He fought valiantly in the First World War so that I would not have to live under the tyranny of a foreign oppressor.

I cannot let the above sentence lie. The truth is that my poor, dead grandfather fought in the Great War because he was ordered to. He always did what he was told. I take after him in that respect.

Monday, November 11th

A gang of Leicester yobs shouted out, 'Hey, John Major, how's Norma?' tonight, as I came out of the cinema. I looked around, thinking that perhaps the Prime Minister was visiting the Leicester Chamber of Commerce, or something, but there was no sign of him. I then realised, to my horror, that they were addressing their yobbish remarks to me.

Wednesday, November 13th

A letter from Bianca.

Dear Adrian,

Thank you for your letter, which Lucy forwarded to me. As you can see from my address, I am living in London. I am renting a small room in Soho at the moment, but it is costing £110 per week, so I won't be here long!

I've got a job as a waitress in a restaurant called 'Savages'. The owner is a bit strange, but the staff are very nice. It would be lovely to see you when you're next in London. My day off is

Monday. How is the novel going? Have you finished your revisions? I can't wait to read it in full!

Love,
Bianca (Dartington)

Thursday, November 14th

Dear Bianca,

Many thanks for your letter of the 11th. I must confess that I was rather surprised to hear from you. I am hardly ever in London, but I may drop in and see you on my next visit. Isn't Soho a dangerous place in which to live? Please take care as you walk the streets. Personally, I am ossifying in this provincial hell.

Lo! is going very well. I have called my hero Jake Westmorland. What do you think?

Please write back.
Yours as ever,
Adrian

Friday, November 15th

The New York Stock Exchange collapsed today. I hope this won't affect the interest rates of the Market Harborough Building Society.

Saturday, November 16th

No reply from B.

Sunday, November 17th

Why isn't there a Sunday delivery in this country? I expect it is because of objections from the established Church. Do the clergy imagine that God gives a toss if humans receive letters or not on a Sunday?

Monday, November 18th

By second post. A postcard of Holborn Viaduct.

Dear Adrian,

No. Soho is not dangerous. I *love* Jake Westmorland. When are you coming to London?

Lots of love,
Bianca

Tuesday, November 19th

I sent Bianca a postcard of the Clock Tower, Leicester.

Dear Bianca,

As it happens, I shall be in London next Monday. Would you like to have lunch? Please write or ring to confirm.

Very warm wishes,
Adrian

P.S. I have shaved my beard off. It was the television pictures of Terry Waite that decided me.

Wednesday, November 20th

Grandma's Christmas card arrived. The shops are full of Santa Clauses ringing bells and getting in the way of legitimate shoppers. My mother said that whilst on duty she saw an old lady shoplifting a Cadbury's Selection Box. I asked her what action she'd taken. She said, 'I turned and walked the other way.'

There is a rush on for burglar alarms. Everybody wants them fitted before Christmas when they fill their homes with consumer durables and Nintendo games.

Saturday, November 23rd

A postcard from Bianca, of the original Crystal Palace.

Dear Adrian,

I have got to work on Monday. The office party season has started, but come down anyway. I will get off early. I look forward to seeing you. Come to 'Savages', Dean Street, at 2.30 p.m.

Love,
Bianca

Sunday, November 24th

Freddie Mercury has died of Aids. There was no time for me to mourn, but I put 'Bohemian Rhapsody', which is one of my favourite records, on the record player.

I laid my wardrobe on my bed (or rather, the *contents* of my wardrobe) and tried to decide what to wear for my trip to London. I do not wish to be marked out as a provincial day-tripper by sneering metropolitans. Decided on the black shirt, black trousers and Oxfam tweed jacket. My grey slip-on shoes will have to do. Set my alarm for 8.30 a.m. I catch the 12.30 p.m. train.

Monday, November 25th
Soho

I am in love with Bianca Dartington. Hopelessly, helplessly, mindlessly, gloriously, magnificently.

Tuesday, November 26th

I am still here, in Soho, in Bianca's room above Brenda's Patisserie in Old Compton Street. I have hardly seen daylight since 3.30 p.m. on Monday.

Wednesday, November 27th

Poem to Bianca Dartington:

Gentle face,
Night black hair,
Natural grace,
Love I swear.
Marry me, be my wife,
Make me happy, share my life.

Thursday, November 28th

Phoned my mother and asked her to send my books to Old Compton Street. Informed her that I am now living in London, with Bianca. She asked for the address, but I wasn't falling for that. I hung up.

Friday, November 29th

God, I love her! I love her! I love her! Every minute she is away, working at 'Savages', is torture for me.

Query: Why didn't I *know* that the human body is capable of such exquisite pleasure?

Answer: Because, Mole, you had not made love to Bianca Dartington—somebody who loves you body and soul—before.

Saturday, November 30th

What did I ever see in Pandora Braithwaite? She is an opinionated, arrogant ball-breaker. An all-round nasty piece of work. Compared to Bianca, she is nothing, nothing. And as for Leonora De Witt, I can hardly remember her face.

I never want to leave this room. I want to live the whole of my life within these four walls (with occasional trips to the bathroom, which we have to share with a fire-eater called Norman).

The walls are painted lavender blue and Bianca has stuck stars and moons on the ceiling which glow in the dark. There is a poster of Sydney Harbour Bridge on the wall between the windows. There is a double bed with an Indian bedspread covered in cushions; a chest of drawers that Bianca has painted white; an old armchair covered in a large tablecloth. A wonky table, half painted in gold, and two pine chairs. Instead of a bedhead, we have got a blown-up photograph on the wall of Isambard Kingdom Brunel, Bianca's hero.

Every morning when I wake up, I can't believe that the slim girl with the long legs who is lying next to me is mine! I always get out of bed first and put the kettle on the Baby Belling cooker. I then put two slices of toast under the grill and serve my love with her breakfast in bed. I won't allow her to get out of bed until the gas fire has warmed the room. She catches cold easily.

I want to please her more than I want to please myself.

This morning, 'Stand By Me', sung by Ben E. King, was playing on Capital Radio.

I said, 'I love this song. My father used to play it.'

Bianca said, 'So do I.'

We danced to it, me in my boxer shorts and Bianca in her pink knickers with the flowers on.

'Stand By Me' is now our song.

Sunday, December 1st

Went to the National Gallery today. We walked around the Sainsbury Wing like Siamese twins, fused together. We cannot bear to be apart for even a moment. The renaissance pictures glowed like jewels and inflamed our passion. Our mutual genitalia are a bit sore and bruised, but it didn't stop us making love as soon as we got back to the room. Norman next door banged on the wall and nearly put us off, but we managed to ignore him.

Monday, December 2nd

I was putting my socks and shoes on this morning, when I noticed a strange expression on Bianca's face.

I said, 'What is it, darling?'

After a lot of cajoling, Bianca confessed that she adored everything about me except my grey slip-on shoes and white towelling socks. As a mark of my love for her, I opened the window and hurled my only pair of socks and shoes into Old Compton Street. I was unable to go out all day as a consequence. I was a barefoot prisoner of love.

Late that afternoon, Bianca bought me three pairs of socks from Sock Shop, and one pair of dark brogues from Bally. They all fitted perfectly. The shoes are *serious.* I felt like a grown-up in them as I walked around the room. I then walked to the Nat West Bank in Wardour Street and removed £100 from the Rapid Cash machine. This is the most I have ever withdrawn in one go. I paid Bianca for the shoes (£59.99), which is also the most I have ever paid for a pair of shoes. Incidentally, it is now late evening and the grey slip-ons are still in the gutter. I *did* see a tramp try them on, but he scowled and took them off immediately, though they looked a good fit.

Wednesday, December 4th

I telephoned my mother today and asked her why she hadn't sent my books on as I had asked.

She screamed, 'Mainly because you refused to give me your address, you stupid sod.' She then went on to say that she had asked our postman, Courtney Elliot, for an estimate of the cost of sending the books by Parcel Post. Apparently, he 'guestimated' (her word, not mine) that it would cost about a hundred quid! She said that my father is driving to London on Friday to attend a conference on Home Security. She said she would ask him to drop the books, and the rest of my worldly goods, off. I agreed reluctantly and gave her the address.

When Bianca had gone to work, I walked to Oxford Street and bought a dustpan and brush, a packet of yellow dusters, Mr Sheen, a floor cloth, some liquid Flash, a bottle of Windolene and a pair of white satin knickers from Knickerbox.

Bianca was thrilled when she returned at 3:00 p.m. to find our room cleaned and sparkling. Almost as thrilled as I was at 1.00 a.m. when she put the satin knickers on.

Friday, December 6th

My father was in a foul temper when he got here tonight. The conference was in Watford, so he had to go considerably out of his way (backwards) in order to deliver my stuff. When he eventually found Old Compton Street, it was 9.30 p.m.

He parked outside on double yellow lines, with his hazard lights flashing. Together, we lugged the boxes of books and plastic bags of clothes four floors up to the room. When we'd finished, my father collapsed on the bed. His bald patch was glistening with sweat. I was glad that Bianca was at work. When he'd recovered, I went down to see him off. Mrs Bellingham had ordered him to be home at a reasonable time. He is obviously afraid of her. As we walked to the car, my father stopped, pointed to the gutter and shouted, 'What the bleeding hell is that?'

His Montego had been wheel-clamped. I thought he was going to break down and cry in the street, but instead he went berserk and kicked at the yellow clamp and shouted obscenities. It was highly amusing to the posing idiots who were drinking cappuccino in the cold wind on the opposite pavement.

I offered to go with him to the outer reaches of London, to start the long, bureaucratic process of declamping the car, but my father snarled, 'Oh, bugger off back upstairs to your cowing love nest.' He hailed a black cab and jumped in. As it turned into Wardour Street, I could tell that it wouldn't be long before my father was whining to the cab driver about his bad luck, his ungrateful son, his fearsome mistress and his feckless ex-wife.

Saturday, December 7th

Spent a pleasant day cataloguing and then arranging my books on the bookshelves I constructed from three planks and nine old bricks I found in a skip in Greek Street. Cost? Nil. In the same skip, I found *Moral Thinking* by John Wilson. It was printed in 1970, before sex came into *The Archers*, however, so I suppose the morality may be out of date.

Bianca came home at lunchtime and asked if I wanted a job as a part-time washer-up in 'Savages'. It is cash in hand, off the books. I said, 'Yes.'

We went to see the Thames Barrier and talked about our future. We pledged that we would not let riches and fame divide us.

I start washing up on Monday.

Monday, December 9th

Peter Savage, the owner of 'Savages', is certainly aptly named. I have never known a man with such a bad temper. He is rude to everybody, staff and customers. The customers think he is amusingly eccentric. The staff hate him and spend their meal breaks fantasising about killing him. He is a tall, fat man with a face like a beef tomato. He dresses like Bertie Wooster and talks like Bob Hoskins of *Roger Rabbit* fame. He wears a C.N.D. tiepin on his Garrick Club tie.

Culturally, he is all over the place.

Tuesday, December 10th

Savage was drunk at 10 a.m. At 12 noon he vomited into the yukka plant in the corner of the restaurant. At 1 p.m. his wife came, abused him verbally and then carried him out to her car, helped by Luigi, the head waiter.

I am reading *The Complete Plain Words* by Sir Ernest Gowers. I am on page 143: *Clichés*. Far be it from me to say so, but I'm sure my writing style will improve by leaps and bounds.

Bianca startled me this evening by suddenly shouting, 'Please, Adrian, can't you stop that perpetual sniffing. Use a handkerchief!'

Wednesday, December 11th

I toil over greasy pots and pans for £3.90 an hour, and the customers fork out £17 for a monkfish and £18 for a bottle of wine! Savage is obviously not as stupid as he looks.

Fogle, Fogle, Brimmington and Hayes, the advertising firm, held their Christmas party in 'Savages' at lunchtime. The restaurant was closed to ordinary customers. Bianca said that the managing director, Piers Fogle, told her that they were in a celebratory mood because they had just won a contract worth £500,000 on the strength of a slogan for an advertising campaign for condoms.

'What the well-dressed man is wearing,' is to appear on billboards all over the country.

Their bill came to over £700. They gave Bianca and the other waitresses £5 each. I, the serf in the kitchen, got nothing, of course. Luigi put two fingers up to Fogle's back as he staggered out of the restaurant.

Saturday, December 14th

We haven't made love for over twenty-four hours. Bianca has got cystitis.

Sunday, December 15th

Bought *The Joy of Sex* in the Charing Cross Road. Cystitis is called 'The Honeymooners' Illness'. It can be caused by vigorous, frequent sex. Poor Bianca is in the toilet every ten minutes. Why is there *always* a price to pay for pleasure?

Monday, December 16th

Savage was in court this morning, charged with assaulting a customer last April. He was fined £500 and ordered to pay costs and damages totalling my wages for five years. He came back to the restaurant with Mrs Savage and his lawyer to celebrate the fact that he hadn't been sent to prison, but after the champagne had been drunk and the tagliatelle consumed, Savage spotted a group of Channel Four executives on table eight and began to abuse them because they didn't show enough tobogganing on their sports programmes.

According to Bianca, Mrs Savage said, 'Darling, do be quiet, you're starting to get a little tedious.'

Savage shouted, 'Shut your mouth, you fat cow!'

She shouted, 'I'm a size *ten,* you callous bastard!'

The lawyer tried to conciliate, but Savage tipped the table up and Luigi ended up throwing his boss out of his own restaurant.

Personally, I would be happy to see Savage chained up in prison, on bread and water, with rats gnawing at his feet—and I'm a supporter of prison reform.

Tuesday, December 17th

Experimented with making very gentle love. I was the passive partner.

Later, we had our first argument. Where are we spending Christmas Day and Boxing Day? In our room? At her parents'? At my parents'? Or with Luigi, who has invited us to his house in

Harrow? We didn't shout at each other, but there was (and still is) a distinct lack of seasonal goodwill. Bianca turned her back on me in bed tonight.

Thursday, December 19th

We woke up tangled together, as usual. Christmas wasn't mentioned, but love, passion and marriage were. We are going to spend Christmas with her parents in Richmond. Her father is going to pick us up on Christmas Eve. It will save me having to buy presents for my family.

Saturday, December 21st

Tonight, Savage promenaded around the restaurant with a miniature Christmas tree on his head, complete with twinkling lights. He kissed all the women and blew cigar smoke at all the men. Luigi led him into the kitchen and propped him up against the sink. Savage then proceeded to tell me that his mother had never loved him and that his father had run away with an alcoholic nurse when he was eight. (When Savage *junior* was eight.) He broke down and wept, but I was too busy to comfort him. The cook was screaming for side plates.

Sunday, December 22nd

Bianca stayed in bed today, tired out, poor kid, which gave me a chance to work on chapter twenty-one of *Lo! The Flat Hills of My Homeland.*

> Jake ran his fingers down the length of her back. Her skin felt like the finest silk, even to his fingers, roughened by years of immersion in washing-up water. She sighed and squirmed into the flannelette sheet. 'Don't stop,' she said, her voice cracking like a whip. 'Don't ever stop, Jake . . .'

Tuesday, December 24th
Christmas Eve

I braved the maddening crowds today and went out to buy Bianca's Christmas present. After tramping the streets for two hours, I ended up in Knickerbox and bought her a purple suspender belt, scarlet knickers, and a black lace bra. When the saleswoman asked me about size, I confessed I didn't know. I said, 'She's not Rubenesque, but she's not Naomi Campbell.'

The woman rolled her eyes and said, 'Okay, she's medium, yeah?'

I said, 'She looks a bit like Paula Yates, but with black hair.'

The woman sighed and said, 'Paula Yates breastfeeding or not breastfeeding?'

I said, 'Not breastfeeding,' and she snatched some stuff off the racks and gift-wrapped it for me.

I agonised in Burger King over whether or not to buy her parents presents. At four-thirty, I decided that, yes, I would ingratiate myself with them and bought her mother some peach-based pot-pourri. I phoned Bianca at 'Savages' and asked what I should get for her father. She said her father was fond of poetry, so I went and bought him a book of poems by John Hegley, called *Can I Come Down Now Dad?* which has a picture of Jesus on the cross on its cover. I also managed to track down a copy of *The Railway Heritage of Britain* by Gordon Biddle and O. S. Nock for Bianca.

Thursday, December 26th
Boxing Day

Richmond

Bianca's mother is allergic to peaches; and her father, the Reverend Dartington, thought that the John Hegley book was in extremely bad taste. Also, I hate Bianca's brother and sister. How my sweet, darling Bianca could have come from such a vile family is a mystery to me. We slept in separate beds in separate rooms. We had to go to a wooden hut of a church on Christmas Day and listen to her father rant on about the commercialisation of Christmas. Bianca and I were the only people to buy presents. Everyone else had given money to the Sudanese Drought Fund. Bianca bought me a Swatch watch and the *Chronicle of the Twentieth Century*, which will be an invaluable work of reference to me. I was very pleased. She was pleased with the Biddle and Nock.

Her brother, Derek, and her sister, Mary, obviously disapprove of our love affair. They are both unmarried and still live at home. Derek is thirty-five and Mary is twenty-seven. Mrs Dartington was forty-eight when Bianca was born.

There was no turkey, no drink and no celebration. It made me long for my own family's vulgarity.

This afternoon, we had to go for a walk alongside the river. Little kids were out in force, wobbling on new bikes and pushing prams with new-looking dolls inside. Derek has now taken a shine to me. He thought I was a fellow trainspotter; I quickly put him right. Bianca and I managed a quick embrace in the kitchen tonight before being interrupted by Mary, who came in looking for her constipation chocolate.

Mrs Dartington had a convenient 'turn' just before dinner and took to her bed. Bianca and I cooked the meal. We had salad, corned beef and baked potatoes. I cannot wait to get back to our room. I need Bianca. I need onions. I need garlic. I need Soho. I need Savage. I need air. I need freedom from the Dartingtons.

There are four beige car coats hanging up in the downstairs cloakroom.

Friday, December 27th

The Reverend Dartington drove us back to Soho in martyred silence. Every time he stopped at a red light or pedestrian crossing, he drummed his fingers on the steering wheel impatiently.

Two days with her family have had a deleterious effect on Bianca:

she seems to have shrunk physically and regressed mentally. As soon as she got back into the room she burst into tears and shouted, 'Why didn't they *tell* me they were giving their Christmas presents to the Sudanese?'

I said, 'Because they wanted to claim the moral high ground and make you feel foolish. It's obviously a punishment because you are living in sin, in Soho, with a lowly washer-upper.'

An hour later, Bianca had sprung back in size and mental capacity. We made love for one hour, ten minutes. Our longest yet. It is quite useful having a stopwatch facility on my new Swatch.

Sunday, December 29th

We went to Camden Lock today to buy Bianca a pair of boots. The whole area was thronging with young people who were both buying and selling. I said to Bianca, 'Isn't it nice to see the young out and about and enjoying themselves?'

She looked at me in a funny way and said, 'But *you* are young. You're only twenty-four, though sometimes I find it hard to believe.'

She was right, of course. I am young, officially, but I have never felt young. My mother said I was thirty-five on the day I fought my way out of her womb.

The cystitis is back. Bianca has reluctantly put the satin knickers back in her underwear drawer and gone back to the cotton gussets.

I am reading a play, *A Streetcar Named Desire* by Tennessee Williams. Poor Blanche Dubois!

Wednesday, January 1st 1992

'Savages' was closed last night, so we went to Trafalgar Square at 11.30 p.m. to see the New Year in. The crowd was like a drunken field of corn rippling and swaying in a storm. For over two hours I lost myself and went with the flow. It was frightening, but also exhilarating to find myself in a line doing the conga up St Martin's Lane. Unfortunately, the person in front of me had extremely fat buttocks. It was not an attractive sight.

When Big Ben struck twelve, I found myself kissing and being kissed by strangers, including foreigners. I tried to get to Bianca, but she was surrounded by a party of extrovert Australian persons who were all over seven foot tall. But finally, at 12.03 a.m. on the 1st of January, we kissed and pledged our troth. I can't believe I've got such a wonderful woman. Why does she love me? I live in fear that one day she will wake up and ask herself the same question.

We went to Tower Bridge today. It left me cold, but Bianca was enraptured by the structural design of the thing. I practically had to drag her away.

Thursday, January 2nd

Got up at 3.30 a.m. and joined the queue outside Next in Oxford Street. The sale started at 9.00 a.m. I got into conversation with a man who had his eye on a double-breasted navy suit, marked down from £225 to £90. He is getting married to a parachute packer, called Melanie, next Saturday.

In my new black leather jacket, white tee shirt and blue jeans, I look like every other young man in London, New York and Tokyo. Or Leicester, come to think of it. For Leicester is at the very epicentre of the Next empire.

Bianca wanted to visit Battersea Power Station today and asked me to go with her, but I pointed out to her that *Lo!* was about to develop in a revolutionary direction and that I needed to work on Chapter Twenty-two.

She left the flat without saying a word, but her back looked very angry.

> Jake pulled the collar of his Next black leather jacket up against the cruel wind that blew across the Thames. He stared down

into the ebbing water. It was time he did something with his life other than help with famine relief in Sudan. He knew what it was. It was something he had fought against—God knows how he had fought! But the compulsion was overwhelming now. He had to do it. He had to write a novel. . . .

Wednesday, January 8th

President Bush vomited into the lap of the Japanese Ambassador at an official banquet in Tokyo tonight. We watched it on the portable television in the kitchen at 'Savages'. Mrs Bush shoved her husband under the table, then left the room. She didn't look too pleased. The television news showed the whole incident in slow motion. It was sickening. The Japanese people looked horrified. They are sticklers for protocol.

Savage has fired little Carlos for smoking a joint in the yard at the back of the restaurant. Savage then drank half a bottle of brandy, three bottles of Sol, stole various drinks from customers' tables and ended up fighting with the palm tree at the bar after accusing it of having an affair with his wife. Alcohol is certainly a dangerous drug in the wrong hands.

Wednesday, January 15th

Jake sat in front of his state of the art Amstrad and pressed the glittery knobs. The title of his novel appeared on the screen.

SPARG FROM KRONK
Chapter One: Sparg Returns

Sparg stood on the hilltop and looked down on Kronk, the settlement of his birth. He grunted to his woman, Barf, and she grunted back wordlessly, for the words had not yet been found.

They ran down the hill. Sparg's mother, Krun, watched her son and his woman come towards the fire. She grunted to Sparg's father, Lunt, and he came to the door of the hut. His eyes narrowed. He hated Sparg.

Krun threw more roots into the fire: she had not expected guests for dinner. It was typical of her son, she thought, to arrive unexpectedly and with a woman with a swollen belly. She hoped there would be enough roots to go round.

She was glad the words had not been found. She hated making small talk.

Sparg was here, in front of her. She sniffed his armpit, as was the custom when a Kronkite returned from a long journey. Barf hung back and watched the greeting ceremony. Her mouth salivated. The smell of the burning roots inflamed her hunger.

Because the words had not been found no news could be exchanged between mother and son.

Jake fell back from his computer terminal with a contented sigh. It was good, he thought, damned good. The time was right for another prehistoric novel without dialogue.

Tuesday, January 21st

A letter from Bert Baxter. Almost illegible.

Dear Lad,

It seems a long time since I saw you. When are you coming to Leicester? I've got a few jobs that need doing. Sorry about the writing. I've got the shakes.

Yours,
Bertram Baxter

P.S. Bring your toenail scissors.

Had a serious row with Bianca tonight. She accused me of:

a. Never wanting to go out
b. Excessive reading
c. Excessive writing
d. Contempt for Britain's industrial heritage
e. Farting in bed

Monday, January 27th

At last reconciled, we went to the National Film Theatre tonight and saw a film about a Japanese woman who cuts her lover's penis off. During the rest of the film, I sat with my legs tightly crossed and at intervals looked nervously across at Bianca, who was staring up at the screen and smiling.

My hair is almost long enough for a pony tail. *The Face* tells me that pony tails are becoming passé. But it may be my last chance to try one. So I am going for it. Savage has been boasting that he has had his for five years.

Bianca has bought a secondhand electric typewriter and is typing *Lo!* She has already presented me with seventy-eight beautifully laid-out pages. It is amazing how much a novel is improved by being typed. I should have taken Mr John Tydeman's advice years ago.

Wednesday, January 29th

U.K. heterosexual Aids cases rose by fifty per cent last year. I gave this information to Bianca as we walked to 'Savages' early this evening. She went very quiet.

I had to wait ages outside the bathroom tonight to clean my teeth. Eventually Norman came out and apologised for the new scorch marks on the frame of the mirror. He has been *told* not to practise in there.

When I got back to our room, I found Bianca reading a pamphlet written by the Terence Higgins Trust.

I said flippantly, 'Who's Terence Higgins when he's at home?'

'He's dead,' she said, softly. The pamphlet was about Aids.

Bianca broke down and confessed that in 1990 she had had an affair with a man called Brian Boxer, who in turn confessed to her that in 1979 he'd had an affair with a bisexual woman called Diane Tripp. I shall ring the Terence Higgins Trust Helpline in the morning and ask for help.

Saturday, February 1st

The first twenty-two chapters of *Lo! The Flat Hills of My Homeland* are now a pile of 197 pages of neat typescript. I keep picking it up and walking round the room with it in my arms. I can't afford to get it photocopied, not at ten pence a page. Who do I know in London who has access to a photocopier?

FLAT 6
Brenda's Patisserie
Old Compton Street
London

Dear John,

I have taken your advice and revised *Lo! The Flat Hills of My Homeland*. I have also employed the services of a professional typist and you will be pleased to see that my manuscript now consists of twenty-two chapters in typewritten form. I consider that, when completed, *Lo! The Flat Hills of My Homeland* will be eminently suitable for being read aloud on the radio, possibly as part of your Classic Serials series.

As you can see, I have enclosed my MS and entrust it into your care. However, I still need to make several minor changes.

Would it be too much trouble for you to photocopy the hundred and ninety-seven pages and send a copy to me at the above address?

Thanking you in advance,
Yours as ever,
Adrian Mole

Tuesday, February 4th

I walked to Broadcasting House this morning. As I struggled to push the big metal doors open, a gaggle of autograph hunters rushed towards me. I reached inside my jacket for my felt tip, but before I could extract it, I saw them surrounding Alan Freeman, the aged D.J. I pushed through them and entered the hallowed reception area of the British Broadcasting Corporation, watched by the stern-looking security staff. I walked up to the reception desk and joined the short queue.

In the space of four minutes, I saw famous people galore: Delia Smith, Robert Robinson, Ian Hislop, Bob Geldof, Annie Lennox, Roy Hattersley, etc., etc. Most of them were being seen off the premises by young women called Caroline.

Eventually the blonde receptionist said, 'Can I help you?' And I said, 'Yes. Could you please make sure that Mr John Tydeman receives this parcel? It is most urgent.'

She scribbled something on the jiffy bag which contained my letter and the manuscript of *Lo! The Flat Hills of My Homeland* and threw it into a wire basket.

I thanked her, turned to go and bumped into Victor Meldrew, who plays the grumpy bloke in *One Foot in the Grave!* I apologised and he said, 'How kind.' He is much taller than he looks on television. When I got back to the room I told Bianca that I had been chatting to Victor Meldrew. I think she was quite impressed.

Wednesday, February 5th

We both woke early this morning, but we didn't make love as usual. We had a shower and got dressed in silence. We went downstairs and had croissants and cappuccino in Brenda's Patisserie and listened to the gossip about the demise of the British film industry. Then, at 10.45 a.m., we paid our bill and walked to the clinic in Neal Street. (We forked out one pound, forty pence to the various beggars who met us on the way.)

We were counselled separately by a very empathetic woman called Judith. She pointed out that, should our tests prove positive, it wouldn't necessarily mean that we would develop full-blown Aids. After seeing Judith, we went for a drink in a pub in Carnaby Street to discuss our options:

a. Have the test and know the worst
b. Not to have the test and suspect the worst

We decided to sleep on it.

Thursday, February 6th

We have both decided to have the test and have pledged to care for each other until the day we die. Whatever the outcome.

Saturday, February 8th

Mr Britten, the greengrocer who supplies 'Savages' with fruit and vegetables, came into the kitchen today and told us that he is going out of business next week. He said that Savage owes him seven hundred pounds in unpaid bills. I was outraged, but Mr Britten said defeatedly that Savage is only one of his many bad debtors. He said, 'If the Bank'd give me another two weeks I'd be all right, but the bastards won't.'

I made him a cup of tea and listened to him ranting on about interest charges and Norman Lamont. I think he felt slightly better by the time he left to make his next delivery.

I rang my mother to tell her about my conversation with Victor Meldrew and found that she has also been seeing a counsellor. A debt counsellor. I have been wondering for some time now how she has been paying her mortgage. Now I know. She hasn't. She has received a legal notice from the Building Society, informing her that the house where I spent my childhood is to be repossessed on March 16th. She begged me not to tell the other members of the family. She is hoping that something will turn up to avert disaster.

I didn't tell her that I have got one thousand, one hundred and eleven pounds in the Market Harborough Building Society. But I did say that Bianca and I would come to Leicester tomorrow. She sounded pathetically grateful.

Sunday, February 9th

When we got to St Pancras Station, Bianca told me to look up.

'You are looking at one of the largest unsupported arch structures in the whole world,' she said. 'Isn't it beautiful?'

'Quite honestly, Bianca,' I said, 'all I can see is a dirty, scruffy roof covered in pigeon shit.'

'It was stupid of me to ask you to look at something further than your own nose,' she said, and stormed onto the train, leaving me to carry our overnight bags.

I'm always forgetting that Bianca is a qualified engineer. She doesn't look like one and since I've known her, she's only ever worked as a shop assistant and a waitress. She applies for at least two engineering jobs a week, but has yet to be called for an interview. She is considering calling herself 'Brian Dartington' on her c.v.

The ticket inspector forgot to punch our three-monthly returns, so our journey to Leicester cost us nothing. But any feelings of happy triumph vanished as we got into the house. My mother was putting on a brave front, but I could tell she was inwardly distraught—at one point, she had one cigarette in her mouth, another in the ashtray and another burning on the edge of the kitchen window sill. I asked her how she'd got into such terrible debt.

She whispered, 'Martin needed the fees to finish his degree course. I borrowed a thousand pounds from a finance company, at an interest rate of twenty-four point seven per cent. Two weeks later, I lost my job with Group Five—somebody grassed on me and told them I was forty-eight.' I asked her to tell me the full extent of her indebtedness. She brought out unpaid bills of every description and colour. I urged her to tell Muffet the true nature of their financial situation, but she became almost hysterical and said, 'No, no, he *must* finish his engineering degree.'

I seem to be surrounded by engineers. Bianca informed my mother that she too was a qualified engineer.

I said jokingly, 'Yes, but she has not built so much as a Lego tower since she left university.'

To my amazement, Bianca took great exception to my harmless joke and left the room, looking tearful.

My mother said, 'You tactless sod!' and followed her into the garden.

I sat at the kitchen table, braced myself, and wrote three cheques: to Fat Eddie's Loan Co. (two hundred and seventy-one pounds); to the Co-op Dairy (thirty-six pounds, forty-nine pence); to Cherry's Newsagent (seventy-four pounds, eighty-one pence). I know it does not solve my mother's housing problem, but at least she can answer her front door now without being hounded by local creditors.

When Martin came back from Grandma's (where he is in the middle of replacing her two-pin sockets with three-pin ones), I introduced him to Bianca. Within seconds, they were bonded. They talked non-stop about St Pancras Station and unsupported arch structures. It is some time since I saw Bianca so animated. They sat next to each other at the dinner table and volunteered to wash and dry afterwards.

I helped Rosie with her English homework essay, 'A Day in the

Life of a Dolphin'. I then went into the kitchen and found Bianca and Muffet droning on about the St Pancras Station Hotel and its architect, Sir George Gilbert Scott.

I interrupted them and informed Bianca that I was going to bed. She hardly looked up; just muttered, 'Okay, I'll be up soon.'

The spare bedroom was full of Rosie's hideous, fluorescent My Little Pony models.

Monday, February 10th

I have no idea what time Bianca came up last night. She must have got into bed beside me without waking me up. All I know is that Muffet and my mother are not speaking and that I am utterly miserable.

11.30 p.m. Worked on *Chapter Twenty-Three: Conundrum.*

> Jake sat in Alma's, the patisserie favoured by the intelligentsia, and scribbled on his A4 pad. Night and day, he worked on his novel. He was already on Chapter Four.
>
> *Chapter Four: Rocks*
>
> Sparg crept through the lush undergrowth. He knew they were there. He heard them before he saw them. They were grunting about their mutual interest in rocks.
>
> Sparg parted a yukka plant and they were there in front of him: Moff and Barf, bathed in sunlight, tangled together. Their limbs were entwined in an intimate manner.
>
> Sparg stifled a jealous grunt and crept back towards Kronk, the settlement of his birth.

Tuesday, February 11th

We get our results tomorrow. I should be agonising and reflecting on mortality, etc. But all I can think about is the way that Muffet looked at Bianca and the way that Bianca looked at Muffet when they said goodbye on Monday morning at Leicester station.

Wednesday, February 12th

Judith told us that our tests are negative! We are not H.I.V. positive! We are not going to die of Aids!

However, I feel that I may well die of a broken heart. Bianca has suggested another day trip to Leicester. She claims that she is tired of London. A feeble excuse. How could anyone be tired of London? I am with Dr Johnson on this one.

Thursday, February 13th

A letter has arrived from the BBC.

> Dear Adrian,
>
> When my secretary handed me your letter and your manuscript of *Lo! The Flat Hills of My Homeland* yet again, I thought I must be hallucinating.
>
> You have more cheek than a Samurai wrestler, more neck than a giraffe. The BBC does not run a free photocopying service. As to your laughable suggestion that your novel be read as one of our classic serials . . . The writers of such texts are usually dead, their work having outlived them. I doubt if your work will outlive you. I am returning the manuscript immediately. Owing to an administrative error, a photocopy *was* taken. I am sending this on to you, though with great reluctance. You really must not bother me again.
>
> John Tydeman

Friday, February 14th
St Valentine's Day

A disappointingly small card from Bianca. Mine to her was a thing of splendour. Large, padded, expensive, and in a box tied with a ribbon.

Savage is in a clinic for drug and alcohol abuse. Luigi went to see him on Sunday and said that Savage was playing ping-pong with a fifteen-year-old crack addict from Leeds.

Saturday, February 15th

Bianca is going to Leicester for the day on Monday, to see my mother. I wish I could go with her, but I am now working a sixteen-hour day, seven days a week. Somebody has to keep my mother out of prison, and I am now the only person in our family who has a proper job.

My duties at 'Savages' now include the preparation of vegetables. It is tedious work, made more difficult by the obsessive attitude of Roberto, the chef. He insists on uniformity of vegetable length and width. I have to keep a tape measure in my apron pocket.

Sunday, February 16th

It is now seven days and nights since Bianca and I made love. It is not only the sex I miss. It isn't the sex. It really isn't only the sex. I miss holding her and smelling her hair and stroking her skin. I wish that I could talk to her about how I feel. But I can't, I just can't. I really can't. I've tried, but I just can't. I held her hand in bed tonight, but it didn't count. She was asleep.

Monday, February 17th

Before I went to work at 6.30 a.m., I wrote a note and left it propped against the bowl of hyacinths on the table.

Darling Bianca,

Please talk to me about our relationship. I am unable to initiate a discussion. All I can say to you is that I love you. I know something is wrong between us, but I don't know how to address it.

Love, forever,
Adrian

Bianca was very kind to me early this evening. She assured me that nothing has changed regarding her feelings towards me. But she was talking to me on the telephone from Leicester. She has arranged to stay another day, to help my mother.

When I got home from work at 11.30 p.m., I re-read the note, which was still on the table, and then tore it up and threw it down the lavatory. It took three full flushes before it disappeared completely.

Tuesday, February 18th

I was very tired last night, but was unable to sleep, so I got out of bed, got dressed, and went for a walk. Soho never sleeps. It exists for people like me: the lonely, the lovesick, the outsiders. When I got home I read Dostoievsky's *The Humiliated and Insulted.*

Wednesday, February 19th

The gods are not exactly smiling on our family. Mrs Bellingham has sacked my father and kicked him out of her bed. She was outraged to find out that my father had been selling her security lights for half price in low-life pubs. He is back living with Grandma. I only know this because Grandma rang me at work, complaining that my mother owes her fifty pounds from last December. Grandma needs the money because she is going to Egypt with Age Concern in June and needs to pay the deposit next week.

I pointed out to Grandma that she has got substantial savings in a high interest bank account. Couldn't she withdraw fifty pounds?

Grandma pointed out that the bank requires a month's notice of withdrawal. She said, 'I'm not prepared to lose the interest.'

I casually asked Grandma if she had seen anything of Bianca. She casually answered that she had seen Bianca and Muffet on the top deck of a number twenty-nine bus, heading towards the town. She threw in a few details. They were laughing. Bianca was holding a bunch of freesias (her favourite flowers). And Muffet looked 'happier than I've ever seen him'. There was a twanging noise as she leaned back in her chair by the telephone and said, 'It doesn't take an Einstein to work that one out, does it, lad?'

Thanks, Grandma, Leicester's answer to Miss sodding Marple.

Thursday, February 20th

I fear the worst. Bianca is still in Leicester. I received a brochure this morning from an organisation called the Faxos Institute. They were offering me a holistic holiday on the Greek island of Faxos, complete with courses in creative writing, dream workshops, finding your voice and stress management. One photograph in the brochure showed happy, tanned holidaymakers scoffing green foodstuffs at long tables under blue skies. Close examination with a magnifying glass showed the foodstuffs to be made up of lettuce and courgettes with a bit of what looked like cheese thrown in. There were bottles of retsina on the tables, vases of flowers and rough-hewn loaves of bread.

Another photograph showed a beach and a pine forest and the bamboo hut accommodation spread over a hillside. It looked truly idyllic. I turned a page and saw that Angela Hacker, the novelist, playwright and television personality, was 'facilitating' the writing course for the first two weeks in April. I have not read her books or seen her plays, but I have seen her on the television programme *Through the Keyhole*. She has certainly got a gracious home, though I remember being struck at the time by the amazing amount of alcohol in evidence. There were bottles in every room. Loyd Grossman made a quip about it at the time, something about 'sauce for the goose'. The studio audience laughed itself stupid.

I closed the brochure with a sigh. Two weeks on Faxos talking about my novel with Angela Hacker would be paradise, but I can't possibly afford it. My Building Society reserves are running low. I'm down to my last thousand.

Saturday, February 22nd

Bianca rang the restaurant at lunchtime and said that she would be catching the 7.30 a.m. train from Leicester tomorrow and would be arriving at St Pancras at around 9.00 a.m. Her voice sounded strange. I asked her if she's got a sore throat. She replied that she'd been 'doing a lot of talking'. Every fibre of me longs for her, especially the bits around my loins.

Sunday, February 23rd

I was on the platform when the train came in and saw Bianca jump onto the platform. I ran towards her, holding a bunch of daffodils I'd bought from a stall outside the Underground on Oxford Street. Then, to my surprise, I saw Martin Muffet step down from the train, carrying two large suitcases. He put them down on the platform and put his arm around Bianca's slim shoulders.

Bianca said, 'I'm sorry, Adrian.'

Muffet said, 'So am I.'

To be quite honest, I didn't know what to say.

I turned away, leaving the two engineers under the engineering miracle of St Pancras Station and made my way back to Old Compton Street on foot. I don't know what happened to the daffodils, but I hadn't got them when I arrived home.

Monday, February 24th

Chapter Twenty-Four: Oblivion

Jake slipped the hose over the exhaust pipe and checked that it was properly connected. Then he put the other end of the hose through the side window of the car. He took a long, last look at the glorious vista of the Lake District panorama spread beneath him. 'How glorious life is,' he said, aloud, to the wind. All around him the daffodils nodded their agreement. Jake took his portable electric razor from his toiletry bag and proceeded to shave. He had always been vain and he was particularly keen to look good as a corpse. His bristles flew into the wind and became as one with the earth. Jake splashed on Obsession, his favourite after-shave lotion. Then, his toilette completed, he climbed into the car and switched on the engine.

As the fumes filled the inside of the car, Jake ruminated on his life. He had visited four continents and bedded some of the world's most beautiful women. He had recovered the Ashes for England. He had climbed Everest backwards, and found the definitive source of the Nile. Nobody could say that his life had been without interest. But, without Regina, the girl he loved, he did not want to live. As Jake slipped into oblivion, the needle on the petrol gauge turned to 'E'. Which would run out first, Jake's oxygen supply, or Jake's petrol . . . ?

Tuesday, February 25th

Got the courage up to ring my mother. My father answered. He said that he has moved back to live with my mother 'on a temporary basis' until she has recovered from the immediate shock of the Bianca/Muffet affair. Apparently, she is too ill to leave her bed and look after Rosie.

He asked how I had taken it.

I said, 'Oh me, I'm fine,' and then big, fat tears rolled down my cheeks and into the electronic workings of the telephone handset. My father kept saying, down the phone, 'There, there, lad. There, there, don't cry, lad,' in a tender voice that I don't remember him using before.

Roberto the chef came and stood at my side and wiped the tears away with his apron. Eventually, after promising to keep in touch, I said goodbye to my father. For years I have thought of him as a feckless fool, but I now see that I have misjudged him.

When I got back to the room, I found that Bianca had taken all her personal belongings, including the photograph of Isambard Kingdom Brunel.

Wednesday, February 26th

I went to a place called Ed's Diner at lunchtime today and had a hot dog, fries, a Becks beer and a mug of filter coffee. I asked for a glass for my beer and then noticed that the other men of my age were swigging it from the bottle, so I pushed my glass away surreptitiously and did as they did. I sat at a high stool at the counter in front of a mini-jukebox. Each selection cost five pence. I selected only one record, but I played it three times.

I used to be able to recite the lyric of 'Stand by Me' off by heart. Bianca and I used to sing along with Ben E. King when we cooked Sunday breakfast together. Our percussion instruments included: a box of household matches, a spatula, and a tin of dried lentils.

In Ed's Diner I tried to sing the words under my breath but I couldn't remember a word.

At the end of the song I was in tears. Why couldn't she have stood by me?

A man sitting on the next stool asked if there was anything he could do. I tried to compose myself, but to my absolute horror I began to sob loudly and without restraint. There were tears; there was snot; there were undignified gulpings and heavings of the shoulders. The stranger put his arm around my shoulders and asked, 'Have you had a relationship gone wrong?'

I nodded, then managed to say, in between sobs, 'Finished.'

'Same here,' he said. Then 'My name's Alan.' Alan told me that he was 'devastated' because his partner, Christopher, had fallen for another man. I ordered two more beers and then I told Alan the whole story about Bianca and Martin Muffet. Alan confessed himself to be shocked and was thoughtful enough to enquire as to my mother's feelings. I told him that I'd phoned her last night and that she'd told me that her life was over.

Alan and I have arranged to meet for a drink at 8.00 p.m. tonight. Am I know, like Blanche Dubois, dependent on the kindness of strangers?

Midnight Alan didn't turn up. I sat in the 'Coach and Horses' for over an hour, waiting for him. Perhaps he met another stranger with a more original tragic story.

I miss her. I miss her. I miss her.

Thursday, February 27th

Roberto stood over me this evening and made me eat a plate of tagliatelle with hare sauce. He said 'A woman issa woman, but food issa food.'

Perhaps it has more meaning in the original Italian.

> Jake handed the envelope containing the money to the sinister man.
>
> 'Quick and clean,' he said. 'They mustn't know what hit them.'
>
> The man grunted and left the Soho drinking den. Jake looked around him, at the tawdry, painted girls, at the bestial faces of the late night drinkers. Was it only yesterday he was in the Lake District attempting suicide? As he rose to his feet, a

young prostitute attempted to procure him. He pushed her away irritably, saying, 'Get lost, baby, I've known and lost the only woman I'll ever want.'

He strode out into the vibrant Soho night, his cowboy boots tapping strangely on the murky pavement. I must get them soled and heeled tomorrow, he thought. As he passed down Old Compton Street, he looked up at the window of the flat above Alma's Patisserie. The light was still burning but he knew that by now all human life had been extinguished. He was a murderer by proxy.

Tears poured inside his heart, but his face was as it always was, hard and unforgiving and without God's blessing.

Saturday, February 29th

I have informed Mr Andropolosis, the landlord, that I have taken over the tenancy, and paid him a month's rent in advance, so the room is now mine. Thank God for the end of this month. It has surely been the worst since time began.

To complete our catalogue of family misery, Grandma was admitted to hospital during the early hours of this morning with abdominal pains. I rang the hospital this afternoon and was told by the ward sister that Grandma was 'comfortable'. If this is true, then she is the only member of the family who is—the rest of us are in total misery.

Sunday, March 1st

I joined my mother, father and Rosie at Grandma's hospital bedside this afternoon. It was the first time I had seen Grandma without her teeth. I was shocked at how *old* she looked.

My mother has lost weight and her eyes looked sore, as though she has been weeping constantly since Muffet upped and left her. After visiting time was over and we were trooping down the ward, my mother said bitterly: 'They're in Hounslow, staying with his brother, Andrew.'

I said, 'I don't want to know, Mum.'

My father said, 'Let it drop, Pauline.'

Rosie said, 'I'm glad he's gone. I hope he never comes back.' She held her hand up and my father took it and steered her through the big double doors at the end of the ward. As we walked alongside the hospital tower blocks, the litter swirled around our feet and I had a premonition of doom.

I almost turned back to say a proper goodbye to Grandma, but I didn't want to keep the others hanging around in the potholed car park, so I didn't. Instead, we went home and had a Marks and Spencer's roast beef dinner each. Mine was quite nice, but it wasn't a patch on the real thing cooked by my grandma. As I was compressing the dirty tin foil trays into the kitchen pedal bin, the telephone rang. It was the hospital, telling us that 'Mrs Edna May Mole passed away at 5.15 p.m.'

I tried to remember where I was *exactly* at 5.15 p.m. I worked out that I was in a B.P. petrol station, helping my father to check the pressure in his car tyres.

I haven't shed a single tear for her yet. I'm dried up inside. My heart feels like a peach stone.

Monday, March 2nd

It is a well-known fact that Grandma and my mother never got on, so nobody was prepared for the positively Mediterranean grief my mother is displaying over her mother-in-law's death: copious tears, breast-beating, etc. This morning she was lamenting, 'I owed her fifty quid' over and over again.

My father continues to astonish me with his maturity. He has dealt with all the death paperwork and haggled over the cost of the funeral with commendable efficiency.

Tuesday, March 3rd

At 10.00 p.m. I rang 'Savages' to tell them that I am staying in Leicester for the funeral on Friday afternoon. Roberto said, 'I'm glad you ring, Adrian. Your flat has been called on by burglars.' He made it sound as though burglars had been invited to tea, brought flowers and left a visiting card. There's nothing I can do tonight. The police have employed the services of a locksmith. The new key is at 'Savages'. I feel strangely calm.

Wednesday, March 4th
Train to Leicester 8.40 p.m.

They have taken everything, apart from my books, boxer shorts and an old pair of polyester trousers. How they got the bed down the stairs will probably always remain a mystery. The policeman I spoke to on the phone said, in answer to my question about the likelihood of their finding the culprits: 'You know what chance a snowball has in hell? Well, halve that. Then halve it again.' He asked if I had insurance.

I laughed scornfully and said, 'Of course not. This is Adrian Mole you're speaking to.'

I am now a man without possessions.

Thursday, March 5th

I went into Grandma's home this morning. Everything was the same as ever. My G.C.E. certificates were still there, framed on the wall. My dead grandad Albert's photograph was on the mantelpiece. The clock was still ticking. Upstairs, the linen lay folded in the cupboard and in the garden the bulbs pushed through the earth. The biscuit barrel was full of fig rolls and her second best slippers stood by her bed. Inside a kitchen cupboard, I found her Yorkshire pudding tin.

She had used it for over forty years. Stupid to weep over a Yorkshire pudding tin, but I did. I then wiped it dry and replaced it in the cupboard, as she would have liked.

Friday, March 6th
Grandma's Funeral

My mother and father, Rosie and I worked together as a team today and managed to give Grandma a good send-off. There was a respectable turnout in the church, which surprised me, because Grandma didn't encourage people to call on her. She preferred the company of Radio Four. She had been known to turn people away from her doorstep, should they be inconsiderate enough to call during the Afternoon Play.

The hymns were 'Amazing Grace' and 'Onward Christian Soldiers'. Bert Baxter sang out loudly, almost drowning the others in the congregation. For an atheist, he certainly enjoys singing in church. As I watched him, I couldn't help thinking wistfully that it should have been him who died instead of Grandma. The vicar said a lot of incredibly stupid things about Grandma being born into sin and dying in sin.

Anybody who knew Grandma knew that she was incapable of sin. She couldn't even tell a lie. When I asked her once if my spots were clearing up (I must have been about fifteen), she answered, 'No, you've still got a face like a ladybird's arse.' She occasionally used such mild profanities, but she was certainly not a sinner.

I don't like to think of her lying under the earth, alone and cold. Still, at least she was never burgled or mugged. She is safe from all that now.

The funeral tea was held at our house. My mother had been up most of the previous night, cleaning and polishing and trying to get the stains out of the lounge carpet.

My father replaced the missing light bulbs and mended the ballcock so that the lavatory flushed properly.

Tania Braithwaite came round to give her commiserations and kindly offered to defrost some vegetarian quiches she had in the freezer. She told us that Pandora had cancelled a lecture and was intending to come to the funeral tea and would be bringing six bottles of Marks and Spencer's champagne with her.

She said, 'Pandora believes in celebrating death. She sees it as a new adventure, as opposed to a rather boring ending.'

Bert Baxter had phoned to ask what time the service started, which reminded my mother that there was no beetroot in the house. So Rosie was given a personal safety alarm and sent round to the corner shop to buy a jar from Mr Patel's shop.

At midnight, I watched my parents spreading a white tablecloth over the dining room table, which had had its leaves fully extended. As they flapped and adjusted the cloth, one at either end, I had a sudden sense of being a member of the family.

Rosie had arranged some daffodils and freesias nicely in a vase and was praised by everyone. Even the dog behaved itself. When we finally went to bed, the house looked perfect; everything was in its place and we Moles could hold our heads high. Grandma would have been proud of us.

After the funeral service, Rosie and I ran ahead of the other mourners to take the clingfilm off the sandwiches and sausage rolls.

Pandora was waiting outside the house in her car. We filled the bath with cold water and put the bottles of champagne into it to chill.

Pandora looked beautifully severe in a black tailored suit. However, I no longer felt in awe of her, so we were able to talk to each other as friends and equals. She complimented me on how well I was looking and she even praised my clothes. She fingered the lapel of my navy blue unstructured Next suit and said, 'Welcome to the nineties.'

The house soon filled up with mourners and I was kept busy circulating with glasses of champagne on a tray. At first, everyone stood around, not knowing what to say, nervous of enjoying themselves for fear of being thought disrespectful to the dead. Then Pandora broke the ice by proposing a toast to Grandma.

'To Edna Mole,' she said, lifting her glass of champagne high, 'a woman of the highest principles.'

Everyone clinked glasses and swigged back the champagne and it wasn't long before laughter broke out and I was fishing the bottles out of the bath.

My mother rummaged in the sideboard and brought out the photograph albums. I was astonished to see a photograph of my grandma at the age of twenty-four. She looked very dashing, dark-haired, with a lovely figure, and was laughing and pushing a bicycle up a hill. There was a man next to her wearing a flat cap. He had a big moustache and his eyes were crinkled against the sun. It was my grandad. Everybody remarked that I looked like him.

My father took the photograph out of the album and went into the garden and sat on Rosie's swing. After a while, I followed him out. He handed me the photograph and said, 'I'm an orphan, son.'

I put my hand on his shoulder, then went back inside to find that the funeral tea had turned into a party. People were laughing hysterically at the photographs in the album. Me at the seaside, falling off a donkey. Me in a secondhand cub's uniform three sizes too big. Me at six months, lying naked on a half moon-shaped rug in front of a gas fire. Me two days old with my grinning, young-looking parents in the maternity hospital. On the back was written, in my mother's handwriting, 'Our darling baby, two days old'.

There was a photograph I don't remember seeing before. It was my mother and father and my grandma and grandad. They were sitting in deckchairs, watching me, aged about three, playing in the sand. On the back was written: 'Yarmouth, Bank Holiday Monday'.

Rosie said, 'Why aren't I in the photo?'

Bert Baxter said, 'Cos you 'adn't been bleedin' born, that's why.'

At seven o'clock, Ivan Braithwaite offered to escort some of my grandma's elderly neighbours back to their pensioners' bungalows while they and he could still walk.

The rest of us carried on until eleven o'clock. Tania Braithwaite, who has been vegetarian for nine years, cracked and ate a sausage roll and then another.

My mother and father danced together to 'You've Lost That Loving Feeling'. You couldn't have slid a ruler between them.

Pandora and I watched them dancing. She said, 'So they're back together again, are they?'

'I hope so,' I said, looking at Rosie.

As I said before, it was a good send-off.

Monday, March 9th
Old Compton Street

I am back in my room with only my books and boxer shorts for company. I have given the trousers away to a young man selling *The Big Issue*. I made a pillow out of my underwear and slept on the floor. I have often wondered what it would be like to be a celibate monk in a bare cell. Now, thanks to burglary and desertion, I know.

I went into 'Savages' to help clean the kitchen. Savage himself was there, released from the alcohol abuse unit and looking fit and athletic and sipping on a glass of mineral water. He commiserated with me on my various losses and said that there was some old furniture in the attic above the restaurant that I could have.

'Just help yourself, kid,' he said.

I can't get used to this new, kind, philanthropic Savage. I keep thinking he must be Savage's long lost twin brother, recently returned from a missionary station in Amazonia.

My room is now furnished with rococo style banquettes and fag-stained *faux* marble tables. Stuff that was obviously thrown upstairs when Savage took over the restaurant. I now sleep on two banquettes pushed together. I have angels at my head and cherubs at my feet. Roberto gave me some cutlery and crockery and kitchen utensils. Most of my fellow workers brought something to work with them this morning, to donate to the Adrian Mole Disaster Fund. I cook on a ring fuelled by a gas canister and I read by a mock chandelier, both donated by Luigi.

Wednesday, March 11th

I rang home this morning. My father is still there, living in sin with my mother. My mother told me that Bianca and Muffet are intending to set up an engineering partnership called 'Dartington and Muffet'.

I cannot bear the thought of Muffet's bony fingers touching Bianca's lovely pale skin.

I cannot bear it.

Thursday, March 12th

Chapter Twenty-Five: Resurgence

Jake sat down at the *faux* marble table and began to write another chapter of his novel, *Sparg from Kronk.*

Chapter Five: Green Shoots

Sparg missed his woman, Barf. There was a part of him that would never be reconciled to her loss.

It was springtime. Green shoots showed through the earth. Sparg left his hut and went outside. He was glad to be outside, for the hut was damp and the damp was rising fast.

Sparg needed a woman, but the only woman in sight was Krun, his mother. Though her face was wrinkled, her thighs were inviting. But it was forbidden by Kronkian law to take your own mother, even if she agreed.

Sparg walked aimlessly up a small hill and then walked

aimlessly down. He was bored. There was firewood to collect, but he was sick of collecting firewood. It did not challenge his intellect. He grunted in despair and wished it were possible to communicate with his fellow Kronkians. It was just his luck, he thought, to be born in prehistoric times.

If only there was *language,* grunted Sparg internally . . .

to be continued

Jake fell back. The intensity of the writing had left him drained and pale. He left his room and walked to Wilde's, his favourite restaurant, where he was greeted by Mario.

'Longa tima noa see, Mr Westmorland.'

'Hi, Mario. My usual table, please, and my usual bottle, well chilled, and I'll have my usual starter, usual main course and usual pudding.'

'And for your aperitif, Mr Westmorland?' purred Mario.

'The usual,' barked Jake.

I've got to finish *Lo! The Flat Hills of My Homeland* soon, but I can't do that until Jake has finished writing *Sparg from Kronk.* I wish he would hurry up.

Friday, March 13th

More businesses are closing around us. Every day, the boards go up at shop and restaurant windows. Every night, I pray that 'Savages' stays financially viable. I need my job. I'm aware that I'm being exploited, but at least I have a reason to get up in the morning, unlike three and a half million of my fellow citizens.

Grandma left my father three thousand and ninety pounds in her will, so my mother is not going to have her house repossessed. This is truly joyous news. It means that I won't have to break into my Building Society savings. I couldn't have seen her thrown onto the street. At least, I don't think I could.

Saturday, March 14th

I received the following message when I got to work this morning. It was written on the back of a paper napkin. 'Forgot G. Left 500.' Nobody knew what it meant or who had taken the message.

Monday, March 16th

Received another brochure from the Faxos Institute. Why are they mailing me so assiduously? Who has put them on to me? I don't know any holistic types. I'm not even a vegetarian and I swear by paracetamol.

I went to the National Gallery today, but it brought back painful memories of B., so I went back to Soho and paid two pounds to watch a fat girl with spots remove her bra and knickers through a peephole. I *watched* her through a peephole. She didn't remove her underclothes through a peephole.

Query: Are there night classes in syntax?

Tuesday, March 17th

I ran out of toilet paper last night and reached for the Faxos Institute brochure to help me out of my emergency, when something about Angela Hacker's face made me pause. It seemed to say, 'Come to me, Adrian.' Her face is nothing to write home about, in fact it's nothing to write *anywhere* about.

I put the brochure down and picked up the *Evening Standard* instead. It has far better absorbency qualities.

11.45 p.m. Can't sleep for St Patrick's Day revellers, so have idly filled in the booking form for the first two weeks in April at the Faxos Institute in Greece.

Thursday, March 19th

Idly filled in a cheque made out to 'Faxos Institute', but I was only trying out a new pen. I couldn't possibly afford the time off work, or the money.

10.00 p.m. The full message was: 'Forgot to tell you Grandma has left you five hundred pounds, love, Dad.' Luigi, who had been away from the restaurant with food poisoning, returned today and congratulated me on 'Alla money ya got'. Naturally, I looked at him blankly. Confusion abounded for some minutes and then came the glorious realisation, which we celebrated with a bottle of corked Frascati.

Saturday, March 21st

The newly benign Savage has agreed to give me two weeks' leave (without pay). I posted my booking form this morning and this afternoon I bought some swimming trunks from a shop that was closing down in the Charing Cross Road. I can't wait to feel the warm Aegean sea on my body.

Worked on *Lo!* with Angela Hacker in mind.

> Jake opened his manuscript book. The ivory handmade paper looked enticing. He took his Mont Blanc pen in his hand and began to write.
>
> 'Sorry, darling,' he said to the glorious example of English womanhood who sprawled opposite him, showing her knickers, 'but the Muse is upon me.'
>
> Then he lowered his handsome head and was at once in Kronk, the home of his hero, Sparg.
>
> Sparg grunted, recognising the hated form of his father in the darkness. His father grunted back. Sparg threw a pebble from one hand to the other. Why hadn't something been invented to

pass the hours of darkness before bed, he wondered. Something like a game such as cards, he wondered. He went back into his hut and pushed the animal skins listlessly around on his bed. He was cold at night without a woman. He determined that he would get up early the next morning and find one and bring her home to Kronk.

Thursday, March 26th

I bought a short-sleeved shirt and a pair of Bermuda shorts from a stall in Berwick Street market. I have never worn shorts since reaching adulthood.

A new Adrian Mole is emerging from the ashes.

Savage turned up drunk and disorderly at the restaurant and proceeded to fire Luigi, Roberto and the whole of the kitchen staff apart from me. He said, 'You can stay, Adrian. You're a fucking loser, like me.'

He has promoted me to *Maître d'*, a position I do not want and cannot do.

Luigi and Roberto sat in the kitchen, smoking and talking in Italian. They didn't seem too concerned. Meanwhile, dressed in Luigi's suit, I was forced to fawn over customers, show them to their seats and pretend to be interested in their requirements. Savage sat at the bar, shouting out the biographical details of his customers as they came in. As one respectable-looking middle-aged couple entered, he yelled: 'Well, if it isn't Mr and Mrs Wellington. He's wearing a toupée and she's paid three thousand pounds for those perky looking titties.'

Instead of going straight back out, or thumping him on the side of his drunken head, Mr and Mrs Wellington grinned and allowed me to show them to table number six. Perhaps they are proud of their artificial attributes. As my recently dead grandma would say, 'There's nowt so strange as folk, especially London folk.'

Poor Grandma. She never went to London in her life.

For the past four days, I have been unable to write a word. The thought of Angela Hacker reading my manuscript has totally inhibited me. However, tonight I achieved a breakthrough.

> He had writer's block. For over five hours he stared down at the mockingly empty page. His publisher was calling hourly. The printing presses were waiting, but still he could not finish his book. Jake looked out of the window, hoping for inspiration. The New York skyline stretched away into infinity . . .
>
> 'Infinity!' shouted Jake, excitedly, and he began to work on his novel, *Sparg from Kronk.*
>
> Sparg had wandered far from Kronk and was standing on a high headland, looking in wonderment at a strange watery mass and a blue line ahead of him. Without knowing it (because there was no language), Sparg was marvelling over the sea and the far distant horizon. Sparg growled and began to descend the headland. He would walk to the far blue line, he thought. It would be something to do. Sparg thought this because there was as yet no swimming . . .

Received confirmation from Faxos Institute that I have a place on the Writers' Course. I am terrified.

Friday, March 27th

Luigi has been reinstated and I am safely back in the kitchen, thank God. Roberto has been allowing me to watch him at work. For most of my life, I have been denied a proper food education. There was never anything to learn from my mother; she stopped cooking real food soon after reading *The Female Eunuch.* Though, ironically, the author of that seminal tome, Ms Germaine Greer, is a renowned cook and dinner party giver.

Thanks to Roberto's kindness, I can now cook pasta '*al dente*' and make a basic sponge cake and I've almost cracked making watercress soup. I now spring from my double banquettes in the morning, eager to get to work.

Plane tickets arrived today.

A new girl started work as a waitress at 'Savages' this evening. Her name is Jo Jo and she is from Nigeria. She is studying Art at St Martin's. She is taller than anybody else in the restaurant. Her hair is braided with hundreds of tiny beads. She rattles when she walks. Her mother is something big in the Nigerian tractor industry.

Saturday, March 28th

Made a *tower* of profiteroles today. Roberto said: 'Congratulations, Adriana! The chocolate icing issa perfection.'

Jo Jo tasted the first one and pronounced it to be 'delectable'. Luigi happened to have his polaroid camera with him, so he photographed me and the tower and Jo Jo. I have pinned the photograph on my wall. I look quite handsome.

Sunday, March 29th

I was still in bed at midday when there was a knock on the door. I never have visitors, so I was a little alarmed. I put my ear to the door, but all I could hear was a peculiar rattling noise. I eventually opened the door, but I kept the security chain on. I was delighted to see Jo Jo through the crack.

She smiled at me and said that she was going to the Tate Gallery.

'Do you want to come?' she asked.

I slipped the chain off and invited her in. She walked around the room and commented on how tidy it was. She stopped at the table where my manuscript lay in its transparent folder and said, 'So this is your book.'

She touched it reverently. 'I would like to read it one day.'

'When it's finished,' I said.

I made her a cup of Nescafé and then excused myself and went into the bathroom to wash and change.

I looked at myself in the washbasin mirror. Something had happened to my face. I no longer looked like John Major.

Jo Jo likes walking, so we walked to the Tate. I was proud to be seen with such a stunning looking woman. I asked her about Nigeria and she spoke about her country with obvious love. She is a Yoruba and comes from Abeokuta.

She asked me about my family and I told her about the tangled web of relationships, the break-ups and the reconciliations.

She laughed and said, 'To work out the relationships in my family, you would need an extremely sophisticated computer.'

I had never been to the Tate, but Jo Jo knew it well. She guided me round and made me look at a few of her favourite paintings—all depicting people, I noticed. We looked at paintings by Paula Rego, Vanessa Bell and Matisse, and a piece of sculpture by Ghisha Koenig called 'The Machine Minders', and then she insisted that we leave before we got bored and our feet started to ache.

As we were going down the steps, Jo Jo asked if I would like to have tea at her flat in Battersea.

I said, 'I'd love to.' We crossed the road and stood at the bus stop, but then, on impulse, I flagged down a black cab and we rode to her flat in style.

She lives on the top floor of a mansion block. Every room is full of her paintings. Many of the paintings are nude self-portraits, in which she has depicted herself in many colours, including green, pink, purple, blue and yellow.

I asked her if she was making a statement about her colour. 'No,' she laughed. 'But I would get bored only using blacks and browns.'

We ate scones and drank Earl Grey tea and talked non-stop: about 'Savages'; Nigerian politics; cats; one of her art teachers, who is going mad; Cecil Parkinson; the price of paint brushes; Vivaldi; our star signs—she is Leo (but on the cusp of Cancer); and her girls' boarding school in Surrey, where she lived from the age of eleven until she got expelled at sixteen for climbing on the roof of the chapel in a protest against the lousy food.

Over a glass of cheap wine, we discussed trees; Matisse; Moscow; Russian politics; our favourite cakes; the use of umbrellas; cabbage; and the Royal Family. She is a republican, she said.

Over a final glass of wine and a plate of bread and cheese, I talked to her about my grandmother, my mother, Pandora, Sharon, Megan, Leonora, Cassandra and Bianca. 'You're carrying a lot of baggage,' Jo Jo said.

We parted at 10.30 p.m. with a friendly handshake.

Before she closed the door, I asked how old she was.

'Twenty-four,' she said. 'Goodnight.'

Monday, March 30th

I ran out of 'Savages' during my break time and bought Ambre Solaire (Factor 8), espadrilles, sleeveless tee shirts, three more pairs of shorts and sixteen thousand drachmas.

I worked on the book late into the night. I am nervous about Angela Hacker's opinion. Added more descriptive words to *Lo! The Flat Hills of My Homeland* and took out more descriptive words from *Sparg from Kronk.*

Tuesday, March 31st

The staff arranged a small *bon voyage* party in the kitchen after the restaurant closed at lunchtime. I was very touched. Roberto cooked kebabs and arranged an authentic Greek salad in my honour. Jo Jo bought two bottles of retsina earlier in the day and we all clinked glasses and swore eternal friendship. Then Savage came in, complaining that Luigi had forgotten to add V.A.T. to somebody's bill, so the party broke up. Jo Jo is good at packing, she said. She offered to come and help me.

I laid my clothes, toiletry bag and manuscript out on my bed before proceeding to pack, and then realised that the burglars had taken my suitcase.

Jo Jo ran to Berwick Street market and bought one of those man-made fibre striped bags, the type that refugees have on the television news. Once I was packed, I debated with Jo Jo on whether or not to take a warm coat with me. She said I ought to, but I decided not to. Instead, I slung a cotton sweater around my shoulders. Everybody has said that Greece is warm in April. My legs look very white at the moment in my shorts, but by the time I return, they will be gloriously tanned.

Hotel Adelphi
Athens
Thursday April 2nd

9.30 a.m.

Dear Jo Jo,

For the first time in my life, there is nobody to wish me a Happy Birthday. I am now twenty-five years old. Which is a millstone in anybody's life. Do I still qualify to be called a 'Young British Novelist'? I hope so.

Other participants in the Faxos Institute course are swirling around downstairs in the hotel lobby, chatting easily to each other. I fled back into the lift when I saw them, and went up to the roof terrace, but Angela Hacker was up there, smoking a cigarette and looking moodily at the Acropolis in the far distance. She is skinny and dresses in white clothes. She was weighed down by ethnic silver jewellery.

I don't know when the photograph of her in the brochure was taken, but in life she looks at least forty-eight. Obviously past it, sexually and artistically.

I didn't thank you properly for that afternoon in the Tate. I keep thinking about the pictures. I particularly liked those painted by that Portuguese woman, Paula something.

All best wishes,
Adrian

Ferry
Friday April 3rd

Dear Mum and Dad,

I am writing this on the first ferry, which is taking us to where we catch the second ferry to Faxos. Angela Hacker and most of the twelve members of the writers' group are already in the bar. The majority of them smoke. You would probably get along famously with them, Mum. The other, more holistic, holidaymakers are looking over the side of the ship, taking photographs or swapping aromatherapy recipes. I am keeping to myself. I don't want to lumber myself with a hastily-made 'friend' and spend the next fortnight getting rid of him or her. It has just started to rain. I will have to stop now and go inside.

Love from your son,
Adrian

Ferry
Friday April 3rd
4.00 p.m.

Dear Jo Jo,

There has been torrential rain for the whole of the three-hour crossing. I am wearing my cotton sweater, but am still cold. I now wish I'd followed your advice and brought a coat with me.

Angela Hacker has been falling down in the bar. The sea *is* choppy, but I think her lack of balance is due more to the copious amounts of retsina she is throwing down her neck. My fellow writers have been laughing non-stop since boarding the ferry. Some private joke, no doubt. I have not yet introduced myself to them.

Bamboo Hut Number Six
8.00 p.m.

The wind is whistling through the slats of my hut. Outside, the sky is grey and dotted with storm clouds. Supper was eaten in the open air, under a 'roof' of palm fronds. Not surprisingly, the ratatouille was cold.

I can hear Angela Hacker coughing from here, though her hut is at least two hundred yards further down the rocky hill.

There was a community meeting at eight o'clock, where the permanent staff and the facilitators introduced themselves and their work. The meeting was held in what they call here the 'Magic Ring', which is on the very top of the hill. The Magic Ring is a concrete base, surrounded by a low wall and covered in the usual palm frond and bamboo roof. There is nothing magical looking about it.

I was most concerned to hear Ms Hacker describe her course as 'Writing for Pleasure'. I get no pleasure from writing. Writing is a serious business, like painting.

There is a man here who wears his hair like yours. I saw him on the headland, looking out to sea. From a distance he looked like you. My heart did a backflip.

My hut is next to the hen-coop. A goat has just put its head inside my hut and a donkey is braying somewhere in the pine woods. If Noah's Ark was washed up on the beach, I wouldn't be surprised.

Best wishes,
Adrian

Faxos
Sunday April 5th

Dear Pan,

You asked me to let you know how the Faxos course was, so I'll tell you about the first day.

The writers collected on the terrace at 11.15 a.m. I sat upwind, away from the cigarette smoke. At 11.30 a.m. Angela Hacker had still not appeared, so a man called Clive, who had seven boils on his neck, was sent to her hut. She eventually showed up at noon and apologised for having overslept. She then rambled on for an hour and fifteen minutes about 'Truth' and 'Narrative thrust' and 'developing an original voice'.

At 1.15 p.m. she sprang to her feet and said, 'Okay, that's it for the day. Write a poem including the word "Greece". Be prepared to read it aloud at 11.15 tomorrow morning.' She then headed for the bamboo bar, where she stayed for most of the day. When I'd written my poem, I went in for a cup of tea and heard her talking about your college in Oxford.

I asked her if she knew you and she said she had met you at Jack Cavendish's house a few times, 'before Jack left his third wife,' she said.

I said, 'It's a small world.'

'Try not to use clichés, darling,' she said.

She's a strange woman.

All the best from,
Adrian

Faxos
Monday April 6th

Dear Rosie,

I hope you like this postcard of the cheerful donkey. There is something about its daft expression that reminds me of the dog.

I have sent you a poem I was forced to write about Greece.

It's time you started to take an interest in cultural matters. There is more to life than Nintendo games.

Love from your brother,
Adrian

Oh Greece, ancient cultured land
You wrap around my heart just like
An old elastic band.
Your hag-like women pensioners
Clad in clothes of black,
Are they unaware of all the services they lack?
Will they be content to watch
The donkey with its load?
Won't they want a vehicle to
Drive along the road?

Faxos
Tuesday April 7th

Dear Baz,

I am here on Faxos with Angela Hacker, whom I understand you know quite well. She and I hit it off immediately and she has invited me to stay at her place in Gloucestershire when we get back. I may be able to make the odd weekend, but I am currently doing research in a restaurant kitchen in Soho for my next book, *The Chopper*, so will not be able to stay for a couple of weeks, as she would like.

The reason I am writing is to say that I hope there are no hard feelings any more over the Sharon Bott affair, because we are likely to be moving in the same circles soon and I would rather there were no acrimonious feelings between us.

Congratulations on finally getting to number one!

Cheers,
Your old friend,
Adrian Mole

Faxos
Wednesday April 8th

Dear John Tydeman,

As you cannot fail to see, if you have noticed the postmark, I am on the Greek island of Faxos. I am a member of a writers' course being facilitated by Angela Hacker (she sends you her love).

She asked us to write the first scene of a radio play, which is something I have never attempted to do before.

I thought you might be interested to read what I have written. I would be more than willing to finish it, if you thought it had merit.

I shall be back in London at 3.00 p.m. on the 15th April, if you would like to talk to me face to face.

On second thoughts, the 16th would be more convenient for me. I shall probably need to rest after my journey.

Here is how the play opens:

THE CUCUMBER SANDWICH

A PLAY FOR RADIO BY ADRIAN MOLE

A room in a wealthy house. A game of tennis can be heard through the french windows. Tea is poured. A spoon rattles in a cup.

LADY ELEANOR: A cucumber sandwich, Edwin?

EDWIN: Don't try to fob me off with your bourgeois ideas of gentility. I know the truth!

LADY ELEANOR (*gasps*): No! Surely not! You don't know the secret I have kept for forty years!

EDWIN (*contemptuously*): Yes, I do. The servant girl, Millie, told me.

A bell rings.

MILLIE: You rang, mum? Sorry to keep you, only I was 'elpin' cook with Master Edwin's twenty-first birthday cake.

LADY ELEANOR: You are dismissed, Millie. You have blabbed my secret.

MILLIE: What secret? Oh! The one about your being born a man?

To be continued

I do not wish to prejudice you in any way, but after I had finished reading this text, there was a stunned silence from my fellow writers. Angela's only comment was, 'You should have spun the secret out until the last scene of the play.'

Good advice, I think.

Anyway, I hope you enjoy *The Cucumber Sandwich.*

Yours,
With best wishes,
Adrian Mole

Faxos
Thursday April 9th

Dear Jo Jo,

The sun has shone for two days now and has turned Faxos into Paradise. The colours are breathtaking: the sea is peacock blue, the grass is peppermint green and the wild flowers are scattered on the hillside like living confetti.

Something has happened to my body. It feels looser, as though it has broken free and is floating.

I have been going to dream workshops at 7.00 a.m. The facilitator is a nice American woman dream therapist called Clara. I told her about a recurring dream I have that I am trying to pick up the last pea on my dinner plate by stabbing it with a fork. Try as I may, I cannot get the prongs of the fork to stab into the flesh of the pea.

For years I have woken up feeling frustrated and hungry after dreaming my pea dream.

Clara advised me to look at the dream from the *pea*'s point of view. I did try hard to do this and, by discussing it with Clara later, I understood that I, Adrian Mole, was the pea and that the fork represented DEATH.

Clara said that my pea dream showed that I am afraid to die.

But who is *looking forward* to death? I don't know anybody who is cock-a-hoop at the prospect.

Clara explained that I am *morbidly* afraid of death.

How do you feel about death, Jo Jo?

I have made friends with the bloke with the beaded plaits like yours. His name is Sean Washington. His mother is Irish; his father is from St Kitts. He is here taking the stress management course, but he hangs out with the writers' group on the bar terrace.

We were both on vegetable chopping duties today and I was complimented by him and others on my expertise. I think I would like to be a chef. I may ask Savage if he'll give me a trial when I get back.

Angela Hacker has forbidden her writers' group to use clichés, but she will not be reading this letter, so I'll sign off by saying:

Wish you were here,
Adrian

Saturday, April 11th

My first fax! It was addressed to 'Adrian Mole, Faxos Institute', and arrived at the travel agent's shop in the town. It was then conveyed to the Faxos Institute by greengrocer's van and delivered to me on the bar terrace by Julian, the handsome bald-headed administrator. It caused a sensation.

Dear Adrian,

Thank you for your letters. I wish I were there with you. It sounds idyllic.

I'm so glad that you feel at ease. When I first saw you in Savage's kitchen, I thought: that man is in *pain*. I wanted to touch you and comfort you there and then, but of course one does not do such a thing—not in England.

I think you have it in your power to become a happy man, providing you can let go of the past. Why not try to live in the present and leave all that baggage behind on Faxos when you return?

I couldn't wait to tell you that I have been offered a shared exhibition of 'Young Contemporaries' in September. Will you come to the opening? Please say you will.

Roberto is complaining that the man Savage has hired to take your place for a fortnight is massacring the vegetables and he now regrets letting you go on holiday.

Everybody at 'Savages' sends their best wishes. Roberto asks if you will bring a bottle of ouzo back for him.

I miss you.

I send you my best wishes as well,

Jo Jo

Hut Number Six
Faxos Institute
Faxos
Sunday April 12th

Dear Jo Jo,

What fantastic news about the exhibition! Of course I will come to the opening. September seems a long way off, though. The spring is so glorious here. I've never seen such colours before.

At our meeting yesterday morning Angela Hacker asked the writers' group to write the first page of a novel.

I wanted to run up the hill to my hut immediately and present her with the whole manuscript of *Lo! The Flat Hills of My Homeland,* but I restrained myself. The book was only a few pages short of completion. Why spoil the ship for a ha'p'orth of tar? (Since being forbidden to use clichés, I find myself using them all the time.)

I worked all day and most of the night on *Lo!* And I think that now the book is finished. This is how it ends:

Jake got up from his computer terminal and paced around his study. He adjusted the painting of a stately African woman that he had recently bought in an exhibition.

He then stared moodily out of the window and watched a child dragging a stick along the ground.

Jake was desperate to finish *Sparg from Kronk.* He could hear the printer banging on his door, demanding the finished manuscript. His publisher had been admitted to hospital the night before with nervous strain, but the ending of his book continued to elude him.

The child outside the window stopped to scratch the stick into the dry earth of drought-hit London.

'Goddit!' shouted Jake, and he leaped into his state-of-the-art typing chair and began to write the end of his book.

Sparg wrestled with Krun, his father, for possession of the stick. He wondered why they were fighting over this particular stick. There were plenty of others lying around.

He looked at his father's old face, now disfigured by anger, and thought: why are we *doing* this? He let go of the stick and allowed his father to take it away.

Sparg sat on the baked earth and thought, if only there was *language,* we wouldn't have to be so damned *physical.*

He poked his finger into the dust. He drew it along. In a few minutes, he had made marks and symbols.

Before the sun had gone down, he had written the first page of his novel. He hoped it wouldn't rain in the night and obliterate his work.

Tomorrow, he would continue his work inside a cave, he thought. What should he call his novel? He grunted to himself and tried out several titles. Finally, he settled on one and hurried to the big cave to scratch it on the wall before he forgot:

A BOOK WITH NO LANGUAGE

Yes, that was it. And he picked up a stick and began to gnaw the end of it into a point.

Jake could hardly wait for the electronic printer to spew out the typewritten page.

'At last,' he jubilated, 'I have finished *Sparg from Kronk!*'

Please let me know what you think, Jo Jo. I really value your opinion.

I gave the completed manuscript to Angela Hacker this morning. She took it from me and groaned, 'Sodding hell. I only asked for one page!' Then she put it into the blue raffia bag that she carries everywhere with her and continued her conversation with Clara about a dream she'd had of being chased by a giant cockroach.

At 11.00 p.m., after spending the evening with my friends, singing on the bar terrace, I got back to my hut to find that the following note had been slipped under my door:

Adrian,

I've skipped through *Lo! The Flat Hills of My Homeland.* I won't waste words. It's typical juvenilia and has no merit at all. *Sparg from Kronk* has been done a million times, dearest boy. But *A Book With No Language*—Sparg's novel—is a truly brilliant concept.

I would like you to come and see me when we get back to London. I'd like to introduce you to my agent, Sir Gordon Giles. I think your originality will appeal to him.

Congratulations! You are a writer.
Angela Hacker

I may be a writer, Jo Jo, but I can't find the words to express my happiness.

My plane gets into Gatwick on Wednesday at 3.00 p.m.

Love from,
Adrian

Tuesday, April 14th

Angela Hacker announced this morning that the writers' group's last meeting was to be held on 'Bare Bum Beach'. My penis shrivelled at the thought. I have never appeared in the nude in public before. 'Bare Bum Beach' is where the extrovert and confident desport themselves. I am neither of these things. However, after three glasses of retsina at lunchtime I found myself slithering over the rocks, heading for the nudist beach.

I was astounded by the ridiculous blue of the sea. The rocks shone pink as I stumbled towards the beach which was the colour of custard. It seemed the most natural thing in the world to shrug my shorts off and embrace the sand. For twelve long years I have worried about the size of my penis. Now, at last, by glancing at my fellow male writers I could see that I am made as other men. I easily fell within the 'normal' range.

At half past six in the evening I turned over and exposed myself to the sun. Nothing terrible happened. There was no thunderbolt. Men and women did not run away, shrieking in horror at the sight of my full frontal nakedness.

I walked into the sea and swam towards the blood-red sunset. I allowed myself to float and to drift. It was almost dark when I swam back to the beach. I did not use my towel. I let the water dry on my body.

I walked back to the Institute in pale moonlight. I took a short cut through the woods. The floor was covered in pine needle debris, every footstep was a crackling aromatic delight.

I walked ankle deep through a glade of soft grass and wild flowers. Then I smelled honeysuckle and felt a tendril brush across my face. I reached the headland and stood for a moment, looking down at the Institute. The kitchen door was open. Out of it spilled bright light, laughter and the delicious smell of grilling meat.

Wednesday, April 15th

10.00 p.m. I saw Jo Jo waiting beyond the barrier. I threw all my baggage down and ran towards her.